Heiligtum

Rosemary Showell

Grosvenor House
Publishing Limited

The right of Rosemary Showell to be identified as the author of this
work has been asserted in accordance with Section 78
of the Copyright, Designs and Patents Act 1988

The book cover is copyright to Rosemary Showell

This book is published by
Grosvenor House Publishing Ltd
Link House
140 The Broadway, Tolworth, Surrey, KT6 7HT.
www.grosvenorhousepublishing.co.uk

This Book is a work of fiction. The characters are products of the
author's imagination. Any resemblance to characters living or
dead is coincidental. The destinations and institutions
mentioned are adapted for the purpose of storytelling

A CIP record for this book
is available from the British Library

ISBN 978-1-83975-142-4

This Book
is dedicated to the memory of
John and Isabella McNamee
and their daughters
Mary and Rose.

Also, by Rosemary Showell.

Lanshoud
Nephilim

Children's book- Flash McKinley and the Mystery of
Rosewood Cottage

Acknowledgements

I offer my grateful thanks to the following people.

To my granddaughter Broghan Showell, a talented young artist, for her gift of the visual representation of the fictional Heiligtum,which is on front cover of this book.

To my good friends, who read my manuscripts.

Elizabeth Morton
Maureen McGeeney
Mary McFeely
and
Margaret Dekker.

Their familiarity with the fictional personalities, is staggering; giving them the ability to approve or disapprove of character behaviour. Thus, they make it easy for me, to keep the nature, temperament, and personality of each character, as they flow from book to book.

Also

These books would never reach print, were it not for the endless cups of tea, support, and encouragement from my husband Arthur.

Contents

Prologue

The gate at Lanshoud, the gate that led to another world was closed and I had closed it...with a little help, from some incredibly special people. The problem was Lanshoud was not the only place that had a gate, there were at least three more and I held the keys to all of them. Gates to where you might ask? In short, your guess is as good as mine. All I can tell you is that the one at Lanshoud appeared to be the way into and out of Hell. Yes, Hell, the Netherworld, the Abyss, whatever you prefer to call it, a place of evil? a place of punishment? Who knows? What I do know for certain is the gate at Lanshoud was a portal to another world. Please try to keep an open mind as I attempt to explain.

My life is complicated. I have no family, but I am not alone in the world. I have good friends who stand by me through thick and thin. I have property, money and now I have Christina a possible sibling of sorts. She looks like me, same eyes, same colouring. I found Christina after my husband died, or rather she found me. Christina's story was like mine. She inherited a fortune and property. She had guardians, caretaker parents and a caretaker husband whom she loved and believed were real, just like me. Her adopted parents are dead, like mine. My husband is dead, Christina's is missing. I inherited Lanshoud in Scotland; Christina inherited Schloss Heiligtum a little castle in Bavaria. I have met my birth father. I met him after I inherited from his will. Christina however had never met her birth father. We did know both our birth mothers were dead.

Heiligtum has a gate like the one at Lanshoud, a portal to another world, a gateway that allowed creatures to pass into our world. I had no idea if it was open or closed but the legends and folklore around the area, that tell tales of the Wild Hunt or Wilde Jagd, as they call it in Germany, suggest it is open. Tales abound in the area around Heiligtum and that led me to believe that the gate there had been opened and if so the danger of it lying open was too great to ignore. It had to be closed and I had the key.

I can imagine what you are thinking. How could I have met my birth father after he died. Simply, he wasn't dead, he just had found a way to go home to his own world. I know how it sounds but there are many academics in the world who believe that we have been visited by aliens in the past. The evidence they say is almost overwhelming. As proof they present stories written in ancient texts or carved into stone thousands of years old, from all corners of the world, or exhibit fossils that don't fit into the evolutionary chain.

Excavating and examining historical sites, it's not surprising that they have come to the understandable conclusion that primitive people may have had help from intelligent, technologically advanced beings. They could be right. Maybe that is a reasonable explanation for the movement of stones weighing anything from 2 to 50 tons or more used to build monoliths or pyramids, Stonehenge, the Statues of Easter Island, the Great Pyramid of Giza, Sacsayhuaman in the Peruvian Andes, the Nazca Lines in the Peruvian desert. The incredible 3D engineering of Tiwanacu in Western Bolivia. I could go on, but I am sure you get the gist.

It's not just the archeologists. The theologians who study the ancient scripts and holy books of the world's religions that describe angels, believe beings with wings flew down from the sky, that they came from a powerful God, the creator of mankind and that they were sent here to guide and help us. Change the name from angel to extraterrestrial being and in our 21st century world this belief takes on a fresh perspective. After all we now know you don't need wings to fly. So, who were the performers of magic described as being half bird, half man? Who were these beings credited with imparting knowledge and who were called Gods?

Who were the prophets and saints who were healers and performed miraculous deeds? Were they magicians?

About ten years ago, my husband and I were fortunate enough see a well-known magician perform. He took six members of the audience, hypnotized them in seconds and persuaded them they were desperate to eat an apple. He then handed each one a whole peeled onion and they happily munched away. Consider this, maybe, just maybe, there really were visitors to our planet and if that was the case how did they get here? Could it have been through a portal in space and time? If these portals exist, where are they? Are they open or closed? If, and only if, they really do exist, like the portals at Lanshoud and Heiligtum, where are they? and where do they lead?

Main Character List (Appearance in Previous books in brackets)

Erica Cameron (Lanshoud, Nephilim)
> A young widow with no living relatives who inherits Lanshoud and a vast fortune from an unknown benefactor

Katie and Gill (Lanshoud, Nephilim)
> Erica's close friends

Jack Docherty (Lanshoud, Nephilim)
> Gill's husband. Lecturer and Historian.

James Anderson (Lanshoud, Nephilim)
> Erica's solicitor and friend

Christina (Nephilim)
> Erica's sister, she only found recently She inherited Heiligtum and a fortune.

Frank Summers (Nephilim)
> Christina's husband

Otto Reinhardt
> German BND officer

Stephan
> Heiligtum's chauffeur

Kurt
> Helga's son and Heiligtum' s handy man

Helga Schroeder
> Heiligtum's housekeeper at Heiligtum.

Eli Laskov (Nephilim)
> Lecturer, Historian, and expert in ancient languages

Doria Van Brugan
> Eli's friend also an expert in ancient languages.

Dietrich Oppenheim
> Leader of a Neo Nazi cell in Munich

Jonah Seagraves (Lanshoud, Nephilim)
> Retired CID Officer

Carmen Valdez (Nephilim)
> Glasgow CID Officer.

Chapter 1

Heiligtum

The chauffeur driven car wound its way uphill through a thick forest of pine trees and emerged onto a single-track road. We had been chatting about various things since we left Munich airport but, in the car, Christina had been curiously quiet, fending off Katie's attempts to draw her into conversation. The road wound steadily uphill and fifteen minutes later Christina said, "we are here. Look, there is Schloss Heiligtum." I reached over to Katie's side to look out the window. There it was, clinging to the side of the mountain, perched rather precariously, on an outcrop of rock overlooking the valley below. It seemed more like a castle than a house. It had turrets and stone walls. It was breathtaking. Rapunzel would not have looked out of place hanging her long hair from one of those turret windows.

"Oh my God! It's beautiful!" Katie said. "It's like something from a fairytale."

Christina in a flat subdued voice said, "It is the Bavarian style. There are others like this. Neuschwanstein, King Ludwig's castle, the one on which Disney modeled the castle in their theme parks, is not far from here. It is near the Austrian border, I will take you to see it, if you like." She didn't turn her head when she spoke, just stared out the window. I had the feeling, now we had arrived she was not looking forward to what we might find here.

Christina introduced Katie and I to the human statue who had come to greet us. She was there waiting on the steps as we left the car, just as Molly my housekeeper, always did when I returned to Lanshoud. Only this woman with the ramrod back, dressed in black, though it was the height of summer, was nothing like Molly. She was younger for a start, early fifties I thought. She had straight black hair, cropped noticeably short and scraped back from her face. She wore a black collarless dress, buttoned down the front and tied with a black belt at the waist, like an old-fashioned maid's uniform but, without the apron.

Helga Schroeder smiled graciously at Christina and welcomed her home and when Christina introduced Katie and I, her acknowledgement was at least civil, though clipped, and cold. We were subjected to a distinctive pained expression as though she had suddenly detected a bad smell under her nose. Scanning me blatantly from head to toe, she made me feel as though I had spilled food on my clothing or mismatched my shoes.

Frau Schroeder led the way into a large entrance hall with a flagged stone floor and a sweeping staircase with a wooden balustrade. It was so polished it reflected the light from the magnificent chandelier hanging above us.

Christina had told me she had a housekeeper like Molly, but Frau Schroeder was nothing like Molly. In fact, she and Molly were like chalk and cheese. I call her Frau Schroeder and not Helga because she didn't believe in using first names, not because she felt in anyway subservient, I'm sure, but more, I suspect, because she wanted to keep us in our place; wherever she thought that was.

The chauffeur Stephan polite and with impeccable manners was at least friendly, as was Kurt the young man who collected our cases and showed us to our rooms. I noticed the Iron Lady was as short and sharp with them as she was with Katie and I. The one good thing was they all spoke flawless English.

My bedroom was large, cold, and sparsely furnished with a huge bed and heavy dark intricately carved wood furniture, so dark it was almost black. There was a wardrobe, a chest of drawers and a small table with one large chair. Even the chair was carved with leaves and flowers and when I looked closer there appeared to be faces all with their mouths open. In fact, all the furniture throughout Heiligtum was this dark furniture so highly polished I could see my face in it

That and the heavily embroidered brocade curtains and cushions gave the place a gloomy look. In my room there was a stone fireplace, clean and polished as though there had never been a fire lit there. Brightening the room, a little, on the walls were paintings of various German beauty spots and one of Heiligtum in winter, it was beautiful, with the snow sparkling in the winter sunshine, gracing the little castle like icing on a cake. The best of all was the view from my bedroom window.It was a breathtaking view of the mountain and the shear black rock face falling away into lush green meadows in the valley below, where a crystal blue lake nestled in the sunshine. Heiligtum had to be one of the most beautiful places in Europe.

Tired after the journey I stretched out on the bed and lay there gazing out on the azure blue sky with its little cotton wool clouds. I felt exhausted and overwhelmed with emotion. I kept living the last few days over and over in my mind. Hot tears stung my eyes and I made no attempt to stop them as they tumbled down my face. I was cold, I pulled the embroidered bed cover over me and buried my face in the pillow and gave in to sobbing, letting go in this place where I knew no one could hear me.

I had looked forward to coming here to Heiligtum. Sometimes, when you are overwhelmed as I had been with drama, fear, indecision, temptation, the best thing to do is to escape somewhere quiet. I wanted to help Christina search for her missing husband Frank but now that I was here, I felt worried, anxious, insecure and I had been feeling that way since I stepped on the plane. Why was I like that? Well, to be truthful I think it was because James didn't come with us. For the first time since that incredible day when I first met him there was no James to speak to, to phone, call or text when I needed him. Oh yes, needed him. How many times have I denied needing him? How long had I spent convincing myself I was some kind of superwoman? Proclaiming to everyone who would listen how independent and strong I was. Now, when he was caring for and supporting someone else, I was devastated, hurt, angry even.

James, the perfect man. I didn't know a woman who wasn't under his spell. Cool calm collected James, the ultimate male protector. It was after all what he was good at. Someone who picked up the pieces when someone else's life fell apart. It was his forte, I suspect he loved to be needed. It was not his strong point. I think it was a weakness in his personality, I just didn't realise it until now. The blessed St James would always find another lame duck to care for. I lay on that bed and sobbed my heart out. I hated him.

How could he do that to me? I may have denied it to everyone, a thousand times, but in truth I thought he loved me, no, I knew he loved me. I wanted to pick up the phone and tell him I needed him, beg him to come, so that I could tell him I loved him. I wanted to say that I was sorry, that I was a fool.

I missed him so much I had a physical pain in my chest, but of course I couldn't call him and now I thought my heart would break with the strain. I wanted to feel his arms around me again, to rest my head on his shoulder, and feel the warmth of his skin through his shirt to feel safe again.

Burying my face in the pillow, I let the tears fall, until eventually I fell asleep; It was over an hour before I woke. My head was pounding. I lay on the bed looking out of the window mulling things over in my mind. Should I give up, could I get him back? Of course, I could get him back, faint heart never won fair maid, well it works both ways. I sat up and I looked for my mobile. I would call him right now. I fumbled about in my bag and when I did find it there was no signal. I would go and find a landline...then I saw my face in the mirror, chalk white face and red raw eyes.

Like most things in the last few years, nothing had gone as planned. Just when I had some semblance of order in my life, everything changed...just like that, bang, fate struck again,and all my plans fell into disarray. James, Katie, and I were traveling to Germany with Christina, who was going to Heiligtum to search for Frank. Then the call came from James, to say that his father's partner in the law firm Galbraith and Anderson, had died suddenly of a heart attack. For James it wasn't just the shock of the sudden death, but the loss of someone who had not only been his father's business partner but his father's lifelong friend. James was needed, he had to stay and take over the open cases of the remarkably busy, now deceased, Adam Galbraith. James could not come to Munich.

Adam Galbraith was a lovely man. I met him on that fateful day when he delivered the news that I had inherited Lanshoud and millions of pounds. He was a gentle, kind man and I knew James was very fond of him. When James said he hoped I understood why he had to delay coming with us to Germany, of course I did. What I didn't know at that time was that James was the executor of the will and that Adam Galbraith's only surviving relative was his daughter Alison, who was a childhood friend of James, and who had been besotted with him ever since. All this information was imparted to my sinking heart by Adam Galbraith's secretary Laura, who attached herself to me at the funeral, four weeks later. Four weeks, because it had been a sudden death and under Scottish law one in ten of every sudden death is referred to the Procurator Fiscal and is sent for postmortem. Adam Galbraith fell into that category.

In that four weeks that followed. I called James three times under various pretexts. He cut the conversations short saying he would call back, but he never did. As the weeks wore on, I felt he was becoming cold, distant, matter of fact, repeatedly apologetic that he could not be there to help us. He advised me to go ahead without him and he would join us later, but Christina was not ready to go, she had things to do first. She intended to stay in Germany till she found Frank. She had arrangements to make, and Katie, not sure how long we would be away, wanted to arrange management of her two gift shops before we left. So, we waited for James and I went to the funeral.

"Mrs. Cameron," the voice said as I followed the mourners into the church. I turned to see Laura the secretary. "It's so nice to see you again. James said you might be coming, he asked me to look out for you as you may not know anyone else here."

"No, he's right. I don't know any of the family, but Mr. Galbraith was so kind to me I wanted to pay my respects."

"Yes, James said as much. It's nice to see so many people have turned up. He hadn't any family to speak of, just his daughter Alison." She looked around. "These people are mostly just friends and colleagues."

At that point James walked into the church with a young woman dressed in black hanging onto his arm. Laura whispered "It's as well she has him. There is no one else. Did you know they were engaged at one time?" "Engaged! No, James has never mentioned it."

"Really! That surprises me. It was a few years since they broke up, but they were engaged for over a year, plans were being made. Mr. Galbraith always hoped they would marry someday. He was fond of James. I don't know what happened. I think it was Alison who broke it off, but don't quote me on that, I could be wrong. Maybe James met someone else, who knows," she sighed. Maybe this will bring them together again. She needs him now and he is not the kind of guy who walks away from his responsibilities."

No, he wasn't. That much was true. I knew that more than anyone. Right then I wished I had never come. What was I doing there anyway? I hardly knew the dead man. I had felt obliged because James was so upset. I thought it was the right thing to do. I stupidly thought James might need my support for a change.

James had been close to this man; he didn't just walk Alison into the church he sat beside her in the front pew. He delivered the eulogy and stood at the door with her, thanking mourners for coming to the funeral. If I hadn't known better, I would have thought it was her partner. I went to that funeral alone and watched James as he provided support for Alison Galbraith and I felt numb. She in turn hung onto him at every opportunity, at the church and as they followed the other mourners to the crematorium; she had her hand on his arm constantly as if to steady herself. They appeared to be a couple. Laura had to correct a former colleague who thought they were man and wife by now.

The service at the crematorium was short but it seemed like an eternity for me, as from a rear pew I watched James, his arm around her, comforting a distraught Alison. When the coffin had gone through the curtains to the strain of Highland Cathedral, everyone turned towards the aisle and led by Alison and James the procession of mourners left the little chapel. As it passed it halted for a moment and James turned his head. I knew instinctively he was looking for me. In that split second, between the heads of the people standing in front, our eyes met. It was only seconds, but I drowned in his eyes and the world around me faded. He stopped and stared, I smiled at him, he just stared for a moment too long and Alison looked up at him and pulled his arm, he had to move on.

Stomach clenched I knew without a shadow of doubt James had a new dependent, a new helpless female clinging to him for support. A new Erica, in the form of Alison, someone to hold up through her dark days ahead. It's what he does and does well, I was the living proof. My hurt allowed my imagination to run riot. They might even renew their engagement. I had my independence now, and so it was time for a replacement. Alison would fit the bill perfectly. Well, I would cope. I repeated my mantra over and over in my head. I am strong independent and rich. I swore to myself I would never depend on him or any man again. My heart was broken for the last time. I didn't know it then, but in the quiet moments of the days ahead, and in the hush of night, and every moment of every day when I wasn't distracted, that little gap between the mourners when I drowned in James' eyes, those bitter sweet seconds frozen in time, haunted my heart. Like a video playing over and over I remembered that small space between the heads and James looking for and finding me in the crowd.

I excused myself and left, declining an invitation to accompany Laura and the other mourners to a local hotel. I pulled over on the way home and phoned Katie to ask her to book the first flight to Munich. I didn't call James again.

There was a light tap at the door. I called "come in." It was Katie.

"How gorgeous is this place?" she asked.

"Breathtakingly beautiful", I answered. Looking back through the window. "How's your room?"

Not as big as this," she said pulling down the sleeves of her sweater, "but just as cold. It's hard to believe it's summer outside."

I pointed "Look at that painting it's Heiligtum in winter, it's magnificent."

Katie studied the painting. "Did you spot the Harlequin?"

"Where?" I went to look.

"There in the corner." She was right, I hadn't noticed the tiny little figure standing among the trees on the approach road. "Christina was telling the truth about the harlequins being here too. Oh! and there's a figurine in my room."

"What do you mean she was telling the truth? Did you think she was lying?"

"I don't know what I think..." she hesitated. "I just don't wholly trust her."

The harlequins had been my birth father Luke's way of leaving reminders that the legendary ghostly wild hunt still rode the countryside at night seeking souls and we had to be on guard. The Wild Hunt. The horsemen who had come through the gates and been chasing him for centuries. The little harlequins were a warning and the home I had inherited Lanshoud on the East Coast of Scotland was full of them.

"Anyway" Katie said "I came to tell you lunch is being served."

I closed my bedroom door and as we walked along the corridor Katie in a soft quiet voice asked. "Have you been crying?"

"I'm fine."

"I didn't ask if you were fine. I asked if you had been crying."

Since it was blatantly obvious, I had been crying and to stop her switching on her motherly mantel, I stopped and pleaded "Please Katie, don't start."

"She waited a moment studying me. "Have you even heard from James?"

"No and I am asking you, if you care at all about my sanity, stop asking me about him."

"I'm sorry," she said "I am worried about you that's all. You haven't been yourself since we got here."

In an exasperated tone I said "Look Katie we are here we to help Christina find Frank and to find the other gate if there is one. I don't want to talk about James anymore. He is busy with his own life. Ok?"

She was watching me closely and the understanding in her eyes hurt me even more. "Ok" she said. "I'm sorry I upset you."

"I sighed, I felt defeated. "No, I'm the one who should be sorry. I know you are trying to help. I just ...I just don't know what's wrong with me, I have everything anyone could ever need yet I feel so down, so lost. Sometimes I think I am losing my mind."

Then we were both silent. After a moment She said. "I want to say one thing then I promise I'll let it go. I won't mention him again". She paused then said softly, "I know you have been down. I can see it, so don't expect me to stand by and say nothing. You are like the sister I never had. I can't stand to see you hurting like this. You say you don't know what's wrong with you, well I can tell you. That tear that stings the edge of your eye, that lump in your throat, that hollowness and pain in your chest, it's a kind of grief, it's love all bottled up with nowhere to go. One way or another you need to let it out. Tell him Erica, pick up that phone and tell him. He loves you; we all know that." She said.

I shook my head. I could feel the tears stinging my eyes. I couldn't speak. She was right of course, only it was too late. I genuinely believed I had lost any chance of a relationship with James, and it was all my own fault, I said "It's too late, he's with someone else."

Katie studied my face, when I didn't speak, she sighed deeply. "I said I will let it go and I will. Come," she put her arm through mine. "Let's go see if we can help Christina." She pursed her lips. "I think this should be a cakewalk compared to the gate at Lanshoud."

I prayed to God she was right, but I already had my reservations. Katie wasn't sure about Christina, well, I felt there was something not quite right about Heiligtum, but I hadn't put my finger on it just yet.

Katie and I had been at Heiligtum for the last few weeks. The idea being that we would wait for James to join us before attempting to find the gate, but it was pretty obvious after I returned from the funeral that James had other plans. So, we settled with helping Christina in her so far fruitless search for her husband Frank Summers. She contacted the local police who came to interview her. She gave them an edited version of the events that took place in Glasgow and voiced her feeling that he may have returned to Germany. They in turn questioned her relentlessly, asking pointedly if her relationship with her husband had been a good one, and why she had employed a private investigator instead of going to the police in the first place.

Christina started at the beginning explaining that as we didn't speak German, she would be translating along the way, she then told them as much as she could without revealing anything that might have her written off as a lunatic. She explained about the private investigator David Baxter's death and about the brutal beating she received from an unknown assailant. They then asked more pointed questions about Heiligtum, about how she inherited, when and from whom. The more Christina evaded answering directly the more they grew suspicious. It was clear from the outset that they believed the missing man was more the concern of the Scottish police as it was in Scotland he lived, worked, and disappeared. They did however agree that he could have returned to Germany and said they would initiate a missing persons alert on their network. They would also be contacting the police in Glasgow and asked for the name of the investigating officer. Christina was forced to name Detective Inspector Carmen Valdez. They left saying they would be in touch.

Christina showed them out. When she returned Katie said. "Did anyone else get the feeling they weren't interested or was it just me."

Christina agreed" No I felt that too."

"I think you should have been firmer with them." Katie said. "You practically helped them to decide it was a problem for the Scots police and not them."

Christina was taken aback by her remark. "I answered their questions what else did you expect me to say? What more could I tell them?" Then a few moments later, with no warning that a breakdown was imminent or the slightest clue she wasn't coping, Christina stood up with tear filled eyes and without apology left the room.

"Great." I said, "that went well. She had no choice; she could hardly tell them the truth about what happened."

Remorseful, Katie said "You're right. Maybe we should go after her."

"No, I think maybe we should leave her for a while." I took a deep breath. "I think those tears have been a long time coming."

I had plenty of things to keep my mind off James and Alison Galbraith. We had been searching for Frank by going through his papers and the clothes he kept at Heiligtum. The truth was Christina had no idea where to start looking. When she hired David Baxter, the private detective in Glasgow, she really believed he would find Frank, but all David's leads led to a dead end, literally, when David himself died in a hit and run and the police were unable to trace the car. Then Christina had almost lost her own life. That assault, the both physical and mental trauma she sustained as a result, left her suffering from sleepless nights and flashbacks that assailed her without warning, leaving her in a state of near panic. Katie and I had witnessed one of those panic attacks at the airport in Munich.

Katie mused afterwards. "You know, that's the first sign of real emotion I've seen from Christina, she's a cold fish. I mean honestly, does she look to you like someone who has lost the love of her life?" In truth, no, she didn't. Katie was right, Christina didn't show her emotions, not to us anyway. I said, "I think she had been too busy fighting for her own life. The implications of his disappearance, the not knowing if he was dead or alive are just beginning to hit her now."

Katie stood up and looked up at the painting on the wall beside her. It depicted a man, suited in armour, plunging a spear into the blood-soaked chest of a soldier in the battlefield. "Did I mention I really do not like this place?" She said hugging herself.

11

"Yes, several times"

She screwed up her eyes. "Well I'm reinforcing my opinion, notching it up a little, it gives me the creeps."

I laughed.

"What? You think I'm joking?"

"After Lanshoud? Yes, you have to be. Anyway, I remember you said it was like a fairytale castle?"

"I did think that...at first... but this place is... I can't describe it. It's a feeling that someone is watching me. That there is someone or something outside my door or just around the corner just waiting to pounce."

"Oh, I see, and you didn't feel like that at Lanshoud?"

"That was different, there were more people there."

"Initially there wasn't. At one point there was only you and I."

"There was a lot of moral support at Lanshoud and I am not feeling it here. I do think it's like a fairytale castle and I enjoy looking at it, at a distance, but in here, well..." she stood up waving her hands around. "Look at it the stone walls, the decor, the enormous doors that weigh a ton. The tapestries with battle scenes of blood and gore, and that tour Christina gave us.... you are not seriously telling me it didn't freak you out a bit? The hall with the pillars and that alter thing in the center, with the stone drains running off it, and the stone seats all around it. How could she live here for so much of her life and not know what it was used for? Looked like human sacrifice to me"

I smiled; she was on a rant. "You're letting your imagination run riot."

"As for the pretty turrets, oh my God Erica, those were chains in those walls, and the cages? What do you suppose was kept in them? They were far too big for cats or dogs. She said she didn't know? I mean seriously, you really think she doesn't know anything? She was brought up here. She speaks fluent German. You would think at some point she would find out the history of this place."

"I am sure she does but maybe she doesn't want to scare us, after all most castles have dungeons of some sort and I suspect chains in these places. I mused remembering something. "Tell you what though. It did occur to me that she is hiding something because she was so insistent that we don't go near the crypt and then she sidetracked when I asked her why. Then when I asked her who was buried there, she said she didn't know."

After lunch Katie and I took our tea into the small sitting room and Christina went to collect some papers she had found. Shortly afterwards, she burst through the door "I think I've found out something important." She was more animated than usual. "I've been looking and looking and finding nothing but invoices and receipts but look at this."

Katie and I were lounging on huge soft comfy chairs, toasting ourselves at fire that had been lit, in this the smallest of the sitting rooms. The fire was necessary because at Heiligtum rooms were all large and cold, with damp patches visible on some of the walls, the walls that weren't covered with paintings of battles or snow-capped mountains or damsels being rescued by knights on horse-back in full armour. These rooms were not conducive to cozy warmth. It was the height of summer but the castle being halfway up a mountain and with thick stone walls that kept the heat out, it was always cold. In that respect it was worse than Lanshoud. Christina waived a letter in the air. "Frank and I usually came here together, for a holiday, but Frank also came himself to deal with matters related to the running of Heiligtum and he would call in on the way back from business trips. Helga told me that Stephan had driven Frank to a business meeting in Munich, the last three times he was here on his own. Frank didn't even tell me he had come here on those occasions. I am used to Frank being away. He travelled a lot because he worked for the travel agency." She hesitated and then added, "of course I now know that was all lies. He never worked for any travel agent. Anyway, according to Helga, the last time he was here was around the time he disappeared, the time I thought he was still in Glasgow."

A chap at the door and Frau Schroeder came in with a tray of tea and cake.

"Thank you" Christina said. Is Stephan here?" She asked.

Frau Schroeder replied. "Yes, I think he is in the garage."

"Please tell him I would like to speak to him."

"I will send Kurt for him immediately."

When the door closed Katie said," she really is the archetypal ice lady."

Christina looked puzzled. "Really! You like her? I thought you would be put off by Helga's formality, but she is alright really."

Katie frowned. I didn't say I liked her I said she was an ice lady."

"Oh" I laughed, "We both thought you said a nice lady."

"Christina smiled. "It's the German personality, sometimes they can appear standoffish and aloof with strangers. Most German people are reserved by nature and they can appear cold. Manners are especially important to them. They tend to treat strangers quite formally. In this country the boundaries of one's personal space are a little larger than most and they are not big on small talk. It takes a bit of getting used to."

"Hmm I figured that. "Katie said, not impressed.

Moments later Stephan knocked on the sitting room door. Christina questioned him at length. "Stephan, these business meetings in Munich, that you took my husband to, do you know who he was meeting?"

"Yes Madam, I drove Herr Summers there on three occasions, to meet a man called Otto Reinhardt. Always it was at Kaffeehouse Rutgart on Marienplatz. On three occasions I left Herr Summers there and collected him an hour later."

"Did Herr Summers say anything to you about Otto Reinhardt? Do you know anything about him? Was he a friend?"

"No, Madam. Herr Summers said it was a business meeting." Stephan frowned trying to find the words. "Herr Reinhardt is an Immobilienmakler." I am sorry I do not know the English word."

"An Immobilienmakler!" Christina was surprised. "An estate agent?"

Christina turned to Katie and I "What on earth was Frank doing meeting an estate agent?"

"Maybe he was thinking of selling Heiligtum" Katie volunteered.

Christina was quick to reply, and it was obvious she was not pleased at Katie's comment. "Frank would not do that without telling me and furthermore Heiligtum is not his to sell. No, it has to be something else".

"I believe he was looking for premises for his travel company Madam." Stephan said.

Christina was quiet. There was of course no travel company, only Stephan was not to know that. How would he know that Frank Summers had been lying about his job?

"Will that be all Madam" he asked.

"Thank you, Stephan. That will be all for now, but I may need you to take me to Munich tomorrow."

"Of course, Madam."

Katie smiled at me and I knew why. Stephan was so stiff, so polite, even I expected him to click his heels together and salute.

Katie lifted her tablet and looked up the name. "Here it is," she said she pointed to the tablet in her hand. There's a website. Reinhardt Immobilienmakler. It even has his name, look, Otto Reinhardt and the address and a telephone number. She turned the laptop around to Christina. Why don't you phone him now?"

Christina called the number. Otto was out meeting a client. His secretary would ask him to call when he returned. He did and she arranged to meet him the next day. "Come with me." she said "Come and see Munich."

Chapter 2

Garmisch-Partenkirchen

We left after breakfast. Christina was to meet Otto Reinhardt at the coffee house on the Marienplatz. She thought it best she should meet him alone. They were to meet at eleven. Choosing that time because that was when the Rathaus Glockenspiel came to life. Stephan dropped us off and Christina told him we intended to do some sightseeing and we would not be returning till evening, so, she would call him when we were ready to leave. She left us there in the Marienplatz which is the central square in the old town and the heart of the Munich. It is a beautiful square with lots of shops and that day it was teeming with tourists most of whom had come to see and hear the glockenspiel.

We followed the people to the new town hall where everyone stood looking up at the figures high above. We stood with the other tourists and at exactly eleven o'clock the bells rang out, and the life-sized mechanical figures of the glockenspiel came to life. We were lucky to be standing beside a group of American tourists and their guide and so we listened to the story. The guide explained it was part of the New Town Hall and had been there since 1908. The tale depicted by the top story of the clock, as the life size figures twirled round and round to the bells ringing out music, told the story of the fantastically expensive marriage of the Bavarian Duke Wilhelm V in 1568. The mechanical jousters dressed in red and blue represented characters from Bavaria and Longthingren. On the next level down brightly, painted figures representing the town's coopers performed their famous Schafflerstanz, the Coopers Dance. According to tradition, the Coopers Dance is tied to the plague of 1517, when the coopers lured the frightened people from their house by performing the foot slapping dance. The whole show lasted fifteen minutes and ended when a small golden bird chirruped from the top of the glockenspiel. It was worth the trip to Munich just to see it.

We fought our way through the crowds and spent the next hour shopping. The shopping was good on Marienplatz, but the crowds were daunting. Christina had said in winter the square was even more busy, filled with the stalls of the Christkindlmark, the Christmas market. With colourful stalls selling wonderfully flamboyant and creative things. I was waiting outside one of the shops for Katie who was at the till, buying a cuckoo clock for her flat, when my mobile rang. Minutes later I saw Christina making her way through the crowds. She looked strange, worried, and pale. "Are you alright?"

She nodded and whispered. "Where is Katie? We cannot talk here; it is dangerous Otto says there are too many ears. Follow me, quickly please."

I felt that little adrenaline chill creeping up my spine. She turned back into the crowd and I called to Katie who had paid for her purchase and was about to start browsing again. Christina was already almost hidden by the sea of people.

"What's wrong?" Katie asked. I want to look at those dolls."

"I don't know, just follow her, quickly or we will lose her in the crowd."

Ten minutes later we were in the car and speeding away from Munich. Stephan drove like a bat out of Hell. Christina, tense and anxious, said "We can't go back to Heiligtum. Otto Reinhart thinks we are in danger. We are going to a house in Garmisch-Partenkirchen. Otto's sister has a holiday home there. Otto will meet us there later tonight and Stephan will stay with us till he comes.

Katie looked at me puzzled. "Stay with us! Why? What's happened?"

Christina didn't answer, with white knuckles she was gripping her seat belt, pulling it forward to allow herself to turn and look out the rear window. She was wide-eyed and chewing her lip.

Somehow from the driver's seat Stephan knew. "He said, "It's alright Tina, we are not being followed."

"Followed! Who would be following us?" I asked.

Christina shook her head. "I don't know Otto said there were people watching us. He said he would explain later. He just called Stephan and told us to go."

Stephan had called her Tina. A big change from the previous formality at Heiligtum. Katie raised her eyebrows at me and mouthed silently. "Tina!" I shrugged I was as surprised as she was. The familiarity implied by the nickname was completely contrary to the very formal way in which Stephan had been addressing Christina ever since we arrived in Germany. Christina didn't react at all. She was lost in staring out the window. Only when we were far away from Munich did she settle back in her seat. She was very pale and looked frightened. Her jaw was clenched, she was holding herself stiff and her breathing was quick and shallow. Fearing another panic attack, like the one she had at the airport, I slipped my arm around hers and gave her a squeeze of reassurance. She gave me a weak smile. "I am so sorry," she said this is my fault I should not have brought you here."

"It's not your fault. We volunteered to come." Katie said.

"Nevertheless, I may have put you in danger." she said looking out the rear window again.

It seemed to take forever but eventually, we came to a little town full of brightly painted buildings decorated with art and flowers. The car turned off the road and we were climbing up a steep dirt road. We passed a few houses and continued to climb the track when we heard the feint sound of bells ringing, not a tinkle, but the deep base sound of large bells.

"What is that?" Katie asked looking out the windows.

Stephan stopped the car. "Cows. They are being brought down from their mountain pasture. We will have to wait till they pass."

We heard deep bellowing and mooing and suddenly there appeared a huge herd of blonde coloured, doe-eyed cows. They calmly split in in the center and walked around the car. Every so often one would stop and look in at us with huge, soft brown, heavily lashed eyes.

"I have never been so close to a cow before" Katie said, "And those bells are the same as the ones we saw in the gift shop this morning. I picked one up, they weigh a ton."

A man on a bike, came at the back driving the cows. One cow stopped and stared at Katie. "Oh my God" She said. "Look at those beautiful eyes, they are huge. Look at her eyelashes. I don't think I will ever be able to eat beef again."

"I didn't realise cows still wore bells." I said. It was surreal sitting there waiting for them to pass, like a scene from the Sound of Music.

Stephan answered. "It is necessary. They wander freely, it helps the farmer to find them when one wanders off and gets lost or when the mist covers the mountain."

When the last cow had moved behind us Stephan drove a little further up the hill then stopped at the only house for about a mile. "This must be it," he said. It was a white stone-built house with a red slate roof, red wooden framed windows with shutters and a red wooden door. In keeping with the alpine theme each window had a painted window box filled to overflowing with flowers. "It certainly fits the description." He said.

The house, the last one on the track was similar to others we had passed. Stephan turned off the road. He stepped out of the car and opened the door for Christina, then did the same for Katie and I. Katie gripped my arm. I knew, I saw it too. Stephan was wearing a shoulder holster under his Jacket. "He's got a gun." Katie mouthed silently."

Garmisch-Partenkirchen is a ski town and was originally two separate towns until the winter Olympics of 1936 when Adolf Hitler forced the Mayors to make it one town. Otto's sister was a skier and she kept the little house, which was no more than a bungalow of sorts, sitting on the slope of a mountain. It had three bedrooms, one bathroom and a large open plan kitchen, with patio doors that opened on to a garden and with a large rustic table and six chairs alongside the patio doors. I looked out but there was a mist coming down fast and nothing to see but dense whiteness.

"Is someone going to tell me what's going on? Why are we here? "Katie asked looking at me as she sat down on one of the two sofa's that lay at either side of an open fire.

"I have no idea...Christina?"

Christina called "Stephan, Otto said there would be basic supplies... would you mind making some coffee?" Stephan didn't move but I put up my hand up to stop him anyway. "Wait, wait a moment. Christina would you please explain why you brought us here?"

"Coffee Stephan, please, or tea if you prefer?" she asked still looking at me blankly.

Stephan didn't move, he spoke gently. "I will of course, but I think it's time to tell them the truth...Yes?"

"I know that," she said resignedly but she still didn't offer any explanation.

Katie shook her head. "This is ridiculous."

"Yes, I'm sorry, it's just... "Christina sat down and put her head in her hands. Then she ran her fingers through her hair and looked up with tears pricking at her eyes. "...I don't know where to start. I know so little. This is all I know. Otto is coming here tonight. This is his sister's holiday home. She is a skier. He said there would be basic supplies and he would bring dinner for us."

She rattled the information out. Irritated I raised my voice "You know that's not what we are asking you. Stephan, what is she not telling us?" His face gave nothing away.

Christina looked up at me sweeping her hair behind both ears. "We are here because Otto believes we are in danger."

"So, you said but danger from what exactly? "I asked.

"I am waiting for Otto Reinhardt, "she repeated. "He said they threatened Frank. Otto didn't even know he was missing. He knew Frank had gone back to Scotland and thought he was safe there." She started rocking back and forth. "Otto said they may have taken him because they want Heiligtum." She looked at me through fear filled eyes. She was obviously scared, and she was beginning to scare me.

I put my arm around her." Who are they? Christina you're not making any sense." She looked over to Stephan.

He said. "They need to know, now. It makes no sense to hide it any longer. You are putting them at risk by not telling them."

Christina waited, looking at Stephan, then she turned to me." He's right," she said I am sick of all the lies, of hiding things. Please Stephan tell them what you know. Explain if you can. Otto can fill in detail when he gets here."

Stephan brought a tray of tea and coffee and placed it before us on the table. He removed his jacket and folded it carefully over a chair, so now, the gun nestling in the shoulder holster was in full view. "There is no fresh milk I am afraid, only this powdered milk." He handed me a mug. I don't like powdered milk at the best of times, but the tea was hot and therefore comforting. He sat down beside Katie who caught my eye and gave me a little smile to make sure his broad chest and the bulging muscles in his arms were not lost on me, they weren't but I was not in the least interested in Stephan.

At this point my mobile rang. I went to get up. Stephan put his hand up. "Sit" he ordered. He rose and walked to where I had left my handbag on the kitchen table and began rifling through it until he found the now silent mobile.

He checked the caller. "Who is James?"

James is a friend, a close friend." I stood up walking towards him my hand out. "I will call him back. You don't have to worry about James."

"I will be the judge of that. Is he your lover?"

That stopped me in my tracks. I was taken aback. "That is none of your business." I snapped, annoyed at his frankness, and thinking I had misjudged this guy.

"No matter," he shrugged his shoulders. "You do not have to tell me, but you are my business and if you want to stay alive... no calls."

"Stay alive!" Katie exclaimed.

Ignoring her, he took the battery and sim card out of the phone and handed it back to me. "And yours." he said to Katie and Christina." He took the sim cards out of both phones and handed them back. Then he sat down beside us.

"Now I will tell you what I know."

I had never heard Stephan say more than a few words, but though heavily accented, he spoke fluent English. "Otto Reinhardt and I go back a long way. We both served together in the Bundeswehr, the German army. After discharge Otto became an estate agent and I a mercenary. My job paid better." he smiled at Katie, who was looking more than a little nervous. "Two years ago, I was employed by Frank Summers, as a bodyguard. He had been approached by a man called Dietrich Oppenheim, on the surface a restaurant owner, in truth, the leader of a secretive and very militant Neo Nazi group. Oppenheim offered Frank a large sum of money for Heiligtum and followed it with threats when Frank declined his more than generous offer. You should know they are not the kind of people who take no for an answer. Frank had no idea why they wanted Heiligtum."

"Like any other Neo Nazi group, they are white supremacists." Jew haters, homophobes, who worship the ideals of Adolf Hitler. Worried, Frank then went to Otto whom he knew was involved in an anti-Nazi group. Otto warned Frank that Oppenheim and his gang were ruthless and saw themselves as the leaders of a movement that would enable a fourth Reich to rise. He gave Frank my name and advised him to employ me, to protect him, when he was in Germany."

"Why did they want Heiligtum?" I asked as confused as ever.

"We do not know for sure, but Otto had his suspicions. His ninety-one-year-old grandfather was in the SS during the war and at one time had visited Heiligtum, with a high-ranking official in the German army. Apparently, the SS had a great interest in Heiligtum. Otto's grandfather has a good memory and his mind is sharp despite his age. His grandfather's stories are one of the reasons Otto became involved with the anti-Nazi group. Frank asked to speak to Otto's grandfather, but the old man refused.

"No, he didn't, "Christina interrupted, "At least I think he may have changed his mind."

"Why do you think that?" Stephan asked. His eyes narrowed as he stared at her intently. "Because I found a note a note from Otto saying that 'He' would speak to him now. I take that 'He' was the grandfather."

Stephan took a deep breath. "Maybe."

Christina cleared her throat and sat back against the cushions. "I didn't understand why they would want Heiligtum. Even if it were to carry out their subversive activities, out of the public eye, it doesn't make sense. It is to remote to use as a meeting place and the roads are often impassible in winter. Heiligtum as you know is not the most welcoming place, it's cold and damp and the upkeep is expensive."

Katie gave me a surprised look but said nothing, we were obviously on the same thought path, so I asked Christina. "If you knew about Oppenheim? How come you said you didn't know Otto Reinhardt." I looked over at Katie, who gave me an *I told you not to trust her look*.

"No, no." She sat up. "I knew there was someone, but not his name. Frank only told me there was a man wanted to buy the castle, that was all. Frank said he was a businessman he wanted it for meetings or something. I didn't know they were Neo-Nazis. Frank didn't tell me any of that. I only found out today when I spoke to Otto. He thinks Oppenheim might have harmed Frank and now will be looking for me. I am so sorry I have dragged you into this."

"You didn't drag us, "I said, "We came willingly to help you find Frank." And of course, to look for the other gate." But I kept silent about that.

"Yes, but I still feel bad, "she said

"Fine then, call the police now, tell them you have information for them." Katie said looking at Christina, not exactly sympathetically.

Christina was wringing her hands. "That is what I intended to do but Otto said no. He said we couldn't trust the police that they had been infiltrated by this group. Otto said they may have Frank and they may be coming for me. When I told him, I had already spoken to the police he told me to come here, that we were all in danger.

"All of us?!" Katie was indignant. "You think Erica and I are in danger? I mean we are just... tourists."

"Hardly." Stephan said. "You came here with Christina from the UK. They will know that. They will already know everything there is to know about you."

I was worried now. "Have I got this right. This is a Neo-Nazi group maybe trying to buy somewhere remote to have their meetings. I don't get why is it so important that they would resort to violence?" Stephan stood up and walked to the window. The rain was now thundering down, and a rising wind battered it against the patio doors. "Otto should have been here by now" he said. "The weather will be slowing him down." He turned "We believe it is not for a meeting or to establish a headquarters. We think there is something valuable at Heiligtum. We think it has something to do with Heinrich Himmler and the SS who visited Heiligtum during the war. We think it has something to do with Christina and maybe you. Because you see, no one and I mean no one at all, has visited Heiligtum since 1945. The only people who have crossed the threshold are the Summers, Frau Schroeder, Kurt, me and now you."

"Who are the 'we'?" I asked "Who are the other people involved? Who was watching and knew we were being followed? Is it the Anti-Nazi group Otto is part of? Are you one of them?"

He pulled the curtains across the window, but before he could answer there was a banging on the door. A voice called out "Stephan it's me." He hurried to unlock the door and a man stepped in quickly to escape the downpour. He was carrying two large bags, one of food the other a nylon zipped hold-all containing our clothes and toiletries which had been hastily put together by Frau Schroeder. Kurt had brought them to Otto at a garage just outside Munich.

Chapter 3

Otto Reinhardt

Otto was not what I expected, that is he was not my idea of what a German estate agent might look like. He was young, early forties I thought and athletic looking. He had black hair, striking blue eyes and a five o'clock shadow on a pale complexion. He looked more like a male model than something as mundane as an estate agent. He removed his jacket to shake off the rain exposing a shoulder holster with a gun tucked neatly under his arm.

Speaking quietly in German to Stephan, then switching effortlessly into perfect English he said, "Christina, I see Stephan has been taking care of you." Loosening his tie, he sat down on the sofa opposite Katie. He undid the strap of the shoulder holster and placed it on a little side table. Katie looked at me, eyes wide. I shook my head slightly, expecting her to comment on the guns, which was silly really, because they were making no attempt to hide them. Stephan handed him a cup of coffee. He took the cup turned and smiled at me. "I realise my sister's coffee is vile, but it will be hot and wet." Leaning forward he held out his hand. "Otto Reinhardt...and you are Erica Cameron I presume since you look so like Christina... and this must be Katie? I would say it is a pleasure to meet you both, but I am afraid there is nothing pleasing about these circumstances. He sat back, looking from one to the other. "You are confused I imagine""

"Very" I said.

"I am sorry, but It was necessary to get you out of Munich as quickly as possible. You had been followed from Heiligtum."

"So, I believe. Do you know who was following us and why?"

25

He eyed me up and down. Studying me, in no hurry to answer. "Yes, Stephan has told you about the Neo-Nazi group and I can only speculate, either they think Christina might lead them to Frank or they have him and now want Christina, either are possibilities we must consider. The people we think are following you, are capable of anything,"

"Does Frau Schroeder know where we are?" Katie asked

Otto shook his head and put the cup down. "No, Christina phoned her from my office. It is better that she does not know where you are, that way she cannot be, shall we say be persuaded, to reveal your whereabouts."

Placing a fresh pot of coffee on the table Stephan said, "Christina told Frau Schroeder that you had decided to go to Berlin for a few days and that is what she will tell anyone who calls."

"And when did you tell her that?" I asked Christina.

Christina looked a little guilty, she said, "I phoned her from Otto's office."

I snapped at her "Oh I see, you told her, but it didn't occur to you to tell us?

Otto sipped the hot coffee and grimaced. "I think I will buy my sister, a coffee machine for her birthday." Then he said "I asked Christina not to tell you anything. I did not want to scare you. Would you like some more coffee?" He held up the pot.

"Well you failed miserably, and I prefer tea," I said icily.

He smiled again. "I am not surprised if this is the best we have to offer. Never mind, Brigitta has a secret stash of wine and I know where to find it."

"I take it Brigitta is your sister?" I asked.

"Yes, and she has good taste in wine, but she does not herself drink coffee and so, we have only this instant to offer."

Christina in a quiet little voice asked, "could we have been followed here?"

"No, Stephan lost them in Munich." Looking up at Stephan he said something in German.

Stephan replied in English. "Yes, only what you said they should know. That a Neo-Nazi group may be involved in Frank's disappearance".

Otto sat back. "Yes, and because of that I believe it is not safe for you to stay here."

"So, you think we should go back to Heiligtum?" Christina asked.

"No, I meant it would be best if you all returned to the UK."

For Katie, the trip to Germany had been relatively pleasant, vacation-like, even though the intention was to help Christina find Frank and search for the second gate. In spite of the drama around our hasty exit from Munich, she said she thought that we were fleeing Munich just to protect Christina. Until that point, I don't think she had even considered that she herself might be in danger.

"You seem to think they would be interested in Katie and I?" I asked, still sipping the hot coffee. Otto took his time to answer, choosing his words carefully he said. "Put simply, Christina is standing in their way and you have a close relationship with Christina. You see they have offered a large sum of money to buy Heiligtum and Frank has repeatedly refused to sell." He stopped to sip some more coffee. He was so casual, lounging back on the sofa. I wanted to knock the cup out his hand.

"Do you have any idea how much you are scaring us? You have us dragged away from Munich in a speeding car, bring us to this Godforsaken place in the middle of nowhere, take the sim cards out our phones" I glared at Stephan "and now you are sitting there as though you are making a social call."

He answered irritatingly smiling again and holding up his fingers as he counted." One, this is not a Godforsaken place, it is one of the top tourist destinations in Germany".

I groaned, I wanted to slap him.

"Two, you must understand these people are in the habit of getting what they want, and they will, if necessary, use violence to get it." He hesitated, watching Christina, then said   "Three, it is likely that Frank has told them by now, if not before, that he cannot sell Heiligtum without Christina's consent."

"Four, Frank has vanished and neither the police, nor the private investigator Christina hired, have been able to find him. Furthermore, the investigator is now dead, his brother murdered, and you Christina" He pointed at her, "were subjected to a brutal attack that left you for dead. That is correct is it not? "Christina nodded. "That is why it is not safe for you to stay in Germany." He said.

"How do you know all that?" I asked.

"We have been already spoken to Detective Inspector Valdez. We know about Lanshoud. We know about David Baxter the private investigator and David's brother Leo, who was your neighbour Erica. D.I Valdez was immensely helpful. She was extremely interested to know that you had come here with Christina." He smiled pursed his lips and nodded. "Though there is no proof as yet, it is not inconceivable that the same organisation, the Brothers, are behind all of it. Do you agree or do you have another possible explanation because...?"

The Brothers?" I interrupted him.

"Der Bruder de Vierten Reich. The Brothers of the Fourth Reich they call themselves. Their aim to restore the ideals of Nazism to Germany

"Are you saying these people followed Frank to Scotland? "Katie was genuinely shocked.

Stephan sat down, mug in hand beside her. "The fact you were in Scotland makes no difference they have contacts everywhere; they have an extensive network throughout Europe. Police in every country keep track of them, as much as is possible.

"You still haven't told me, why they want Heiligtum?" Christina asked again, looking from one man to another for the answer.

"No because we don't know why they want it but..." Otto stared her straight in the eye, "I suspect you know something. Frank was hiding something from me, he said there was a story around Heiligtum, but the story was not his to tell and he was desperate to find out how much my grandfather knew. I use that word loosely. Joseph Bachmiere is not my grandfather, merely a friend of my family whom I have been close to since I was a boy. He was my grandfather's best friend and when he died Joseph took his place in my life. He is an old man who is hanging onto life by a thread and whose memory is not always good but Frank felt he still might still remember something. Look…" he became insistent. "Stephan and I have people who can help but we need to know what we are dealing with. What is the secret that connects you and Erica?… Lanshoud and Heiligtum?" He saw my face. "As I said, we know about Lanshoud."

There was silence. Christina looked at her hands, she began rubbing her left wrist, the one that had been almost severed in her attack.

Stephan had been watching her closely. He spoke gently to Her. "Christina, we cannot help Frank if you do not help us." As she looked up at him, eyes moist, as though she was looking for him to tell her what to do, there was no way the relationship between them could be mistaken by the people in that room."

I answered for her. "And we will tell you nothing, until you tell us the truth about who you are? Why we are really here and how you know so much about us?" I had doubts about these men from the moment the car had sped away from Munich carrying us to that house. Now that they were here, well, I spoke angrily "Really you expect us to trust you. You are both armed, an estate agent and a chauffeur? I put my hands up. For all we know you could be part of the very Neo-Nazi group you are warning us about, and this could be just some kind of set up?"

Otto smiled, he reached into his hip pocket and took out a wallet. He placed it on the table and turned it for me to see. It was an ID. I could see a photograph and a crest and a black bird, standing upright with its wings spread. Christina leaned over lifted the wallet, she studied it and looked up and met my eyes. He is "BND!" She looked at him. "He is a Federal agent."

"Federal agent?" Katie repeated looking at him blankly.

"Yes," Christina said. "MI5… CIA… the German equivalent…"

"In our country Katie we are Bundesnachrichtendienst. BND for short.

Christina picked up on the 'We' straight off. "We?" she looked up at Stephan.

"We are both BND." Stephan said quietly

Christina was stunned. Looking at Stephan more it seemed with hurt than surprise, her voice almost a whisper. "Stephan? All this time?" To me she said "I should have known. I should have realised."

Otto stood up and stretched. He walked over to the window and peered out into the rain. "Stephan was there to protect you. We knew two years ago that Oppenheim was sniffing around Heiligtum. We knew or rather we suspected his reasons for wanting it. There is evidence that suggests he is involved in an occult circle." He turned to see Christina's reaction.

"Occult?" You mean...black magic?" Katie asked

"Exactly. You must have read articles or at least seen one of the countless documentaries about the relationship between Nazism and the Occult. During the war they searched for objects believed to have supernatural elements that could be used as weapons, the Spear of Destiny, the Ark of the Covenant. You know of this?" he asked.

Both Christina and I knew. Katie had never even heard of it."

It is strange that you have not yet encountered this theory Katie, if not by reading then on TV."

"So, you are saying Hitler was involved in black magic?" Katie persisted.

"There are many historians who have rejected the idea but when you consider Hitler's meteoric rise to power and the immeasurable number atrocities carried out by his regime well..." He sat down again. "While Hitler was in power the whole world was turned into a battleground. Millions died. The Jewish race almost annihilated. Faced with that level of evil, it is not difficult to understand why some may think demonic forces were involved. Even if Hitler was not a believer, he was certainly surrounded by people who were. It is a known fact that Hitler never made a serious decision without consulting a horoscope drawn up for him by an expert astrologer." He paused. "The point I am trying to make is that it may be that the Brothers believe there is something powerful, something supernatural at Heiligtum. Of course, it is nonsense but the fact that they believe it means they will stop at nothing to get it and we don't even know what it is they are looking for. All we know is that if there is something there it cannot fall into their hands."

"If you believe it's all nonsense, Why do you care?" I asked"

"Because to them it is symbolic. Anything they believe to be supernatural or to have a unique power they can use; they will use to manipulate people. Hitler believed his power came from his possession of the Spear of Destiny. The sword that pierced the side of Christ. You know of this?"

I nodded yes. I said. "I know Hitler believed possession of that spear, the Holy Lance, would give him the power to rule Germany." I was worried just a little that Katie might say something, but she didn't.

He continued. "According to legend possession of the Spear would make its owner invincible. History and legend tell us many rulers who rose to power while the spear was in their possession, Charlemagne, Barbarossa, Herod the Great, Constantine, Justinian, Napoleon, the list is extensive, all lost their power or died when they lost the spear as did Hitler. On the 30th of April 1945 at 2.10pm the American forces took possession of the spear. Eighty minutes later Hitler killed himself in the bunker in Berlin. Nonsense or not, when Hitler took it from the Hoffburg museum, he believed in its power, even though not all historians accept it was the original. An interesting fact is that the spear was in the possession of the American General Patton whose job it was to return it to the Hoffburg Museum. There is a conspiracy theory that he did not return the original, but that America kept it, and that is how they rose to be a world power. However, General Patton returned a spear to Austria and on his way home he was involved in a car accident. He was the only one injured and he died twelve days later. As you see the legend and the mystery around a powerful talisman holds great interest to those who believe in its magic. We know the Spear is now in safe keeping, but it was not the only thing the Nazi's were searching for. Intelligence from our operatives who have penetrated one of the groups of Brothers has led us to believe that they are searching for another relic of similar talismanic legend and it's possible the brothers believe it is hidden in Heiligtum."

"What other relic? "Katie asked

"It could be anything." He shrugged. "Anything from the Holy Grail to Noah's ark."

"We sat in silence for a moment, then Katie said. "I have never understood, given the defeat of Hitler and the Nazis and the exposure of the horrors of World War Two, how anyone could become a Neo- Nazi. Their minds must be twisted,"

Otto thought for a moment. "Twisted and closed" he said They are no different from religious dogmatists. They have a blind certainty that locks up the mind so tight, they do not even know it is imprisoned."

Katie, Christina, and I had no appetite, the stress of the day had taken its toll, but we did have some wine but only when Stephan insisted it would help us to sleep. Frau Schroeder had packed a huge dinner that tempted us eventually to eat a little. In the bag were slices of roast pork with crackling and horseradish, roast chicken, German sausage, a selection of cheeses and breads, pretzels, apple strudel and what Stephan called Helga's homemade Raderkuchen, which were little twisted sugar doughnuts, mouth-wateringly delicious and highly addictive. She had also packed Lowenbrau beer, Prosecco, and Lemonade. She had made sure we were not going to be hungry. The men ate well but had only one bottle of beer each. They encouraged us to eat and poured the wine, but I for one had lost my appetite. Christina picked at her food and we drank little.

Otto told us about Anton Bachmiere. "He had been to Heiligtum as a young man during the war. When I talked to him about it, it was obvious that he was uncomfortable. I could see he was afraid of someone or something and was for a long time unwilling to say anything." Otto reached for a beer and drank from the bottle. Putting the bottle down he leant forward on the table and said. "Frank was anxious at the persistence and the increasingly aggressive behaviour of Oppenheim, he needed to know why they wanted Heiligtum. He offered a financial bribe to Bachmiere and it was snapped up. I then arranged the meeting between them, and I listened as Bachmiere told his story. He told Frank he was only 18yrs old when he was sent to Heiligtum and he knew nothing of the place, but he listened to the other soldiers stationed there. He said they were afraid and desperate to leave, so much so that they were told any man who left his post would be shot. There was talk among the men that it was haunted. That some powerful ancient evil resided behind a gate under Heiligtum and that Hitler believed he could harness that power to help him win the war." Otto hesitated. "If I say they were looking for a gate, does that mean anything to you?" He paused, sat back in the sofa and looked from me to Katie and then to Christina waiting for a reaction, when there was no response, he grunted." Ladies, your silence speaks volumes."

Christina shaking her head said, "I can't believe that Frank was dealing with this and I knew nothing about it. I mean why would he not tell me?"

Otto drained his beer. "He probably didn't want to worry you."

Stephan opened a bottle of wine. Christina held up her glass and as he refilled it, she asked him. "So, you knew about all of this?"

He hesitated for only a moment. "Yes." There was no emotion in his voice or his manner. He said coldly, "If you want to see your husband again Christina you need to tell us why they want Heiligtum. If any of you know anything, you have to trust us."

"I replied. "You are asking us to trust you Stephan when you have obviously been lying to Christina for a long time."

"It was my job. I was protecting her," he answered, his voice flat, emotionless. "I did not tell her lies I simply omitted the truth."

Lying by omission, well two could play at that game. "I see, well in that case, it is a pity that we cannot help you. I for one have no idea what these people are looking for at Heiligtum," I was not about to trust anyone I hardly knew; I had learned the hard way and was not about to make the same mistakes again. Christina and Katie followed my lead, both remained silent. "So, what now?" I asked, "how long are we here for?"

"There are other officers working on it They will be tracking the Brothers. You will be here overnight, then I suggest you return home. It is not safe in Munich we will fly you home from Berlin."

"No! Christina exclaimed. "Heiligtum is my home. I am not leaving without Frank

Otto voice changed. He spoke harshly. "I was not asking you. For you will be returned to the UK tomorrow. Your passports are in the bag with your clothing."

"Christina" Stephan said softly "The BND will find Frank, there is nothing you can do, and they could eventually find you here."

"You just said they are everywhere. They could just as easily find us in Scotland.

"You will have police protection there, that has already been arranged."

"We have BND protection here, what's the difference" Christina asked."

"Otto snapped back. Your flights have been arranged. You will be escorted home tomorrow." He was not taking no for an answer. "Meanwhile I suggest you get some sleep. We will be leaving early tomorrow."

The holiday home had two bedrooms, one with twin beds and one with two sets of bunk beds. "Brigitta has four boys." Otto said "These are adult size bunks; you should be comfortable there. Stephan and I will take the twin beds." As I said good night, he said. "Heiligtum means Sanctuary, did you know?"

I stopped.at the door and turned. "Yes, I did."

"May I ask what Lanshoud means?"

"It's Dutch. Originally the house was called Lans Haute. It means Spear Hold or Lance Hold" I waited for him to react, but he didn't. I guessed he already knew why. Though he feigned surprise.

"A house named in Dutch in rural Scotland. Any particular reason?"

"I don't know. Maybe the original owner came from Holland."

"Interesting." he said, as I closed the door.

The wine we had consumed helped us to sleep well, but I woke feeling slightly hung over and with a pounding headache.

The other two were still asleep. Pulling on jeans and a tee shirt that I had left lying at the foot of my bed. I tiptoed out of the room and checked the other bedroom; the door was slightly ajar but not enough for me to see if the men were still asleep. I wanted to peek to see if they were still sleeping but the door might creak, so I didn't. The kitchen was empty. I filled a kettle and drew back the curtains. It was around 8am and the mountain was shrouded in a bright white mist. I looked in the cupboards for some Paracetamol or Aspirin but couldn't find anything. Creeping quietly to the bathroom, I found there was nothing in the cabinet there either. Back in the kitchen I stepped outside onto the patio, it was deathly quiet, and I couldn't see any more than two feet in front of me, only a small patio and grass at my feet and a wall of dense white mist. The noise from the kettle boiling covered the sound of Katie who padded through in bare feet, still in her pyjamas. I nearly jumped out of my skin when she put her hand on my shoulder.

"Sorry". she said "It's pretty creepy out here; that mist is thick."

"It will probably burn off when the sun comes out. Tea?" I asked her.

She groaned "I have a blinding headache." Flopping down onto a chair and rubbing her eyes, leaning over the table, she folded her arms, closed her eyes, and rested her forehead on them. Without moving a muscle, she said "you might as well pour some for Christina, she is just coming."

"Did you sleep ok?" I asked.

"Yes, but I woke up feeling lousy. And you know" she lifted her head, indignant. "I only had two glasses of wine."

"Probably the stress and excitement yesterday. I woke up with a headache too." I thought she did look awful. I said," before you ask, I can't find any painkillers."

"Where are the men?" She asked.

I shrugged grinning "Bed I suppose."

"Bed? Still in their kip? They are priceless. I thought they were our self-appointed bodyguards."

A moment later Christina appeared. Yawning she looked around." Where are Stephan and Otto?"

"Oh, our bodyguards? Still in bed I suppose." Katie said with disingenuous smile.   Christina frowned. I asked her if she would like tea and poured her some for her. She turned back and walked into the hall and knocked lightly on the men's bedroom door. There was no reply so, she pushed it open. She turned and called back. "They are not here." She checked the bathroom, then tried the front door. It was locked. "Where are they?" she asked still looking at the door.

Katie and I went to the door I looked through the letter box. "The cars are gone." I said completely confused.

"Maybe they have gone for bread or something?" Katie said. "Or milk." she said weakly under our withering gaze.

"It's almost eight thirty. Otto said he would waken us at six." I looked at Christina's pale worried face. "There is something very wrong here" she said.

Chapter 4

Faces in the Mist

Christina sat down at the table rubbing the back of her neck. Elbows on the table, her head in her hands, her thick auburn hair spilling over her face, she groaned. "I feel as though I have been battered all over, my head is bursting."

"Mine too," Katie said. "I don't suppose you have any painkillers?"

"I might have some Paracetamol, I'll get them." She stood up pushing her chair away, staggered and almost lost her balance. She was as white as a sheet.

Katie sitting beside her caught her arm? "Hey, sit down I'll get them. Where are they?"

"They're in my bag, It's on the floor beside the bed." She sat back in the chair, stretching her neck back. "I feel so ill. As though I have had too much alcohol, but I didn't, did I?"

"No. I don't think so." I filled a glass with water from the bottle in the fridge. "Here, drink this, it might help." Placing the glass in front of her I watched her sip it slowly, thinking to myself that she looked worse than I felt.

Katie called from the bedroom. "Erica, could you come here a minute." There was an edge to her voice, so I hurried through. "Our bags are gone," she said. She stood in the bedroom looking at the floor, turning around and around. "The bags, they're gone, everything's gone, our handbags, the hold-all, everything, except this." She lifted a bulky carrier bag. "They left my cuckoo clock."

I looked on the floor, under the bunk I had slept on, thinking maybe I had kicked my handbag underneath. I looked behind the little set of drawers between the beds, in the wardrobe, nothing. Katie pulled the duvets off the beds. "They have left us with nothing, no phones, no money, no clothes. I have nothing but my pyjamas. Why in God's name would they take our clothes?"

I went to the front door, Katie followed me. It was locked. I looked through the letterbox. "Both cars have gone." I said confused. My brain was working overtime. Had they maybe taken our things to give to whoever was taking us to the airport? But why would they take absolutely everything. "I don't understand." I said.

Katie's voice faltered as she realised." They're not coming back, are they?"

Katie and Christina sat at the table nursing their tea. Christina moaned; she was massaging her temples in a circular motion to ease the pain.

I watched her for a moment then, "I have a headache too," I said quietly, realisation beginning to dawn.

She looked up at me blankly, what I said hadn't registered. She shook her head. "They can't have just left. It's ridiculous to think that they would steal our bags, lock us in and just drive off. There must have been someone else here."

I sat down in front of her. "They didn't lock us in completely, the patio doors are unlocked. Anyway, what are you suggesting, that they have been taken? Someone kidnapped them and took our things at the same time. No, sorry, that too is unbelievable."

She looked over at the patio." They locked the front door but not the back?" I nodded yes. "But that's bizarre," she said.

"I'll tell you something even more bizarre." A thought had been slowly taking root in my equally throbbing head. "I think we've been drugged. I think our drinks were spiked." She stared at me blankly.

Katie eyes widened. "Of course. Oh my God! I think your right"

I asked Christina "Don't you think it's strange that we all have headaches and are feeling lousy this morning."

Her eyes narrowed as though she was trying to process what I had just said, then she was incredulous. "Are you suggesting Stephan or Otto spiked our drinks?"

"Yes" I said.

"No, there is no way Stephan would have been party to that."

"Really?" Katie smirked. "The man who has been lying to you for the past two years could not possibly be involved in deception." Christina looked up at her, shaking her head, she still had a sort of spaced out look about her. "Well the field is pretty narrow since there was no one else here." She had refilled her cup and was leaning against the sink behind Christina. Speaking directly into Christina's ear she said quietly. "Well I know it wasn't me and I would bet my life it wasn't Erica who spiked the drinks. So, if it wasn't them, who does that leave?"

Christina turned and stared at Katie. "You think it was me?" She was shocked.

Katie hesitated only long enough to remind me that Christina was not on her list of her favourite people. She backtracked. "I am simply asking who else do you think it could be?"

Christina looked at me for reassurance." Is there any proof we were drugged?"

"I said "Yes, I think there is, unless you can trash my theory by explaining how two federal agents who claimed to be protecting us, up and left in the middle of the night. How they came into our room and took our bags, without waking us. How they drove off in not one but two cars, practically right outside our bedroom door and in total silence. How did they manage that? Don't you think if nothing else the engines would have wakened us? If you have another explanation, please tell me."

The fact was the hallway was very small and our bedroom was the one next to the outside door and driveway. It would have been extremely difficult if not impossible to open and shut the outside door without making a noise, let alone drive two cars away.

Christina was silent her head obviously clouded; I could see she was trying to process things. Whatever they doped us with, it had affected her more than Katie or me.

"But why would they just leave us. I don't understand... and...and take our things? No." Christina shook her head. "Stephan would not do that to me."

"No!" Katie smirked. "Is that because he is more than just your chauffeur?"

"What are you suggesting?"

"Oh, come on. I've seen the way he looks at you and calls you. '*Tina*'..." she imitated Stephan's accent.

Christina was aghast. "Stephan has been a friend to me, at times when I needed one and no more than that." She spat out the words.

There was an awkward silence. I gave Katie a look and tried to smooth things over. "It's obvious he is very fond of you, that's all she is saying."

Christina became defensive. "Stephan has always been someone that Frank and I could rely on. I know he called me Tina yesterday, but I have no idea why, and I was as surprised as you were. Only Frank calls me Tina." She was really upset by Katie's comment. "I simply know Stephan well and I do not believe he would do anything to hurt us."

Katie almost laughed; she could be like a dog with a bone sometimes. "You know him well do you? Well how come your chauffeur dropped a rather obvious bombshell when he sported a gun and told you he was a BND officer? You were as surprised as we were, if not more."

Christina started to respond then faltered, "I don't know, I don't understand any of this.   If they are both federal agents, they would not have abandoned us like this. Something happened last night. There has been someone else or more than one person involved in this. Maybe the Brothers, the Neo-Nazi's"

"Either that or Stephan and Otto are not the federal agents they claimed to be, and their story and their ID's are false. How long have you known Stephan?" I asked her.

"He has been employed at Heiligtum as a handyman for the last five years or so. Then he became our chauffer two years ago. When we came over for holidays, he ran us everywhere and when Frank came alone, he relied a lot on Stephan. He is a good man. Frau Schroeder adores him." She said.

I couldn't imagine Frau Schroeder adoring anyone. "Think about it. Why would a federal agent spend all that time working at Heiligtum?"

"It doesn't make sense does it?" Katie asked Christina.

"Yet if their story wasn't true, why did they bring us here?" I posed the question as much to myself as to them. I was at a loss to understand, then it occurred to me as I looked at them, I had jeans and a tee shirt, they had nothing but pyjamas." Where did you put your clothes when you changed last night? "I asked.

"In the holdall" they both said at the same time.

"I left mine at the foot of my bed. They must not have seen them; they just lifted the bag and the jackets." I continued thinking out loud. "They left us food but no clothes or any form of communication...why? They lock the front door but not the patio doors...why?" I turned around and looked across the open plan kitchen and living room to the front window, a plate glass window that didn't open. "Everything was planned." I said. "I don't believe they forgot to lock them I think they didn't lock them because they wanted us to go out the patio doors or they left them open to let someone or something in." A sudden chill made me shiver.

I was trying to get my head around it when Katie said. "No, they wanted 'you' to go out the patio doors. They didn't miss your clothes, they left them deliberately. They took our shoes from the floor beside our beds but not yours. I looked down at their bare feet.

Katie made some toast and we ate it to help with the nausea we were all feeling. "We need a plan," I said "but first, Katie while you're on your feet, lock those patio doors, will you? Christina, we need to go for help and there is no point in Katie or I going because, we can't speak German."

Katie turned." How is she going to go? She's got no shoes." She opened and closed the heavy glass door.

Christina said "And I have a bigger problem. This is what Frau Schroeder chose from my lingerie drawer." She stood up and held up her hands. She wore only a silk and lace camisole and shorts.

"There's no key." Katie said still struggling with the doors."

"They took the key. Just put the handle down, that seals the door from the inside." I said looking at her full, long sleeved, shirt type, pyjama top.

"What size shoes are you? "I asked Christina.

"A five." She said.

"Good, you can wear my shoes then."

Katie was sliding the door back and forth. It won't lock."

"I'll get it, it's a bit stiff. "I walked over to the door slid it open, closed it, sealed it, and put down the handle to secure, it at the same time saying. "We are all around the same size. Christina you could wear my jeans, and Katie's pyjama top." There was no comment. I turned around and they were both frozen, staring at me. "What?" I asked. "Oh, I know it's not hygienic, but we have no choice and that's the least of our worries. "They didn't answer. They were staring. Speechless, Katie lifted her hand and pointed, the look of horror on her face made me afraid to turn around. Christina said quietly "Erica walk over here. Don't look round." I walked over to her, chills running up and down my spine as I realised they were looking not at me but at something behind me. As I reached them, they both held on to me and I turned around saw what they saw, and fear gripped me like a vice. Five grey faces fading in and out of the swirling mist. Christina started shaking violently.

I whispered their name on a breath, my mouth too dry to speak. Fear and disbelief that they could be here and in broad daylight, had paralysed my voice and I could feel blind panic settling in. I tried deep breathing to control it, something James had taught me when he noticed I had a habit of holding my breath when I was stressed. The faces faded out and in the mist. One came so close to the glass I could clearly see the grey parchment skin stretched over the skull-like face. Christina gave a loud moan of despair, a horrible gut-wrenching sound that vibrated in my ear making my heart pound in my chest and my hands shake. I caught her just as she started sinking down on her knees. I whispered in a croaked voice. "Katie help me move her, the hallway... quick." We held onto Christina's arms and pushed her towards the door, the only place in the house where there were no windows, thinking there at least we could no longer see them, and they could not see us. In the hall we let her sink to the floor and Katie closed the door behind us. Christina sat back against the wall her arms around her knees, her head bent, her face hidden by her hair. Katie sat down beside her, pity showing on her face, realising as I did that seeing them again had taken Christina back to the time she had been brutally beaten and left for dead. Katie put her arms around her." They can't come in and they can't see us in here. We're safe here."

She's right Christina." I said sitting on the floor beside them. "In every encounter we have had with them, they have been unable to cross the threshold. I don't know why but it's the truth."

There was no response. I lifted her head, it was limp, her face pale white and her eyes glassy as though she was didn't even recognise me. "Christina," I patted her face. She didn't respond.

"Is she alright?" Katie's worried face loomed over me.

"She's in shock? She's as cold as ice."

I put my arm around Christina and let her head fall onto my shoulder. It was not surprising she had become like this, since the last time she had been in contact with one of these beings she had been beaten within an inch of her life and left for dead. Sick barbaric torture is how the police surgeon described the attack. I remember when my parents were killed and then my husband Paul died, my whole life was torn apart. Katie and Gill had struggled with supporting me. There were times when I sank into a deep depression, when I was so afraid of life, when the pain of loss was so great, I felt my heart would burst and I just wanted to escape reality. So, I would close my eyes and I go to a happier place in my mind. I shut out everything around me and hid in my special time and place, where nothing had changed and where my family were still alive. Looking at Christina now I believed she had escaped in her mind to a similar secret shelter, away from the terror and horror facing her.

Katie and I knew what they were, this was not the first nor last time we would see these creatures, the legendary riders of the Wild Hunt. Christina who had heard our stories and who had been brought up with German tales of the Wilde Jagd, the ghost riders of the night, also knew who they were, and she knew to be very, very afraid. They came in the night, or in the mist. They had terrorised us at Lanshoud. Christina had survived a violent attack on her life at their hands. They were beings of darkness, from another time and another place and they were subservient to the wishes of their infernal master. The terrifying thing was that they were out there now in broad daylight.

We sat in silence, listening for any sound that meant they had entered the house. We huddled together chilled by our fear. Within a few minutes the tapping started just like at Lanshoud. That same harrowing nerve-wracking beat. Not just on the patio doors but on every window in the house. Drumming into our brain like a malevolent heartbeat. We huddled together on the floor outside the bathroom door in the middle of the hall. I was so scared I just kept saying over and over *"they cannot come in; they cannot come in"*. The drumming seemed to go on for an eternity. It was at least a half an hour before it faded and stopped.

"Do you think they've gone?" Katie asked in a whisper.

"Yes, I think so, "I whispered back. I lifted Christina's head off my shoulder. She was still limp and chalk white with closed eyes and shallow breath, but at least she was breathing."

Summoning every bit of courage, she could muster, Katie stood up and said, "I am going to take a look". She lifted a pole I hadn't noticed before; it had been lying in the corner tight against the wall. There was a hook at the top. It took me a minute to realise what it was and then I looked up and there, in the ceiling, was the door to a loft. Katie peeped through the kitchen door. "Thank God." she said sighing with relief. "The mist has faded, and the sun is out." She bravely stepped into the kitchen the pole held in front of her like a battering ram." I can't see any sign of them."

I stood up and pulled Christina, who unresisting got up with me. I walked her to the sofa while Katie, not without trepidation, checked the windows. "The mist is completely gone from the front" She said again. She walked over to the kitchen cupboards opening and closing them, till she found what she was looking for. "I knew I saw this somewhere," she said taking out a bottle of brandy. She poured some into a glass. Here give her this, this will help her."

I poured a little into Christina's mouth, she coughed almost choking on it. I tried again this time she swallowed and before

44

long the color returned to her cheeks. "It's alright Christina" I said," they are gone." she stared blankly at me. Just rest." I said, lying her down on the sofa.

Katie brought a duvet from the bedroom and wrapped it around Christina. She stood looking down at her and asked me. "What are we going to do with her?"

"I think just leave her to sleep."

Katie sank down onto the other sofa. "No clothes, no money, no phone and I am not keen on going out those patio doors. I think I need some of this." She took a swig from the bottle and handed it to me. I said "No, one of us needs our wits about us."

"Take a sip it will help you."

She was right of course, and I did. Just a sip, then another. I sat down beside her, we both watched Christina. "They are creatures of night." Katie said. "They won't come back in the daylight."

"They did this morning. They did when James and I had the car crash. "We have to get out of here."

She studied me. What are you thinking? I can practically see the wheels turning."

"I was thinking that pole, it's for a loft. The hatch is in the hall. Maybe there is something up there we could use."

"Like what?"

"I don't know and there's only one way to find out." I lifted the pole and Katie said, "Hang on there is a torch in that drawer." She got it and followed me. I hooked the pole into the ring on the hatch and pulled, nothing happened. I twisted the ring and it clicked releasing the lock. The hatch door fell down and Katie shone the torch into the space revealing a set of metal ladders. "Ladders," I said. "Well, if they have bothered to put them in, they must store something up there. Katie shone the torch onto a ring on the ladder and I hooked it with the pole and pulled. The ladder slid down slowly in sections. I went up first shining the torch into a loft space the size of the house. Just to the right of the hatch was a switch that turned on overhead strip lighting, revealing a space packed with cardboard boxes, cases, and basket hampers. It was awkward, we had to stay bent over because the loft was only about five feet high in the center and sloped down towards the eves. Still, we spent around half an hour in the cramped condition, opening boxes and cases. They held various things like books, mostly in German, one was in English, 'Secret History Files, Camp 020, MI5 and the Nazi Spies.' There was one box with bags and wallets of every shape and size. The cases held jumpers, trousers, jackets mostly men's. We opened case after case and searched through them looking for something that we could wear. "Don't you think that odd they are all in different sizes. They are mostly men's but there are some women's clothing." I said raking through one of the larger cases. "It doesn't really matter though; we can use these whether they fit us or not."

"Erica" she almost whispered. Does this look to you like something a mother with four boys would keep? "She was holding a knotted leather whip. She reached further into the box and held up chains and handcuffs, a box of surgical instruments, a cattle prod. She jagged her hand lifting out a wooden baton studded with nails. With a look of horror, she dropped it back in the box, wiping her hands on her pyjamas as thought though they had been contaminated by it. "It's got dried blood on it and look a box filled with passports. Who do you think all this belongs to? She swallowed hard, then in a quiet voice said. "We really need to get out of here."

"I was struck dumb for a moment my mind racing to make sense of what Katie had found." "This is not a holiday home for Otto's sister is it"? She shook her head. I took three hooded jackets from the pile that looked as though might fit. They were clean but smelled stale as though they had been stored there for a long time. "These might have belonged to the people whose blood stained that baton."

Katie said quietly. "We have no choice."

Katie went down first, and I threw down the three jackets, she picked them up and piled them on the floor. I came down and she helped push the ladder back into the loft. She picked them up and carried them through to the kitchen while I pushed hatch back into place and locked it. Then suddenly she screamed." Erica she's gone. Christina is gone." I ran in the patio doors were wide open. The duvet lay on the floor and there was no sign of Christina.

Chapter 5

Christina's Disappearance

"Where is she?" Katie cried, her eyes wide with shock. She turned around and around as if eventually she would find Christina lying on the floor. I was just as bad; I was staring out the patio doors as if she would suddenly reappear. The mist had completely cleared, and the sun was shining, I was close enough to the doors to feel the warmth of the sun on my face, but my blood had turned to ice. There was no sign of Christina or the entities. "They have taken her" I said, almost in a whisper because my mouth had gone dry and I could hardly speak. I was stricken with guilt. We had left her alone and that was my fault. I turned to Katie. "We left her, oh my God Katie what have we done?"

Katie was standing as if rooted to the spot, she shook her head. "No, no, it isn't our fault, because they had already gone, remember? They had gone before we left her alone, the mist had gone." Her eyes were huge, her face as white as a sheet. She looked out the doors. "She must have gone with them."

Stunned by her reasoning. I asked, "Are you serious?"

"Yes," she was almost pleading, "She must have gone out after them. I told…" she hesitated as if considering what she was about to say. "… I told you I didn't trust her."

"You are actually suggesting Christina walked out there of her own free will? That's madness. You saw the state she was in. She couldn't even walk." Katie wasn't giving up. "About that. You're going to hate me saying this, but I think she deserves an Oscar for some of her performances."

I was almost lost for words. "How can you even think that? You are living in cloud cuckoo land if you think for one moment, she went out that door willingly."

Katie held up her hand. "I know, I know what you're going to say. "She mimicked my voice. "For God's sake Katie, they beat her to a pulp and left her for dead."

I nodded "Yes, pretty much, because you would not be even thinking that way if you had seen her in that hospital bed, seen her body broken from the terrible beating she took. Even when the hospital staff said they thought physically she might survive, mentally she might never recover, yet you think she walked out there. I shook my head denying any possibility that Christina had walked out those doors. "No, never, there is no way on God's Earth she would have gone willingly. They have taken her."

Katie sniggered. "And how exactly did they do that? Since supposedly they can't cross the threshold without invitation, and they cannot survive in daylight. Have I got that right?"

"What do you mean?"

"I mean how can you be sure they can't enter unless invited? Remind me where that came from?"

The shock of Katie's seemingly unsympathetic reaction to Christina's disappearance calmed me a little. I backed away from the doors and sat down at the table. "Paddy told us, don't you remember? That night in the kitchen at Lanshoud when we were scared out of our wits. Caleb was possessed, and Paddy told Molly not to invite him in, but she did anyway. When Emilio came to Lanshoud, he stood at the door until Alice invited him in. We didn't realise at the time; it was because he could not cross the threshold until he was invited. Paddy was right, and I completely forgot that fact, the night the thing impersonating Jonah came to Lanshoud. The phone rang just as I had the opened the door and I turned to take the call and when I turned back Jonah was still standing there waiting for the invitation. It was so obvious and still I didn't see it. If I had remembered then, I would have realised it wasn't really Jonah."

Katie grunted. "You do realise you are just confirming what I think, which is that she either walked out to them or she invited them in, and they took her, which is it?" She sat down at the table in front of me and leaned over. "I can't help it, either way my gut instinct is not to trust her. Erica we are here in this mess because Christina told us some cock and bull story about being in danger and having to flee Munich. Now look where we are."

"No Katie, that wasn't her story, it is what Otto told her. She wasn't lying, she was genuinely scared. I watched her in the back of the car."

The words had barely left my lips when a scream, a gut-wrenching wail of despair, the cry of someone in terrible pain or in terror of their life, echoed across the mountain. It chilled me to the bone, it turned my blood to ice and my legs to jelly and it stopped Katie's rant. It came from a distance and it was no ordinary scream, it sounded like someone being tortured and begging for mercy. Visions of Christina and the brutality of the last attack on her raced across my mind.

We both stood up. Katie grabbed my arm, she was trembling. So terrifying and prolonged was that cry that we stood for what seemed forever, hanging onto each other. I felt panic creeping in, I would have fled the room, but my feet had turned to lumps of lead. It stopped. There was a deep silence. A few minutes passed, and my heartbeat returned to normal as did my sanity, to a degree. I sank back into the chair my legs feeling rubbery. "I can't just do nothing I have to go out and see, maybe they have left her out there." I don't know why I even said it. The cry had come from a distance.

Katie pulled open a drawer in the table." "I saw knives in this drawer." She reached in and grabbed a meat chopper and handed me a large carving knife. It felt good to hold, even though I knew it was probably useless against what was out there."

Expecting to see something dreadful and with the flesh on the nape of my neck crawling, we crept carefully towards the patio doors. Holding myself together as best I could and with Katie wielding her meat chopper, I opened them. Instead of horror, in complete contrast, we met the beauty of an Alpine summer. The fresh morning air scented with newly mowed grass, wafted in the open door. It assaulted my senses and confused my mind, as did the scene in front of me. Sunshine, flowers growing in a rockery, an emerald green lawn stretching out and sloping down, so that the edge could not be seen, and in the background the dark shear rock face of the mountain rising vertically into the clouds. The scene should have calmed me, but it didn't because it was all wrong. Yes, the mountain was magnificent, but so close it was claustrophobic, it was exquisite but so powerful and overwhelming it just heightened my anxiety. Everything was wrong. There was no birdsong, no whisper of a breeze, no rustling of leaves. Nature was silent, waiting, listening like we were, for the next cry. There was no sign of anyone or anything.

I was holding the knife in front of me with both hands struggling to control my trembling. While Katie stood beside me holding her meat chopper high, ready to strike the first thing that moved, it was a few moments before we were brave enough to step out onto the patio. When we did, we could see a cable car climbing high and the shape of passengers on board. Could the cry have come from there I wondered. Did the mountain carry the sound like an echo? Where else could it have come from? We went slowly and carefully over the lawn and down the sloped grass. It ended in a boundary wall, but there was nothing else, not even a path, just rocks, long grass, and wildflowers. The grass was damp and the air chilled. Katie in her pyjamas, and the blue parka and trainers she had found in the loft, was shivering violently. I took her arm as much to steady me as to steady her. "Do you think that scream was her?" She asked, now subdued. I knew it was Christina, I just knew but I didn't answer because I thought that instinctively Katie also knew. I strained my ears. The silence was deep and unnatural. Not a bird, nor a breath of wind broke the stillness, until Katie spoke." I'm sorry," she said.
There was nothing there and nowhere anyone could be hiding, so we walked back huddled together, checking the driveway and the other side of the house, where only untamed bushes grew. It was eerily silent. I felt grief and guilt and fear all rolled into one.

"What now" Katie asked." We should get help. Other people will have heard that cry. We should go down to the town, someone may have called the police, we can explain."

"Explain? How do we explain this? That we think it's the riders of the Wild Hunt that have taken Christina, in broad daylight. How do we explain that in English to Germans? Oh, and we can tell them an estate agent and chauffeur, who may or may not be federal agents, brought us here yesterday, then stole our clothes and bags and vanished."

"It does sound crazy."

"Yes. There is no point in even trying. Stephan told us the police had been infiltrated by the Neo-Nazi's. They may be looking for us. We can't risk speaking to the police. I think we should leave, go back to Heiligtum. Frau Schroeder will help. We just keep walking through the gate, down the road and try and find a taxi. I don't want to go back in there and there is nothing we can do here. We have no money, but we could get a taxi and pay for it when we get there."

And so, we did just that. We left through the gate and down the road until we saw other houses and eventually people.

Garmisch-Partenkirchen is a beautiful romantic Bavarian town, with brightly painted houses with some of the facades elaborately decorated with paintings. It is surrounded by snow-capped peaks and lies near the Zugspitze, Germany's highest mountain and so, it has long been a playground for hikers and skiers. In that town full of prosperous locals and tourists our shabby old-fashioned jackets and dishevelled look made us stand out and caused people to stare. The first shop we came to was a small supermarket, the woman serving behind the counter looked up with a smile, then looked me up and down and lost the smile as fast as it came. I politely asked her if she spoke English. I explained I was looking for a taxi. Maybe she didn't speak English, though the word taxi is universal these days. Or, maybe it was because we didn't buy anything, at any rate she rattled out a few words in German turned her back and continued stacking the shelves. We hurried down the hill till we reached the town square, where the designer boutiques and shops sold high quality traditional handicrafts and beautiful Bavarian costumes, and there, outside a cafe, was a white BMW with a taxi sign and even better the driver spoke a little English.

There was no doubt he was suspicious of our state of dress and unkempt look. He seemed reluctant at first to take the fare but when we explained it would be to Schloss Heiligtum, and that we were guests there, he changed his attitude very quickly. Within the hour the car pulled up in front of Heiligtum. The driver was not happy when I asked him to wait, till I went in for money. I was half hoping that Frau Schroeder would have appeared and paid him but there was no sign of her. I asked Katie to wait with him and left her telling an elaborate tale of how we had been robbed. I don't think he understood any of it, but he listened politely. I had left euros in my room; it only took a couple of minutes to get them and I gave the driver a generous tip which amazingly changed his attitude even more. He even smiled and waved and wished us an enjoyable holiday. He then drove off like a Madman leaving Katie and I bemused." What did you do to him?" I asked.

Nothing." She said. "I have no idea why he took off like that. Where's our Helga then?" She asked in an ...I don't like the woman, tone of voice. "I see she's not running out to meet us this time."

"She probably hasn't heard the taxi."

The doors of Heiligtum were unlocked, which reinforced Katie's belief that Helga and Kurt were around somewhere. I was not so sure, there was a deathly hush about the house. Katie went upstairs to wash and change, and I went to look for Helga only I couldn't find her. The sitting rooms, library, study, and dining rooms were all empty and pristine, not a chair or cushion out of place. However, the kitchen looked as though she was not far away. A floured board with a sheet of rolled pastry and a rolling pin lay on the work surface. There was a knife, flour, butter, and sugar lying beside a bowl of peeled and chopped apples. The apples had been steeped in lemon juice and water, but they were already browning as though they had been sitting there for some time. Two pies finished but not cooked lay beside them ready for the oven, a wood fired stove which was still warm. She wasn't in the kitchen garden either. I tried the laundry room and storeroom. The cloakroom was empty. I thought she might be in the garage talking to Kurt, she wasn't, and

I couldn't find Kurt either. I walked about the castle, calling, but there was definitely no one to be found. I looked in on Katie who was already in the shower to tell her that I was going for a shower. I told her I couldn't find anyone so, Helga and Kurt must have gone out, but I thought it very strange that the doors had been left unlocked.

Sometime later I came into the kitchen to find Katie rummaging in the fridge, she turned around her arms full of bread and ham and salad. She didn't even look at me. "It's a nuisance," she said "the light in this fridge isn't working." She put the food on the table and began buttering bread. "I was just thinking, maybe Helga and Kurt decided to take some time away from here because Christina had gone off with us. In which case they may not come back anytime soon. We could be on our own tonight or even longer. Don't you think this schloss or castle or whatever you want to call this place is creepy enough in daylight let alone when it's empty." She gave a huge sigh. "I hope to God they come back tonight. I for one do not fancy staying in this place, just the two of us, no thank you."

I tried to lighten her mood. "Oh! I see, you have another option up your sleeve then. Is there a 5-star hotel I didn't notice on the way here? or are you planning on camping, in which case where's the tent?"

She wasn't amused. "There had better be another option, there has to be. What if the Brother's come here looking for Christina? Or worse, the Hunt." I don't think we should wait. I say, just phone the police now." She started slicing the ham with a large knife, using much greater force than the soft ham needed, and cutting more off the joint than we would ever eat. Furthermore, she was banging the knife hard enough to damage the wood of the table. I've known Katie a long time, I knew she was afraid and trying hard to keep her cool and I knew what I was about to tell her might just push her over the edge. When I didn't answer she looked up. "What? What is it?"

"The phones are dead and before you ask me to put the kettle on…" I flicked the switch. …The electricity is off too. It went off just as I came out of the shower."

"A power cut. Honestly! What next?" She shook her head. "No, no, please don't tell me we have to stay here alone, in this place, without lights, or a phone, seriously?" She pushed her chair back and got up shaking her head, "No it's not going to happen."

"Don't panic, if and only if Helga and Kurt don't come back today, there is bound to be a generator. We just have to find it."

She laughed hysterically, then sarcasm dripping from her tongue, she said, "a generator hmm..." she put a finger to her lips."... "Let me think, now where would they keep a generator? I'll just guess, shall I? Oh! yes of course, the cellar," she raised her voice." Well I am not ever, ever going down a cellar again, do you understand me? especially in this house and before you say it, neither am I going to hang around here alone while you disappear down one." She hesitated "Where is it anyway?"

"Behind you. It's not locked, and it does have electricity or did when I tried it before the power cut."

She looked at the innocent brown wooden door. "It's not locked. Oh my God I thought it was a cupboard or I would not have been sitting so close to it." Her voice was getting higher, she ran her hands through her thick tangle of black curls, something she always did when she was nervous, worse I could hear the edge of panic creeping into her voice.

I tried to calm her. "Katie I would never ask you to go down a cellar, after what happened at Lanshoud, but I may have to go down or we will be left alone in the dark with nothing but candles."

She nodded, "Oh yes, exactly, and in an old castle in the middle of nowhere."

Katie sat down again, put her elbows on the table, her head in her hands and groaned. A moment later she lifted her head. "Why don't we just walk out of here? Maybe camping is not such a bad idea."

"Well for a start it's miles away from anywhere, we are halfway up a mountain, remember? Have you forgotten; the legends of the Wild Hunt abound in this part of Germany? You know as well as I do that it was the riders of the Hunt, we saw at Garmisch? They found us there, they can find us here. We are safer in doors, than out. Just keep in your mind, they cannot come in unless we invite them."

"No but they can terrorise us They've done a pretty good job on that front before. It is possible to die of fright you know."

"Stop it. We are not going to die of fright. We can close the curtains and plug our ears,"

Katie didn't stop. "Yes, but if we do that, we won't hear the Brothers coming. Maybe they took Otto and Stephan and now they'll come for us."

She was wearing me down. I was as worried as she was, but I was damned if I was going to cave in. I snapped at her. "The Nazi's are not going to come here, if they had wanted us, they would have taken us with Otto and Stephan.

"Maybe they didn't take them, maybe it was the Hunt."

"Now you are being ridiculous, do you think the riders of the hunt would have taken our bags and clothes too? We need to calm down and work on the premise, we are on our own tonight. Right now, we have to find a torch or some candles before it gets dark." I opened the door of the oven. "At least it's an Aga but it's almost out and it might be the only heat and light we have. So, we need to find wood."

"There is wood in a basket over there in the corner."

I checked the basket, "good, we will be able to boil a pan of water, but there's not enough wood to last the night." A thought crossed my mind. "There is probably wood in that cellar."

Katie was hugging herself. Biting her bottom lip, she shook her head. "I can't. I can't go into a cellar".

"Well I'm not going alone. It doesn't matter anyway. We need to be calm. It's almost three o'clock. Frau Schroeder or Kurt will probably be back soon. In the meantime, we need to find keys and lock the doors."

"That's another thing, why would they leave without locking up?"

"Maybe, because the house is so isolated, they don't expect intruders."

"Look, try to stop worrying, just make those sandwiches and I'll find the wood. There might be some outside the back door, I'm sure I saw a bunker of sorts there." I went to the half-open kitchen door that led into the hall, when I heard a noise coming from the front of the house. I heard the front doors open. I froze signalling to Katie, holding a finger to my lips.

I could hear footsteps in the hall. A deep male voice, that was definitely not Kurt called out to someone in German and an equally deep voice answered. Katie crept over beside me. "Is it Kurt?" She whispered.

I answered. "No, and they are in the house."

She whispered again. "We can't get out of here; they will see us."

Footsteps... they were coming. "Go... the cellar... it's open, quick." I pushed her towards the cellar door. She resisted. I grabbed her arm. "We have no choice." I pulled open cellar door cringing as it creaked, and I pushed her into the darkness closing the door behind us. I stood just behind the door straining my ears, but all was silent. I knew we had to move down the stairs and find somewhere to hide, but my fear of this being the Brothers, come to find us, had not taken over my fear of dark cellars. Over the past few years, I had learned that evil was a real, tangible thing. Not just something that bad people do. Not the murderers, not the rapists and the child abusers, not even the Neo- Nazi's upstairs. Nor was it just the stuff of horror stories. I knew it was a presence that walked in our world under various disguises. Katie and I had experienced this evil as it came into our lives disguised as Emilio and as Chloe. It charms, seduces, deceives, and manipulates mankind into doing its will. As it may have done with the original Nazi's and now their new evolution upstairs. But Evil has a weakness. It needs willing subjects. It needs us to cooperate. It needs us to say come, "come into my home," "come into my soul."

I had to make a choice, and this was the right one, or so I thought. Those men upstairs may have been seduced by evil, may have invited it in, but they were just men. The cellar was just that, a cellar, a storage room, nothing to be afraid of. What we faced in the cellar at Lanshoud had been invited in. It was not of this world. It was more dangerous than any Nazi.

In the pitch darkness, Katie stood, too afraid to take a step. With the power cut. there was no point in looking for the light switch. As my eyes grew accustomed to the darkness, the pale watery light that leaked from under the door, enable me just to see the top step and no more. I felt the wall, it was rough, cold, and damp. "We have to go down." I whispered." We must find some-where to hide."

"No, I can't." she almost cried.

"Shh...they will hear us. We must go down. Sooner or later they will come in here. I'll go first. I am going to move slowly one step at a time, we can do this."

We crept down the stairs, painfully slowly, afraid of falling, till we finally reached the last step. Katie hung onto my arm, she was shaking with cold and fear. I kicked something, and it rolled it sounded something made of metal. We froze again, listening for any sound from the kitchen...nothing. I reached down and felt the stone floor. Sighing with relief, I thought, what were the chances of me finding a torch." It's a torch" I whispered as I picked it up. I couldn't believe my luck. I found the switch, but it was dead. I unscrewed the back, and rolled the batteries, rubbing them like I had seen my father do. It spluttered for a moment then sprang into life. I shone it around, over the boxes and ladders, the stacks of wood and dust sheets covering furniture. Until, with chills running up and down my spine, I saw the beam land on a black robed and hooded man, sitting on a crate.

Chapter 6

The Body

We both froze, afraid that if we tried to run, if we made any sudden movement, the thing, still, silent, might like a sleeping dog suddenly spring to life and attack. My heart was hammering in my chest and my hand shaking, making it difficult to hold the beam steady on the seated figure. I couldn't see its face, it was hidden in the folds of a black hood, its hands lost in the black robes that covered its feet. There was no sound of breathing, no way of knowing if it was alive, no way of knowing if it was even human. A putrid odour of decay was making my stomach churn. Katie covered her mouth and retched.

Terrified of waking it. I stepped back slowly, holding onto Katie, pushing her gently towards the stairs. Then with my back pressed against the cold damp stone I started up, one step at a time watching for movement, trying to keep the beam of light fixed on the figure, even though my hand was trembling. Moving painfully slowly we climbed up the steps, until about five stairs from the top, the torch spluttered a few times then went out. That was it, no longer looking back, we ran for our lives up the last few steps. Almost at the door I stumbled and fell onto Katie, who staggered though the door and fell straight into the arms of Otto Reinhardt.

We hadn't screamed, we hadn't even cried out, so afraid were we that the figure would lift its head and we would be faced with the death mask of a rider from the Hunt. As a result, Otto and Stephan were as startled as we were, so, when I stumbled out the door after Katie, I found myself staring down the barrel of a gun.

"Erica! "Otto exclaimed in surprise."

Katie looked up into the face of the person who had caught her. She was shocked but for only seconds then recognition kicked in. "You... It's you...you piece of shit." Katie screamed at Otto as he held her close with one arm. "Get off me" She punched him in the chest and pulled away. "You left us there, you left us in that place with no clothes, no money and at the mercy of the riders. How could you? You said you were there to protect us."

Otto's face was a picture. I think he swore in German. He said angrily, "What are you talking about you madwoman, we have been looking for you all day. What riders?" Katie struggled to free her arm, but he held onto her. Keeping her at arm's length he looked at me. He said "We left you! Yes, we left you for a few hours and when we returned you were gone." Still holding Katie, who was struggling like a chicken, he had just caught, he asked me. "What is she talking about? What riders?"

Katie made another swipe at him. Through clenched teeth she hissed. "You said you were there to protect us, you. You b…" She was struggling for something bad enough to call him.

We were spared her rant. She was stopped in her tracks when a sharp voice asked. "Where is Christina? Katie cringed as Otto, still gripping her arm, spun her round to face Stephan. Mouth hanging open, she just stared at Stephan, who asked again "Where is Christina?" Katie was struck dumb for a moment. Then she wrenched herself away from Otto. "Take your hands off me." She said again spitting the words at him as she freed her arm and pushed him away.

I stepped between Katie and Stephan before she could say something she might regret. "Christina disappeared," I said "we don't know where she is."

"Disappeared where did she disappear? Do you mean she is somewhere in the castle? When did you last see her? Did she go down the cellar?" Stephan was angry.

Katie's eyes went wide. "No, she' s not here, she disappeared in Garmisch."

"Disappeared in Garmisch! Are you serious? You left her there!" Stephan was incredulous.

Katie groaned. She said each word, enunciating slowly as though she was speaking to a child, or someone with a learning disability. "In English, disappeared means someone has gone, and you can't find them, so, you don't know where they have gone. They have disappeared. Does that make it clear?"

Otto bit back at her. "Somehow, you, do not understand. Not giving truthful answers to a B. N.D officer could see you behind bars. Tell us what you know. You said you looked for her and could not find her. Where did you look? Go over what happened, minute by minute."

My heart sank, they were giving me a bizarre feeling of guilt. "She just vanished; she was lying sleeping on the sofa. We only left her for minutes, when we came back, she was gone. There had been no sound of a struggle, it looked as though she had just walked out the patio doors. We looked for her in the area around the house, but there was no sign of her." I didn't think telling them about the screams at that point, was a good idea and I harboured a fragile and irrational hope that Katie wouldn't either. "We were terrified." I said, "We didn't think you were coming back, and we thought Christina had been abducted."

"Or she chose to leave" Katie added quickly.

"So, you thought to leave her in Garmisch even though there was a chance Die Brueder could have taken her." Stephan said harshly, in a voice coloured by anger.

"No" Katie said we did not think it was Die Brueder. I thought she had walked out, and Erica thought it was the...

"Katie" I cried out stopping her.

"The what?" Otto persisted.

Katie rather coldly replied "No, as I said we thought she had walked out"

Otto sighed. "You are lying about something. You will tell me the truth. You said she was sleeping on the sofa. You left her there and went where?"

Kate said "We were in the loft because..."

"The loft!" Confused he asked, "Why were you in the loft?"

Katie glared at him. "I am trying to tell you if you would let me finish a sentence. Clothes, we were looking for clothes because you took ours, remember?" Oh, by the way, and now that we are on the subject, you took everything else, why did leave the clock. Cuckoo clocks not your style?"

"What is she talking about?" asked an enraged Stephan who at this point had, I think, come around to Otto's opinion that we were mentally unhinged. "We did not take your clothes." He told her. "Why would we take your clothes? You crazy woman." I suspected he was embarrassed to show his concern for Christina in front of us, so he was covering it up with anger.

"It's coming out all wrong." I said "Stephan we did not abandon her. We tried to find her. Even though we didn't know where to start looking."

Unconvinced Stephan snapped. "You could have gone to the police station and reported it."

"We don't speak German how could we explain?" I asked.

"The same way you managed to explain to the taxi driver to bring you here. If you had gone to the police, they would have found someone who spoke English." Otto threw in.

"Oh, come on, you know we would have been written off as hysterical tourists. Christina had only been missing a few hours. They would not have seen it as a problem unless they heard the screams." Katie said casually dropping the bombshell on an already heated conversation.

"You heard her scream?" Stephan asked and his face showed everything. In the little time I had known him, his most obvious trait was that he never showed emotion. Stephan was what my adopted Scottish mother would have called Po- faced, meaning he was devoid of expression, constantly serious, always with a disapproving look about him. Until it came to Christina of course, just the mention of her name seemed to melt him. There was no doubt in my mind that Stephan loved Christina and he was devastated she was missing. I knew how that loss felt, and I felt shame that we had left her, even though I knew there was nothing we could do.

I began to feel a bit lightheaded, nauseated, with feelings akin to the panic attacks that I had felt when Paul died. The truth was I was weary of dealing with fear that amounted to terror at times. I was sick of fear that forced me to lie and deceive. At that moment

61

I had reached the point where I believed it didn't matter anymore. I wanted to tell them the whole story and get it over with. I sank down onto a chair.

"Are you alright Erica" Otto asked "You are very pale. Would you like some water?" Katie filled a glass and handed it to me. I sipped it slowly. "Look "I said. "Katie didn't say we heard her scream, we don't know if it was Christina. The screams echoed across the mountain; it could have come from the cable car. We don't know what happened to her, that is the truth. We ran, we fled that house because we were terrified not of Die Brueder but of something much worse." I put my head in my hands on the table. "I am weary of secrets; I am weary of lies. I am weary of fear, of disbelief and ridicule. I will tell you all I know, all of it and believe me you may regret gaining this new-found knowledge, you may never have a good night's sleep again."

Otto stood opposite, he placed his hands on the table and said "You are intriguing me now. What have you been hiding? You must tell us the truth, or we cannot help Christina or you."

"I will tell you everything, but right now, you must take a look down there." I pointed the torch, "There is something, someone, in the cellar". Both men looked at me with complete disdain.

"What were you doing down there?" Otto asked Katie, much the way you would ask a naughty child.

Katie still irked by the inference that we had neglected Christina replied in kind. "Oh, we were just exploring, you know, passing the time like you do in an empty castle, in the middle of nowhere, when there is no one around. Which reminds me, you don't happen to know where Frau Schroeder and Kurt are by any chance? They seem to have disappeared. I mean you surely didn't just leave them here, when you knew Die Brueder had been hanging around." She smiled sweetly at him.

Otto leaned forward inches from her face, and for a moment he was lost for words "You are the most exasperating woman" he said.

She faced up to him. "Yes, it's a gift I have, it helps me to deal with useless cops who go for a jaunt and leave defenceless women alone."

"You, defenceless," he laughed. "No clothes, no money, you do not speak German, yet you manage to get a taxi to bring you here, let yourself in, find food," he looked at the table "and go exploring in the cellar. Oh! wait... yes, I forgot, you did the same in my sister's loft. I see there is a pattern there."

I interrupted their standoff. "The power's off Otto, we were looking for a fuse box or a generator, in the cellar. More importantly there's what looks like a man sitting on a crate in the corner. He is dressed in black robes with a hood, we couldn't see his face."

Otto looked over at Stephan. He sighed, the kind of sigh you give when someone terrified of spiders tells you they have just seen one. He pulled the torch from my hand

"It's dead, "I told him.

He shook the torch, slapped it on his hand a few times and of course it sprang to life. Waiving me out of his path, looking down the open door into the darkness, he spoke in German to Stephan who nodded and told Katie to sit down."

Stephan started after Otto when with a sudden urge to warn them I called out "Wait." They both stopped. "You don't understand. "I said.

"What don't we understand?" Otto asked. "You said there is a man down there. I will go take a look."

"Yes, but it may be dangerous, it looks like a man but... "I hesitated, not sure what to tell him. "It may be something else."

"Something Else. You think Die Brueder followed you here? Had you even considered that before you left my sister's house and ran here." Otto gave Stephan a look that spoke volumes. "Well I wouldn't worry I don't imagine they would be hiding in the cellar, but I will check it out anyway."

I muttered to myself. There are worse things that walk this earth than the Neo Nazis and that gun will not protect you.

Otto stopped" What did you say?"

I said, "There is something bad down there, be careful."

"Well we will soon find out." He ignored me and went down the cellar stairs anyway. Stephan told us to move away from the cellar door as far as we could, without leaving the kitchen. We were chilled with fright, so we pulled chairs close to the Aga for warmth. Stephan followed Otto.

"Do you think he is telling the truth about not leaving us in Garmisch. Katie asked. Do they did come back?

I sighed. I felt a drenching tiredness. "I don't know, maybe, probably. After all they came here looking for us."

We sat, staring at the open door, listening as Otto found and loudly challenged the figure in German then English, then there was silence. They were down there for ages. We could hear them talking. When they came back, Stephan closed the door behind him and went on his mobile speaking to someone in German. Otto pulled up a chair beside us. He took a deep breath. "It appears we may have found Frank Summers."

Within a couple of hours Heiligtum was buzzing with police, a forensic team in white plastic overalls and hoods and electricians in green overalls. The body was taken away and electricity restored.

"What happens now?" I asked Otto. "You said it may be Frank Summers."

"Yes." He said, "the body has been here for some time, but there are some unusual factors that make identification difficult."

"Such as?" I asked.

"The body had been drained of blood prior to death and dressed in black robes. The forensic examiner was able to say it was a white male in his forties. A note had been pinned to his chest. It said we are coming for you. In English.

"So, it may not be Frank." I asked

"It is too soon to say. He took a deep breath. "You will stay here tonight; we will stay with you. You will have police protection"

Katie said. "Oh! You mean like the last time, that makes me feel so much safer."

Otto started to answer her then decided there was no point. Katie lavished her sweet smile on him again. He continued "The plan is taking you to a safe house in Munich, in the morning,

Police protection will be there for you. You will have to stay in Germany until you have been interviewed by the local police. Tonight, we start at the beginning. You will tell me how you met Christina. Your relationship with her. Why you came here. How well you knew Frank Summers?" Which was not at all of course. "It is time for the truth," he said. "I want to know about the riders you speak of. As for now. I think it would be better if you go to your rooms and get some rest. There are four armed police officers staying overnight with us. So, you will be safe. Is there anything else you need?

There was no argument. I said no and thanked him. We were heading out of the kitchen when he called. "There is only one more thing. There was a strange message on your mobile from someone called Eli. Who is Eli?"

"Eli Laskov is a friend. He is looking after my business in Glasgow. What was the message?"

"There are many missed calls from him. The last message reads…" He took out a notebook,

"For your life and your sanity, do not go near the gate. It is worse than before. You must speak to Doria Van Brugen she knows all. So, who is Doria Van Brugan? What does this mean?"

I shook my head "I don't know, I honestly don't know."

Chapter 7

The Van Brugan House.

From the moment he said her name, I thought I sensed a change in Otto's attitude. "Doria Van Brugan? It sounds Dutch." I said, wondering if maybe she had known the Vansterdams. Maybe she had been in the employ of Luke my birth father. Eli had said she knew about the gate, therefor it might be that she had been in the inner circle of people paid to protect Luke.

Otto said, "Dutch she may be, but she lives here, in Germany, in Berlin to be precise."

"That's handy." I said.

"If you already know who she is, why were you asking us?" Katie asked dryly.

His response was sharp. "I know a Doria Van Brugan lives in Berlin. I know she is a widow who pays her taxes and has a driving license. That is all. Now I would like you to tell me what you know about her, and what it is she knows, and where is this gate you have not to go near?"

Shaking my head, I said "I told you, I have no idea who she is."

"Your parents were Dutch."

"What's that to do with anything?" I asked sighing.

"Just answer the question please"

"Yes, well, that is, my adoptive father Wilhelm Vansterdam was Dutch. My mother Mary was Scots born.

"And your birth father, where was he born?" Otto asked pulling out a chair and settling himself down at the table.

"I don't know where he was born."

"Not Scotland then? I thought since he left you Lanshoud...

"Possibly, I don't know. I didn't know of his existence till after he died."

"But surely there were papers left behind at Lanshoud."

"Yes, of course but none to say where he was born."

"According to Detective Inspector Valdez of the Glasgow police, there is some mystery around your father and his death. and of course, the disappearance of Frank Summers."

"Yes, she is a very suspicious person" I said smiling sweetly.

His tone changed from soft to sharp. "My dear Erica," you seen to think sarcasm is an acceptable response to my comment. Make no mistake, I will not accept glib replies, you are no longer in Scotland. Since you arrived here, a body has been found, the owner of this castle has disappeared, and it is now a major investigation involving the police and the BND. He waited for my reaction to the implication of my involvement in a crime. I didn't react. He continued. "According to Inspector Valdez, you are in the habit of evading questions. Let me make it clear. I expect you to cooperate with the German authorities, the fact that you have been given police protection does not absolve you from answering questions truthfully. So, when I ask you the following questions, I expect truthful answers. Am I making myself clear?"

"Perfectly" I snapped back. "What do you expect me to tell you when you seem to know more about Doria Van Brugan than I do?"

"We have traced her, but the woman is a recluse and we have no more information. So, let us start with this gate Eli speaks of, and where is it ,and what is its importance?"

"I don't know."

"I think you do." He became loud. "Since Eli sends you a warning not to go near it."

"Well you are wrong, because I really don't know where it is, but if you let me speak to Eli, I might be able to find out."

He took my mobile from his pocket and slid it across the table. "Call Eli. Find out what he knows."

Katie was quick. She stuck her hand out "Eh, where's mine?" She asked indignantly. "You took my mobile too, remember?" He reached in his pocket and passed her the mobile."

"Katie picked it up" it's dead."

"Yes, apparently we could not access a charger to suit yours. Anyway, your mobiles have no signal here. The landlines have been connected now and you may call Eli from there."

Eli was relieved when I called. I told him we were all well. I explained the landlines had been down at the castle and we had no signal on our mobiles. He accepted my story so readily that I realised what an expert liar I had become. I was very careful what to say because I had no doubt that the BND would have tapped the phone. I asked Eli about Doria. It transpired he had known Doria for years. She had been a lecturer and his mentor when he studied Classical and Ancient languages at Oxford. Eli had not heard of her for many years, but he knew that she had married a Dutchman and now lived in Germany. She was an expert at identifying ancient manuscripts and he had a hunch she may have heard of the gates. Doria was a recluse and did not have a telephone so, he had written to her, when he first found the box with the keys,

He told her about finding the keys and reading about the existence of the four gates. He also told her about my inheriting Lanshoud. She did not reply. He thought one of two things, either Doria knew about the gates and was afraid, or she had died. Then suddenly, the day after Christina, Katie and I left for Heiligtum, a letter had arrived from Doria. Eli had been trying to contact us since. He was relieved to know we were safe and anxious to tell me that Doria's letter contained a warning about the gates. She was more than willing to speak to me but only me. She wanted me to come to her, but she specified she would speak to me and only me.

"How old is she Eli?" I asked. "She must be a good age, if she was a lecturer when you were at Oxford?"

"Yes indeed, late eighties at least, if not more. Her letter was short and to the point, containing only the warning about the gate, and that she would speak only to you. Her handwriting was difficult to read, thin and spidery. Do not go alone Erica. If you need me, I will fly over and go with you."

"No, thank you Eli but I will be fine. I will call you when I know more."

"Please go soon and let me know."

"Wait, you didn't tell me what the warning was?"

"She was not specific. She will only speak to you."

"Ok. I will let you know what happens as soon as I can." I said wondering how it would go down with Otto. However, because he had been listening into my conversation with Eli, there was no argument with Otto. He was intrigued by this mystery of the gate and highly suspicious of our involvement with Christina and Heiligtum. He no longer insisted on my return to Glasgow the next day, now he was taking me to Berlin.

"I'm not going home tomorrow." I broke the news to Katie who was packing her case.

She spun around. "Oh my God! I knew you were going to say that. Shaking her head, she said, "don't tell me, let me guess. Oh! I know, you want to look for Christina, even though half the German police force are probably out there right now, searching for her." She flopped on the edge of the bed. I just knew you wouldn't go without looking for her. She sighed heavily. "Please Erica, think about it, it's just not safe here."

"Look Katie, you can go, they will fly you back. I don't mind, I'll be fine."

Katie shook her head." No. I am not leaving you here."

"Please Katie, if you want to go home tomorrow, just go. but I'm staying. I am going to see Doria Van Brugan."

Groaning in frustration Katie pleaded, "What can we do here? nothing. So, why not go home where it's safe, at least until you get some news. You could write to this Doria woman like Eli did."

I sat down beside her." No, I need to know now. If Eli has reason to worry, then so do I. It's not safe at home either, is it? It's safer to stay here, you know that. We have bodyguards here and they know what we're up against."

"But that's the whole point, they don't know what we are up against. They don't know about the riders and even if you tell them they won't believe you. They are focused on the Neo Nazis. Thinking they have taken Christina and her husband. Don't go Erica, just come home with me.'"

"I am going to see Doria tomorrow. Otto is taking me to Berlin in the morning. I am not changing my mind."

"Oh, you drive me mad sometimes...fine, I'll stay."

"No! because you don't have to."

"Yes, I do, because you don't get to spend... how long does it take to go to Berlin?

"5-6 hours. We will have to book into a hotel when we get there."

"Oh, really, well I am coming with you, because it's enough that you would have him all to yourself cooped up in a car, but you don't get to spend a night in a hotel with that guy all on your own,

The thing about Katie was she always made me laugh. "Ok, I hugged her. "I am glad you're coming with me."

"I don't suppose they have brought our week-end bags back from Garmich- Partenkirchen?"

"You are right, they do have them, they took them to stop us from trying to leave, while they were gone. Stephan is bringing them to us now."

We left after breakfast, around nine the next morning, taking overnight bags, knowing we would more than likely stay for more than one night. We had not gone far before Otto started asking questions. I talked a lot to Otto, on that journey to Berlin. We talked about the skeletal faces swirling in the mist, at the patio doors. I told him we had seen these beings before. Otto was familiar with the legend of the Wild Hunt or Wilde Jagd as it was known in Germany, but as I expected he dismissed out of hand, our having seen them that day. He politely suggested it was nothing more than the vivid imagination of two frightened women. Who were left terrified by the isolation, the mist and Christina's disappearance?

He said, "the mountain mist and the eerie silence it brings with it, can disorientate even the most experienced climbers. It creates shapes. It swirls and changes giving an appearance of life, and the movement coupled with the silence spawns an ominous sense of presence. You are not the first to have seen faces in the mist and you will not be the last."

He asked Katie and I to go over the story again and again. He knew nothing of the attic full of clothes and had phoned his sister. Completely confused she said she thought the attic was empty. She had never stored anything there. She said she had never been up there. He could not explain the fact we thought we had been drugged. He said again and again, he and Stephan had been called away and had left us securely locked in. He could not explain the open patio doors and insisted they had also been locked. "Try not to worry," he said placatingly. "Stephan will find Christina. He is working with an expert team."

"Is that so?" said Katie from the back seat, where she was sitting, arms folded, listening to the conversation. Oozing sarcasm she continued." Would they be the same expert team who found Frank? Oh! no wait, sorry, that was us."

He smiled at me. "This is a long journey, but we will stop for lunch and coffee. Why don't you tell me about all about Lanshoud?"

"You have spoken to D.I. Valdez. So, you already know all there is to know."

"No, you and I both know there is far more to your story."

"The truth is so bizarre you will refuse to believe anything she tells you. "Said the voice from the back seat.

"Try me." He insisted. What have you to lose?"

"My self-respect," I said.

"Tell me again. Valdez may have missed something."

"That woman doesn't miss anything," Katie said

"You are not a fan of hers then, Katie?"

"I think that would be putting it mildly," I said.

It was to be a long journey. I started at the beginning. I told him about Paul's death, my inheriting Lanshoud and the vast fortune. I told him about Molly and Alice, about James and Gill and Jack and the belief that we had been terrorised by the riders of the Wild Hunt. I told him about the parapsychology team who came to help. I did not at this point think it was the right time to tell him about Michael, Rafe, Gabriel and Uri, I added only Jonah and the C.I.D.

Two hours had passed, and he had listened intently, interrupting only when there was a word or a phrase in English, he didn't understand. Valdez had told him all about Christina. She had told him about the murders of David and Leo Baxter, and I told him about Eli and Antique Treasures. When I had reached the part where we came with Christina to Heiligtum. I said "Well! Say something."

He slowed the car and pulled off the road onto a side road. "It is an incredible story. I am how you say, dumbstruck. I don't understand how you have kept this a secret for so long. How the authorities and the press have not gotten hold of it."

Katie jumped in with. "It has stayed secret so far because until now, she only told people she could trust."

"I assure you; you can trust me Katie."

"Thanks, but I'll reserve judgement on that one," Katie replied almost falling over in her seat as Otto took a sharp turn towards Nuremberg.

The sky was heavy with clouds and before long there was the pitter patter of raindrops on the windshield. Otto pointed out a little restaurant nestling among the trees where he had reserved a table for lunch. It was a lovely old-fashioned place with seating for no more than twenty diners. Solid oak furniture graced with real china dishes, fresh flowers on every table and exceptional food. It was exceedingly popular, full of well-dressed customers, who made Katie and I feel a little self-conscious about wearing jeans. The owner, an elderly gentleman knew Otto well and made a fuss over the two ladies whom Otto introduced as his friends from Scotland, who were touring Germany. He shook hands when we left and handed Otto a basket with pastries and drinks for the rest of our journey and provided Otto with an umbrella to protect the ladies from the now pouring rain."

"Thank you, that was a lovely meal" I said to Otto as we climbed back into the car.

"Yes," Katie said, "a genuinely nice owner too. Does he make a fuss over all the police and BND officers? What I mean is do you offer him protection in return? "she asked with a smirk.

I gasped "Katie!" Honestly?"

Otto did a double take, then said. "Well Katie, I see you are very observant. I am impressed at how very quickly you assessed the situation. Extortion, protection money, yes of course, it subsidises our income." He looked at her shocked face in his mirror. Are you surprised? Or should I say shocked?"

"More like disgusted." Katie said.

Otto laughed aloud" You watch too many gangster movies Katie, Gerhart is my uncle, my mother's brother and my Godfather. I understand your assumption, but I can assure you there are no corrupt officers among my colleagues."

With egg on her face Katie, now subdued, ran her fingers through her tight curls, as she always did when she was put out, and apologised. Otto accepted her apology with grace and having drank two large glasses of wine Katie soon fell asleep in the back of the car.

The weather was deteriorating, dark heavy clouds hung over-head, and heavy rain began battering the windshield, I felt relaxed. The warmth and comfort of the car, and the hypnotic metronome-like beat of the windshield wipers passing back and forth, were making me drowsy. Otto was concentrating on the road when he suddenly said. "There are, as you British say, a lot of holes in your story." Parts of it do not connect. May I ask some questions?"

"Why? I have already told you all I can."

"With respect Erica. I don't think you have. I think you are hiding something because you feel you have to." Otto's tone was light, friendly. "I must admit after the things you have told me. I am intrigued."

"I have already answered your questions as honestly as I could." I was so tired now. No, tired was not the right word. I was weary and I needed someone to lean on. I had been hoarding my secrets for so long, they had slowly eaten a hole in me, and my will to see this mission of finding the gates, through to the end, was ebbing daily. I missed James. Katie, much as I loved her, was no substitute and now there was something oddly comforting about this man. This man I hardly knew. This handsome man with dark hair and piercing blue eyes. The strong jaw with hair so black the shadow of it remained after every shave. Intelligent, resourceful, and kind, his precise accented English and his impeccable manners were charming and slowly they lulled me into a sense of security, and I caved in. There was no decision or thought involved. I just instinctively trusted him. I was ready to share all, and I knew in order to stay sane, I needed to offload these secrets, share the burden. I had reached the limit I could cope with. For me Christina's disappearance and finding Frank Summers body, was the last straw. No more secrets. If I told all, the worst that I could see happen was they could write me off as a lunatic.

Over the next few hours, I told Otto the secrets of Lanshoud, about Luke Treadstone as he was known when I met him, my father, the interdimensional time travelling alien, who had somehow travelled through Hell and opened gates that were portals into our world. I told him about the finding of the keys, the gate at Lanshoud and what we found there. The other houses. The possibility of other siblings.

I must give credit to Otto for when I told him about all I knew, he didn't bat an eyelid and that was not quite the reaction I expected. It made me consider the possibility that he knew far more than I suspected. I described the search for my identity and the discovery that my life till that point had been a web of deceit. I told him about meeting Christina, her subsequent brutal attack and finally, in for a penny in for a pound, I told him about the how we were rescued at Lanshoud. When I finished, we sat in silence? Otto was stunned. He said he was lost for words. He looked shell shocked and I knew for certain he believed every word. As for me, well, like a repentant sinner who has just been given absolution I felt a huge weight lifted from my shoulders.

He asked more questions, of course he did, but even allowing for the language barrier I was amazed that Otto seemed to accept what I was telling him was the truth. There were no disparaging remarks like those flowing during my interrogation by Valdez. Otto simply listened, asking me to clarify a few things here and there. He had known a little of my story from information he had gathered from the Glasgow police. It turned out he had spoken to Valdez more than a few times. He explained that when they discovered Die Brueder interest in Frank Summers and Heiligtum they traced Frank and Christina's whereabouts to Glasgow. It was at the time Christina had gone missing in Glasgow, that they were referred to D.I. Carmen Valdez, the officer in charge of Christina's case.

The traffic was slowing to a crawl in both lanes. Moments later a siren wailed in the distance and an ambulance went screaming past the car followed by a fire engine. The cars had slowed and stopped completely.

"An accident?" I asked.

"Yes, probably some madman. It is common to find people testing their cars on the Autobahn, where there is no speed limit. It happens a lot, but our traffic police are exceptionally good at dealing with it. The traffic will move again soon." And it did.

By the time we reached the hotel in Berlin it was evening. The heavens had opened and driving sheets of wind and rain battered the car. We ran for shelter splashing through ice cold puddles. Gerhart's gift of an umbrella was useless against the power of nature and we arrived at the reception desk looking like drowned rats. There was a living flame gas fire blazing in the lounge. After dinner, Katie and I curled up beside it, basking in its warmth while Otto ordered drinks. He had changed from his formal suit and was dressed casually. It made him look more approachable. Though when he reached to lift a glass, I could see the shape of a gun at his waist.

"I was just wondering if the address you have for Doria will be easy to find?" I asked.

"Yes, she lives In Potsdam near the river Havel about fifteen miles south west of Berlin's City Centre. This hotel is halfway there, so, tomorrow it will not take us long to get there."

"I don't feel right about just turning up." I took a sip of the wine Otto had suggested. I prefer red but it was a genuinely nice German Riesling, that smelled flowery and almost perfumed.

"It's delicious." Katie said, holding out her glass for more.

He refilled it. "She asked to see you did she not?" You are not arriving uninvited."

"No, but she is an elderly lady with no telephone."

Otto said, "I understand. Perhaps deliver a note first? Asking when it would be convenient to call."

"Yes, that would be better."

"Write a note, the hotel will have it delivered."

We spent the rest of that night discussing the events of the last year. It was I suspect an awfully expensive wine and so fine on the palate I drank more than I should, which was in hindsight his intention. He asked more questions, one leading to another. Katie filling in detail. Feeling more relaxed than I had in a long time I spoke about Jack and Gillian, about Sean David's birth, about our plans to turn Lanshoud into a hotel and finally the more he questioned I finally told him about Mike, Gabe, Rafe and Uri. Katie filled in details about Emilio Mendez and how he had fooled us all. By the end of that evening he knew everything there was to know about Katie and I and we knew nothing about him. Still my instinct to trust that man was strong. Sometimes in life you do the wrong things for the right reasons.

The reply was handed to the reception the next morning, scrawled across the bottom in a spidery hand were the words *come tomorrow at eleven*. There was no signature.

Eli said she would see me and only me. Katie decided to do a little shopping while Otto took me to Potsdam. He parked the car near the house overlooking the river. He handed me the umbrella and pointed to the house. "I will be waiting here, call if you need me. Keep your mobile in your pocket."

The sky was a depressing grey that morning. In the outskirts of Berlin sheets of fine rain swept over the land creating a mist that billowed like clouds over the Havel river. Everything was grey and hushed and there was an unworldly silence, broken only by the hum of the car engine. The Van Brugan house loomed in front of us, a sad relic of better times. A neglected house, whose windows and doors had fallen into a state of disrepair. Faded paint peeled from rotting wood and an overgrown hedge spilled onto the weed strewn path. As I opened the gate that hung loose from its post, the metal hinges screeched loudly, breaking the silence and loud enough to bring a woman to the door.

She was a middle-aged woman, dressed in an apron. She didn't speak but she was obviously expecting me. When I introduced myself, she nodded with only a hint of a smile. She rattled away in German and at the time she ushered me in, indicating that I should follow her through the house, which was as old and tired inside as it was outside. Showing me into a sitting room she signalled for me to wait while she knocked gently on a connecting door. There was no reply at first, she waited patiently then knocked again. This time a voice called out. The woman opened the door, spoke to someone and then leaving the door open she gestured for me to go in. "Frau Van Brugan" she said. I stood for what seemed like ages not sure if I should go in uninvited. Then in English a woman's voice called sharply. "Come through here. Close the door behind you."

The old woman sat at her desk in a room surrounded by books. Every inch of wall was covered with bookcases. They crammed the shelves. Hard backs, paperbacks, huge dusty old tomes. They were piled in teetering towers in every corner of the room and stacked in piles on every piece of furniture. She stood up from her desk with difficulty and leaning heavily on a stick, she surveyed me from head to toe. Her hair was as white as snow and scraped back into a bun at the back of her head. She was dressed in a long dark red skirt a pale blouse fastened with a strange gold broach at the neck and a cardigan too large for her slight frame. I felt nervous. I held out my hand and spluttered out. "Good morning Frau Van Brugan. Thank you for seeing me. I am Erica Vansterdam, though I was married, and I am now Erica Cameron." There was no response she continued to stare. I twittered on. "Eli sent me. He said I should speak to you, because you knew something about the gate at Heiligtum and, I am very pleased to meet you."

She ignored my outstretched hand.

"You have a birth mark." she said. It was more of a statement than a question. Surprised because I had one but never told

77

anyone about it. I said "Yes I do, but it's so small that I forget I have it. I need a mirror to see it but... how do you know about it?"

She ignored my question. "It is on the right side of your back just above the waist. Show it to me. Come around here. Show me." I did as I was told

"Now turn around." Even though she wore spectacles she picked up a large magnifying glass and waited till I took off my jacket and pulled up my blouse. She studied the mark at length. "Yes, you are one."

"I am sorry I don't understand. What do you mean one? One what?"

"Sit down" she said blatantly, and rudely, ignoring my question again. I did and we sat in an uncomfortable silence while she continued to study me. "There are four, "she said.

"Pardon? Did you say four? I am sorry, four what?"

"You are being difficult. There are four. Do not pretend you know nothing. I know you closed the gate at Lanshoud. I know, foolish girl, you come with no armour, no defence, to close the gate at Heiligtum." She was talking in riddles.

The door knocked and the other woman brought in a tray with tea and biscuits. Doria snapped at her, they argued in German. The woman plonked the tray on a desk and handed Doria a small glass with tablets in it. She spoke firmly to Doria, who finally lifted the glass poured the tablets into her mouth and washed them down with a glass of water from the tea tray. Then she slammed the glass down on the tray and grunted. The woman whom I eventually discovered was called Marta, poured out the tea and handed me a cup. She held out milk and sugar, and smiled at me, I took some milk and thanked her. She glowered at Doria and left. Sipping the hot tea mostly to calm my nerves. I asked again." What did you mean about the four?" but Doria just stared at me.

"Four" she said angrily. Why do you not see, there is always four, four houses, four gates, four babies." She started shouting. "There is always four. One gate has been closed but they all must be closed. If not, they will come through and all will be lost. It is near time. The ice caps melt, volcanoes erupt. Tsunamis kill thousands. It is a sign of their coming."

Cryptic again. "By them do you mean the Wild Hunt, the riders?"

Foolish girl, so dangerous, the riders are only the forerunners, they always have been, they pave the way. She raised her voice. You don't know what terrible force you are playing with. The four, the four. she cried. It is always the four."

I thought great, she's mad as a hatter, she's lost it. I was wondering why on earth Eli had sent me here, when Doria suddenly gave a deep sigh and dropped her head onto her chest. For a moment I thought she had fallen asleep. Then painfully, she stood up and walked, leaning heavily on her stick again. She opened a drawer in the middle of a bookcase and handed me a large brown package. "This is what you came to find. This is how they will come. The four. It is valuable take it and go."

She hit a bell and Marta came running, smiling apologetically, to show me out. I thanked Doria and left. Walking back to the car I turned and looked back at the house. The curtain twitched and I thought I saw two faces at the window I couldn't tell if they were male or female but Doria was not alone in that house.

The rain had stopped, and the sun had come out. "Is everything alright?" Otto asked, "you seem a little upset."

"No, it was awful, I don't think she is right in the head. I couldn't hold a conversation with her she was rude, aggressive almost. She knew I had a birth mark, no one knows about. She kept talking about four, everything was four. She gave me this though." I showed him the package, she said it was what I came for. Let's just leave Otto. I don't like it here. I'll will open this on the way"

As soon as we were out of sight of the house, I opened the envelope. It contained, I thought a large drawing and some papers, but it wasn't a drawing, but a print, on yellowed waxy paper. It depicted four riders on horses, their dress, biblical. They wielded swords and their horses trampled men who cowered in terror beneath their hooves. An angel flew in the sky above their head. I had seen this before.

I asked Otto to pull in somewhere. He stopped at a layby. With chills running up and down my spine I had realised what it was and why she had kept saying the four. The words were sticking in my throat. "That's why she kept saying "the four". That is what will come through the gates. I have seen this before at Lanshoud, in the cellar. It's a copy of a woodcut. A 14th century woodcut of the Four Horsemen of the Apocalypse

Chapter 8

The Café in Potsdam

As we drove back to the hotel, Otto suggested that we stop for a coffee. It was a charming little café with wooden armchairs and soft cushions. To crown it all we had a window seat bathed in sunshine and overlooking the river. The aroma of freshly made coffee and pastries, made on the premises, filled the air. To my delight they sold a decent pot of tea, not the quality of Scottish blend of course, but an acceptable alternative. It was no longer raining the dark grey clouds had gone, instead fluffy white cotton wool clouds floated across an azure blue sky. It was shaping up to be a lovely day. In any other circumstances I would have been relaxed and happy, but I wasn't because my mind was elsewhere, mulling over the horrific implications of the print and the letter.

"You are upset" Otto said not looking at me but stirring his coffee then licking the milk foam off his spoon. Tell me what you are thinking? Is it the letter?"

I shook my head. "It isn't that, not the letter, not yet anyway, since I can't read it, it's written in some kind of script. It will have to wait till I can get it to Eli. Eli will either be able to translate it, or he will know people who can. No, that's not what's upset me." I stirred my tea watching it swirl round and round like the thoughts in my head. "Luke, my birth father, was a brilliant young scientist in his own world. He was working on time travel when he passed through what we call Hell. Luke said no one who entered Hell was ever allowed to leave. He believed that the technology he had developed to increase the speed of light had allowed him to pass straight through. Furious, Hell's master, as Luke called him, sent the Wild Hunt to find him and drag him back. The Wild Hunt, the night horsemen, written off as myths, yet who have terrorised so many people, in so many nations for centuries. Luke said he had entered and left Hell through a portal, a kind of a wormhole in time and space and he was thrown from it onto Earth in Roman times."

Otto was listening intently, but he made no comment, so I continued. "Since that day he had never aged. He was my father, but he was younger than me when I met him." I paused "Can you imagine being faced by a man younger than yourself telling you he's your father? I was already living in a dream world, wondering about my own sanity and Luke turning up just about finished me. It was unbelievable."

Otto's face was expressionless. "You're not saying anything." I said nodding my head and smiling. "You don't believe any of this, do you?" He didn't answer. "Well, I'm not surprised really. I mean why would you? It's sounds like fantasy, like a pure work of fiction. That's what I thought it was. I felt just like that, I couldn't get my head around any of it. I wanted to run away. Pretend it wasn't happening. It was my friends who stopped me from falling apart." Silence, he still didn't comment.

I liked Otto, I felt safe with him, he was a good listener and had always seemed interested in everything I told him, but this time it was different, he seemed distracted, looking around the cafe. Of course, I knew he was there because he had a job to do and he might just be humouring me, playing along, because I was somehow a link to whatever the Neo-Nazis were searching for. Whatever it was they believed was hidden at Heiligtum.

I felt tears pricking my eyes. Quite suddenly and for the first time since all of this began, I had an overwhelming feeling of homesickness. I didn't know this place, nor did I speak the language. I hardly knew this man sitting in front of me, and I was afraid. Afraid that what Doria had given me was the forerunner of disaster.

I wanted to be home again, back to the days when in my blissful ignorance, I was happy with Paul. Sitting on the sofa with my feet up, watching and laughing at sitcoms like Friends or Frasier on TV or even a horror movie. Cuddling up to Paul because the movie was scary. Snacking on wine and crisps. Now, that was all gone, that part of my life no longer existed and had never been real in the first place.

My mood was spiralling to reach an all-time low. I was on the verge of dissolving into a deluge of tears, when a strong soft hand touched mine. He stroked my hand as he enclosed it in his and with his other hand, he gave me a tissue. I took it and blew my nose, feeling to sorry for myself to even be embarrassed.

He looked straight into my eyes, eyes that were blurred with the tears that I was desperately trying to keep under control. His gaze was soothing and caring, his voice soft and low he said. "Erica, try to trust me. I do believe you." I remember thinking he was reading my mind, when in a firm voice he said again," you are safe with me. I am here to protect you and I believe everything you have told me. Now listen carefully to what I am about to say. Do exactly what I tell you. Now, pick up your cup." I looked at him blankly. "Do it," he said sharply.

I lifted the cup and sipped my tea; it was getting cold. As I reached for the teapot, covered in a hand knitted tea cosy, Otto, always the gentleman lifted it and poured the still hot tea into my cup. When he put it down, he scanned the room again, stopping to watch a man and a woman who had entered and taken a table near us. He nodded "Carry on Erica. Carry on with your story. I am listening. Please keep talking. I will explain why, for now just keep talking."

I cleared my throat and pulled myself together. "Luke tried to get home. He travelled back and forth over time, crossing every corner of the earth, searching for a way back, looking for the other portals he knew existed. Eventually he learned of the existence of four, he called them the gates. He searched the world till he found those gates, moving on and changing his name when people noticed he wasn't ageing. One at a time over centuries, he found them. One in Scotland, one in Germany, one in Italy, and one in France. He found a way to open them with a device he made to look like keys. At first, he was afraid that one of the gates might lead him back to, and trap him in, Hell, but he was so desperate to return home he tried anyway and found, to his horror, that he could not enter them from this side. So, over hundreds of years, he built the four houses around the gates to conceal them until he could find a way to get safely through. These houses are Lanshoud, in Scotland. Schloss Heiligtum in Germany, Castello Delcancello in Italy, and Chateau Langedechu in France.

When I first met Luke, when he appeared in the kitchen at Lanshoud, he was working at CERN in Switzerland on the Hadron collider. He had heard of the outstanding achievements of a young scientist called Rory Gemmell who was working there on a special project. This young man was working under the radar of the authorities and Luke believed that sooner or later, the work that Rory was doing, would open yet another portal. So, Luke found employment at CERN with the sole motive of sabotaging Rory's experiments. Luke said he had crossed a line and he believed Rory would eventually do the same, it was only a matter of time. He said that in everyone's lifetime they do things they regret, things that cannot be undone. He tried to stop Rory Gemmell making the same mistake he had."

"Yes, that makes sense," Otto said in a strange voice, not looking at me but at yet another couple coming in for coffee. "Keep talking," he said, but I had faltered so he added.

"I see now that Heiligtum, the similarities in your inheritance and the resemblance between you and Christina are the reasons why you believe Christina is your sister?" He touched my hand again. Had I not been so emotional, I might have considered the gesture intimate and inappropriate considering he was a Federal policeman and had made it quite clear it was his job to protect me. Yet, somehow it wasn't like that, his touch was warm, soothing, comforting like a balm for my spiralling panic. "Try not to panic, take deep breaths." he said. Yet again sensing my thoughts he added, "Stephan will find her. I have no doubt of that."

"But will she be alive and well, when he does?"

"That I cannot say," He was listening now but again watching other customers.

"There is something else. Something that has worried you since you spoke to Frau Van Brugan" he said, still checking out the other tables."

I almost laughed. "Seriously? You think I am worried? No, terrified is closer to the mark. I am terrified that these gates are the way into our world for the four horsemen, who according the Book of Revelations will bring, war, famine, plague, and death. They will destroy mankind and I am the one holding the keys that close those gates. Don't you see?" I was almost pleading. "Christina and Frank were the only people who could have helped me find the gate at Heiligtum and now they are missing or dead."

Otto chose that moment to drop a bombshell, he said. "They are not dead. The body found at Heiligtum was not Frank Summers."

I was aghast." What? You knew this and you didn't tell me? How long have you known?"

"I received a call when you were with Frau Van Brugan. I would have told you, but you had other things on your mind. Consider this, if they haven't killed Frank, then it is more than likely they are both being held somewhere. As I said before, I believe what you saw at my sister's house was no more than an optical illusion, caused by the mist around the mountain and your previous experiences of apparitions at Lanshoud. It is therefore more likely that the Brothers have them and it would not be in their interest to kill them, not if they need them to find what they are looking for at Heiligtum."

He was right if course. "Who was it then? the body, I mean"

"That, I do not know yet."

I am not sure when I began to feel uneasy. It was like a gradual awareness seeping into my consciousness, an animal instinct, a primordial warning of approaching threat that created a chill causing the hair to stand on the nape of my neck.

Otto turned and looked across the room, staring at something. Following his gaze, I saw her, an old woman, dressed in a long grey coat and headscarf. She seemed out of place among the other customers. Even at a distance I could see the bright red lipstick smeared across her mouth. The hat with the hat pin, sharp and dangerous. I watched as the waitress served her coffee and a pastry and exchanged a few words with her. As the waitress walked away, the old woman turned and looked right at me. That look sent a chill, tingling my whole body. It was the old woman from the Glasgow Art gallery and Museum. My blood was now running cold through my veins. I turned away and picked up the teaspoon and started stirring the tea. I was thinking, stop it, don't be so stupid, it can't be her, not here in Potsdam.

I shivered violently."

"Is there something wrong?" Otto asked." Are you cold?"

"No, I am just a little jittery."

"Jittery?" he frowned. "I do not know that word."

He made me smile. "No, I don't suppose you do. It's the effect of letting my imagination run riot."

"Yes, that I understand perfectly. No, you must talk to me as though there is nothing wrong."

Confused I asked, "What do you mean?"

Otto said, "look at me Erica. Look at me and smile."

Surprised I said, "I am looking at you."

His next words made my blood run cold. "I know you feel her presence as I do. I need you to keep talking. Can you do that? Tell me about your friends, smile, laugh if you can, flirt with me."

"Flirt with you!"

He was grinning away at me. "That's better. Tell me about Gill, bring her into your mind. Focus on her. Tell me all the good things about your friend, smile Erica and do not look round."

Bewildered as I was, I realised he was deadly serious. I smiled as broadly as I could throwing myself into the game pretending what he was saying was incredibly funny,"

"Keep talking about Gill, raise your voice then listen carefully to my replies. I am going to talk about how we are going to leave here in the next few minutes," he said laughing.

I nodded to let him know I understood. "Oh, I know she has always been like that. Gill is such a man-eater. You know, when we were young, I used to despair of trying provide shoulders for all her jilted boyfriends to cry on."

He took out his mobile phone. I hadn't heard it ring or buzz. He looked at it as though he was reading a text, then left it on the edge of the table saying, "there is a door behind you it leads to the toilets and through it there is another door that leads onto the side of the building. Don't move till I tell you to." He lifted the teapot to pour the last of the tea into my cup and at the same time knocked his mobile onto the floor and it slid under the table. I looked under to see if it was near me, but he had already found it.

I feigned disapproval. "That was careless, is it damaged?"

"No" he said, "keep talking about Gill."

I drank some tea. "It wasn't unusual you know for Gill to have more than one guy on the go at a time." I was trying hard, really hard, to focus on his smiling face and not look round.

With a big grin and a low voice, so low I had to strain to hear him he said, "When I tell you, go to the toilet, go out of the back door that leads onto the side of the cafe. I have put the car keys in your bag. Run to the car, start the engine but sit in the passenger seat. I will go to the counter and pay the bill. You will have to run as fast as you can when you reach the outside door. Do you understand?"

"Of course, you are right." I said, "but the thing about Gill is she is happy now. She has been a different person since she met Jack, and she is a wonderful mother to Sean David."

He nodded smiling. "Now go, but do it slowly, and tell me where you are going."

I stood up. "You will have to excuse me. I am just going to pop to the ladies' room." I looked around as though I was looking for the toilet sign. I noticed the two couples and the old woman watching us. Fixing my eyes on the sign that said 'Dames' I left the table, walking slowly, smiling at the waitress on the way.

Without knowing why, I ran for my life out that that cafe, at the same time fumbling in my bag for the car keys. I had no sooner climbed into the driver's seat, started the engine, moved to the passenger seat, when Otto was climbing in the car. He hit the accelerator and seconds later the car, tyres screeching, was speeding out of the car park. He drove like a racing driver. He must of have been hitting 90mph. I didn't speak to him for fear of breaking his concentration on a road with multiple bends, that took real skill to navigate. I just sat frozen, my knuckles white from gripping my seat belt.

When finally, we pulled into the hotel car park. I asked what that all about. "Was there a demon in that café? I have seen the old woman before."

"A demon!" He repeated" Then obviously amused he said, "yes, I suppose you could call them that. There was more than one. I saw them while I was waiting for you outside Frau Van Brugan's house. I stopped at that cafe so we could lose them."

"Why didn't you tell me?"

"I didn't tell you because you are not a good actress, it would have shown in your face."

"So, you think they followed us to the Doria Van Brugan's house?"

"No, we were not followed from the hotel. I would have known. They were already there when we arrived."

"Do you mean they knew we were coming?"

"No, I think it was just coincidence."

"The old woman," I said. "You said I felt her presence, you were right I did, and so did you."

"Yes, but those demons, as you call them, are only servants, just as dangerous, though they are only flesh and blood."

Katie sat in a Lotus position on one of the twin beds. I was packing the last of my things into my overnight bag. "Am I getting this right? You are talking about the biblical four horsemen? You think that maybe the four gates are there to allow the Four Horsemen of the Apocalypse to enter our world? To bring the end of time by destroying the human race. Wow! Even given what we've been through, that is way too farfetched."

"I hope you're right, but we won't know till Eli can get the letter translated. Come on," I said as I struggled to get the zip across the bag. We should hurry. Otto is waiting downstairs in the lounge."

"Well I am packed and ready to go when you are. "Listen to that wind out there," she said getting off the bed to look out the window. She stood there while I checked the room and the bathroom to make sure we hadn't left anything behind.

"Right, I am ready," I said.

Katie called me to the window. "Come and look at this." A white voile curtain covered the window that overlooked the square at the back of the hotel. A strong wind was picking up, blowing leaves across to where Otto stood talking to two men. They were young, very tall, and well dressed.

Katie said. "In the lounge waiting for us is that what you just said? Is that what he told you? I knew there was something odd about him, and them. I couldn't put my finger on it at first but then I realised, they are just standing there, looking at each other, as though they are having a conversation, but no one is actually speaking. Don't you think that's peculiar, look at them"

I looked out. "Maybe they are just waiting for someone. Maybe waiting for us. They may be friends of his"

"Maybe but he told you he would be in the lounge waiting for us. You know something Erica? For a supposedly intelligent woman you can be very naive sometimes. I sat in the back of that car, all the way here, listening to you spilling your guts to that man. You trust him, you told him everything and you know nothing about him."

"Not now Katie, please. I just want to go home." I pulled on my coat. "Are you coming? We will miss the flight."

As soon as we had reached the hotel. Otto had said it would be safer if we went home. He arranged the flights and was taking us to Berlin Airport. He taken care of everything. The hotel bill had been paid and the flights. Katie's reply to that was, "it's no skin of his nose. The BND will be Paying for that."

She lifted the edge of the curtain. "They are still down there, look, they haven't moved an inch. They are just standing looking at each other, now don't tell me there isn't something queer about that.

Curious, I put my bag down and walked back, to look down to where the three men stood. At the exact same moment, like a highly trained unit, they snapped their heads round and up, to look directly at me. Later I couldn't shake off the feeling, they had heard us, even though we were on the third floor. The thing is, no matter how much you trust someone, when someone else sows the seeds of doubt in your mind, as often as Katie did in mine about Otto, the weeds begin to grow, and they get bigger and bigger, as they are fertilised by each new disparaging observation. When it came to that kind of gardening, Katie was an expert.

Chapter 9

Return to Scotland

The captain announced the descent and the air stewards walked up and down the aisle checking seats were upright and seat belts were securely fastened. I woke Katie to tell her to fasten hers. I have never been able to sleep while travelling, whereas Katie was out like a light the minute the plane took off. Which was a blessing in disguise, because she would, in all probability, have continued her rant about Otto all the way from Berlin to Glasgow. Now at least the aircraft was into descent before she could start again.

I asked her what had changed. I knew she liked Otto, she had said so and it was obvious he liked her. Apart from anything else, although I am sure the funds would not have been out of his own pocket, he had paid our hotel bill and our flights. He even, I suppose because he had special clearance, delivered us safely to the actual door of the aircraft.

Katie gave a huge sigh, "of course I liked him. So did every other woman in that departure lounge. What's not to like about that tall, lean, hungry look, broad shoulders, and eyes blue enough to drown in. That guy is expensive looking eye candy, but my instincts are fairly good, and they kicked in. There was something not quite right about him. For a start there was no chemistry. Tell me, did you feel any chemistry between you? Like the kind you have with James?"

"Oh, for God's sake Katie."

"Ok, ok. She held up both hands I was just illustrating my point. There was no chemistry between us, and I am not going to even start on trust, and as for reliability, well, all I can say is just think back a few days."

91

I love Katie, but when she has an issue with something, she is like a dog with a bone. I quickly changed the subject. "We will have to phone a taxi soon as we land. I did text Eli, but he is the only one in the shop today." Katie looked out the window she didn't say anything. "Did you hear me?"

"Yes, don't worry, it's sorted. I ordered one while you were batting your eyelashes at the eye candy,"

The flight arrived as scheduled. Ever since the armed terrorists, the ones that were taken down by a baggage handler, drove their car through the glass doors into the main terminal at Glasgow airport, taxis have not been allowed to pick up passenger anywhere but in the car parks. The taxi firm I have always used, take details of your flight, and contact you around ten minutes after the aircraft lands. They tell you where they are parked, the type and colour of the car and the driver's name. At the baggage carousel I asked Katie to check her mobile to see if she had a text from the taxi driver.

"No need this driver will come into the terminal to meet us."

Surprised I asked, "what firm is that?"

"I am just going to nip to the toilet." She said rushing off."

I waited, then wandered over to where there was an overhead screen showing the relatives and friends waiting for the passengers. I thought our taxi driver would probably have a board with Katie's name on it, but I couldn't see any. Either he wasn't there yet, or I wondered what taxi firm she had called that had not given us any means of identifying their driver. Suddenly among the sea of faces, I saw him. Of course, she hadn't hired a taxi, she had called James.

She floated back out toilets. "Watch. my... bag" I said through gritted teeth. I'll be back in a moment." When I came back, she gave me a knowing look. "I guess you spotted him then?"

"Yes, I spotted him."

"I could tell." She said running her hand through her hair, touching her cheeks and lips. "The hair, the blusher and the lippy." She laughed."

"I freshened up, just the same as you did."

"Of course, you did. C'mon, best not keep him waiting."

Annoyed I said, "he's a busy man Katie you shouldn't have called him."

"Thanks for picking us up James". Katie said as he kissed her on the cheek." I got a row from Erica for not phoning a taxi."

"Oh, it was no bother. I'm glad you called me. It feels like ages since I've seen you." He leaned over and pecked me on the cheek. He took our bags and as we left the airport saying. "It's nice that Jack and Gill have come down from Lanshoud and arranged this weekend for us. It's been a long time since we have had a get together.

Surprised I asked "They arranged a weekend? I didn't know anything about it."

He looked at Katie, confused. "I did tell Katie when she called me yesterday."

Katie had a smug look. "Sorry, I meant to tell you, but you had gone off with Otto to see the Van Brugan woman and it slipped my mind. Gill has gone to a lot of trouble. She is making dinner for us all tonight. Eli is coming after he closes the shop.

Sensing I was not happy. James asked. "Are you ok with this? Gill and Jack are expecting us because Katie said you would want to go there straight from the airport."

"Sorry, yes I am ok with it. It's just a surprise that's all. A nice one of course."

James understanding said. "But not so nice when it's sprung on you. "Would you rather go home first?"

Katie piped up. "Well, actually I would quite like to go home. Would you mind dropping me off first? I'll come later. I will bring my own car to Gill's tonight."

She was unbelievable. I knew she had planned all of this and the need to go home first was all part of her scheme. If she went to her own flat it would mean James driving through Glasgow's rush hour traffic and for James and I to get back through that traffic, to Gill's home in Bearsden, meant James and I would be alone in the car for at least an hour.

"Of course. I'll drop you home first." James was as obliging as ever and completely oblivious to the fact Katie was playing him."

I glowered at her. "Katie" and as if she didn't know this already," I said "it would be unfair to have James running about all over the place. So, either he drops me at your place, and we go later to Gill's, or we go straight there now. Which would you prefer?" Both scenarios screwed up her plans, so she caved in. Straight there we went, through heavy Glasgow traffic to the leafy suburb on the outskirts of Bearsden.

Jack answered the door with a beaming smile and swept Katie and I into the house shouting to Gill, "come out here woman, would you look at what I have found on our doorstep."

"Shhh." Gill came quickly, flicking a tea towel at him. I have just got Sean off to sleep and this big Irish foghorn keeps waking him." Gill looked wonderful, her eyes were bright and shining and her skin glowed with only a faint blush on her cheeks. She wore a flowered apron with traces of flour on it, evidence, as was the air filled with the scintillating smell of warm scones, that she was, I think, in the best place she had ever been. No longer the wild party animal flitting from man to man. Now, as a wife and mother, she was idyllically happy. We threw our arms around each other, and I cannot tell you how good it felt to be again among friends, real friends who were like the family I never had.

Gill asked Jack to put the kettle on, while we had a quick peep at Sean David. The baby lay snuggled in his cot under a blue fleece blanket. His favourite bear was tucked under the cover beside him. His head with its mop of hair, the same auburn as mine and not ginger like his father's, lay on a white pillowcase, the corner of which, had been lovingly embroidered by Molly and Alice. In blue thread, it read Sean David and beside the name a beautiful and exquisitely crafted angel. How appropriate I thought, for this little miracle, the little boy whom the messenger Abdiel had described as a gift.

"He will waken soon. He goes down for the night at around seven and wakens up again around two, I can't wait for him to sleep through the night. He is Jack's son, he hollers his head off when he wants attention. He has the most adorable little pout. He squeezes out a tear or two and Molly and Alice or my mum come running. Though I wish they would run during the night. Jack and I are shattered from lack of sleep. He was so spoiled at Lanshoud."

As I suspected she would, Gill had invited James to stay. I fully expected him to decline but he didn't partly because Katie hung on to his arm and begged him not to go. She said. "it is so nice to be all here together; we have been through so much and I feel safe here." Truth be told I was glad he stayed. Tonight, when Eli came, we could go over everything together.

Sean woke up and Katie and I played with him. We sat on a rug building towers with brightly coloured cloth cubes, only for Sean to knock them all down again, which he found hysterically funny.

"Gill you have become so domesticated." Katie said sinking into the lush sofa with huge cushions as soft as pillows. "I can't believe you actually made those scones. They taste fresh out of Gregg's."

"Well you can thank Molly for that. She has been teaching me how to bake." Gill beamed at the complement.

"We spent the next few hours talking about Lanshoud and how Jack was settling in to managing the estate. I had given him a sizeable budget for the general maintenance, but the plans for turning Lanshoud into a hotel or a venue were on hold, because Antique Treasures was surprisingly turning over a regular profit and Eli had some ideas for expansion in that area.

Jack was cooking that night. James followed him into the kitchen leaving us to chat about babies and motherhood with Gill. Katie and Gill went to bathe Sean, who was getting cranky which Gill said signalled bath and bedtime. Left alone on the sofa with a glass of wine, I mulled over the implications of the print and letter and my inability to do anything about Christina or her husband. I worried that I would have to back to Heiligtum alone, because there was no guarantee anyone else would go with me. Even if they did, I wasn't sure I had the strength physically or mentally to go through it all again. Would Otto be there to help? He escorted us to the very door of the plane, but said nothing about seeing us again, he simply wished us a safe journey home. Which was odd, considering how close we had been over the last few days. The more I thought about it the more a dark cloud seemed to be gathering over me. What if there was no Otto this time and no James. I had a headache, the kind that usually turned into Migraine, the kind that only a power nap would relieve. I was so tired. The wine and the comfort of the sofa helped me to relax to the point I closed my eyes and dropped off, only to be woken when I felt a hand touch mine.

"Sorry, I didn't mean to wake you, but your glass was about to fall." James was standing over me and had taken the glass out my hand. "Are you alright? You look exhausted."

I sat up and rubbed the back of my neck that was aching from the way I had been lying." I'm fine. I haven't been sleeping well, that's all. With everything that has happened I feel my head is all over the place. Our flight was at the crack of dawn this morning. Katie slept on the plane, but I've never managed to do that."

"I put your bag in your room. Why don't you go and have a lie down? We can wake you when Eli comes."

"There is no point. I won't sleep."

"Well you gave a good impression of it. I didn't know you snored so heavily."

Mortified and hoping it was a joke, I cried "I don't snore."

"Yeah, that's what everyone says, but since you were asleep you wouldn't really know would you? So, I will enlighten you." He then gave a good impersonation of me with my head back, my mouth wide open and sounding like Peppa Pig. I punched him playfully, he had made me laugh.

"You don't look happy. Tell me, is it the separation from... by the way I am quoting Katie here... separation from Otto, one of the most gorgeous men she has ever seen? Whom she hastened to add has a dark side that you are completely blind to."

I sighed. "That's nonsense." He doesn't have a dark side that's just Katie being Katie and doing what she always does."

"Oh! Well! Quick to defend him. Katie was right then; you do have a soft spot for him. She did say he was at your side constantly.

"Don't be ridiculous James. Otto was just doing his job."

"He was certainly doing something. Takes you to his sister's holiday home and abandons you there."

"He didn't abandon us; he explained all that."

"Katie thinks he did." He was irritatingly smirking now. "He drove you to Potsdam. He paid for your hotel, he took you to see Doria Van Brugan and waited outside for you. Then he took you for coffee, brought you back to Katie. On top of all that he then arranged and paid for your flight home and hand delivered you to the aircraft. That is some service, I hope he was well paid."

From his tone of voice, I didn't know how to take that last remark.

He suddenly realised I wasn't laughing. "I'm sorry, I was just winding you up. I know what Katie's like. Have I stepped on a raw nerve?"

"Of course, you haven't. Why would I have a raw nerve where Otto is concerned. He was just a security officer doing his job and he did it well. I felt safe when he was with us and so did Katie, only she didn't tell you that did she. James, I needed the support he gave us. I am scared, really scared. I'm not sure I can go through all this again. I would give all the millions back just to feel safe again. Life was good when the biggest problem I had was what to make for dinner. I used to say to you I felt like Alice down the rabbit hole. Now I feel I am about to go through the looking glass, and I don't have the skills, or the knowledge to survive. I don't know what I am dealing with. Is it the Neo Nazis? Is it the Wild Hunt or the Four Horseman of the Apocalypse or are they one and the same? If this were a movie, I would say the plot was ludicrously far-fetched and the leading lady, me, was ridiculous and incompetent. I am not educated enough; I am not skilled enough. I have had this dumped on me and I stupidly thought I had won the jackpot. A mountain of money, a home I could only have dreamt of. I felt like Alice in Wonderland. Instead. the truth is I have faced the shades of Heaven and Hell, science fiction and horror and I am terrified of what I will have to face next." I shivered violently.

"You're cold?" He said sitting down beside me on the sofa. He handed me the glass of wine I had almost dropped. "Here finish this" I could feel his closeness. Feel warmth radiating from him. Coupled with the familiar comforting scent that was James, I found his nearness overwhelming and my hand trembled when I took the glass.

"No, I am fine. I feel panicked sometimes and no matter how many people, are around, I feel very alone. I feel they are being nice, but I am sure no one wants to face those demons again. Everyone else has the ability to just walk away at the first sign of trouble."

I was on the verge of tears. He reached over and took my hand in his. His hands were warm and soft and strong. He said, "Erica I..." he hesitated as though he were considering something carefully. "We all love you. Everyone under this roof would stand by you through thick and thin. You will never be alone. We spoke about it before you came. We all are in this together."

Eli arrived around 7pm, immaculately dressed as I knew he would be, in his black suit, white shirt, bow tie and waistcoat. His black shoes shining like a mirror. With Sean David now safely tucked up in bed ,we sat down to dinner at eight. We ate and talked.

Eli was excited to hear about my meeting and couldn't wait to see the print and the letters. He studied the print carefully saying it was one he was very familiar with. "It is a copy of the most famous of Albrecht Durer's Illustrations of the Apocalypse, created in Nuremberg in 1498. It is the Four Horsemen of the Apocalypse. Death, War, Famine and Pestilence." He placed the print on the table. "And now the letter" He picked up the two pages very carefully, peering closely at the script through his wire framed spectacles. "These pages may be yellowed but they are not old, and the ink is not faded. He rubbed the page between his finger and thumb, admiring the silky texture and the thickness of the paper. It feels like velvet, it is silent when you turn the page. This is vellum. It is made to last."

"What's the difference between paper and velum? "Katie asked.

Eli explained. "Vellum in these days, is often just another name for high quality paper. Real Vellum is traditionally made from calf skin or sometimes other animal membrane. It is less porous than paper, so ink is less absorbed. If you look you, can see the ink lies on the surface and each letter seems to stand out. It does not crinkle like paper. There is no sound when you crush it.

The language is Aramaic, Old Aramaic. A language of the middle east, of the Jewish people across the Holy Land. It would have been the language spoken by Jesus and the Apostles." He looked up at our faces and smiled to see that we were, as always, riveted when Eli educated us. His voice with its heavy accent was soft, deep, and soothing. Jack did tell us once, that when he worked in the history department at the University and Eli was a guest lecturer there, Eli's voice nearly hypnotised the students.

Eli continued. "It is the main language of the Talmud. Whoever wrote this is undoubtably a scholar of ancient languages and therefor, though I cannot be certain, I presume it was written by Doria. She was you know my teacher and mentor at Oxford, where she taught ancient languages.

"Ah!" said Jack who was walking around the table refilling glasses. I wondered how you knew her. Is this then why it is in Aramaic? Is it for your eyes only?"

"Oh Eli, how romantic. it makes you sound like James Bond". Gill said.

Eli smiled and said" Doria knows I can read this, but not many people can, so, it is likely she was afraid it might fall into the wrong hands."

"But you will be able to translate it? I asked?"

"It will take me some time, but I can do it."

I asked him a question that had been on my mind. "When you called my mobile and left a message you said Doria Van Brugan knew something. What did you mean?"

Eli settled back in his chair. "When I knew you had gone to Heiligtum. I contacted her to see if she knew anything that would help you. If she had any idea what the Nazi's might have been searching for in Heiligtum, either during the war or now. She told me to send you to her, at Potsdam. May I ask how you found her?" Did you talk much?"

"No, to be truthful Eli, I felt she wasn't very friendly. She mentioned the gates, said I was foolish to come to close them without armour, whatever that meant. She asked me about my birth mark, it's on my back, the right side, above my waist. I can't see it except in a mirror. Doria took a Magnifying glass to look at it and then bizarrely said I was the first, but she wouldn't explain what she meant."

He took his spectacles off and rubbed his eyes. "Four gates, four keys, four houses, four children to inherit." Eli said.

"Otto took you there and sat outside waiting?" Jack asked me, giving James a knowing look that Katie didn't miss, she was right in there.

"Oh yes," she said, "he was super attentive; followed Erica everywhere like a puppy dog."

Although I had already told them everything about Christina's disappearance Katie had obviously felt duty bound to fill in the little details, of how distraught we were, when we discovered we had been abandoned. How Otto had dismissed the idea that it was the riders of the hunt we had seen in the mist. How he had claimed to know nothing about the clothes and things in the loft at Garmisch. How when he was meant to be meeting us in the hotel lounge and instead was talking to two strange men outside."

"Do I take it you didn't like him Katie?" Gill asked

"Oh no, "Katie said, "It would be difficult not to like him. He's male model material He is charming, good looking and well-mannered. It was very difficult to see past all that."

"But Katie managed anyway," I said to Jack and James' amusement.

"What else did Otto tell you about Oppenheim and Die Brueder. "James asked.

Just what I told you already, that they want something they believe is at Heiligtum. Something powerful and occult and they will stop at nothing to get it. Otto called Oppenheim a reptile, a cold-blooded killer with no morals and with a band of sadistic psychopaths at his disposal."

Jack laughed. "He didn't mince his words then".

"Otto believed they have taken Frank and Christina, but he repeated several times, that Stephan will find them'"

Jack asked "Did he not think it could be Heiligtum itself he is after. Maybe he wanted it as a remote headquarters for his organisation. Like Himmler did with Wewelsburg."

Eli nodded. "You could be right Jack, it could be Heiligtum itself he wants. Doria told me Schloss Heiligtum was furnished like an emperor's palace, rich brocades, Persian carpets, solid oak furniture and tapestries on the walls. Is that so Erica?" he asked me.

"Yes, it is exactly like that."

"Then it is not out of the question, that this the very reason they want it. Neo Nazis are as fanatical as the SS they emulate. In 1934 Heinrich Himmler acquired Schloss Wewelsburg in Westphalia. He turned it into a Camelot for the SS. He furnished it accordingly. In the same expensive furnishings as Heiligtum. Beneath the Great Hall there was a large stone circular vault with twelve black pedestals. It was known as 'The realm of the Dead.' It is believed by many historians that magical rites were carried out there."

"There is a vault like that at Heiligtum and Otto said Himmler was there during the war. Christina showed it to us."

"Do you have any idea what the occult object they want might be?" James asked. "Could it be the gate?"

Eli said, "I doubt it, there is little or no documentary evidence that these gates exist. It could be anything. The Spear of Destiny lay at Lanshoud. It is possible something equally valuable lies at Heiligtum."

Gill had made deconstructed rum babas for dessert. Jack was supposed to be serving it while Gill went to check on Sean. But Jack was engrossed in conversation, so Gill served instead. I offered to check on the baby, but Gill said "oh he is fine, listen you can hear him laughing." We could hear Sean on the baby monitor, he was restless, not crying but making little noises and clearly giggling. Gill said." He talks to his teddy bear, the one Jonah bought him. He will not be parted from without kicking up a fuss."

James asked Jack and Eli again, did they really believe it was something occult? Oppenheim and his gang were looking for and did they think that had something to do with the body in the cellar being dressed in black robes. Having lectured on history and the Second World War at Glasgow University the question was right up Jack's street. Being German born of Jewish parents, born of a father and grandparents who died in Auschwitz, Eli was also an expert.

The desert was too tempting to lie forgotten as Jack and Eli settled back into what they liked best, in depth discussion on historical matters.

This is delicious Gill" James said pouring the rum over the desert. "To Jack he said, "I thought all the theories of the Nazis being involved in the occult was dismissed by most historians as being pure conjecture." James said.

Eli nodded. "Yes, that is true but not all historians. Personally, I believe it to be true. It cannot be proven of course but just look how Hitler surrounded himself with occult. Look at the uniform. The SS symbol of the black uniform and the black cap with the death's head insignia. The SS, their name synonymous with brutality and murder. Look at the exceptional cruelty of experimentation carried out on Jewish men, women, and children and on prisoners of war. It beyond belief that any sane rational human beings could stoop to such levels of sadism, as was carried out on concentration camp inmates."

Jack said "It is well documented that Hitler regularly consulted an astrologer before he made strategic decisions about invasions. British intelligence had a department that used astrologers and psychics simply to counteract any occult activities carried out by the Nazi's. Still, as you say, it is not a wide held belief among most historians.

People look for magic and myth when reality is out of step. It is otherwise difficult to explain how a nation like Germany, who produced cultured geniuses like Einstein, Beethoven, Bach, Von Goethe, and Freud and many more like them, allowed itself to be led to destruction by a group of sadists, misfits, and undisputed criminal. All, led by a poorly educated and psychologically unbalanced painter."

The men talked for hours. The detail of their conversation into the depth of the savagery, that an otherwise cultured nation, had descended into was depressing. Gill, Katie, and I left them to it and took our tea and coffee to the sitting room. We talked about lots of things and by eleven clock I was falling asleep. I said good night, went to bed and conked out the minute my head hit the pillow.

I woke startled, not knowing what had wakened me. Had I heard something? Was it a dream? There were no streetlights outside Gill's home, but there was a full moon that shone through the window, where I had forgotten to close the curtains. The pale light shone on my bed but didn't penetrate to the corners of the room. My mobile lying on the bedside table said it was exactly 2am. Instinctively I felt there was something wrong.

Was there something lurking in those dark corners of the room. I strained my eyes to see. Floorboards creaked, not inside, but outside my door. Shivering, drawing the duvet around me I watched the door. Fumbling, finding the light switch on the bedside table, I chased the darkness away. Nothing hidden there. I froze, listening, watching the door handle, afraid to take my eyes off it. I could hear breathing. Someone was there right outside my door. I held my breath, my muscles tensing with fear. Then I heard movement of footsteps, going down the stairs slowly one at a time, then silence. Relieved, I took a deep breath. Thank God, I was such an idiot. It was probably just Jack or Gill going down to the kitchen. My head on the pillow, the duvet wrapped tightly around me and with the bed light left on, I watched the door until my eyes began to grow heavy and I fell into a dream filled sleep. A sleep that was later shattered by a heart-rending scream, a shriek of horror, of terror, that chilled me to the bone. It stopped my breath and sent my pulse racing. I couldn't breathe the horror of that wailing sound would live with me forever. That sound was coming from Gill, who had also heard footsteps, and gone to the nursery to find an empty cot.

Chapter 10

The Missing Child

I woke not sure if I had been dreaming or if the scream, I had heard was real. The sound was followed by raised voices. I listened intently. I heard Gill crying out for Jack and then there was a commotion outside my door. I heard James' voice too I got out of bed and opened the door to see Jack and James running down the stairs. Gill was standing watching, obviously distressed.

"Is he here?" Gill cried pushing past me into the bedroom. Her face was chalk white. She was dressed in a white camisole and white pyjama shorts and with her long dark hair streaming behind her she looked like a ghost.

"Is who here? ..." No answer... "Gill what's wrong?" Again, no answer. Wild-eyed she just stared at me; her lips held tightly together as though she couldn't bear to speak the words. I thought maybe she was sleepwalking; it was something she did as a child and when we were students.

Turning to the window she looked out, put both her hands and her forehead against the cold glass of the windowpane, and gave a moan that I can only describe as the sound of anguish. Visibly shaking, she was staring out into the pale darkness of the moonlit street. "Gill" I said quietly. She didn't seem to hear me. Still thinking she was sleepwalking I touched her arm tentatively, worried that I would startle her. She spun around and looked at me with crazed eyes.

"Gill, who are you looking for?"

She turned and gripped my hands. "He's gone" she said.

I started to ask who was gone but at that moment, on some subliminal level, I knew who she was looking for, but I didn't want to go there, it was too horrible to contemplate. She pushed me out of her way and ran across the hall straight into Katie's bedroom. I followed her.

Katie having heard the scream had just opened her door. She was standing there looking child-like in pink fleece pyjamas, rubbing her eyes, and pushing her mass of black curls behind her ears, when Gill crashed into her and sent her flying back onto her bed. As though Katie didn't exist Gill went straight to the window. The widow in that room looked over the garden at the rear of the house. It was dark and impossible to see anything other than the grey outline of trees, as the tall dense conifers filtered the moonlight.

"What the hell!" Katie cried out, still lying on the bed propped up on her elbows, not attempting to get up. "What's going on?"

"Where is he?" Gill pleaded looking from one to the other. Did either of you lift him?" Her voice trembled with panic.

I knew then for sure. "No, there's no one here." With a sickening feeling I asked her. "Gill what's happened? Is it Sean?" At the mention of his name she sank to her knees on the plush blue carpet, moaning like an animal in pain. I knelt beside her, but she got up quickly. I followed her as she ran back into the nursery, she was desperately looking around as if the baby could still be somewhere in that room, and somehow, she had missed him. It was as if her mind was refusing to accept the gut-wrenching horror of the empty cot.

That beautiful white cot, with the blue pond full of bright yellow ducks painted on its base, lay empty. The snowy white pillow, with Sean's name embroidered on the corner, still held the imprint of the baby's head. At that moment I felt a wave of nausea and I had to grab the door post to steady myself. The impact of the empty cot, and the footsteps in the night sunk in.

Gill stood trembling. "He's gone, my baby Erica, someone has stolen my baby," she said through tear-soaked eyes. She sank to her knees again laying her head against the cot, her knuckles white as she gripped the cot bars. "It's my fault, I didn't get up. I heard him cry and I didn't get up."

A car engine roared into life. "Where did Jack and James go?" I asked her.

"Jack and James have gone to find him. Erica, someone came in here and took him from his cot."

"Oh my God Gill." I knelt beside her turning her around to cry on my shoulder. I looked up at Katie who stood with her hand across her mouth, horror making her lost for words.

Gill was distraught. "He's gone Erica." She said gulping back tears. She rattled out the words. "I heard footsteps. I thought It was someone going to the toilet. The monitor is right beside me. Sean cried, just once. He does that a lot when he turns over in his cot. I didn't get up." She put her head in her hands, wiped the tears from her eyes and repeated. "I didn't get up; I didn't get up."

She sat back, weeping loudly. "I was so tired. When I didn't hear him anymore, I thought he had gone back to sleep. It's all my fault. I looked at the clock, it was only two o'clock, he wasn't due his feed until six. Someone must have been in the room with him when I heard him cry. Someone has taken him." She stood up suddenly, wringing her hands. "I have to look for him. Jack and James have gone to find him. I must help them."

"Oh Gill." Katie said reaching out to hug her, but Gill pushed her away. "I have to get dressed," she said still gulping down tears. "I have to help them find him," she said as if she expected them, to find him lying in the street.

She staggered into her bedroom and we followed her. "I have to look for him," she kept saying over and over. She pulled on jeans and a hooded jacket, then stood tall for a moment taking deep breaths in a brave attempt to pull herself together. Running back to the nursery she went straight to the cot and lifted the little pillow pressing her face into the soft white cotton. I thought my heart would break when she whispered," I will find you baby, Mummy will find you." She then went calmly downstairs.

Seemingly unaware that we were following her, she walked straight to the front door. I called out, "Gill wait, I'm going to ring the police they'll want to speak to you." Deaf to my plea she lifted a jacket from the coat stand and opened the door. I caught her just in time to stop her running out into the street. "Wait, Gill, you can't go out there. You need to stay here because..." I almost said if...when they find him..." She was pulling away from me... "when they bring him back, you will want to be here. "I struggled with her pushing her back from the door as Katie ran to close it.

Katie with her back against the door, her voice soft with sympathy said, "Jack and James are looking for him. We'll call the police, but they will want to speak to you Gill. You need to stay here."

Her eyes swollen with still more unshed tears, she let me guide her to the sofa where she sat with her head bent over her knees and her hands over her head. She was rocking back and forth, moaning. It was the most awful sound I had ever heard.

"Someone came in the night and took him. They took my baby." She looked up at me. What time is it? He'll be hungry, he will be calling for me." She put her head in her hands again clutching and almost pulling her hair out. Suddenly she stopped, frozen, she looked up at me again and her voice changed to a deep cold tone. She looked straight into my eyes and asked, "Who took him?" My heart sank as I sensed the accusation. "Who took him Erica, do you know? "

I dialled the emergency number to find someone had already called it in. A car had been dispatched and would be with us in minutes.

I wasn't surprised that Gill asked me, so pointedly, who took him. We all knew that Sean had been a miracle. His gestation had been less than five months. Other forces, forces for good had been at work the night James and I were rescued by the messenger Abdiel. The night Abdiel said my friend would be given a gift. Sean was that gift. A precious irreplaceable gift of a child to an infertile couple. I sat on the sofa opposite her not knowing what to say because I knew exactly what Gill was suggesting. The last time we stayed with them, the phantom riders from the Hunt had made their presence known outside this house. They had followed me, looking for my father Luke. No one could blame Gill for thinking they had followed me again.

"It's not the Hunt Gill. The gate at Lanshoud is closed. They can't come through anymore. They can't have taken him."

Her tone was sharp, angry. "No? Then who Erica? What else are you mixed up in? "She spat each word out. "What foul thing have you brought to our door this time?" "I know it has something to do with you." There was venom in her tone, and I was gutted by her vitriolic outburst. I felt a wave of nausea again. I was devastated by what looked like hatred in Gill's eyes. Never for a second had I considered she would blame me, but I was not so naïve, as to not realise she had good reason. She had listened to the conversation the night before about the Neo- Nazi's having cells across Europe, also, I had told her something else that only James knew. After Christina recovered from the brutal attack that nearly killed her, she asked James to help her make a will. At that time, she believed two things, one that Frank may have been killed by the same people who tried to kill her, and two that I was truly her sister and since she had no other family, she made me her heir. I couldn't know for sure, but I had to consider Die Brueder might be holding Christina and Frank. If so, they may have extracted all sorts of information from them. There was a distinct possibility that they could have taken Sean, in order to blackmail me into revealing what was hidden at Heiligtum. Maybe like Himmler they already knew about the gates and Christina knew I had the keys.

Katie looked up at me, still with her arm around Gill she shook her head. She said, "she doesn't know what she's saying, she doesn't mean it. she's just upset"

Gill pushed Katie away. In a voice as cool as ice she said, "oh I know what I am saying alright and so do you and she knows I mean it."

My heart was thumping so loudly in my chest, I was sure they could hear it. There was nothing I could say. I knew that, like me, she was thinking if not the Hunt, then who? I didn't know which was worse. Die Brueder? or Lamashtu the demon, the child stealer, who had insinuated herself into James' life as Chloe. Could she, at that time, been looking to steal the precious child gifted to Gill and Jack. The thing impersonating Jonah had been her accomplice, they had fooled us all. How many more were around us? Taking the shape and form of people close to us. Yet, how did these demons enter our world if not through the gate, the portal at Lanshoud that led to their world, to their space and time. I repeated "Lanshoud's gate is closed Gill, it's not the Hunt."

"Yes, but there are three more," she bit back, "and you have just been to Heiligtum. What did you bring back with you? You didn't find the gates there, did you? You don't know if they are open or closed. What did you bring back with you Erica?"

Had someone or something followed me here? Any of that was possible. I felt so sick I could vomit. I walked over to the window. Jack and James had taken both cars and probably driven off in opposite directions. A pointless exercise since it was almost three hours since I heard first heard the footsteps outside my door.

"Did you hear anything during the night? Gill asked Katie."

Katie said "No, I only woke up when I heard your voices outside in the hall."

Probably making her hate me even more I said "I heard footsteps too, earlier, around 2am. I thought it was you or Jack getting up for the baby."

Gill didn't even look at me. I looked up at the clock it was now 4.45am almost three hours had passed, whoever took Sean could be miles away by now. Gill stood up, pulling her jacket round her, she put shoes on her bare feet and headed for the front door again. Katie tried to stop her.

Gill was calm, she held up her hand. "Let me go, I want to go out, he might be near. I want to search the house, the garden, the street, waken neighbours. Someone might have seen something. I have to ask if they've seen him."

Katie with silent tears filling her own eyes, didn't let her go. "Gill, please, sit down, the best thing we can do is wait here." She stopped. "Wait! Listen!" Cars screeched to a halt outside the house. Katie sighed with relief. "They're here."

Morning had also arrived, though it was hard to tell. It was almost darker than the previous moonlit night. Clouds completely covering the sky, like a grey quilt, heralded the threat of heavy rain.

Jack came through the door first, ahead of James, and the first of the police to arrive. Pale with red eyes, he went straight to Gill. She threw herself into his arms, looking up at him. He shook his head, answering the silent plea, the question she didn't ask. She sobbed on his shoulder. He said, "there was nothing, the streets are empty but there's a police car outside now. They will find him." He stroked her hair, "They will find him darling, they will find him," he repeated, in a low weak voice with no hint of conviction.

The two C.I.D officers were the start of an army. Within the hour there were as many as six cars, with uniformed police and more C.I.D. Two vans with hyperactive excited dogs and their handlers. A forensic team, who trailed into the house, in white hooded suits, carrying cases and plastic sheeting and rolls of yellow 'do not cross tape'.

A young woman in uniform introduced herself as police constable Sheila Collins from the incident team. She sat down beside Gill and Jack, her eyes full of pity, her obvious aim to reassure them. "Mrs. Docherty we will do everything in our power to find your son. Every police station across a wide area, has been called upon to dispatch cars. There will be C.I.D. Teams of dog handlers, forensics, all working to find your son. They'll check CCTV's in the area and make door to door enquiries. If he is not found quickly, the media will be asked to launch an appeal for witnesses. Gill covered her ears and buried her head in Jack's shoulder, as if everything Sheila Collins was saying, made the nightmare more real. For me it was a nightmare that was about to get worse. I heard her voice before I saw her.

"Well, well, here we are again Mrs. Cameron." Standing behind me like the Sword of Damocles, was last person I wanted to see. I didn't even turn to look at her. I waited till she came to me. She sidled round the sofa, smiling, then turned to Gill and Jack. "Mr. and Mrs. Docherty, I am very sorry that you are going through this terrible event" Her voice was soft showing genuine pity. "We have met before. If you remember, I came to your home when Mrs. Cameron and Mr. Anderson here," ... she nodded towards James who had come in at her back... "were involved in a car accident. I am Detective Inspector Carmen Valdez."

"Of course, we remember you" Jack said dryly, "you are not exactly easy to forget."

"Thank you, I will take that as a complement." Valdez chose to ignore his derogatory tone. She then rolled out the same sentence they all did. "I realise how distressed you must be, and I want you to know we will do everything in our power to find your son." I..." She was interrupted by a uniformed constable asking for three items of the babies clothing, to give the dogs a scent they could follow.

Gill was still clutching Sean's pillow that she had lifted from the cot. Jack held out his hand "Gill, the pillow" Gill shook her head and clutched the little pillow tightly to her chest. Jack reached to take it from her. "Gill, the pillow will have a strong scent"

Valdez in a display of empathy, that I was surprised she was capable of, said "No, don't take the pillow from her, she needs it. I am sure you have something else. Favourite soft toy or unwashed clothing will do Mr. Docherty, preferably what your son wore yesterday."

Jack stood up "Yes of course I'll get them. "Gill, I can't remember exactly..."

Gill looked at Jack witheringly, as if to say, really? You can't remember what our son was wearing yesterday! Instead she said, "In his laundry basket, a white vest, a white tee shirt with blue dinosaurs on it, and little blue dungarees with Thomas the Tank Engine on the front or maybe ..." she looked up at Valdez" Would the cot sheet be better?"

"Not the sheet." Valdez said, "Nothing from the cot. Forensics will want to swab those for DNA"

"For Sean's DNA?" Gill asked confused."

"Yes, and for the DNA of anyone who handled the baby last night. I need to ask some questions Mrs. Docherty. Do you feel able to talk to me just now?"

"Yes," Gill nodded frantically "I want to talk to you, I want to do anything to help find him" she said almost pleading again.

"Good, then let's start with how many people were in this house last night, who they were and why they were here." She looked at me with raised eyebrows.

In her usual abrupt manner Valdez asked me to make tea and coffee. James offered to help and followed me into the kitchen.

"Are you ok?" he asked lifting cups from the cupboard and laying them on the work surface, while I started up the coffee maker and filled the kettle.

"I'm fine," I said, though it would have been obvious to him I wasn't. I had a king-sized lump in my throat that made my voice croak. I looked up at him.

"What? What is it you're not saying?"

Trying to keep the tears back I told him, "Gill blames me."

"She blames you for what?" He studied my face "Stealing the baby?" He almost smiled.

"No of course not, but she does blame me for bringing trouble to her door. Remember the Hunt, the last time we stayed here?"

He shook his head "No, you're imagining it. Gill knows that wasn't your fault, she would never blame you."

"Well she does." I swallowed hard. "She asked me what foul thing I had brought to her door this time?" Tears were now burning my eyes.

He gave a deep sigh and said, "Gill is distraught, she's in shock, she doesn't know what she's saying. She will blame herself, Jack, you, and anyone else she can lash out at, and then regret having ever said anything, when they find Sean."

"Do you think they will find him soon?" What if they don't find him?" I turned away and walked to the other side of the kitchen and started filling the milk frothier on the coffee machine. I had a tightness in my chest, that was almost pain, but I was also ashamed of feeling sorry for myself. "Gill is my friend, the closest thing to a sister I have, now when she is going through hell and with every bone in my body, I want to help her, she's shutting me out."

James followed me across the kitchen. He caught my arm and turned me round to face him. "It's all in that silly head of yours. We are all upset. Look, they will soon have almost the entire Scottish police force out there, and they will move heaven and earth to find that child. Trust me, Gill will see things differently when they do. "I wiped my eyes. He pushed my hair away from my face and tilted my chin up, he was studying my face but I couldn't even look at him and after only a moment's hesitation, he kissed me full on the lips, so soft, so gently that I forgot everything, where I was, the fear, the horror, the dismay. I simply drowned in his arms. It was the safest place in the world. I was secure, too afraid to face reality. I wanted to stay in there like that forever. My bubble was suddenly broken, and I pulled away from James when the voice said "I guess the tea's not ready then? Valdez was leaning on the kitchen door with a face like thunder.

I handed Gill a mug of coffee, but she shook her head. I put it on the table beside her. Jack lifted it and put it in her hands, this time she took it and held onto it, but didn't taste it let alone swallow it. Katie sipped hers slowly. She too was holding back tears as she tried to stay strong for Gill.

Another detective asked Jack to go with him around the house, while he took notes. He wanted detail about each guest who had stayed in the house on the previous night, their relation-ship to Gill and Jack and which room they had slept in. He asked Jack when Eli had arrived, when he had left and why only he had not stayed overnight.

Valdez asked the exact same questions of us. I guessed they compare notes. She had already spoken to Jack and James outside the house when she arrived, still she asked them again and again, where they went and why they had left the house in such a hurry. More importantly why they left in separate cars, and in opposite directions. James said they had driven in opposite directions to see if there were any other cars around, in the empty street. It had been what Jack asked him to do.

"Carmen" a CID officer called. Valdez went to speak to him.

There was a crocheted throw on the sofa. Katie lifted it and wrapped it around Gill, holding her close as she did. Then we sat there, the four of us. We sat in silence like a tableau, no words of reassurance left to give, no platitude that could bring any comfort. We couldn't even look at each other, so deep was the sorry we felt. There was nothing else we could say because repeating, 'they will find him' again and again was no more than just empty words and soul destroying to listen to. We all knew there were no guarantees. So, we just stared at the floor or watched the forensics people walk back and forth with clear plastic bags containing Sean's clothes, his bedding, and some soft toys.

From where I was sitting, I could just about hear the conversation between Valdez and the other C.I.D guy. I heard her say, "That changes everything, make sure the parents are debriefed separately."

Valdez returned and introduced Detective Sergeant Martin Cassidy. She stepped back to allow D.S Cassidy to speak.

"Mr. and Mrs. Docherty, I just want you to know that we are working hard to recover your son. Right now, there are police on the street doing door to door enquires, teams of dog handlers are searching woods and fields in the area. and police cars from all over Central Scotland are on high alert and will be looking for a car carrying a baby."

Valdez added "I am sorry Mrs. Docherty but in order to help us we need you to leave the house. Is there somewhere else you could stay?"

"What! No! "Gill cried. "We have to stay here in case they bring him back."

Valdez said. "The moment he is found we will bring him to you, wherever you are. I am sorry Mrs. Docherty, but we must insist. There is no sign of forced entry. The locks on doors and windows are intact, which suggests the perpetrator either had a key, or was already in the house. The house is now a designated crime scene."

"Are you suggesting one of us took the baby." Katie asked shocked. "Are we suspects?"

Cassidy answered. "We simply have to rule you out. We need you to accompany us to the station for further questioning. Mr. Docherty and Mr. Anderson left the house. We need details of why and where they went."

Valdez said, "P.C Collins will assist you to gather what you need. We can arrange for anything else to be brought to you." She asked Gill again." Do you have somewhere else you can go? Do have family or friends you can stay with?"

Gill said "Yes, my parents live in Glasgow." And as if she suddenly remembered "I have to call my mother, now, she will be devastated,"

After a long telephone conversation with her hysterical mother, and her aggressive idiot of a father, who was threatening to kill Jack for not looking after his daughter and grandson, Gill asked if they could stay at my flat. Overwhelmingly relieved that she had even considered staying at my flat. I said "Of course," I looked over at James whose hint of smile said I told you so.

Valdez continued to quiz Jack about the sequence of events leading up to Jack and James returning to the house. The seriousness of the comments about their leaving the house was not lost on James or Jack. Both stunned and angry Jack got up. "Are you really implying I am responsible for my son's disappearance?" Jack looked as though he wanted to punch her.

James quickly caught Jack's arm and in a placating tone said, "sit down Jack, it's procedural. They have to do this."

"Your friend is right. I am not suggesting anything Mr. Docherty, simply letting you know what will happen next."

That day was the worst day in Jack and Gill's life. Valdez spoke to them about the importance of a TV and Press appeal. Gill would have none of it. She was a mess, hardly able to hear, let alone say Sean's name, without crying. She fell apart every time, so no one was surprised when she refused to do it. When she said she couldn't face it, Jack said he would do it alone. Valdez tried hard to persuade Gill and when she couldn't, to her credit, Valdez said she understood completely and if they felt they were not ready then she or Cassidy would conduct the media interview.

Cassidy who stood listening to Valdez was gentle but firm. He said, "Mrs. Docherty I realise how difficult this would be for you, but the truth is, that the audience and hopefully whoever took your son, will see his photograph on their television screens. From experience I can tell you people will only see photos of a child, with as much effect on their emotions as an episode of Coronation Street or EastEnders. He is then only a doll to them, a stolen possession, rather than a living breathing child. You don't think you can do the interviews because you are too upset, too traumatised, but if you do, the general public will see and hear an appeal from a desperate mother. A woman asking for help to find her baby, her only, precious child, ripped away from her in the night. I urge you to reconsider for you son's sake. An appeal from you will move the hearts of thousands of people and might persuade anyone with information to come forward." His plea was enough to sway her, and Gill agreed to do the interview.

It was the day from hell. We were all interviewed separately at the police station. I was shown into a room with nothing in it but a table, with a recording device on the top and four chairs. The table lay side on against the wall, and on the wall opposite there was a large mirror. I had seen enough crime dramas to know it was viewing mirror, allowing the police to watch and listen to the interview undetected. I was left sitting there for a least twenty minutes, long enough for me to worry myself into a state of anxiety. I was sure there were people watching my every move from the other side of the mirror. It was nerve-wracking. I was so nervous about being interviewed by Valdez that I must have looked guilty of something.

They came in together Cassidy and Valdez. Cassidy was friendly, apologised for keeping me waiting, asked me if I wanted tea. Valdez said nothing. Valdez wore a smart grey skirt suit. With a dazzlingly white silk shirt, her gleaming black hair, dark eyes, and olive skin, her smart but casual clothes gave the impression of a woman who spent a great deal of time in front of a mirror. She might have fooled most people into dismissing her as ineffective, but I knew differently. This lady was not a pushover, but a force to be reckoned with and her very presence unnerved me.

Cassidy explained that this interview was being recorded and immediately switched on the machine. He stated who was in the room. It was only when he asked me if I wanted a lawyer that I realised I was a suspect. "Do I need one?" I asked suddenly worried. "Am I being accused of something?"

"No" Cassidy said. His manner still friendly.

"Not yet," Valdez added stony-faced.

"You are just helping us with our enquiries." He said as he placed a thick file in front of him with my name across the top.

By the time I got out of that room I was a wreck. I knew the minute I saw her that Valdez would try to trip me up in some way and she didn't disappoint. The fact they had a file on me was even more unnerving. On top of that, her interview techniques were more like an interrogation than an interview. I knew she had spoken to the police in Germany, Cassidy told me that, so I was waiting for her to go for my jugular and predictably it didn't take her long.

In a voice all sweetness and light, she pointed out how difficult it must be for me. "It seems to be a pattern in your life Mrs. Cameron, the disappearance of people around you. Your late husband Paul Cameron, David and Leo Baxter, Frank and Christina Summers and now little Sean Docherty." Her facial expression and tone oozed sympathy. "My colleague here, DS Cassidy, found your file quite fascinating "She smiled "and had I to agree with him that you do have a remarkably interesting life."

Cassidy agreed. "I have to say, it does read like a novel Mrs. Cameron."

I said "Yes, well, since Inspector Valdez probably put it together, I expect it does read like a work of fiction." I smiled sweetly at Valdez thinking I could play her at her own game. That was a big mistake, for three reasons, that woman was clever, she didn't like me, and it didn't pay to antagonise her. I had enough contact with Valdez in the past, to know she didn't like me and would go for the jugular at the first chance she got. I already had butterflies in my stomach. I had to keep reminding myself that I was a witness and not being accused of murder, or something equally bad. In fact, anything might give her an excuse to lock me up and throw the key away. At least Cassidy was there, I thought maybe, he might soften her a little. He at least appeared sympathetic, whereas Valdez I believed to be totally incapable of sympathy, empathy or any other supportive emotion. Her emotional spectrum seemed to sweep from tolerance to persecution in minutes. I remember thinking maybe she had been bullied as a child, or maybe she had been a punch bag for a wife-beating husband. No, the latter was way off, for a start there was no ring on her ring finger, neither was there a pale indent that would indicate a piece of gold had ever rested there. Anyway, Carmen Valdez was nobody's fool, she would have beaten a man like that to a pulp.

"I have been looking forward to having another little chat with you." She said, her smile so wide it bared her sparkling white teeth and made me feel like Red Riding Hood being interviewed by the wolf. I wondered if she had deliberately left me waiting, to make me nervous, in which case her tactic had been a resounding success.

She nodded to Cassidy and he switched on the recording device on the table and stated who was in the room.

"Do I need a lawyer? "I asked again.

"Why do you think you need one?" Valdez asked.

"I don't know."

Cassidy answered reassuringly. "You are a witness Mrs. Cameron. You don't need a lawyer, but keep in mind this interview is being recorded and may be used in evidence in court. You are just here to help us with our enquiries, answer a few questions."

"So, let's cut to the chase." Valdez said with a more serious face. "DS Cassidy and I have been discussing the peculiar behaviour of Mr. Docherty and James Anderson in the early hours of this morning." She sat back in her chair, pursing her lips, waiting a moment, studying my face, long enough for me to wonder if that had been a statement or a question. The silence was becoming uncomfortable. Then she said, "He is just as confused as I am, as to why Mr. Docherty, when he discovered the baby was missing, ran out of the house and into his car and how he persuaded James Anderson to do the same?"

"You did see them run down the stairs?" Valdez asked

"Yes, I did."

She looked at Cassidy who shrugged. "When you think you might have seen something, especially when you are wakened suddenly from sleep, friends telling you, you were mistaken, might make you think your eyes had deceived you in the first place."

Frustrated I repeated." They didn't tell me anything. I saw them run downstairs from the empty cot."

"I beg to differ" Valdez said leaning forward her hands clasped on the table. Bizarrely I noticed her knuckles were white, making me think she was tense, ready to pounce. Forcefully she said, "did you actually see the empty cot before they ran downstairs?"

I hesitated, shook my head. "No"

"Did you hear any sound from downstairs that could have been an intruder?"

"No"

Raising her voice, a little she said. "You saw them run down the stairs. Did you notice if either of them were carrying something?"

"A shawl or a blanket?" Cassidy asked.

"A small bundle?" Valdez asked with an innocent look on her face, as though she had no idea of the implications of what she was asking. "Were either of them carrying a coat?"

Stunned for a moment, I didn't know what to say. It was obvious they were suggesting, or at least trying to make me wonder if Jack had harmed Sean and covered it up. I felt angry, "No! I know what you are suggesting. They were not carrying a child. Why are you even asking me that? Jack loves Sean: he is a special baby. Jack believed he was infertile, they both thought they wouldn't be able to have children. Someone broke into their home and took him, and you are wasting time questioning me. Shouldn't you be out looking for him?"

"A special baby? Do you mean I.V.F? "She asked.

"No, he was... a little miracle." Just saying it made me remember how precious their son was to them and how devastated they must be right now. "They may never have another child." "I said, feeling a tear sting my eye."

In a very condescending and irritating manner, Valdez said, "Now, don't upset yourself Mrs. Cameron there are plenty of people out there looking for him. just you concentrate on what happened in the Docherty house. Now, let me correct on one point, no one broke into their home last night. The kidnapper either had a key or he was already in the house when they locked the doors. There was no evidence of forced entry."

Cassidy feigning concern said." It's really important that we hear your view of the events of last night. Did The baby seem distressed in anyway, before he was put in his cot? Do you know if he was given any medication? Calpol or Nurofen or anything like that?"

"No, he was fine, he is a happy baby."

Without pausing Cassidy added "Are you aware if either Mr. or Mrs. Docherty were having an affair?"

"What?! "I was taken a back. It was unbelievable, really. "An affair! Are you joking? What has that to do with anything?" I pushed my chair thinking I had had enough, but within seconds my sanity kicked in, and I realised I couldn't just up and leave. "I'm not even going to justify that with an answer it's just ridiculous. You saw the state they're in. You can see how close they are."

Valdez jumped in with. "May I remind you that your statement is being recorded and may be used as evidence in court. Answer the question please."

I was exasperated, she knew it and she didn't give a dam." Jack and Gill are devoted to each other." I said angrily. "Neither of them would even look at anyone else."

"Again, Mrs. Cameron, the last comment is just your opinion." She said. "Try and stick to facts. After all I daresay they wouldn't tell you if they were."

There was a knock on the door to tell Valdez there was an important call for her. She stood up, pushed back the chair and stepped forward to the open door.

When she returned, she spent the next hour quizzing me over and over on my relationship with Gill and Jack, and their relationship with each other. Cassidy asked about Sean, about his birth, even about Gill's pregnancy. It was obvious to me then they either knew or had found out something about Sean's birth, that had made them suspicious. She asked me about Sean the night before, how he was? Was he fractious or unsettled? What time was he put to bed? Who fed him? Who put him to bed? Did his parents check on him during the evening? Which parent and how often?

We went around and around in circles, as she changed the way she asked the same questions, over and over. The most unsettling thing of all was her repeated focus on Jack and James leaving the house in the early hours of the morning. Cassidy told me CCTV at local shops had picked up James's car, but Jack had gone the other way into the countryside. He asked again what I thought was the reason they split up and gone in different directions. I told them Jack and James had split up to try and find Sean, but even as I was repeating that I realised how it sounded and with a cold chill running down my spine I realised that they suspected Jack of removing his own son from the house, if not something worse.

The door knocked and she was called out again.

"Neither are having an affair". I called after her. "I know both of them too well."

She stood holding onto the door said. "One more thing do you know of anyone who had a grudge against them. Or against you for that matter. Maybe we are looking in the wrong direction. What were you doing in Germany last week? Oh! yes, that's right, a little holiday with Christina Summers? She waited "but you found a body at Heiligtum didn't you?" She didn't wait for an answer. "Helping the BND with their enquires, were you? Don't bother explaining, I have spoken to Reinhardt. You do lead an exciting life, Mrs. Cameron. "Her face changed. "Well, let's hope you are telling the truth, because if Jack and Gill come tumbling down that hill, you will be the one tumbling after." Her tone changed to a lighter note. "Cassidy will show you out. Don't leave the country anytime soon, we may wish to speak to you again, soon."

James was waiting for us in the car park. Katie who had been subjected to a similar grilling said she had been asked the same questions. She was shell-shocked by questions they had asked her, appalled at the idea they were suspecting Jack or James.

James gave me his car keys and said he would meet us later at my flat. He had been interviewed by Valdez and she had asked him to stay behind as she wanted more background information. It was voluntary, James could have refused, but he said it was better to keep her sweet.

"Sweet! Good luck with that, she is as bitter as Gaul that one." Katie growled. "Blaming Gill or Jack is just" ...she hesitated... "cruel, just cruel."

James sighed. "The parents are always the first suspects. Don't read too much into it." To my annoyance, he went on to defend her. "Carmen is alright really, it's just the job that makes her seem hard." He said he was staying behind not only because Valdez wanted him to, but to support Jack and Gill, who would have to go through the ordeal of the media and press appeal and were still being interviewed after Katie and I left.

Outside the police station, the rain was thundering down. The angry looking sky, in a surreal display of sympathy, emptied gallons of tears onto the grey city below. It was a thoughtful gesture, but the rain was incapable of washing away the horror of that morning. Though James had parked his car, just around the corner, we were still soaked through by the time we reached my flat.

The first thing I did was turn on the T.V. to the B.B.C news channel. At that point it was halfway through the appeal. We saw Jack amidst flashing cameras, sitting calm and in control, focusing on one person at a time, as he tried to answer the questions being fired at him. Beside him was a pale washed out wreck of a woman, almost unrecognizable as our beautiful vivacious Gill. She looked gaunt. She had wound her hair into a bun, the hair scraped back from a face etched with misery. She read from a sheet of paper that trembled in her hand. Her voice faltering as she pleaded with the TV cameras and the journalist's cramming before her, to help find her baby. She begged the kidnapper to look after him. She was beyond crying, her eyes were heavy and raw looking, the epitome of grief. Pathetically she said. "He will be hungry, it's almost his lunchtime. He always takes his breakfast, but he likes to nibble at lunch time, some cheese, fruit and yogurt and some milk. He's a big baby, he needs full cream milk. Please, Sean will be crying for me. He is a good baby, her voice trembled?" Jack put his arm around her. "Please, please bring him home. He needs me."

If that plea did not incur sympathy in her audience, nothing would. Katie and I listened and cried, or maybe sobbed was a better description, because it was loud, wet crying, the kind that needs umpteen tissues to mop up. It was the unleashing of pent-up emotion, finally released and strong enough to compete with the weather outside. We sat on the sofa hanging onto each other watching two people we both loved being torn apart with grief.

I had cried a lot over the last few years, but I had never seen Katie cry like that. Pain and sadness seemed to have the opposite effect on Katie. She hid her emotion under a blanket of indifference that made her seem cold, unless you knew her well enough to realise it was just her way of coping. A skill she had learned during the loveless marriage she walked away from.

Katie always had an endearing childlike quality about her, that as a young student had made her appear vulnerable. She was a shy, pretty bride, who unwittingly tied the knot with a weak-willed man, totally dominated by his manipulative mother. The endurance and survival of those few years of marriage, and the inevitable divorce, changed Katie forever. Disillusioned with life she could have turned bitter, instead, though her looks remained pretty and childlike, though she joked and laughed and pretended to be man-hunting for rich and handsome Mr. Right, Katie didn't need anyone. It had taken time to build her confidence again, she had become a successful businesswoman, who had grown a large retail business around her gift shops. She had an eye for the unique gift and an instinct for what might appeal to all ages. As a result, she was a resounding success in the business world. She was strong, confident and competent and I had never seen Katie cry, since the day she had said goodbye to the excuse for a man she had married. Once she had dried her eyes, she pronounced with conviction, he was simply not worth shedding tears over, and she would never cry over him again. Sean's disappearance, well, that was a different matter, it had found a crack in the protective shell she had built around her heart, and now the long-held grief was pouring out.

We watched the media interview again on the Sky News channel, as Jack and Gill told how Gill had last heard Sean on the monitor at 2 am and how they had later found the empty cot. They pleaded with the TV audience, and the twenty or so reporters, for help to find Sean.

Jack said "Sean is a beautiful baby, he has very distinctive auburn hair and bright green eyes. Please, if you have seen him or have any information, call the number on the screen, or contact your local police station."

Gill her voice breaking pleaded again to the kidnapper to look after her baby and bring him home. Though it was heartbreaking to watch, we watched the recording again and again, dismayed at the questions being fired at them by the Press, more than a few of which carried a suggestion of neglect. The reporters jostling with each other to be heard, were all calling out at the same time, a chaos that DS Cassidy had to bring under control, warning them to speak one at a time, or he would bring the interview to a close. Controlled, the still insidious questions continued, one barbed arrow at a time.

"Mrs. Docherty you said you heard your son cry at 2am, why was it nearly 6am before anyone called the police?"
"Mr. Docherty do you mind telling us why you left the house at just before six?" Did you take your son some- where?"
"Had you been drinking the night before Mr. Docherty?"
"There were other people in your house Mrs. Docherty. Who were they?"
"Were you having a party Mrs. Docherty? When did you last check on your baby?"

125

"Who looked after your son while you partied Mr. Docherty?"
"Was he a difficult baby? Crying all the time Mrs. Docherty?
"How did the kidnapper get in? Were your doors unlocked?"

The questions were fired like bullets, straight at the heart and they all hit the mark. From the first hint that these reporters, whom she had hoped would help them find Sean, were looking no further than at his parents, and from the tone of their questions, brutal, hinting that she and Jack knew exactly what had happened to Sean, at first bewildered then devastated Gill. The last straw came when a reporter from the Daily Enquirer asked bluntly where Jack had left the child, and what state Sean had been in. He then asked Gill, did she think they were all fools. Gill was so shocked, she reached blindly for Jack, seeking his hand, seeking his strength to help her answer. Though Valdez made no attempt to intervene DS Cassidy brought the interview to an abrupt end and refusing to engage with the reporters anymore, he ushered Jack and Gill out of the room away from the clamor of journalists, who were hellbent on asking more questions.

Katie sat quietly thinking. She plucked a thought that had started to grow, not only in her head but in my own too. "A reward, a reward for information leading to the return of baby Sean Docherty, that's what we need to do Erica. I want to post a reward. I want to make sure we get the bastard who did this."

"Yes, I agree, a substantial reward for information. We will talk to them soon as they get here."

It was almost two hours later before James appeared with Jack who was half carrying Gill, who looked on the verge of collapse. Jack persuaded her to lie down, she wouldn't eat or drink anything, she didn't want to talk. She was physically and mentally exhausted. I heard her whisper. "Tell them Jack" as he followed her into the bedroom.

He came out about ten minutes later. He said, "The stress of the morning has taken its toll, she fell sound asleep as soon as her head hit the pillow."

Jack would not or could not rest, he took coffee and sat nursing the mug.

126

"What did she mean, tell them?" I asked. "We watched the interview. It was awful, those reporters..."

"No, not that, that was bad enough, but Gill's parents..." he shook his head "... They finished her." He looked up at me his eyes tired and worn. "They had the same opinion as some of those reporters. They called Gill's mobile when they saw the TV interview, Gill, started to explain what was happening, but stopped mid-sentence. I asked her what was wrong? She just stared at me, she wasn't speaking, just listening. When I saw her start to tremble, I got up and took the phone off her. I had to prize it out of her hands. She had frozen with shock. Her mother with that half-baked idiot of a man who calls himself her father, shouting the odds in the background, were calling her unfit to be a mother and responsible for losing their only grandson."

Katie sighed deeply. "Poor Gill, I knew her father was a headcase, but her mum always seemed ok."

I agreed. "That was all she needed right now."

James sat down beside Jack. "If it helps you to know, the police always suspect the parents, it's procedural"

"It doesn't." Jack snapped

Have they no leads?" I asked him.

"It's not a lead exactly, but they know how they got in. I think we would still be at the station if Gill's mother hadn't phoned. You see her mother had a set of keys for our house, while we were at Lanshoud. She was checking the house for mail, only she lost the keys last week but didn't bother to tell us because she thought she had just mislaid them. Somewhere in her own house. It was only when Gill told her there was no sign of forced entry, that she remembered. They are both being interviewed now."

I made some bacon rolls, but no one could eat. We talked about the reward. Katie and I offered £10,000 for information leading to Sean's recovery. Jack was pathetically grateful. James called Valdez and told her. She said she would set it in motion immediately.

I wanted James to stay but he said he had to leave I told him where we had left his car, I pointed from the kitchen window, he followed me to see. He stood close as we looked out the window. I wanted to ask him to stay so much, but I couldn't find the words. I wanted to cry on his shoulder. In utter selfishness, I wanted him to comfort me. Then I noticed Katie out of the corner of my eye watching us and I felt bad. Who would comfort her? I told him he was welcome to stay, and he hesitated for a moment, then he said he had things to do and so he went home. He said Valdez had his mobile number, she would call him if she had any news.

Jack didn't last long; he almost fell asleep on the sofa. Katie too went to bed. I was tiding up, and taking some things from the freezer for breakfast, when I heard a noise at the door. It sounded like the letter box. I went quickly to the door and saw the white unmarked envelope laying on the floor. I opened the door, but there was no one there. I ran to the window and looked down on the rain lashed street, but the street was empty. I opened the envelope carefully. There was only a few lines written on a single sheet of paper. It was torn from a writing pad and written with ink from a ballpoint pen. The letters looked the same script as those on ancient document that had been given to me by Doria Van Brugan, the letter with the Four Horseman. It was late, I was tired. I knew Eli had been called in for interview by the CID and had spoken to Jack. He was coming for breakfast. I was too tired to do anything about it tonight. This letter could wait till morning.

Chapter 11

The Letter

I spent yet another night tossing and turning in my bed, trying to find a comfortable position that would encourage me to sleep. My brain was working overtime, going over and over the events of the previous night, seeking anything that might be a clue as to who could have taken Sean. The last thing Gill said to me was, "he will be crying for me Erica, he will be shouting Mummy." That struck a chord so deep that I was heartbroken for her, and worried sick that something I had done, may have brought this misery to her door.

I got up around seven, the living room door was closed but I could hear the murmur of voices. Listening carefully, I could tell one was Jack, the other was a male voice. It wasn't James, as I first thought it might be, but a distinct and familiar Aberdonian accent, it was Jonah. I opened the door inhaling the aroma of freshly brewed coffee and I did an immediate double take. The man Jack had been talking to stood up. For a moment I thought I was mistaken, it wasn't Jonah, for he had changed so much he was almost unrecognisable. No longer the overweight, retired, detective inspector; in the old brown leather bomber jacket and jeans he always wore. Instead by some magic, he had been remodelled into a younger looking version. He was smartly dressed in beige, expensive- looking jeans and a smart casual navy safari-style jacket. He wore a checked shirt, chosen to draw the colours of the jeans and jacket together. The belly, that usually hung over his belt had disappeared, instead there was a flatter stomach and a visible waist. Even his hair had been cut into a style that took years off him.

"Hello...I'm sorry...do I know you? "I asked. He grinned. I said "You remind me of a good friend. Are you related to Jonah Seagraves by any chance?"

"That's what I said," Jack added from where he was ensconced on my cream leather recliner. He had a tartan rug wrapped round his shoulders, that made me think he had been there all night. "Personally, I think it's down to a good woman or sudden world shortage of doughnuts?"

Jonah laughed sheepishly.

Beside the immaculate grooming of the new Jonah, Jack looked awful. He still wore the clothes he had on the previous day and he was unshaven. He didn't look as though he had had any sleep at all.

Jonah opened his arms and enveloped me in a fatherly bear hug, "Jonah," I cried "I am so glad to see you. When did you get here? And how have you affected this transformation. You look wonderful "I said returning the hug.

"Och, my GP gave me a lecture on my state of health. Told me I wouldn't see my 60th birthday if I didn't buck up my ideas. I went on a low carb diet, that's all."

"Really," I said, "and did he also tell you how to colour coordinate your clothing and get a designer haircut? Is there something else we should know? Or who we should know?" Now he was grinning like a Cheshire Cat. I sat down, crossed my arms and said, "You might as well tell me now, because Katie will get it out of you the minute she wakens up. So, let's start with what's her name?" He made me smile too, because I could tell he was really happy; in a way I had never seen him before. "You are blushing Jonah Seagraves, so you might as well spit it out."

"Alright, alright, I'll tell you. Her name is Valerie McGuigan, Val for short. She was a Detective Sergeant in the force, we worked together on a case years ago and got kinda close then. A few months ago, by shear fluke, we bumped into one another on a train, literally bumped into one another. The Edinburgh train slammed to a halt when the driver saw a fallen tree on the rails. I was standing reading something on my phone, when the impact sent me flying across the carriage and I landed, sitting, on her lap;

damn near killed the lassie. It was only when she said. "Jonah Seagraves get your fat arse off my knees, that I realised who she was. Well, I bought her dinner in Edinburgh, by way of an apology for landing on top of her." He smiled again remembering. "Ah, she's a fine woman, you'll like her. She's a looker too, and a real smart cookie. She is retired now like me so, we have been seeing a lot of each other. In fact, we were going away for the weekend but then James phoned, with the awful news about Sean. In serious tone of voice, he said "I saw the press interview and I came immediately of course, but here's the funny thing. I was going to a hotel, but James insisted I stay with him. When I arrived at his flat and rang the bell, it just after 10 pm, there was no reply. Then I found a text on my phone to say he had left a key with his neighbour. I got the key, went in, the flat was empty. There were no more messages to say where he had gone, or when he would be back, and he's not answering his phone. I found this on the coffee table." He handed me a sheet of paper from a notepad. It read,...

"Jonah, I am sorry I cannot be here to welcome you, please help yourself to anything you need, fridge and freezer are full. The bedroom with the door lying open is yours, for as long as you care to stay. I have left fresh towels on the bed."

Jonah shrugged. "I sat up till midnight watching TV, expecting James to come home. Eventually I fell asleep in the chair so, I just went to bed expecting to see him in the morning. This morning there was no sign of him and no message. I sent Jack a text. He told me he was up and staying with you, and to come over here.

"That's unusual isn't it, it's not like James. "I drew my dressing gown tighter around me, the room felt suddenly cold "Have you tried calling him again this morning?"

"No, I expect he will call me when he gets my message."

Jack stretched and yawned. He rubbed his red watery eyes, he was weary with both physical and emotional exhaustion, "Jonah has been speaking to a contact in the Glasgow police," he said. "They have found Sean's pyjamas, the ones he was wearing last night."

131

Jonah said. "They found them less than a mile from the house, in the woods, near the edge of the road."

Not sure if that was a step forward, I asked "What does that mean? Is that good or bad? Is that a lead to which direction they went?"

Jonah shook his head. "This abduction was well planned, so much so they managed to take the child, out of a house with five adults in it, all of them in bedrooms a stone's throw away from his: His mother with a child monitor on her bedside cabinet, right next to her ear"

"Gill heard him cry, she just didn't get up." Jack said. There was no mistaking the bitter tone in his voice.

I quickly added. "Gill said he only sounded as though he was turning over in his cot. It was no more than a whimper he made. She said he did that all the time. There was no reason for her to think there was anything wrong?"

Jack exhaled deeply. "Except there was a lot wrong."

I was annoyed with him. This was not the first time I had seen him like this. When Gill had first discovered that by a miracle, she was pregnant, infertile Jack immediately turned sour and accused her of having an affair.

Jonah had picked up on his mood. "To be fair to Gill, a stranger lifting a sleeping child from his cot, during the night would normally find kicking it up a fuss, before they reached the stairs."

Annoyed that Jack seemed to placing blame at Gill's door, I reminded him, "you were in the same bed as Gill, what did you hear?"

Sensing the tension Jonah quickly changed the direction of the conversation by saying. "About the pyjamas. Erica, you asked if that was good or bad. I believe the kidnappers would expect the police to use tracker dogs, and most likely have thrown the pyjamas out of the car window to give the dogs a false scent. The dog handlers would then focus on that neck of the woods. Meanwhile the perps have just driven off in the opposite direction."

"Perps?" I repeated his word. I have never heard that term before."

"Perpetrators of the crime."

"I see. Oh God! Jonah, that's not just bad, that's awful. Now I have a mental picture of Sean, frightened, crying and freezing in the cold night air, as they stripped him of his pyjamas."

"Jack said "It's the same stretch of road I drove along I was looking for the car that took Sean? I am still under suspicion. The police will think I threw the pyjamas out my car window." When Jonah didn't disagree, as Jack obviously expected him to, Jack sat up and stretched. "I think I'll just take this coffee through to Gill, if that's ok?" He wandered off.

"I do feel sorry for them both," I said

Jonah nodded, "I know lass, it will not be easy to help them. "Though I hear the chief investigating officer is Carmen Valdez. If she is the C.I.O. no stone will be left unturned. Valdez is like a dog with a bone, she will gnaw away at the evidence till she gets answers. Have they found out how they got in yet?"

"Yes, they think they may have had the key that Gill's mother lost. Gill said her mother kept the combination of the alarm on a piece of paper wrapped around the key," Jonah grimaced. I said, "I know."

"I know, she knows now how stupid that was. Believe me, between Gill's father, Jack and Valdez, she has been made to feel a guilt that will haunt her forever, especially God forbid if they don't find Sean."

I kicked off my slippers and curled up on the sofa, there was something comforting about talking things over with Jonah. "What I don't understand was how did they get him out without any of us hearing them? Do you think they drugged him?"

"More than likely, but of course there are other ways."

"What other ways?" He looked me in the eye but seemed hesitant to voice his thought. Suddenly I realised why, and it horrified me. "They could have smothered him. Is that what you are hinting at? But why? What would be the point of that? If they are traffickers, they couldn't sell him or if it were for ransom, they would have no child to bargain with."

He was sitting forward on the chair, his hands clasped, with his arms resting on his knees. He was looking at the floor, hesitant as though he were yet again reluctant to voice his thoughts.

"Please Jonah, tell me what you're thinking? it cannot be any worse than what runs through my head.

He looked up "Erica, it may not only be men we are dealing with?"

"What! You think there's a woman involved? It might better if there was. A woman would cope better with a frightened child, a woman would nurse him, comfort him, the contact with a woman's softness would perhaps remind him of his mother. He might not have cried when he was lifted, because he thought it was Gill who was lifting him." I was babbling and I knew it, but I was clutching at straws, anything was better than the thought he had been smothered.

Jonah said, "not all women have maternal instincts, anyway that's not what I meant." Look, there are four ways they could have taken a baby from that house, without waking the adults. Either he was drugged, you were all drugged and unable to hear him cry, he was smothered or..." He hesitated

"Or, what?" I repeated "You are doing it again Jonah, just say it? Look, I wasn't drugged. I was wide awake when I heard foot-steps in the hall and in the morning, there was no sign of a hango-ver or anything like that in any of the others so, what is the fourth way they could have got him out of the house? Tell me?"

"Ok Erica, your life has been dogged by other beings before. Are you one hundred percent sure Sean has not been abducted by something other than human?"

Before I could answer a bedroom door opened, and someone went into the bathroom. I stood up. "That's probably Katie or Gill. I better get the coffee on" I started clearing up, I had spent the night with exactly those thoughts, creating a private hell in my own mind, and now, sitting quietly the just two of us, he had invaded that hell. I could hear Gill's voice again, when she said, "*What nightmare have you brought to our door this time Erica?*" I felt faint, a wave of nausea overtook me, and I staggered.

Jonah stood up. "Sit down lass." He caught my arm took the empty cups I had been collecting out my hand and guided me to sit. "None of this is your fault, but we have to consider the possibility that the Riders of the Hunt are involved. Remember that is an area Valdez and her team know nothing about and are highly unlikely to take seriously. We are going to have to deal with this on our own."

"I think Gill blames me. She more or less said so. In fact, she definitely said so." I felt tears pricking my eyes. She asked. "*What horror did you bring to our door this time Erica,* "I was really upset. I told her the gate at Lanshoud was closed. There is no way the Hunt could come through. The whole gate had disappeared. I told her the gate is closed forever." I rolled out the mantra I had repeated to myself during the night, over and over again? They could not have come through. It was not the Hunt who took Sean. No one would have invited them in. They could not have crossed the threshold."

Jonah's voice was as gentle and kind as he could possibly be when he reminded me. I had gone to Germany, to Heiligtum, where there was another gate that might be lying open. Where I had found a dead man in the cellar? Where I had got myself involved with the BND and Die Brueder. That there was a pattern of disappearance, Christina and Frank had disappeared and now Sean."

I was hurt when he said, *"I got myself involved."* At that point I believed the blame for Sean's abduction was being left at my door. How could I blame anyone else for thinking that when I had spent the night thinking the same thing?

"Who told you about Germany? I asked, "was it Jack?"

"No, James."

"James! really! And does he think I am to blame? Because he didn't mention that to me."

"Don't start getting paranoid. No one is blaming you, especially not James. He is the last person in the world who say anything negative about you, and don't pretend you don't know that, anyway, it's not just the riders of the hunt we have to consider. Remember at Lanshoud both Lamashtu and my doppelgänger integrated themselves into your life as Chloe and me? What if someone in the house the night of the kidnap, was not who they seemed to be. Remind me who was there, and did you notice anyone was acting strangely? Think back, tell me who was there that evening."

"Only Jack and Gill, James, Katie, Eli and me."

"Was anyone acting out of character? Did anything about them seem different? What did you talk about, what did you eat?"

I went over that night with him minute by minute. Right up to the next morning and police arriving. There was nothing unusual.

He said "You didn't think it strange that Jack went tearing off in a car and persuaded James to do the same. You see from where I am sitting, that there was an odd thing to do."

I jumped to their defence. "Jack thought he might see the getaway car and follow it."

"Hmm, and when you saw them going down the stairs, did you notice if either of them was carrying, a coat or a jacket?"

Shocked I said "No!"

"No, you didn't see, or no they weren't carrying anything."

"Valdez asked me that, surely you are not suggesting...?"

"I am not suggesting anything. I'm just reminded you that I was impersonated by a demon at Lanshoud and not one of you noticed anything was wrong. What did you talk about that night?"

"I take it James told you about the letter and the print?"

"Yes, he did."

"That was the main topic of conversation, that and my meeting with Doria Van Brugan. Die Brueder, the BND and what happened to Christina at Garmisch- Partenkirchen"

Did you all go to bed at the same time?"

"More or less. Eli went home as he always does. Gill went first, she was tired and said she had to get up early for Sean. Katie and I went at the same time and Jack and James sat up talking for a while. I don't know when they went to bed. There was nothing that seemed unusual about that evening"

Jonah nodded. "Something was different about that night. Keep going over it in your mind."

"I have, trust me, right now it's all I think about."

A bedroom door opened and closed. In a low voice Jonah said, "Keep this between us for now."

It was midday and still nothing had changed. There had been no contact from the police. Both Jonah and I were still unable to contact James. I phoned the offices of Galbraith and Anderson. Although Adam Galbraith had died, out of respect for his memory James had retained the name of the firm of solicitors. Laura, the secretary, answered the phone. She hadn't seen James. He had not come into the office that morning, but had left a message on the answering machine, telling her to cancel his appointments for the next few days. He gave no explanation. She said she thought it strange because James had employed a new solicitor, who was due to start work in two days' time. It was unusual for James to just go somewhere without telling anyone in the office where he could be reached, and so out of character that Laura said she was beginning to worry.

In my flat the atmosphere was dreadful. Jack spent his time watching news channels and Gill spent most of her time staring out the window. Both said they could no longer just sit around doing nothing. Though they were not allowed into their home Gill insisted the police said nothing about her returning to the surrounding area. She was determined to go and speak to her neighbours or to search the woods around the house. Anything other than just sitting in the flat doing nothing.

Jonah suggested that was a bad idea. "Listen to me Gill. I understand why you want to do that, but you will not find anything in the woods. If there was anything, the dogs would have found it by now and uniform have been doing door to door enquiries. Look at it this way. How did you get here?" he asked Jack."

"Police car, they smuggled us out the back entrance of the police station, away from the press and TV cameras who had stationed themselves outside the front."

"Exactly," Jonah said "and if you turn up at the house now, they will follow you back here and camp outside. You will be hounded every time you try to leave. It's a waiting game Gill. The best thing you can do is sit and talk and go over everything you did in the last few days. Look for anything that seemed strange to you. When you were out and about with Sean in the last few weeks, can you remember anything unusual. Did any strangers speak to you? Did you see anyone watching you or just looking at Sean? Talk about it together, where you went, what you did. People talk to babies. Did any stranger speak to Sean? Think back over the last month. Look for anything you thought unusual."

Around one o'clock Eli phoned, he was on his way over. He had managed a good bit of the translation and was anxious to share it with us. When he appeared around an hour later and Katie opened the door to him, she said he looked tired but excited. Dressed as always in his suit and waistcoat, his white shirt gleaming, shoes transformed into mirrors by vigorous polishing he was as spruce a tailor's dummy. His bow tie, one of his extensive collection, and the only bit of colour Eli ever added to his clothing. Strangely his bowtie hung untied around his neck. He first expressed his sympathy to Jack and Gill, "My dear friends, I have not the words in my vocabulary, that can express the profound sadness, I feel at the ordeal you are going through. If there is anything at all I can do to help, please let me know."

Gill, pale and thin, dressed in black leggings and a black top with a tiny floral print that further drained her complexion of colour, wore no makeup, and had scraped her hair still damp from the shower, into a tight ponytail. She stood up embraced Eli and thanked him. I could see the shock on his face at the change in her.

Sitting down beside Katie, Eli removed his spectacles and discreetly wiped a tear away. Katie nudged him and pointed to the loose ends of his bow tie. With a look of surprise and horror, as though we had seen him naked, he expertly tied it. "Forgive me, I have been forgetful. It is my preoccupation with the awful events of yesterday. I too was interviewed by the police. A most unsettling experience. Believe me I was anxious to help, by remembering every detail of that evening. The Detective Inspector who interviewed me managed to make me feel that I was guilty of something and that I was making a poor job of concealing it. It was so disconcerting. That and the translation of the script has left me a little absent minded and apparently unable to dress myself."

Jack smiled. "Valdez, yes, we know her well, she does that to everyone. Don't let her get to you. How are you doing with the translation? "he asked.

Eli nodded. "I have some good news. Erica, I believe you need no longer concern yourself that it is your responsibility to save the world, by preventing the Four Horsemen of the Apocalypse from coming through the gate."

They all laughed. It sounded ridiculous said aloud. Crazy really, that I had ever considered, even for a second, that I might be responsible for a task of such biblical proportion. Yet, the possibility of just that had haunted me since day Doria Van Brugan put the letter in my hand.

"Well I bet that's a relief," Jonah said with a slight smirk and a poorly disguised helping of sarcasm.

Eli removed his specs again and wiped them with his spotless handkerchief. "I have not yet finished the translation, but I have most of it and quite simply it tells of four gates and how through these gates will come the horsemen. It says they are sent, by their master, to search the Earth and bring back the one who escaped from Hell. It is quite clear. It uses the word *Tara'a* which in Aramaic means Gates and *Sheol* which in Aramaic means Hell. The same words as are used in the original Gospel according to Matthew, chapter 16 verse 18 *Tara'a Sheoltha*. The Gates of Hell."He beamed, "And there we have it. Erica, there is nothing apocalyptic in this letter.

He delivered that news as though he were expecting a round of applause. When there was no response, he looked around our blank faces and realised, we didn't understand. Obviously disappointed, he tried again, tapping the paper with his forefinger. He said, the document included a print depicting the Four Horsemen of the Apocalypse. In the text it merely says horsemen." He wagged his finger. "Not specifically four horsemen. He surveyed us again, as though he was expecting us to have at last grasped a modicum of the magnitude of his findings. Perhaps he was expecting gasps of surprise, followed by intelligent comments. We just looked at him. I wanted to say something without sounding completely stupid, but Katie beat me to it. Katie was never good with silent moments, in company. It made her uncomfortable and predictably she filled the gap. "Oh! I see what you mean, I get why it's good news. It's because it's different horsemen, or there are more horsemen than we thought and less would have been more in this case." Everyone stared at her. I sort of understood what she meant, still the word gobbledygook sprang to mind.

Eli, perplexed, was silent for a moment, he looked at her as though he were studying a new species of animal. "Not quite, let me explain. Over the centuries it is possible many people may have read this document, which is I believe, is no more than a letter of warning written by Luke Treadstone. Why do I think the author was Luke you might ask? Well, I think it was Luke, because we know he was a traveller through time and space. We also know he came through a portal and landed on Earth, in Jerusalem, at the time of the Roman occupation. A time when Jesus and the Apostles walked the land, a time when Old Aramaic was the common tongue. Yet the letter itself was written on a type of vellum which is relatively new and therefore must have been written centuries later. At a time when reports of the Wild Hunt first appeared in Europe. I also believe Luke wrote in old Aramaic simply because he knew there would be few able to translate it. Then at some point during, or after the 15th century, it came into the possession of someone who was able to translate it. I surmise they were unfamiliar with the legend of Wild Hunt. You see as far we are aware the Wild Hunt was unknown in the Middle East, at any point in its history, therefore, someone translating old Aramaic might naturally presume horsemen coming through the gates of Hell to be the biblical four.

"Why do you think it is specifically after the 15th century that the print was added." I asked.

Eli reached inside the document folder and held up the print of the horsemen, "Because it is a print of Albrecht Durer's woodcut, from Durer's Apocalypse, which was published as an illustrated book. The first edition, which was written in German text was not printed until 1498. It seems to me that it was Luke who wrote the letter, and someone else added the print. I am aware I am repeating myself but bear with me. Look at it bit by bit. We know it was in Jerusalem that Luke came through the portal. We know he was a highly intelligent being who landed there in the time of Christ. A time when Romans occupied the land, a time and place when Old Aramaic was everyday language and Luke, in order to survive, would have learned the language. He may have written the letter in old Aramaic, in the hope that if it fell into the wrong hands it would be difficult to translate. Then we have these facts. The legend of the Wild Hunt originated in Europe and can only be traced back a few centuries. The Vellum he used is not that old and again did not come from that area of the world. There is no record of the Hunt ever appearing in the Middle East. No mention in any historical document. Finally, this letter only mentions the gates and the horsemen, there is no mention of Death, War, Famine and Pestilence, which would iden-tify the horsemen as those of the apocalyptic prophesy. Is that a little clearer?"

All except Katie said "yes."

I spoke up first." I don't understand why Luke would want to hide it. Surely anyone finding it would just think it was no more than a story."

"I told you I have not yet finished the translation. But I believe it is more than a story I believe he kept it hidden because it tells the exact location of the four gates."

Do you know how Doria came by the letter in the first place?" Jack asked

"No. I didn't even know it existed, though I did know she had something. Many years ago, when we worked together, she told me she had a secret. A terrible secret she dared not share with anyone. I was intrigued of course, and I tried many times to worm the information from her, but all she would tell me was she had a rare document in her possession which confirmed the existence of portals to another dimension. She called them The Gates. That is why, when you were at Heiligtum, I sent you that cryptic text. I suddenly remembered that document. I knew Doria had become a recluse and that she had settled somewhere Germany. That in itself I found strange because Doria is Jewish, and like me she lost a whole generation of her family to the Holocaust."

"I have just remembered something too Eli. "I held up my letter. " This came through the door last night; it's the same script isn't it. I handed it to him, he carefully removed the letter from the envelope and studied it.

"Yes, it is. "He peered at it closely. "Though the ink is ball-point and the paper cheap and mass produced, the writing is Old Aramaic." He scanned the page examining the writing. "This is very strange, you see there are very few people, only serious scholars, who in today's world could write in Old Aramaic. You can see these letters are written by different people; the hand is different. Look at the slant of the letters and how the writing in this one is spidery and uneven ,suggestive of an unsteady or elderly hand. This my dear is a new and very recent warning but the subject is the same. I immediately recognise Tara'a and Sheol and this word here is the Aramaic word for..." He stopped dead. He took out his handkerchief and cleaned his specs. It was obvious he was stalling.

Jonah said. "Eli what is it? It's obvious you read something. Just tell us, it can't be much worse than we already know."

Eli swallowed hard and looked at Jack. Jacks face was pale. "Just say it Eli. What is the word?

"Yld, it means boy."

Chapter 12

The Penthouse

Eli said he had to leave; he was always keen to be home to his wife before dark. He offered Jonah a lift back to James' flat, since Jonah had come down from Aberdeen by train. However, James lived in a penthouse flat overlooking the river Clyde. As that meant Eli doing an elongated detour, Jonah insisted he would take a taxi, as he was not yet ready to leave. Jack pressed Eli to stay. He said he was deeply concerned about the word 'boy' in the text of the letter. He worried it might refer to Sean.

Eli did not deny there was a possibility that it might refer to Sean, but he said, until the letter was translated in its entirety, there was no way of knowing. He apologised." I am sorry Jack, but I must go home now. I need my books and privacy to study this letter. It may have nothing to do with Sean's kidnap"

Jack threw his hands up. "Nothing to do with Sean. Then why this letter, now, and through Erica's door? Why here? I'll tell you why, they put it through this door, because somehow, they know, that we are here. For God's sake Eli, think about it, why write about a boy in the same context as the gates? Why else would they put a sheet of paper in Old Aramaic through Erica's door, in a language that she can't read, and few can translate? Furthermore, why now? I'll tell you why. The boy in that letter is my son. They put it through this door, because they followed us, they know we are here. They know about you. They know everything about us. That letter is about Sean and you know it," he growled, "For God's sake, Jonah tell him"

"I don't need to," Jonah said calmly, "he gets your point, he just disagrees with it."

Eli nodded. "Yes, you may be right in that they know everything about us, but still the word boy may not refer to Sean. I must translate the rest to be sure.

Jack became loud and animated. "Then do it here. I can help you Eli, I am going mad doing nothing, stay longer, please." He pleaded. "Continue to work here. I can help."

"No, I am sorry, I cannot." Eli explained that the problem for him, was that though the script looked the same as the original document, the word boy seemed out of context, and the spelling of some of the words suggested either, the author was not fluent in old Aramaic, or the words were mixed with some kind of dialect. Jack tried to force Eli to guess. Eli said he would not hazard a guess, that might lead to the belief that the boy the letter referred to was Sean, when it might be completely wrong. "I need time, I need my books and my notes, bear with me. I will do my best to give you an answer as soon as I can."

Jack begged him. "I am sure you will, but you need to do it here, now. This could be a clue to where Sean is. Eli, please."

Eli said he could not, or I wondered would not, translate any more of the words that night. Jack was infuriated, he wanted Eli to look on the Internet with him. He said working together they might fathom it out.

Eli refused point blank. He was emphatic. "No, you will only hinder my progress, this is not your area of expertise. I work best alone. I must go home Jack." He lifted his papers and stood up.

Jack stood up quickly and stepped in front of him. He towered over Eli. His face red, his finger stabbing the air, angry and aggressive, he said, "no, you listen to me, you are not going anywhere. I have known you for years Eli and I know the kick you get out of translating old scripts. Well you don't get time to play around with your little hobby this time, not when it's my son's life you are dealing with." He loomed over Eli, the finger now inches from his face." You will stay here till you have answers"

Eli was taken aback, his faced paled with shock at Jack's outburst. Jonah immediately stepped between them and put a hand on Jack's chest but didn't push him. "Back off Jack, cut the guy some slack. You need his help and you are not gonna get it with that attitude." Jonah was loud, firm and with a hint of threat that was enough to bring Jack to his senses.

Gill jumped up and grabbed Jack's arm, horrified, she pulled him back from Jonah. "Jack what are you doing, sit down."

For a moment or two there was a horrible standoff, then, allowing Gill to pull him, Jack backed away from Jonah, hesitated, then sat down. Katie and I sighed with relief and Gill apologised to Eli.

Jack snapped at her "Don't you apologise for me. That man can buy time for Sean, but no, as usual, he must rush back to his wife; apparently the little lady can't cope after dark without him. "He pulled his arm away from Gill, "For God's sake somebody give him a phone, "he shouted. Can he not just phone her." He stormed away to the bedroom.

That last remark seemed just too much or Eli, the gentle elderly man was stunned and shaken by Jack's outburst. He gathered his notebooks and his pen, put them in the old brown leather briefcase and headed for the door. Jonah went after him.

I followed them. "Eli I am so sorry. That's not like jack."

I heard Gill in a low voice say, "That's exactly like Jack."

Eli put his hand on my arm. "It's alright my dear, please don't apologise, I understand. Jack is in pain. He feels useless and cannot cope and so he lashes out. Who knows how any of us would behave given these circumstances?"

"That doesn't make it right Eli ." Gill said.

Eli sighed." Perhaps not but it is, I am afraid, the nature of the beast. I promise you Gill I will do my best to find out, who is the boy referred to in the letter and who might have written it. I have friends and old colleagues who will help me if necessary, and I will call you as soon as I have news. Tomorrow is Sunday and Antique Treasures is closed. I have all day to work on this. Please if you have any news, let me know."

Gill stood up to say goodbye. She said "I will and thank you Eli. I am very grateful for your help and deeply sorry for my husband's behaviour."

"Please do not be distressed, I have already forgotten."

I gave Eli a hug and he left with Jonah, who insisted on walking him to his car.

Jonah came back still annoyed with Jack, who had returned and now sat sheepishly on the sofa beside Gill, who was obviously still upset with him.

Jonah stood in front of him." Poor show Jack." Though Jonah said it quietly, it seemed to rile Jack again.

Jack wasn't backing down. "Do you blame me? "he asked. We need him here, but he's always like that, running off because his wife doesn't like the dark."

"You big Irish idiot." Jonah said." You are so self-absorbed. "How long have you known Eli eh? If not as a friend, at least as a respected colleague. Have you ever, in all these years, met his wife? Or spoken to his wife? No of course you haven't. Didn't you ever think that strange?"

Jack sat quietly, not sure where this was leading

Jonah sighed heavily." He is going home to his wife, who is in an urn beside his bed. She died in childbirth fifty years ago. He has no family. His mother and father, and the child who was his older brother, died in a concentration camp. He survived because he was only four weeks old. A German neighbour took the infant and passed him off as her own. After the war he was adopted by a Jewish family and brought up in Israel."

The atmosphere in the flat was terrible. Gill went to lie down in the bedroom and told jack not to follow her. Jonah called James again but there was still no answer. He was about to call a taxi, but I said I would give him a lift. "Maybe he is home now but has lost his mobile."

Jonah said "Naw that's unlikely. On the whole men don't lose their mobiles, that's a woman thing. Women change their bags, their jackets, their coats. They move around the house and leave their phone on surfaces and can't remember where they left them. Men always have their mobile in trouser pockets and when they use it, they put it back.

Jonah suggested Jack come with them, to get him out of the house for a while, and it would give me company on the way back.

Jack looked at me." I have a better idea. You stay here. Give me your keys and I'll take Jonah. If James isn't there, we can take a look around and see if there is any clue as to where he has gone.

Jonah shook his head." I don't think so mate. C'mon, have you got a bottle in that bedroom? I can smell it from here. Come along, by all means, but you aren't driving any car tonight."

I pulled up in the car park in front of the high-rise flats. My intention had been just to drop Jonah off, but he said, "I think you should come up; you might find it interesting."

"It's a bit late for visitors." I said

"If he is in," Jonah said, "he will be expecting me, and anyway and I am sure he will be glad to see you."

There was an elevator up to the flat, it had a glass wall on the river side. As it rose it gave panoramic views of the River Clyde. Night had fallen and the city lights twinkled, like a myriad of stars that rivalled those in the sky. I thought it was beautiful. The lift doors opened, and we stepped out to find only one door on this top level. It was an unassuming plain wood door, with no name and no letter box. "Mail is collected from a box at the entrance." Jonah said.

"Just one door! Where is the neighbour you got the key from?" Jack asked

"One down" Jonah said, "This is the penthouse, there is only one flat on this level." He put the key in the door and opened it, stepping back to allow me through first. I stepped into the entrance and stopped dead.

Jack at my back almost walked into me. "Bloody Hell," he whispered

Jonah said "That was my sentiment exactly, when I stepped through the door last night."

I had secretly wondered what James flat was like. He was a busy man, and with no woman around the house, I imagined it would be the no- frill, functional type of bachelor flat. It was therefore a shock when I stepped through that door. Immediately the motion sensor lit the hall and turned on lamps in an enormous living space. It was so impressive it took my breath away. The oak floor was so highly polished I could see my face in it, and the entire wall that formed the corner of the building was floor to ceiling glass. The river and the city lay spread out in front of us like shining jewels. I gasped with surprise and Jack swore.

A large leather corner suite in a pale grey colour, with polished claw-like feet at each corner, sat in the center space. A solid square wood coffee table, inlaid with marble, lay in front. Pale pink scatter cushions drew their colour from a pink wall behind. It had a panel from floor to ceiling that sat proud of the wall and in its center hung an oil painting. A soft light above shone on the painting of a garden, steeped in sunshine, with a winding path. A young woman with long red hair, in a cream floating dress, walked with her back to us down the path. The garden at either side of the path had flowering bushes. Flowers that were the same pale pink hue as the wall. Cylindrical pewter and round ceramic plant pots, holding fig, palm and umbrella trees were scattered around giving the feeling that the garden in the painting extended into the room. In front of the sofa, in the very center of the room, a square, light grey, stone column stood. Reaching from ceiling to floor, it had a television set in its center and at the base a wide circular glass, about three feet deep, that enclosed a log fire. The whole look was insanely beautiful.

Jonah said, "watch this." An ornate carved wood and brass box sat on the coffee table. He opened it, to reveal it was actually part of the table, and inside were two buttons. He touched the first button and immediately the log fire burst into flames. "Took me ages to work out how to switch it on last night. Now, watch this". He pushed the second button and the wall panel that held the painting slid back to reveal a drinks cabinet. It was full of bottles, crystal glasses, snacks and cocktail mixers. He shrugged, "it's not perfect, of course. You have to walk to the kitchen for the champagne and ice. That's, of course, providing you can locate the concealed fridge in the first place."

"This is unbelievable" Jack said. "Are you sure? I mean one hundred percent sure; you've got the right flat?"

"Oh yes, Jonah said, "his mail is lying on that table" The table he referred to, was a dining table to seat twelve, that lay parallel to one glass wall. "There's more, follow me." We followed him, "He left me a note saying this was my bedroom. You know, when James offered to put me up, well, he's a single man, so I would not have been surprised to find I had a pull-down sofa bed to sleep on. I did not expect this." Jonah opened the bedroom door, into a huge beautifully furnished room, with a double bed and an ensuite bathroom fit for a King. The bathroom was almost the size of the bedroom. An antique-style bath, on claw feet, lay close to another glass wall, and in the center, there was another living-flame fire, set again, in a stone pillar. "These are gas fires, "Jonah said "the pipes are in those stone columns."

"It's amazing. I love the fire," I said, "but I don't think I could comfortably bathe in front of that glass."

Jack laughed. "Even with binoculars they would have a hard time seeing you in here."

"From the ground yes, but this is on the flight path to the airport," I said

Jonah smiled. "I don't think that would be a problem. They would be on the decent by now and would only have time to blink and wonder at what they saw."

I sat down on the bed. and looked out at the blue velvet of the night sky. The bed was so soft it must have been quilted with goose feathers. I smoothed the lilac embroidered throw. "What is this Jonah? This cannot be James' flat"

"She's right, "Jack said, "he never bought this on a solicitor's salary."

"I know, I know, I spent last night pondering that one. I had a look around. There are two more bedrooms like this, both ensuite and expensively furnished, but take look at the state-of-the-art kitchen."

We followed him to a long white kitchen with a pine floor. It had white sliding panel walls and a floor to ceiling window at the far end, overlooking the west end if the city. In the center, end to end, stood two curved islands with lights to match their curve suspended overhead. One held a sink and the other an induction hob. Both had white leather bar stools."

Jonah pulled out a stool. "Take a seat Madam. I am about to dazzle you with the latest technology." He passed his hand across one of the little glass squares on a wall panel. It immediately slid back, to reveal a drinks dispenser with rows of buttons, and a barista style coffee maker. Jonah slid back another panel, revealing crockery and cutlery. He placed a cup under one of the pipes, now madam," he said, "We cater for all tastes. Earl grey, Lap-sang Sichuan, Herbal or just plain English Breakfast?"

Bemused by it all, I went along with his game. "I Sir am a creature of habit; I prefer Scottish Blend." I said, tongue in cheek, "but It will probably taste awful anyway. I don't imagine that machine actually brews the tea."

Jonah pursed his lips. "Well now, that's where you're wrong. Look at the label madam. Scottish Blend, the genuine article. As for coffee." He swept his hand in the air, there are nearly twenty different varieties of beans here. It took me a while to find this, and I wouldn't have found it at all if I hadn't wondered what this square bit of glass on the panels were for. Just slide your hand across the panel, this one opens the fridge freezer. He waived his hand over the glass and part of the kitchen slid over to reveal the contents. "Take a look, there is enough food in that fridge to feed an army, and it's one of new models that contacts your smartphone when you're out shopping, to let you know when the food inside is out of date"

Jack, not impressed, grunted "Why didn't you mention any of this morning?"

"I had a feeling no one knew about it. I could have told you, but It wouldn't have had the same impact as seeing it for yourself."

"You must have a theory Jonah; you always have a theory." I said, wandering over to look out the window.

"Several but they are all flawed"

"For example?" I asked.

"Well, he walked over to stand beside me, looking out over the city. "This place is not James' style."

"No, I agree, it's not." I said, thinking about James and how down to earth he was.

"He isn't a flash dresser, or a collector of flash cars." Jonah continued." he doesn't throw money around. He has no airs and graces and he works hard for a living. So, Let's assume he did buy and furnish this place. The mortgage alone would be more than his salary could maintain."

"A big win in the lottery?" Jack suggested.

"It would need to be millions to sustain this place."

"Rented, already furnished? I suggested. "Or maybe, is he is just looking after it for someone else?"

"The rent would be phenomenal," Jack said "but you're right, he might be a caretaker. I mean apart from the mail, is there any evidence that it belongs to either James or someone else?"

"That's more likely," Jonah agreed, "but there is a connection here, and it's in the painting of the woman in the garden. Come back to the sofa, stand back and look at it."

We stood in front of the painting. "I don't know why I didn't see the connection the first time" Jonah said "Look at the evidence. Take in the fact it's an oil on canvas, so expertly painted it looks like a photograph. The subject matter is a woman with long red hair walking in a garden, surrounded by trees. She has her back to us, so, we can't see her face. Now look very closely." He pointed, "she is walking toward the trees with a key in her hand and there in the distance, between the trees, can you see it."

I moved closer, studying the canvas "Yes" I pointed "there, it's a gate, a tall gate almost completely concealed."

"Look familiar?" He asked.

"It's the same as the one we found at Lanshoud" I felt a tingle in my spine.

"Here," he said, handing me an ornamental silver magnifying glass he took from his pocket. I took the liberty of borrowing it from your flat. Now look at the gate through this.

I peered at the gate. It took a minute, but when I saw them, I shuddered. "The eyes, I see them, the slanted lizard-like eyes behind the bars of the gate. "It's horrible, they look as though they are staring right at me."

"Yes, cleverly painted to do just that and that's not all. "Jonah said. "I spent a long time studying this last night. Look at the trees carefully through the magnifier." I did, but I couldn't see anything.

Jack had a look "Is it that key? There?" He touched the canvas. "A key on the trunk of the nearest tree. Look there", he pointed to another key on the path. "Three keys" he said.

"No, there's four". Jonah pointed to one nestling in a pink flower. We stood silent for a moment studying every corner of that beautiful work of art. Then Jonah said, "if I were to make a guess, I would say that woman is meant to be you or Christina, and the key in the woman's hand is Lanshoud's, the others are for the other three gates. You know, until I looked at this, other than the mail, I couldn't connect James to anything in this place. The suits in the wardrobe are Saville Row and look unworn. In fact, every item of clothing in this flat has a designer label."

"What about the mail? I asked Jonah, as I walked over to the table and picked up an envelope. "Is there something here that might give a clue?"

"Probably, but I am not about to open it, in case he comes back today, with a perfectly reasonable explanation for all of this."

Jack and I went back to my flat, but Jonah stayed in the penthouse that night. He said that James might come back, and if not, he would do a bit more digging, as he put it. On the way back I talked to Jack about the way his anger was affecting Gill. He was contrite and knew he was in the wrong. Yet he made no excuse, nor even tried to defend himself.

Katie and Gill were in bed by the time we got there. We tiptoed in, in order not to disturb them. As Jack said good night, he whispered a suspicion that was already taking root in my own head, thus ensuring me another sleepless night. He said, "I have a suspicion our James may not be who he appears to be, but then in your world, people never are they?"

About half an hour later, just as I put my head on the pillow, my phone pinged with a text. It was Jonah, it read.

"*Come over first thing. I have found something. You have to see this.*"

"I text back. *What? What have you found?*"

"*You have to see for yourself. I don't want to put it in writing, wait till morning, I will text you if he turns up or I hear from him.*"

"*Don't do this to me Jonah, give me a clue*", but there was no reply. He had hung up. I tried calling him but just got *Sorry, I am unable to take your call right now. Please call again later.*

Jonah opened the door of James' flat. He looked at Katie and I and said. "Do you know it's after seven? I seriously expected you to turn up at five, which was a worry, as I need my beauty sleep."

I said. "You must be joking, you need your beauty sleep! How much sleep do you think I got last night? I called you and called you and you didn't answer. You are the most frustrating person Jonah. Just tell me, is there still no word from James?"

"No! I called him again this morning and I am quite sure you did too. Where's Jack!? He asked, "I thought he might have come with you."

"Gill wanted him to stay."

"Still no word about Sean then?"

"No, nothing. DS Cassidy told Jack they had followed several leads, from people coming forward with information, but they were all dead ends. Are you ever going to tell me what you found that was so important?" I asked following him across the room

Katie was standing at the floor to ceiling windows. "You really weren't exaggerating." She said. She stood for a moment, mesmerized, then she wandered around, taking in the expensive furnishings, the glass fire and then the painting. "Your right about that painting. That's you on there. The hair, the keys, the gates. It's too much of a coincidence, that is obviously meant to be you". She wandered off checking out the other rooms.

"Jonah," I raised my voice "What did you find last night? I haven't slept a wink wondering what you could have found"

He headed towards the kitchen." Have you had any breakfast?" Without waiting for an answer, he said "no I didn't think so, sit down, take something to eat and I'll show what I found, you have to see for yourself."

The aroma of freshly brewed coffee filled the air. There was a plate of fresh croissants, butter, and jam, on the first island. I perched on one of the bar stools alongside it. Their freshly baked smell was making my mouth water.

"Have you been out for these?" I asked him

"They were delivered this morning," He poured out tea and coffee, serving my tea in a beautiful china cup and saucer. "They are on regular order apparently, from a baker in Byres road. I will check that out later, see who placed the order,"

He sipped his coffee leaving a moustache of fine foam across his top lip. "How was Gill this morning? She seemed really annoyed with Jack last night."

"No wonder, do you blame her? He was ridiculous. He had no right to speak to Eli like that. Eli was trying to help him, and he wasn't giving him an inch".

Jonah nodded. "Jack is under a lot of pressure just now. He feels helpless and guilty that his son was abducted from right under his nose. He'll be worried that the police are suspicious. Now that James has gone off somewhere, he probably realises, if the police find that out, it will look even worse."

"Why is it worse?"

"Because historically parents are the perpetrators, Jack and James left the house and drove off that night. Until the police find out what happened to Sean, Jack and James are in the frame. Yes, it was wrong of him to take his stress out on Eli, but I think we need to cut Jack some slack."

You are probably right, but I felt so sorry for Eli and I didn't know about his wife, none of us did. How did you know?"

"Inside info."

"What! you did a background check on Eli?"

"I did a background check on everyone" Jonah changed the subject quickly. "What's Katie up to out there?"

"Oh, she's just nosing around."

Katie had finished her unescorted tour of the penthouse. She came through the door with her hands behind her back; she was excited. "Which room are you sleeping in?" She asked Jonah. She was holding something behind her back.

"The one beside the front door, why?"

"It's just as well or you would have had some explaining to do, because I found these under the bed." She dangled a pair of red stilettos from one hand and a red silk teddy from the other.

Jonah looked perplexed. "What were you doing looking under beds?"

"I saw a red heel peeping out from under the bed, and that's not all. Come and see this." We followed her through to the master bedroom. She opened the door of the wardrobe with the Saville row suits. She pushed a button that Jonah had failed to notice when he discovered them. The whole cupboard full of suits slid out from the wall and split in the centre into two sections. Each section then turned and the whole thing slid back into place. Now instead of a man's wardrobe, it was a woman's wardrobe. With a flourish Katie said, "I have therefor deduced a man and woman share this bedroom."

"You don't look surprised." I said to Jonah.

"No, nothing about this place surprises me anymore. I missed that one, but I found something similar. This place is a regular little funhouse."

Katie still dangling the shoes, said to Jonah, "do you know?" She ran her hand through the dresses. "These clothes all designer and size 8."

Jonah grunted "No, I thought they were all out of Primark."

"Well, Katie said. "I am sorry to say this, but if this place belongs to James he doesn't live here alone. I had a look through the drawers. There's a lot more of these expensive clothes, perfumes, and jewellery. A woman living here would explain the splashes of pink in the decor. The whole place has a woman's touch." Katie gave me a meaningful look.

"What?" I asked her "You think he is living here with someone."

"Yes, there is definitely a man and a woman living here. There's too much stuff, sort of together stuff, if you know what I mean."

"No, I don't know what you mean." I said, trying to work out what she was getting at.

Katie put on her serious face, and as though she had suddenly morphed into Sherlock Holmes and cracked a big case, she said quietly. "Well, apart from the obvious fact they are sharing a wardrobe, in a flat with several wardrobes, there are both male and female toiletries in the bathroom. That big bathroom, the one with the bath at the window and in the drawers, there are birth control pills and condoms. There's more." She sat down on the bed, kicked off her shoes and slipped on the shoes she had dangled in front of us. The red four-inch heel stilettos, with large red satin bows at the heels "These are Louboutin." She said looking straight into my eyes. "Ring a bell?"

Jonah asked." Louboutin? And the significance of that is?"

Katie sighed as if Jonah's ignorance was unbelievable.

"They are by designer. Christian Louboutin. They would cost between five and eight hundred pounds a pair. They are shoes to die for, but that's not what I was getting at. These shoes are quite distinctive and there will not be many of them around." She raised her eyebrows at me. "Well, c'mon, don't you recognise these? We talked about them. Remember when we first saw them?" She waited till she saw the realisation hit me, she said "that's right, you got it."

I must have gone pale because Jonah asked "What? What about them? Apart from the ridiculous amount of money spent on them."

Still looking at me Katie answered him. "They were on Chloe's feet when she came to Lanshoud."

Chloe, the demon Lamashtu, the child stealer, here, living with James. How could that be. I couldn't even process it at first, then I felt sick, chilled to the bone, then faint. I sat down on the bed beside Katie. "Sean, oh my God! Could she have taken Sean? What if she has? What could we do? How could we even tell Gill that it was a possibility? She is already in a fragile state. This will destroy her." I looked up at Jonah. He knew well the detail of our last encounter with Chloe. I asked him "Is this what you found last night?"

"No, a pair of red shoes, no matter how unique, would not convince me of anything. I am afraid, there is more."

Chapter 13

The Painting

Jonah walked back through to the living space and pointed. "Last night I was studying that painting, when I noticed the frame was thicker on one side than the other. A strange thing to find on such an expensive frame. I rubbed my hand over it, and I found there was a small mechanism under the wood. I fiddled with it, but it didn't seem to do anything. Later, when I used the button in the box on the coffee table, allowing the wall panel to open and reveal the drinks cabinet, I tried it again. This time when I touched the mechanism this happened.

We watched as the wall with the painting slid back revealing the drinks cabinet. Jonah touched something on the paintings frame, and the cabinet slowly swung out from the wall like a door opening. Concealed behind it, lying on shelves from floor to halfway up the wall, and hung on the wall, were guns, knives and even hand grenades.

Katie reached over to touch them." Are they real? "She asked.

Jonah caught her arm and stopped her. "Don't touch them. You don't want to leave any fingerprints on these things. They're real alright."

I was lost for words; my brain was working overtime trying to make sense of what my eyes were seeing. I finally said "Surely those guns are proof this is not James' flat? It cannot belong to James. He couldn't use these guns. Like the rest of us at Lanshoud, he had to be taught how to use a simple handgun. He was as ignorant as we were. Maybe if he was just caretaking this place, he doesn't even know about this hidden panel.

Jonah didn't answer. He reached over and lifted a large cardboard box off the bottom shelf. He took the lid off and handed it to me. "Take a look," he said.

The box was full of mobile phones, passports, driving licenses, credit cards and ID cards, for just about everything. I sat down on the sofa and put the box on my knee. The first passport I picked up belonged to James, except, it didn't, for though the photo was of James, the passport was in French and in the name of a Jean-Claude Bouvier. I cannot described how I felt as I sifted through passport after passport. All were in different names, but with one thing in common, they all had a photograph of James. I laid the passports one by one, side by side on the coffee table. There were four in all. Three burgundy European, with the names, Jean-Claude Bouvier. Ernst Sternberg and James Anderson. The other was a blue American passport, in the name of Alex Mooney. When the implication of these multiple identities hit me. I felt sick. I didn't want to believe it. James not James, if this had to happen again, could it please be anyone but James. I suddenly felt weak and stupid. I looked up a Jonah and the pity in his eyes made me worse. I was truly the biggest fool on the planet. I had a horrible sense of Deja vu."

"Breathe." Katie said, sitting down beside me, she put her arm around me. "C'mon honey, big breaths." She looked up at Jonah shaking her head.

I couldn't stop tears stinging my eyes. "Not again" I said to her choking them back, "not again Katie."

How many times had I been in that dark place where someone close to me and been lying about everything? My husband and my parents. I believed in who they were. I loved them, I believed they loved me. Instead they were on the payroll of my alien time-travelling biological father, known as Luke Treadstone. God knows who or what he really was. Then there was the charismatic Emilio Mendez and Chloe Harkins. How many more would there be before there was no one left in my world whom I could trust. Jonah still standing, looked uncomfortable and lost for words. He walked over and closed the weapons cupboard turning it back into the drink's cabinet. Pouring out a little Brandy into a small crystal glass, he said, "here drink this."

"I shook my head. "I can't, I'm driving."

"Not today you're not." He said putting the glass in my hand. I took the glass and sipped it. I was reminded of the day at Lanshoud, just like this, when I was feeling faint, and choking back tears, because I had just discovered my husband had another identity. Why did it now have to be James? If someone was lying and playing sick games. Why could it not have been someone else?"

Jonah picked up a passport and said, "it's maybe not as bad as it looks, by that I mean it may not be criminal activity." He picked up the cards as though they were a pack of playing cards and flicked through them, He could well be a government agent MI5 or MI6 or something like that."

Katie as stunned as I was, looked up at Jonah "Who cares what he is? How could he do that to her? How could he? When he knows how many times, she has had to face that kind of deception. He has made a complete fool of her"

"I don't think it's personnel." Jonah said. "He fooled us all."

"You know it's more than that to her. It's another betrayal, that's what it is. Someone else close to Erica who has been lying to her, deceiving her, pretending to be someone he was not." I said "She's right, maybe I have gullible written on my back." The way my mind was working right then, it was a relief when Jonah said that James could be a government agent. From experience, I was thinking something much worse. At least if he worked for the government, I could understand why he had to keep that a secret.

"What did you mean Jonah? What kind of government agent? I asked him."

Jonah picked up one of the passports. "Well, he's maybe MI5, or MI6 mostly likely."

"Can you find out?" I asked him.

"Naw, these guys are well protected. There no way of getting that information "He was sifting through the cards, checking them, laying them out again, like a game, matching them to the passports. He picked out a green American Express card. "John Elliot." He tapped the card on his hand. "There is no passport or any other ID with the name John Elliot. If James doesn't turn up soon and we want to trace him, we start by looking for John Elliot."

"Katie looked confused" Why? Why exactly are we looking for John Elliot?"

"Jonah held up the card. "Because there is only one card here with that name, all the rest including James Anderson have matching passports. To me that suggests the possibility that James might be out of the country, traveling under the name of John Elliot. You know yourself, James is often away, and he tells you what? He has gone to see a client. Somewhere else in the UK, or he is away at a conference? No one questions that. Why would they? He was a partner in the firm. If they need to speak to him, they contact him on his mobile. He has a perfect cover. The only odd thing, this time, is that, at the office of Galbraith and Anderson, his secretary doesn't know where he is, and she can't contact him either."

"Assuming we even want to find him? Where would we start?" I asked

Jonah sat down. "Look" he said, I've talked about this before. Valdez is not what you think she is." Katie threw her eyes up. Jonah ignored her. "Get her on side and we have access to passport and all sorts of other information."

"Get her on side." I almost laughed. "I tried that before. She didn't believe a word I said.

"Aye, I know that," he said, "but we have a secret weapon now."

"What's that? "Katie asked

"Not what's that, but who's that? My Valerie, that is who it is. She and Valdez go back a long way. Valerie was a DI when Valdez was a raw recruit. She took Valdez under her wing and they have been friends ever since."

"What do think Valerie could possibly say to her that would change anything?" I asked

"Look Erica, if you agree, I will tell Valerie everything and if she agrees to help, which I am sure she will, I honestly believe she'll get Valdez on side. That is, as long as you are happy with Valerie knowing everything"

Not convinced I said "Jonah I was honest with Valdez once before, granted I didn't tell her everything, but I didn't lie to her either. I once told her as much as I could without, of course, going into detail about Luke or the angels or Emilio. She would have had me locked up if I had. No, that woman has a starting point of treating everyone as a liar. She knew I was hiding something and since then, I feel she has been out to get me."

"I don't doubt that she is out to get you, that's her job, but trust me, the way around that is for her to hear the truth with no holes bard, from somebody she trusts, and that person is Valerie. You have a think about it."

I stood up "I don't need to think about it. I have had enough. If Valerie is willing to help, then great. You know what? I am passed caring who knows. I want to go home now."

He said "I understand how you feel, and I think that is the right attitude to take"

I asked how much he had told Valerie already. He said, "Only the basics. I told her the story of how we became friends, but it was a heavily edited version. I will speak to her tonight". He started putting the passports and cards back in the box. He put the box back in the cupboard closing it over to form the drinks cabinet again.

I went back to the kitchen where I had left my jacket and bag. I wanted out of that place. I came back and Katie was still ranting on about what a lousy rat James was. I wasn't surprised at how quick she was to judge him. That was Katie's style. She never gave anyone an inch but me, I should have been giving James the benefit of the doubt. I knew Jonah believed this was James' flat. I wanted him to be wrong. I wanted James to be the man I always thought he was but instinctively I knew Jonah was right.

I stopped Katie's rant by asking. "What about you Jonah? Is this the James you know? Did you ever see any sign of this other James?"

He nodded, looked at the floor for a minute, as if he were considering what to say, then he said, "in truth, yes." He looked at me gauging my reaction, "but only recently, only since the night

Sean was taken. Since then there have been a lot of things that don't add up. Sit down for a minute. I am going to propose a scenario to you."

I did as he asked. It was obvious he was choosing his words carefully. "James knows I am a highly experienced, though retired, detective from the serious crime squad. Yet he invites me to stay in a flat with concealed weapons. He didn't leave me any instruction on the panels on the kitchen walls, the TV remotes or how to switch on that weird futuristic excuse for a fire. He knew I would poke around with panels and knobs to get things working. In fact, he might as well have handed me the weapons on a plate. So, I'm working on the premise he knew I would find guns and the passports. He leaves one card behind. Five identities in a box and only one credit card with no matching passport. Which suggests that he might have accidentally left that card behind. Very careless for an undercover agent, or was it because he knew, when I found it, I would conclude that he is travelling under the name of John Elliot. You know., I think James wants me to look for him. Then there's the letter through your door. Someone sent you an important message in that letter but written in an ancient language. That is bizarre unless it was James, because James knew Eli would translate it. Then there's that flight of Jack and James down the stairs the night Sean went missing. What if James knew the child was in danger? Could James have taken him, drugged him, put him in his car, came back and waited till Gill found him missing. Then he races down the stairs with Jack, but he takes his own car, possibly with the sleeping child still in it and drives off in the opposite direction from Jack. That is what made Valdez suspicious, remember. Now back to that letter, who wrote it? There are only two people that we know who might be able to translate it, Eli who had obviously never seen it before and Doria Van Brugan. If I were hedging my bets. I would say that James, alias John Elliot, is in Potsdam with Doria and possibly so is Sean. Maybe James took Sean there for his own safety, maybe he knew of a danger and couldn't tell anyone. He couldn't phone so he gets a letter put though your door saying Sean was safe, knowing Eli would translate. I think, if we can find John Elliot, we will find James and we will find Sean."

Two days later, Jonah brought Valerie to meet us at my flat. Jonah was right in a way, she was a looker, as he called her, but not in a pretty feminine sort of way. She wore close fitting mid blue jeans and a dazzlingly white v necked top. She was slim but looked strong and well-toned as though she worked out at the gym a lot. She had short light brown hair, cropped around a face that looked sculpted with the firm angles of high prominent cheekbones and slightly slanting brown eyes. She was not shy in the slightest and gave me the same sort of impression I had when I first met Valdez, that this was a strong confident woman. The difference between DI Valdez and this retired DI was that when Valerie smiled, which she did a lot, her whole face softened. I instinctively liked her, and it was obvious that she and Jonah were close. Before she came Jonah insisted we tell her everything and pointed out that she could not help if we concealed the involvement of supernatural or paranormal activity. He actually said that he thought that was the reason we had so much trouble with Valdez, instinctively Valdez knew we were hiding things. With Valerie we needed to be upfront and honest and that way we would have her on side to deal with Valdez.

Over dinner with Jack, Katie, and Gill, we told Valerie the story so far. She listened, she questioned, and she said she was fascinated and intrigued by the whole story. She wanted to help.

Two more days passed and there was still no word of Sean or James. Gill unable to face food, was fading away to a shadow, she looked worn and haggard, as though she had aged ten years. A ray of hope came when Eli finished the translation of the letter which had been posted through my door. He explained it had been difficult, as the person writing it had misspelled some words, but the gist of it was that the boy had been taken to a safe place across water."

"Across water! "Jack exclaimed "What does that mean? He has been taken across water"

Eli held his hand up. "Please allow me to finish," he continued. "He has been taken across water and will in time be returned to his mother."

At that news Gill, convinced it was about Sean, burst into tears and Jack started firing questions at Eli, but there was nothing else Eli could tell them. It seemed, as before, it was just a waiting game.

We talked about the absurdity of someone using the ancient language to convey a message. "Who is there who knows about Sean who could write in that Language?" Jack asked.

Eli answered "There is one person I know of, though she maybe a little rusty. But that does not explain how it was delivered by hand through this door."

"Do you mean Doria Van Brugan?" I asked.

"Yes," Eli said.

"But she is recluse and living in Germany. There is no reason to think she would even know about Sean or is there?" Gill asked.

"She knew about everything else. About Lanshoud, about the four houses. She even knew about my birthmark." I turned to Jonah" Jonah tell them what you found."

Jonah told them about the flat and what he found there. Gill and Jack were shocked and Gill at first was unwilling to believe it was James that could have taken her son and cause them all this grief.

Eli sat silent, as the rest of us tossed over possibilities. He suddenly said. "I have a strong feeling there is a connection. I ask you to hear me out as it may sound too farfetched.

"Go ahead Eli." Jack said quietly.

We all listened intently as Eli spoke. "Let's suppose Sean was in danger of some kind that we as yet no nothing about. What if James took Sean to Doria for his own protection. James knows that Sean is no ordinary child. What if he knew there was an immediate threat to Sean and had to take him to safety? You know Gill, you would never have allowed James to take him. Maybe he had to act quickly, maybe he had to take him to someone who would understand. The clue is in the letter. I think he may have taken him to Doria and the remote house in Potsdam.

He left a clue .He knew that I was around and could translate a letter that could not be read if it fell into the wrong hands. Now I have two questions. Do you think this is possible? and where is James?"

Since that day when we came back from the penthouse, the day Jonah brought Valerie to meet us, an intense misery had gripped me. A feeling of hopelessness worse than anything I had ever felt before. Now, almost a week later, it still hung over me. Jack and Gill had something to focus on, a lead, a hope that Sean was with James, but I couldn't see how that was good news, given we didn't know who James was anymore. No longer was Sean the focus of my thoughts, instead it was James. I wanted them to find Sean, of course I did, but what if they found James with Sean or if he turned up with Sean? What if he claimed to have taken Sean in order to protect him? How could we ever believe anything he said when he had obviously been concealing so much. I tried not to think about James, but he was all I thought about, every minute of every day. Every time I closed my eyes, I remembered how close we had been. I had trusted him implicitly. What was wrong with me? Almost all the people I had ever been close to, have lied and deceived me and now James was another one to add to that list. Like a puppy I seemed to have a pathetic sense of loyalty, because, even though every instinct in my body was telling me it was James who took Sean, I still didn't want to believe it. Even though it was staring me in the face, that he had been living with another woman. I couldn't believe it, not because there was insufficient evidence to prove it, but because I just couldn't bear to believe it.

Katie came with me to buy some groceries. We bought two coffees from Costa and sat in the car park chatting. I offloaded to her. "How could James even consider living with Chloe Harkins. It just isn't possible. He knew what she was."

Katie's said, "Not to begin with he didn't He was duped like the rest of." She pondered. "Chloe openly tried to seduce James, but he always appeared to resist her charms. If he had succumbed to her blatantly obvious advances, surely one of us would have noticed."

"You would think so," I said "but what if we overestimated his ability to resist her? After all there was that night at Lanshoud, when I saw the scantily dressed Chloe standing with the half-naked James at his bedroom door? Maybe they had an affair before we discovered she was the demon Lamashtu."

"Oh no …you're not thinking…oh my God, surely not". Katie shivered and I did too. She said You think Chloe took him. Her face had paled at the thought that, Lamashtu the Mesopotamian child stealing demon, had taken Sean. It was a terrifying thought."

"Yes, I was thinking that, because as much as we all pretend, Sean is no ordinary child. Abdiel told James and I he was a gift. Sean may well have alien DNA like Christina and I and may equally be in danger from the same things that are hunting Luke."

"Jonah didn't think it was Chloe," she said. Meanwhile I was thinking What did Jonah say. *A pair of shoes wouldn't convince him of anything.* Well what else could it be. I was thinking that if the owner of those Louboutin shoes was not Chloe, then was there another woman around. If so, I would have to accept that in my fear of love and loss again, I had lost James for good.

Katie thought a moment then she asked. "could James be a transvestite?" She saw my face and said, "no I suppose not he's a size 8"

As Jonah predicted Valerie met and very quickly won over Valdez. She then brought a slightly friendlier version of the old Valdez to my flat. Valdez came into my home and greeted me by holding out her hand and saying, "truce?"

Relieved, and after only a moment's hesitation, I smiled and took her hand. I then had a strong urge to wipe my hand clean on my jeans, because she waltzed past me, smiled at everyone in the room, saying. "You know Mrs. Cameron, you have a lot to thank Valerie for, she is the reason I don't have you in a cell right now. You could have told me all of this before, instead you have wasted an incredible amount of police time."

Katie gasped and I wanted to land one right on Valdez' chin but I pulled myself together for Gill's sake and smiled sweetly.

"Thank you for coming to help, Detective Inspector. I am grateful. Please take a seat. Can I get you something to drink?"

"It's my job to help you" she said dismissively, and I'll have a coffee, milk and two sugars if it's not too much trouble." I made the coffee and served it at the table, with cake that Valerie had brought.

I poured Valdez' cup first and handed it to her, she said "just leave it there to cool. I have some questions that need answers. She was smiling at me again, and that unnerved me. She said, "you know with a little effort on your part I think we will be able get on well together."

I didn't pour it over her, which was what I felt like doing. Neither did I call her Carmen and agree to be best friends forever. I answered all the questions she asked me, politely, with a civil tongue but through gritted teeth. I was annoyed that she asked each question more than once, restructuring the way she asked it. She would then ask Jack or Gill or Katie for conformation that I was telling the truth, even though I knew she already had all these details from Valerie. Valerie who had spent a whole evening being briefed by Jonah, then another evening reiterating it all to Valdez.

When she had finished grilling me, she said." It's an incredible story and if were it not for Valerie and Jonah and your friends. I probably would not have believed a word of it".

Yes, that was another insult.

She continued "However, incredible as it seems and reluctant as I am to believe it, it explains a lot. Now, I have to check out the detail of this fantastic tale and I will try to find James by first tracing this John Elliot. As for you Mrs Cameron I would like you to start practicing telling the truth."

Practicing telling the truth! She spoke to me like I was a recalcitrant teenager. She left telling Valerie she would be in touch. I saw her to the door my mouth saying, "thank you for coming," my mind envisaging me helping her out the door with a boot up her backside. When I came back to the living room, they were all laughing, while was fuming.

Everyone aspired to Jonah's theory that James was an under-cover agent. Listening to Katie, it was evident, in her eyes he had become some kind of James Bond character. I on the other hand was haunted by the possibility, he was another 'minder' put in place by Luke or possibly even worse. Yes, I actually considered the possibility that James wasn't James but had been taken over by another Emilio or Chloe. Another demon who stole Sean because the child had been gifted by the angels. I envisaged a nightmare scenario, where James had integrated himself into our lives. That he was one of these creatures who stalked our world, looking for my birth father Luke, hunting Luke because their master wanted him for passing through and escaping his dark domain. Sean would be a bargaining tool in their hands. No more than an object, something to exchange for the keys of the four gates. Gates that were portals, that would allow them to walk or ride at will as the Wild Hunt. They would have free reign to ride anywhere on our planet, reaping souls, killing at will. The portals might take them to the time and dimension that Luke had returned to, where if they found him, they could drag him back to Hell. The very possibility of that terrified me. What if I were put in the position of exchanging the keys for Sean?"

Now almost a week later the deeper I sank into my self-contained misery, the more I had to listen to everyone's opinion of James. What they thought of him, which was all good of course. I remembered the kiss in the kitchen, the morning Sean went missing. James had been sweet and kind, understanding how much pain Jack and Gill were in. I asked myself, why then? If he knew where Sean was, knew what had happened to him, knew the agony that Gill and Jack were suffering, why did he not to do anything to alleviate it by contacting them. Maybe he had, of course, maybe he had arranged for the letter to be written and delivered. I wanted him to be an undercover agent because the alternatives were worse.

Valdez might be a pain, but she was a good detective. Only 24hrs later she called Valerie to tell her a John Elliot had been recognised as James from CCTV at the airport had flown from Glasgow to Munich almost three weeks ago. From CCTV at Munich airport they knew he had been picked up by a white

Mercedes. They had footage of the driver and she wanted me to come to the station to see if I recognised him.

Katie and I went to the station together. The street outside was quiet, there were no longer hordes of reporters gathered there. I wondered if they had been forced to leave or if they had left of their own accord because Sean was no longer front-page news, we were shown through to a room with a table and four chairs, with nothing else but a laptop and a carafe of water? The policewoman who showed us through to the room said DI Valdez was in the station and would be with us shortly. Shortly turned out to be over an hour later.

"Sorry to keep you waiting," she said when she finally came through the door.

"We have been sitting here for over an hour" Katie complained as she had been doing relentlessly for the last forty minutes.

Valdez snapped at her. I am a busy lady so shall we get on with this? She opened the laptop that lay on the table, brought up the footage and fast forwarded it to Munich airport and a white Mercedes pulling up outside. Moments later we saw a man walking towards the car. His face was hidden by a baseball cap, but I knew by his build and his walk that it was James. He got into the front passenger seat and the car pulled away without us being able to see the driver. Valdez opened another page, this one showed what looked like the same car. It had stopped at a filling station and the driver who was also wearing a baseball cap got out and went into the shop, pulling the cap further over his face. By a stroke of luck, as he left the shop a helicopter passed overhead and for a split second he looked up. Valdez hit the key on the laptop and the image froze. "Do you recognize this Man?"

Yes "It's Stephan, "Katie said.

Valdez waited for me to comment. "Yes, his name is Stephan he is the chauffeur from Heiligtum."

She closed the laptop. "That's all I need to know. You can go now."

"Wait. Have you any leads on Sean yet?"

"No." She checked her phone.

"What about James?" Katie asked

"They lost sight of him after the filling station. The German police are looking for him. Don't hold your breath, they didn't manage to find Frank Summers. Hand on hip she looked at me. "I don't suppose you have any ideas?"

"No." I said. She didn't know about Doria or Potsdam and I wasn't about to tell her. I intended to go there myself.

Chapter 14

Revelations

It seemed to me Jonah's suggestion that James may have taken Sean to protect him, was a definite possibility. If he was a member of any of the security forces, he may have discovered a threat to Sean, from people like Die Brueder. Sean would be a powerful tool in their hands, a perfect bargaining tool to use for the keys. It was the only thing that made sense and Potsdam would be the ideal place to hide him.   Stephan was also a security agent and he had picked James up at the airport. I asked Jonah if it were likely that German and British security forces would communicate. Would they both know about the Neo Nazi cell, Die Brueder, in Munich and he said "Oh yes, without a doubt. James, Otto and Stephan could be working together."

When Katie realised what I intended to do, she wanted to come with me. Worried that it would be dangerous, I told her I was just going to find out if James had taken Sean to Doria.

"Why do you think he would take him there? How would he get him out of the country?

"I don't know how he got him out. I am sure MI6 have ways and means. As for Doria she knows everything about Luke and the gates, she would understand why Sean was special and how Die Brueder could use him. That house is remote and the perfect hiding place. Also, James could have got Doria to write the letter in Old Aramaic knowing that Eli would translate it, just to let us know Sean was safe. Can't you see that makes sense?"

"I'm coming with you." she said

"You are not, and you can't tell anyone, not till I have gone. Gill needs you. Jack is drinking a lot. He's argumentative and you know he has a dark side when he drinks. Gill is vulnerable Katie, she needs you here and if he does get out of hand, just call Jonah, he'll soon deal with him.

"Jonah will go mad if you do this on your own. Honestly, Erica I think it's bad idea."

"Probably, but I'll be fine. At best I will find James and Sean, at worst, Doria will send me packing." We talked it over. It was better that she stays with Gill. I was perfectly capable of going on my own.

I planned for the next day. I booked the first flight I could get to Berlin's Tegel airport. It was at 10.30am the next morning on a budget airline, A direct flight there is under two hours, then allowing for another 30 mins by taxi from there to Potsdam, I could be in the hotel for mid-afternoon.

I lay in my bed that night fantasising about how wonderful it would be to find Sean and be the instrument that brought him home. Then it was meeting James and what I would wear. I intended to look glamorous, sophisticated, independent, and very capable. I would conceal the fact I been in his flat and look surprised to find he was with Doria. He would be both shocked and impressed that I had found him and got to the bottom of Sean's kidnap.

I couldn't sleep at all that night. I swung between thinking it was the right thing to do and worrying that it was a terrible mistake. and Doria would be angry that I had come back, but I had to do something. I was going mad waiting around thinking Gill and Jack believed that Sean was taken by Die Brueder, to blackmail me or the Hunt. I finally fell asleep around 5am and my alarm went off at six.

I wasn't worried that I hadn't had much sleep. I would sleep on the plane, all the way to Berlin, or so I thought, but it didn't quite go to plan, mostly because I had never travelled abroad on my own before. Things I had taken for granted I suddenly worried about. Had I remembered my passport, my euros, my bank, and credit cards, my mobile, my tablet. Everything seemed to go missing at the bottom of my bag, never in the place I had put them. I went too early to the airport in case the heavy morning traffic on the motorway made me miss my flight. As a result, I was too early for check-in, but I just browsed the shops and bought a magazine to read. Then I worried I might not find the gate, so I went through passport control too early. I felt nervous and must have looked it, because when I walked through the screen, the customs officer double checked my bag and frisked me even though the alarm hadn't gone off.

In the departure lounge, I bought tea and sat for a while people watching. I decided to go to the gate, that way, I thought, it would be less stressful than looking for it when the flight was called. I found the gate and sat drinking more tea out of a disposable cup, at a gate which wasn't even opened yet. I sat there for ages, continually checking the flight details screen. Looking around for the toilets. I had two choices, I could go to the toilet first, but I didn't want to lose my seat, or I could wait till we were in the air. As time went on nature called and I had to go. I gathered up my hand luggage and jacket and got in the queue of the busy ladies' room, of course that's when the flight was called. I had waited too long to go, but go I had to. I made it back to the gate just before it closed,

I was so glad to be on that plane and looking forward to some sleep, but that was never going to happen. When I booked, I thought I was lucky to get the only seat left on the flight. It turned out to be at the back of the plane. It was an aisle seat, right outside the toilet door. In the middle seat and the window seat there was an overweight German couple, who throughout the flight consumed large amounts of fluid. Unfortunately, they both had weak bladders. The Frau also had a hearing problem, which meant her husband had to raise his voice when he spoke to her and he did that a lot. The stewardess with the trolley had to repeat everything, loudly, several times, as she served the lady with her numerous drinks and snacks, and purchases from the trolley. The gentleman, and I use that term reservedly, had, because of his girth, a problem with his elbows, which he repeatedly jammed in my ribs. He of course apologised profusely in German. I think he was telling me the seats were too small.   Just when I thought it couldn't get any worse the stewardess announced our approach to Berlin and just as the seatbelt sign came on, she announced the descent had been cancelled. There was a runway problem and our flight would be circling until we had been given permission to land. The aircraft circled for another forty minutes before landing. By the time I arrived in Berlin I was a washed-out wreck, from lack of sleep.

It was mid-afternoon before I reached the hotel. As I collected my key the receptionist whose English was as good as mine, handed me an envelope. At the same time telling me I had just missed the man who left it.

"Did he leave a name?"

"No Madam. I did ask" she said, but he gave no name, he did say he would come back."

Inside the envelope was a card with a message in it, it read. *You are in danger. Don't attempt to leave the hotel till I come back for you.* There was no signature.

"What did he look like?"

She thought for a moment "He was not tall, but not small."

"Medium height?"

"Yes, that is it. He had light hair."

"Blonde?"

"Yes, blonde hair."

"Did he speak German?"

"Yes, but he had no accent, he was German."

Back in the room I lay down on the bed. For a brief moment when the receptionist told me about the man, I thought James had found me. When she described the man, I thought maybe James had asked someone to deliver the card although he definitely had not written it. The moment I read it I knew it wasn't from James, he had very distinctive cursive handwriting. I was worried now. Someone knew I was here, but who? The description didn't match anyone I knew. He would come back for me it said, well I was not going anywhere with a stranger. I thought of leaving the hotel before he came back, but the card said I was in danger. I didn't know what to do and I was so tired I couldn't think straight. I closed my eyes.

It was half past seven before I woke up and that was only because Katie called." It's half past six. I thought you were going to let me know when you arrived."

"Sorry, I lay on the bed and fell asleep. I looked at my phone. Actually, it's half past seven here. Berlin is an hour ahead." I didn't tell her about the stranger and the card.

"What are you going to do now?" She asked

"I am going to freshen up and get some dinner. I am going to wait until tomorrow, to go to Doria's, I think." I yawned." I will need a good night's sleep and a clear head."

"Ok, well, take care and keep in touch,

"Don't worry about me. I will speak to you soon."

It was after eight when the room telephone rang to say the gentleman had returned and was waiting for me in the bar. Nervous, I was sure of only one thing, I was going nowhere with this stranger. The bar was busy and noisy with music playing in the background. I looked around for a blonde-haired man. I couldn't see one. I was about to take a seat on a bar stool when a familiar voice said. "Hello stranger." I spun around to find a smiling, beautiful red-haired woman in a vivid green cocktail dress. It was such a transformation that at first, I didn't recognise her then I realised who it was, and I couldn't believe it. "Chris…" She cut me off, laughing.

She held her hand up, I recognised she was warning me. "Yes, it's me Elise. I have changed I know, but it is me," she said laughing."

I stood up, she hugged me. "Keep smiling," she whispered. "Go along with it, there are people watching." She took my arm. "Come, Hans has a table in the corner." Then she said aloud. "Oh, I am so pleased to see you. It has been such a long time."

She took my arm and led me towards a table. I could see the blonde-haired man sitting there. "Here she is Hans my old friend, she has come all this way to visit us."

He stood up. "It is so nice to finally meet you. Elise has told me so much about you." He kissed me on the cheek. "Keep up the pretence." he whispered.

The table was in a dark corner of the bar and the tables near us were empty so, we could not be overheard. "Christina, what's going on? Where have you been? What happened at Garmisch-Partenkirchen?"

"It's a long story, let me first introduce you to my husband Frank."

"You are a Frank Summers? Really? What happened? Were you both kidnapped by Die Brueder?"

"No, it is a long story," he said. "We will tell you in time, but for now just eat." The table was laden with bar food, finger food, that I needed no encouragement to eat.

"How did you know I was here?" I asked

"Eli found out last night, he called Doria. We have been living with her Erica. James is there and Sean."

"So, it was James who ..." Frank stopped me in mid-sentence. Quietly he said. "it is better if we do not discuss anything here. Small talk only. Perhaps about your flight." Again, I needed no. encouragement. I kept the conversation going with the story of my fellow passengers. We left the hotel an hour later. I was worried. They had told me they were taking me to James and Sean but still hadn't given me any details.

It was dark by the time we pulled up outside the Van Brugan house, in fact it was pitch black. There was no moon that night, it was hidden behind a blanket of dark clouds, and without street-lights, in the isolated setting, the darkness was intensified. In fact, the house itself was no more than a dim shadow. It was difficult to see where we were going.

Frank took a torch from the car. "We need to move quickly" he said, "but hold hands, mind your step and stay close and silence please, until we are inside."

Shutters had been closed over the old windows of the rundown house. Drapes had been drawn over the shutters to prevent even a peep of light escaping. We followed Frank and he led us up the path to the front door, which had been covered with storm doors. The whole place looked deserted. He knocked lightly with the torch, three times on the door and as if someone had been waiting behind them, the doors were opened almost immediately. Christina stepped back and ushered me through. Frank followed us in, and a woman locked the door behind us. No one spoke, and in the gloom. I couldn't see the woman's face, but she was too tall to be Doria's housekeeper, who had been a small stout lady. Then, when she opened the door to the dimly lit sitting room, I was a surprised to see it was Helga Schroeder the housekeeper from Heiligtum.

Two men stood up to greet us, as Christina walked through the door in front of me. I felt a flutter of excitement, so sure was I, that one of them would be James. Hoping he was as glad to see me as I him. Frank said he would be here. I thought he would be waiting for me, but when Frau Schroeder stepped aside, I saw it was Otto and Stephan.

"Hello Erica, I am so pleased to see you have arrived safely". Otto said.

"Come here and sit-down girl." A voice said from a high-backed chair at the fireplace. There was so little light I couldn't see her, but I knew it was Doria.

Christina knew I was looking for James and sensing my disappointment she touched my arm and whispered. "Soon but sit down first. We have some things to explain then I will take you to him."

I nodded and walked over to Doria. "It's very nice to see you again Frau Van Brugan."

She looked me up and down and grunted. "Are you hungry?"

"No, thank you, I have eaten. I am anxious to see Sean." I said, "and James Anderson I believe he is also here."

She grunted again and looked up at me in silence for a while. Then said. "They are alive and in this house. For the moment that is all you need to know. Have patience child it is for your own good. Now sit down."

I did as she asked. No one spoke, she was like a dowager queen holding court. Then she said to me. "You will have to be prepared. There is much to tell you. There is much you do not know. We are all in danger here. Even with these two to protect us," she waved her hand at Otto and Stephan, "One wrong move and all will be lost. Helga bring some brandy she is going to need it and…" she waived her hand in the air again. "Go down, all of you, I would like to speak to Erica alone."

The room was large and very poorly lit by old mahogany lamps with shades, once cream, now brown with age and neglect. Doria sat in her high-backed green studded velvet chair, the velvet on the arms rubbed and worn with years of use. The chair sat close to the tall mahogany fireplace that was graced with brass candle sticks, a loudly clicking mantle clock and an ornate gold framed photograph lying face down.

Doria looked older than the last time I saw her, though it had only been just over a month. She looked both pale and tired and as worn as the room and the whole house did. The colour in her navy pleated skirt with matching heavy knit cardigan was faded. Her grey hair was sparse and thin but still with a few waves that were reminiscent of curls in earlier days, it had been cropped short since I last saw her. I remember thinking Doria must have been pretty in her youth, perhaps still would be if she just smiled occasionally. She sat without speaking, with her eyes almost closed. She sat, like that, silent and still, for so long that I began to wonder if she had fallen asleep. Then moments later as though she had been startled awake, she said impatiently, and though I had kept her waiting, "You may ask your questions now. Come along, what's keeping you? We don't have all night. They will be here soon, we have to go down, down with the rest."

"Who will be here? Go down where?" I asked

She sighed deeply, ignoring my question she then said sharply "Don't you want to know who you are? How you came to be this rich woman you are now? How I know so much about you? How we knew you would come here tonight?" Both her tone and manner were aggressive, and I was surprised and beginning to feel nervous.

"Of course, I want to know   I just don't know where to start. I have so many questions."

She grunted again.

I cleared my throat. "Ok, how did you know I was coming here tonight?"

"Eli," she said

"Of course." I said realising Jack or Katie must have told Eli I had gone to Potsdam.

I thought for a moment. "How do you know me? When Eli sent me to you, you knew I had a birthmark that only my adopted parents and my late husband knew of."

She pointed to the mantlepiece. "There is a photograph there, take it and look at it."

I did as she asked and sat back down on the chair. In the heavy gold frame was a wedding photograph. I gasped when I realised the groom was Luke. He looked the same age as he was when we met him in the kitchen at Lanshoud. The bride was a pretty girl in a long, but simple, white lace dress. She had no veil just a circlet of flowers on her hair and she carried a bouquet of roses.

"You recognise him of course, but not her, is that right?"

"Yes, it's Luke Treadstone."

"Ah, yes, that is what he calls himself now."

"Who is the bride?" I asked

She leaned forward smiling her tone gentler than before she said, "I think you can guess that my dear."

"No, I have never seen her before." My heart was fluttering, I had chills going up and down my spine. I was thinking, could the bride be my mother? Was that what she was hinting at. "How did you come by this?"

She didn't answer at first. Just took a sip of her brandy and put her head back to rest on the chair-back, then stayed that way for what seemed like an eternity, again I thought she had fallen asleep.

"Frau Van Brugan are you alright? Should I call someone?"

She opened her eyes and shook her head. Sipping a little more brandy, she pointed to the photograph. "The girl in that photograph, the bride, she was my daughter."

"Your Daughter! Your daughter was married to my father?"

"Yes, and..." she shook her finger her at me..." I was totally against that marriage." She sighed heavily. She closed her eyes again and laid her head back. "I grew up in France in a little town called Lyons-la-Floret in Normandy. I knew well the man you call Luke. At that time, he called himself Bertrand Montal. He was a friend of my father when I was just a child and so I knew what he was. She stressed the word what, saying, what he was and not who he was. "I watched my father grow old while Bertrand never changed. I knew he had never aged and now, when I was a grown woman and married, he was courting my daughter. My beautiful daughter Marianne."

My heart was thumping so hard I was sure she could hear it. In the kitchen at Lanshoud Luke had told me Marianne, was the name of my birth mother.

Doria continued. "She loved that man with a passion I could not dampen. She had been unwell a few times. The local doctor misdiagnosed her, and she became more and more unwell. Bertrand asked her to marry him and I could no longer stand in her way, because by that time Marianne was ill with a debilitating disease. Bertrand promised to take care of her. He promised she would never want for anything. "In my heart I knew he loved her and so I gave in. I just wanted her to have some happiness in her life. He tried to cure her, and he did make her well for a while, but she could not have children. She so desperately wanted a child and so Bertrand gave her one. He used his sperm to fertilise her eggs." She took another sip of her brandy and closed her eyes again. It was as if she needed to close out everything around her in order to bring back memories. I sat in silence patiently waiting.

She rubbed her eyes "There were four test tube babies. A practice unheard of in those days. He implanted one in her womb and, aware she may not be able to carry the child, he planted the rest in three in other women, surrogates, and so there were four babies born. They were all girls, all with Marianne's red hair and green eyes."

Suddenly it made sense. Of course, that would explain the photograph of the four babies. It was in the box we found at Antique Treasures. The box that held the keys of the four gates. "Am I one of those babies? Is one of those babies Christina?" I asked

"Yes, she is your sister and you have two more."

"Have you met them? Do you know where they are? Eli told me, that you know where the other gates may be. Find the gates and you will find your sisters." She closed her eyes again. "Have you any other questions?"

"Yes," my heart was thumping in my chest, so nervous and excited was I, of the answer she might give. I asked, was your married name Belliere?"

"Yes, my first husband was Francois Belliere."

"Then your daughter was Marianne Belliere, my mother."

She opened her eyes and looked at me. "Yes Erica, Christina is your sister and you have two more, and I am your Grandmother."

She watched me, as I let it sink in. I had a family a real family, a grandmother and three sisters. The shock left me speechless and emotional. I was looking at my grandmother. I couldn't believe it. Doria was smiling, it transformed her face. She pointed to a box of tissues on her side table. I took some and took a gulp of the brandy.

She let me sniffle away and continued. "Bertrand, or Luke if you prefer, had a problem, because the Hunt was catching up with him. He knew it was not safe for Marianne, he decided to leave. It was always easy for him to move around. He had a personal army of people who worked for him, in many countries, and he paid them handsomely. The Vansterdams who became your parents and your husband were part of that army. Frank Summers is one of them, he was allocated to Christina. As it got nearer the birth and Bertrand knew the Hunt were close. He evaded them and escaped taking my pregnant daughter to the Netherlands to a town called Delfshaven in Rotterdam." Her voice was breaking. Her eyes moist with tears, she said. "I never saw my Marianne again. The stress of the birth was too much for her." A sip of Brandy again and another pregnant pause. "Bertrand had you both smuggled out of the Netherlands and taken to Scotland. Marianne died on route."

She closed her eyes. Silence again. Only the ticking of the mantle clocking counting the seconds, waiting for her to speak again.

Her eyes popped open. She leaned forward staring at my face. "Do you know your mother called you Camille"?

"Yes, Luke told me"

"Camille is my middle name." She said almost proudly.

My head was reeling, everything was at last making sense, especially the photograph that we found in the box, the photograph of the four babies, at last I understood. "Does Christina know she is my full sister?" I asked

"Yes, she does, and it is time for you both to know the truth. I am of an age when what is in my memory cannot always be recalled. So, if you have questions ask them now."

"I have so many. I hardly know where to start. "Why is Christina with you? How did she get here? She disappeared from a house in Garmisch- Partenkirchen, we heard her scream it as awful."

Doria nodded. "The Hunt were seen. Otto knew they were following you and Die Brueder were following Christina"

"And yet Otto and Stephan left us there. We could have suffered a fate worse than death."

"Otto knew you were safe inside that house. He took you there and reinforced the protection that was already there. He did not expect you to up and leave."

"Protection? What kind of protection? We had none, Katie and I were left to fend for ourselves. We were at the mercy of what was out there."

Doria shook her head. "You were never in any real danger. "That house was used as a safe house, during the war, for Jewish people escaping the Nazis" The same protection you have at lanshoud was put on that house."

I said "Jewish people! Of course, that explains the cases and clothes we found in the loft."

Doria continued. "During the war. The German Jews, escaping the Nazis were taken to the house in Garmisch- Partenkirchen, from there they were brought here, where they stayed until they could escape to other counties. That house and has the same protection as here."

"I don't understand, what protection do you mean the German police or BND were protecting us?"

Doria took another sip of her brandy. "Have you really not guessed? Even though you have seen them, you have met and spoken to his kind before? You have been blessed child, you met the Archangels and are alive to tell the tale, and James told me you both met a lesser rank of that kind. You met a messenger after a car crash."

His kind! I was stunned, what was she saying? Otto was a messenger? Otto was like Abdiel, was she saying he was an angel? I pictured in my mind, the first time I saw him. The kind charismatic incredibly handsome man, she was right, he had the same piercing blue eyes, that like the Archangels, they seemed to hold some inner light. I used to call them gas flame blue eyes. "Is Otto a messenger?" I asked

Doria thought for a moment. "No Otto is not a messenger. Yes, he is like Abdiel, but he is a higher rank. Otto is Othniel, he is a guardian."

"And Stephan?"

"Stephan" she said is human and in the employ of Luke Treadstone."

"In the employ? But how can that be, Luke is gone forever." I said.

She laughed. "Remember who we are dealing with. Time travel is an addictive hobby. Anyway. the firm of Galbraith and Anderson was setup by Luke to deal with salaries, estate maintenance etc."

I used to think my life was no more than a hallucination, like Alice I had fallen down a rabbit hole, into a strange new world, but Alice was better off than me. At least she knew the Mad hatter was mad, from the moment she met him, and well, the March Hare had buck teeth and ears to give the game away. At that moment there was an almighty crash on the window behind me, that made me jump. Then the steady tap, tap, tap that I was so familiar with, that haunted my dreams.

"They are here" Doria said.

Chapter 15

The tunnel

Stephan burst through the door. "You must come now Madam, they are gathering,"

Doria took the walking stick lying beside her chair and leaned on it heavily. Her face was etched with pain as she struggled to stand on arthritic joints. Stephan held out his hand to assist her but as a sudden wave of emotion washed over me, I stepped forward and said "please, let me help you Frau Van Brugan." She didn't answer, she was staring straight ahead as though she were waiting either for the pain to settle or to get her balance. I tried again holding out my arm. "Frau Van Brugan. Grandmother. Won't you take my arm?" She smiled, her eyes became moist and she nodded her head.

With my newfound grandmother leaning heavily on my arm I followed Stephan into the hallway. Here the tapping was reaching a crescendo. He opened a door that led to a brightly lit cellar and ushered us through. Doria struggled a bit with the stairs, but with my help, she reached the bottom. Stephan had said the rest were down here and so I expected to see Frank and Christina with James and Sean but, to my surprise, there was no one there. I looked around it had the usual junk only better quality than usually found in cellars. No people, only remnants of years gone by, old dining chairs, mirrors and table lamps, prints and paintings lying against the walls. Rolls of left-over wallpaper and an old black Bakelite telephone, a three-legged coffee table and some old suitcases. Curtains and cushions heaped in plastic boxes. Paint tins, boxes of tools, various ornaments all piled high and a very large Victorian type solid oak wardrobe, there were no other doors.

"This way" Doria said pointing her stick. "Over to the wardrobe." Stephan opened the double doors of the huge wardrobe and pushed to one side the coats that were hanging there. He reached down among boots and shoes lying at the bottom and released a catch. It was like a scene from the Lion, the Witch, and the Wardrobe. The back-centre panel swung open and away, but when we stepped through, instead of Narnia there was just as strangely, a very large well decorated room. A room with plastered white walls, several beds, old but comfortable upholstered chairs, occasional tables, a bookcase full of books, a writing desk and against the far wall a dining table and chairs. The floor was even carpeted. It was weird, this hidden room, that looked in better condition than the rooms upstairs. Christina, Frank, Otto, and Helga were already there, sitting quietly, listening to the increasing clamour from outside.

"They try to scare us with their shrieking and screaming," Doria said.

There was a wheelchair in the corner. Frank brought it forward for Doria, who sank heavily into it, sighing deeply. Stephan pulled the coats back into place and closed the door. "There are more than usual out there tonight," he said to Otto.

"Yes" Otto said, "they have been getting bolder. Something is riding with them."

There was no sign of Sean, but two of the beds seemed to be occupied, one with an adult and one with a sleeping child. A child too big to be Sean. With a sinking heart I realised the man was James. He was so badly injured I didn't recognise him at first. His face was swollen and heavily bruised. There were stitches above one of the black swollen and closed eyes. His head had been shaved in places, to allow scalp wounds to be stitched. He lay still, very still. Shocked, I could do no more than whisper. "What happened to him?" Even in the state he was in, I knew it was James. I sat down on the edge of the bed and put my hand over his, it was cold, so cold, and there was no response. "James, James it's me, Erica." There was no movement, no attempt to open his eyes.

185

A strong soft and gentle hand touched my shoulder. "He is sedated, but he is healing; there are no serious injuries. You need not worry Erica, he will recover," Otto said quietly.

Otto, Doria had said, was a guardian. I looked up at him now with new eyes. Why did Doria have to tell me about him? Why hadn't I seen it for myself? The blue eyes, lit from within, shining brighter than the table lamps scattered around the room. I had seen eyes like these before. The deep but gentle voice, the aura of calm that cloaked him. This will sound crazy I know, but there was a scent about him that I should have remembered, recognised. No, maybe scent is not the right word, but it was as though I could smell a scent, as if I had more than five senses. As if I had another sense that lay somewhere between sight and smell. One that enabled me, when my body decided to use it, to recognise the essence of goodness, the scent of purity. It floated like elusive wisps in the air around him.

I felt faint and put my head in my hands. I thought maybe the brandy was affecting me. When Otto again said again James would recover, on some subliminal level, I knew, without any doubt, that he would, and the feeling of nausea left me.

"Who did this to him?" I asked

"Die Brueder," Frank said. "Though Otto has suspicions there is someone much more dangerous involved. We don't yet know how they got Sean out of his home, but they took him to Heiligtum. Stephan traced them there and contacted James. They have worked together before."

I did a double take there. Worked together before! When Katie and I came back from Munich and told James about Otto and Stephan, he didn't bat an eyelid. At that point I realised that he probably knew what had happened in Munich all along. James, I didn't want to believe that he had been lying to me, but at that point even more so than when Jonah took me to the riverside penthouse, I was faced with the solid proof that I didn't know James Anderson. He might as well have been a stranger.

Frank added. "They work for security forces, similar organisations. James in the UK, Stephan and Otto in Germany,"

"Where did they find him?" I asked him.

"At Heiligtum. Stephan and James went to Heiligtum and between them they managed to get Sean out and bring him here, even though James had been attacked and severely injured."

Confused, I said, "If James is a government agent, I don't understand why the UK government would have allowed him to go Heiligtum? Obviously, this was not government business?"

Frank answered, "You are wrong, it was government business. Die Brueder are part of a European wide Neo Nazi movement. There are terrorist cells in almost every country in Europe. It is very much in the interests of the British government to know what they are up to."

"Where is Sean now?" I asked. Because of the strange world I lived in, where nothing was ever what it seemed, where almost everyone I was close to had an alter ego, I had already begun to think the impossible. I remembered how short a time Gill's pregnancy had been, only a few months, not the standard forty weeks, still, Sean had been a full-term baby. What I was thinking was beyond belief, so I asked again. "Where is he? Where is Sean?"

Christina pointed to the sleeping child. Even though I was thinking exactly that. Even though I had no doubt she was telling the truth, it was still unbelievable. How could this be Sean? Sean Docherty hadn't reached his second birthday. How could that child be Gill's son? Admittedly he had the same red hair but from the size of him that boy was at least four or five years old.

Otto reading my mind said quietly, "the recent growth spurt is the last one. From now on he will behave and grow to manhood like any human child"

I was stunned, "Like any human child! What does that mean?"

Those deep blue eyes looked into mine. Calmly, he said, "I know Doria told you."

"Told me what? I don't understand." I couldn't take it in. I knew Sean was a miracle child, but this! Not human, that was insane. Gill was pining for her baby boy; she would be ecstatic when I told her they had found him. I had dreamt of being the one who would find him and bring him home. What was I supposed to say to her now? He is no longer a baby. He's ready for school now. Oh, and by the way he's not human."

I watched the little boy curled up, sound asleep on the bed. He wore blue jeans and a pale blue hooded sweater with Spider-Man on the front. His long thick eyelashes fluttered on his pale skin as though he were dreaming. I almost shouted at Otto. "How can this be?"

Otto said. "Abdiel told both you and James on the night of the car accident, that there was a gift for your friend. Sean was that gift."

"How do you even know about that? About the accident, I mean. Do you have some weird method of communicating?"

"Yes," he smiled, "it's called a mobile phone." He was laughing at me; I could see it in his eyes.

"What is Sean then? If he is not human."

"Please don't worry Erica, though he is of our race, he will be the physical embodiment of his parents. Sean will grow to be a man his parents will be proud of. When the time is right, like all our kind, he will be called upon to serve the Supreme Being, here on earth."

They were all sitting quietly, listening, watching my reaction. Christina got up, walked over, and put her arm through mine. She squeezed my arm. "Look at him, don't you think he looks like Jack, and he is a strong little boy"

"I don't understand, how he can look like Jack when he has none of his Jack's genes?"

Otto said, "yes, but that was all part of his design. Sean was sculpted, manufactured, to look like his parents. He will now grow and live like any other male child. There are many of our kind in this world Erica, we walk among you. I know no other way to describe it. He was made for Jack and Gill."

I shook my head. "But they won't know him, they are looking for their baby, as is practically the whole police force in Scotland. How in God's name, can I turn up with a five-year-old and pass him off as Sean?" I had a sudden vision of me trying to explain this to Valdez. My heart sank."

Otto said "He is Sean. When they see him, they will have forgotten his age. I promise you, they, and all around them, will recognise him as their son. You will remember the truth, but only you and Christina, because the genes you both carry from Luke's race allow you to remember truth. Look at your mobile you will find proof of what I say. Look at your photographs and texts. There is a message from Gill."

I tried to stop my hand from trembling as I scrolled through my mobile looking for a message from Gill. It was incredible, there were multiple inexplicable entries. I had to sit down. I was looking at photos of Sean growing up. Not just one or two but in albums in the gallery on my mobile. There was a video of him learning to walk, then he was aged two or three learning to ride a tricycle. There was even a video of Jack teaching him to swim. There were multiple photos of Sean taken with Gill right up to the age he looked now, but what floored me was the last text message. The text read.

So glad you are bringing Sean home. When he called us, he told Jack he was having so much fun with Frank and Christina, he might just stay in Germany a little longer.

I felt suddenly faint again. I was gulping air. Christina said, "sit down here in the chair, take a deep breath, put you head down on your knees." She knelt beside me. "It's a lot to take in. I know, I have been where you are, but everything will be fine we are all here for you Erica." She hugged me. You are going to be alright you have your family around you"

My family! I had family! I had a sister, a brother-in -law and a grandmother, for me that was wonderful.

Frank came over with a glass, "drink this it will make you feel better," he said.

"No, thank you." I pushed the glass away. I have already had enough brandy to last me a lifetime."

"It's water" he said.

The night was a long one. Doria, Helga, who had been very quiet, and Christina, had fallen asleep. I was tired, but the three hours of sleep I had in the hotel that afternoon, had made me less so. My brain was hyperactive, trying to compute all the things I had just learned. We talked through the night, the three men and I, while the screaming and banging from the Hunt outside, went on relentlessly.

"Is there any possibility they could get in?" I asked Otto.

He hesitated. "Normally, they would not, as you know, they have to be invited. However, there is something more powerful riding with them."

"Like what?" I asked

"The dark Lord has many generals in his army. There are demons of a much higher order and who very powerful." He said.

"I told you we saw them in the mist at Garmisch- Partenkirchen. We thought they had taken Christina. Did they take her? How did she escape and come here?"

"She was never taken by them in the first place. Frank was watching the house. When she wandered out, he took her and brought her here."

"But Frank wasn't there!"

"Yes, he was, we left Frank to watch you. He was in a parked car nearby."

The night wore on, the clamour never lessening. Still only the men and I were awake. I wondered aloud. "Why are we down here? Is it safer? If they do have something more powerful with them and they break in, surely we are even more trapped in here, than we would be upstairs."

Frank stood up and drew back a curtain on the wall behind the bed Sean lay on. It revealed yet another door. "It is an escape tunnel," Otto said. "It leads from here to the nearby church, which does have protection. It was part of the escape route for the German Jews and allied airmen, shot down during the war. They were brought here from Berlin and taken to Garmisch-Partenkirchen, they were then taken through safe houses in Belgium and from there to the UK. There was an elaborate network orchestrated from this place, and the house I called my sister's, in Garmisch- Partenkirchen

I exclaimed "That explains the things we found in the loft. There was so much there. Suitcases full of clothing. I…" I stopped dead mid-sentence, there was an almighty screech, an incredible sound that, chilled me to the bone. And it was right outside the door.

Otto cried, "they are in, quickly waken them, we have to go."

The next frantic minutes saw Frank lift the still sleeping Sean, who didn't even stir, and open the door to the tunnel. Helga followed him pushing Doria's chair through. Christina grabbed my arm." Come on Erica we must move: She pulled me towards the door.

I resisted her. "James. What about James?"

"Otto will bring him. Now please move."

I stepped through into a wide tunnel brightly lit by the powerful torches that Doria and Frank carried. The tunnel was cold and smelled of damp and decay, but the ground underneath my feet felt solid enough. There was a cry of pain from James, I turned back but Christina handed me a torch and pushed me ahead of her. "Keep moving, "she said "unless you want us all to suffer a fate worse than death." James cried out again, it was awful to listen to. I couldn't see what was happening to him which made it worse. I stopped. though Christina kept urging me forward, then minutes later Otto and Stephan came through the door with the limp body of James in a canvas stretcher. Christina went back and bolted the door behind them.

The tunnel was hollowed out of solid rock. Water tricked down the wall in places and disappeared through cracks in the uneven floor. I followed the wheelchair listening to the whimpers of pain from the now conscious James. Helga pushed the wheel-chair steadily ahead. She stopped when the tunnel took a bend and walked in front of Doria to unbolt another door.

Otto told me later that the tunnel was around a mile long and was centuries old. It had been built as an escape route from the old church which had originally been a Benedictine monastery. The monastery itself was destroyed by invading Turks in the late 14th Century and rebuilt by loyal Bulgarians. The tunnel had been built then to allow the Monks to escape to safety when they came under attack and had once led all the way to the river, but that section had collapsed. He told me that my grandfather, Doria's husband had discovered it when they were building the house and had found this section remarkably well preserved. They found medieval pottery in it and some manuscripts which Doria had in safe keeping. The tunnel was then utilised during the war as part of an escape route for the Jewish people fleeing the Nazi's.

The tunnel eventually ended in the crypt of a church. It was creepily full of old stone coffins. We made our way past them to stone stairs leading up to a door that opened at the front of the church beside the altar. Doria's wheelchair was left behind and with Helga and Christina's help she managed the stairs. The church was in darkness, but the moon had come out from the clouds and shone through the stained-glass windows, illuminating the alter and the rows of highly polished pews. Rows of tiny candles creating a bright glow, burned in a rack beneath the statue of the Virgin Mary, left there by parishioners seeking favours from the mother of Christ. I had imagined the church was a ruin perhaps even without a roof. Instead though hundreds of years old it was in a good state of repair and well cared for. The altar was dressed in immaculate white cloths and polished gold candlesticks holding tall white candles. The moonlight shone through the roof windows illuminating the gleaming gold tabernacle. Hymn books lay at the end of the pews and stacks of printed literature lay on a small table at the door. Christina sat on one of the pews near the altar and took the sleeping Sean from Frank. Helga and Doria sat beside her. The pews were too narrow to hold the stretcher. Frank went to the back row and with my help turned one around and we put the two together and Otto and Stephan gently put the stretcher there. They walked up to speak to Doria their voices echoing loudly in the cavern that was the empty church. They then went back down the stairs for Doria's wheelchair.

James was awake. He smiled at me. I sat down beside him. I took his hand in mine, he squeezed my hand. "You are real," he said, his voice no more than a whisper. "Would it be corny if I said I thought I had died and gone to heaven?"

I whispered back. "Yes, very, I expected something more original from you."

He grimaced. "How about, you are a sight for sore eyes."

I laughed, "that's just as bad."

"Damn, I have lost my street cred then."

His voice sounded coarse and dry. "Could I have some water, then I might manage the right words."

I called out to Christina, she pointed to a door near the side alter with the statue and votive candles. "Try the sacristy. There is a sink in there"

I brought a glass of water, held his head, and helped him sip the water. He cleared his throat. "Now I'll try again. Erica Cameron, I love you, I can't believe you are here with me. Is that better?"

"That's a big improvement." I whispered smiling. I wanted to cry but I bit back the tears and gently kissed his dry split lips.

"Does that mean the feelings are mutual?" he asked. "and not just that you are sorry for me?"

"Of course, I love you James, I am just a stupid fool who wouldn't admit it. I ..."

We were interrupted by Otto and Stephan coming back. Stephan went to speak to Frank. Otto stopped beside us. "How are you James?" He asked pulling a bottle of tablets from his pocket. Is it time for some more painkillers?"

"No more thanks I want some time to talk to Erica."

"No take them James, please." I insisted. "I am not going anywhere. If you fall asleep, I will be here when you wake up. I promise." I held out my hand to Otto, he put two tablets in my hand. I helped James to swallow them, with the water left in the glass. Five minutes later he was asleep.

"He is exhausted." Otto said "It is only the pain and discomfort that keep him awake. He is bruised and cut on every inch of his body. He cannot lie comfortably in any position."

"Otto you are sure he will be ok?"

"He has no internal injuries. He is young and strong. Don't worry, he will heal quickly."

Wondering what would happen next, I asked "And are we safe here? Can the hunt get in?"

193

"They do not even know that we are here. They are not the most intelligent species in the universe. They are evil, obedient, and stupid. Even if they found their way through the wardrobe, which is unlikely, they would not dare enter consecrated ground."

"But what about the thing you said rides with them?"

"It is the reason we have to leave as soon as dawn breaks," he looked at his watch, it is 5 o'clock it will be soon. We are going to Heiligtum."

I heard a child's voice. "Sean has woken up," I said. Confused I asked, "Are we going back through the tunnel?"

"No, we leave for Heiligtum."

"Who do you mean by us? Who is going to Heiligtum?"

"We all are," he said, sitting down beside me. "Erica the only way to stop this is to find the gate and close it. Stephan and I will help you. The one that rides with the Hunt brought them here, to where James thought Sean would be safe, but he may not be safe until the gates are all closed. We leave as soon as dawn breaks. Christina and Frank are anxious to go home. Helga has not seen her son Kurt for weeks and we cannot leave Doria here alone. We have prepared, there is a large motor home waiting outside. We will travel together. It will take five or six hours for us to get there. From there we can arrange for Gill and Jack to come and take Sean home. You have the keys. Together we will find the gate."

By the time night had faded away. The sun shone brightly on a sky with clouds no more than streaks, as though a child had drawn a white pen across the blue sky. The six-berth motor home was new and very comfortable. Four seats with seatbelts at the front. A table with wrap around seating at the rear, that folded down into single and double beds and two more beds that folded down from the roof. It was a perfect place for James to rest. The kitchen had a cooker and microwave and a shower and toilet. Sean was so excited at travelling in the big motor home. More to pin him down than any other reason, Otto let him sit at the front, on the child seat provided by the company they hired it from. Doria sat beside him because she got travel sick in the back. Stephan, Otto, and Frank shared the driving. We stopped only once, for an hour. To Sean's delight we stopped at McDonald's and he had a happy meal. The children's meal with complimentary toy. We arrived at Heiligtum around three. Helga had called Kurt and he was waiting for us in the driveway. He went immediately to Frank; it was obvious something was wrong. Christina went to find out. "Come ,she said "we can go in but be prepared." She ran back to Frank.

Prepared for what? Well it was unbelievable, the castle had been trashed, vandalised. Beautiful vases and clocks smashed to smithereens. Paintings lying on the floor, their canvas slashed with a knife. Nazi graffiti painted on the walls. Tapestries torn to shreds. They had been in every single room, looking for something, because according to Kurt there was nothing missing.

Chapter 16

The Tapestry

Christina was in tears, "Who would do this? Who would destroy beautiful irreplaceable paintings and tapestries?" She buried her head in Frank's shoulder, shutting out the horror of the devastated room, only to lift her head seconds later her face red with anger. She furiously rattled out in German, what I took to be a threat to kill the people who were responsible for this carnage. She quickly curtailed her language, when she noticed Sean was standing beside her, looking up with a worried, completely bewildered expression. She leaned down and hugged him. "It's alright Sean, I am just angry with the bad people who did this."

I said, "Does he know what you were saying?"

"He speaks fluent German." Otto said, smiling with raised eyebrows.

I laughed. "Nothing surprises me anymore."

Kurt arrived later that day. He was shocked and defensive, as it had been his job to check the Heiligtum while everyone was away. He asked Frank if he had called the police. Christina said," no, we should wait. There is little or nothing the police can do, and their presence would hinder our search for the gate."

Kurt spoke to Frank in German and Frank answered back in German. Then Frank said, "he is asking about the insurance, but there is none. It would have meant too many prying eyes."

Helga and Kurt catered for dinner and Sean was put to bed early, excited that Mummy and Daddy were coming the next day. Exhausted from stress and travel, we all opted for an early night. Deciding the mess would be better tackled the next day.

"What about James?" I asked no one in particular.

Kurt said he would check James regularly during the night, but I had already decided it was something I wanted to do, and so I insisted I would sit with him. Helga lit a fire in his room and Frank took a mattress from the next bedroom. I slept on the floor that night. Luckily, James slept all night and I only woke in the morning when he knocked over a glass, as he tried to fill it with water.

"Let me get that for you." I threw back the duvet and got up quickly to help him.

"Have you been there all night?" he asked, sitting up and holding onto the strapping over his cracked rib.

"Yes, I am a genuine little Florence Nightingale." I poured the water and sat on the bed to help him drink it. He sipped it slowly. "How are you feeling?"

"I have a splitting headache. I was dreaming. I was in a farm. There were lots of pigs around. But when I woke up, I realised it was just you snoring."

"Me snoring! Never. I do not snore."

He laughed. "Yes, that's what they all say."

"Frank left you some painkillers, but you should eat something first. Are you hungry?"

"A little"

"That's a good sign."

"How do I look?"

"You look as though you had a few rounds with Mike Tyson, and it looks like he won the match."

"Dam, has he spoiled my good looks?"

"No, since you didn't have any in the first place."

"Touché," he said laughing.

"What time is it?""

"Around six, what would you like? Coffee and toast?"

"Yes, thank you," he said groaning, and again attempting to sit up."

"Take your time, I slipped my arm round his back, feeling the firm muscles under the soft skin, I was ridiculously nervous touching him, as he leaned towards me, while I propped the pillows.

197

"He sat up upright. looking around the room. What is this place? Where am I?"

"It's Heiligtum."

"Where? He looked bewildered for a moment, then he said "yes it's…He hesitated. … wait, I know…it's Christina's home in Germany."

"Yes, Heiligtum. Don't you remember coming here last night?"

"No. I don't remember much."

Now I was worried." James what's the last thing you remember?"

He lay back on the pillow and rubbed his head. "This damned headache, I don't remember anything."

"Don't you remember coming here yesterday, in the motorhome?" He looked at me blankly.

"A motorhome! I was in a motorhome?"

"Look, take a minute. I'll go and make some coffee and toast." I squeezed his hand. As I opened the bedroom door he called after me to wait. I turned back, a cloak of unease creeping over me. He looked bewildered; he kept rubbing his forehead."

"What is it?" He didn't answer. "James do you remember me?"

He looked perplexed at my question. "Of course, I remember you. I just don't remember coming here."

I came back and sat on the edge of the bed. "What do you remember?" Before he could answer there was a gentle tap at the door. "Come in." I called.

The door opened and Otto came in. "Good morning. it is early but I heard voices. How are you both this morning? "Did you sleep well on that mattress Erica?"

"Yes, thank you I did"

"And James how are you this morning?

"A bit confused and with a headache. I don't remember coming here, at least not yesterday and in a motorhome of all things. Why was I in a motor home?"

"What is the last thing you do remember?" Otto asked.

James lay back and closed his eyes when he opened them, he said. "It's coming back. I remember coming here with Stephan. We found the boy, Sean. Oppenheim and his mob Die Brueder were holding him here. Is he alright? It's all a bit hazy. Have I been in an accident in this motorhome you talk about?"

Otto said "Sean is safe? There was no accident. You were severely injured, you were tortured, you took a beating from Die Brueder. I hypnotised you and erased the experience, in order to give both mind and body time to heal. That and strong painkillers will account for the memory loss. You have slept through the past few weeks, dropping in and out of consciousness. Stephan and Frank rescued you and took you to the Van Brugan house in Potsdam. There is no need to worry, you are healing well, and you will soon be back to normal."

"Will he get those memories back? "I asked. Selfishly I was thinking of those precious moments in the church when he told me he loved me."

"I could hypnotise him and bring them back" I was a little embarrassed when he said, "I know why you ask this Erica, but would you want him to relive the moments of torture. Would you want him to live with that stress? It could change the James you know forever."

I made my way along the dark corridor and down the main staircase. Heiligtum is a gloomy place with dark wood panelling halfway up walls. Walls heavily decorated with paintings and tapestries, weapons, and bits of armour. A creepy place to be in, on your own. I hurried to the main staircase. A staircase wide and made of highly polished wood, it swept down into the main entrance hall. I then went slowly, creeping quietly, presuming everyone else was still sleeping. The doors to the rooms on the ground floor lay open and I stopped, for, from my elevated viewing point, I could see the extent of the damage. The mindless vandalism was displayed before me. Shards of pottery and glass, smashed period furniture, ripped cushions, and shredded canvas. All that beauty, the work of skilled artists through the centuries, destroyed forever by mindless hooligans. The malicious destruction of these treasures was devastating. Almost every room had been ransacked. At the foot of the stairs a solitary piece of tapestry lay, about the size of a face cloth. I picked it up. Though faded, the colours and style were familiar, it was part of a garden, grass, and trees. There was another larger piece outside the dining room door, longer, about the size of a tea towel. Looking at it there was something hauntingly familiar about it, though I didn't remember seeing the tapestry before.

The dining room had been destroyed, the beautiful highly polished table that sat at least twenty people, was littered with the remnants of tapestries and paintings torn from the walls. I picked up a few and found another piece the same texture, colours, and style, but it though it depicted grass, it had been ripped through a greyish circle. that looked like stone. I took the three pieces of tapestry and went back along the hall and down the few steps that led to the kitchen. To my surprise Christina was already there. She sat at the table, already dressed in a bright white hoodie and blue jeans, her long red hair scraped back from her face. She was nursing a mug of coffee. She was also very pale, and her eyes were red and swollen from crying.

"You're up early. "I said

"I couldn't sleep. I woke up in the middle of the night and remembered what had happened, I couldn't get back to sleep. The mess Erica, she swallowed tears, the beautiful irreplaceable things lost forever."

I put my arm around her shoulder. "I know its soul destroying, but they are only possessions Christina. It could have been much worse. They are dangerous men. Frank, James, and Stephan could have been killed saving. We could have been killed if we had come here earlier." I sat down beside her. "What I don't understand is why Die Brueder would destroy all these valuables. They could have simply taken it and sold it on the black market.

"It wasn't Die Brueder who did this. Otto told me last night. It was the Hunt. Dietrich Oppenheim knew about the Hunt and local people had reported seeing them recently in the vicinity of Heiligtum. Oppenheim thought he could control them; Otto said he performed a ritual that summoned them. He then foolishly gave them permission to enter Heiligtum and they killed him and took his men. His was the body that you and Katie found in the cellar. The hooded cape was a warning they were around. They came back, it is not Die Brueder but The Wild Hunt who are responsible for this destruction." She looked at the pieces of cloth in my hand. "Have you started clearing up already."

"No, but wait, I will explain, but I am supposed to be making coffee for James". I started to rise from the chair."

A voice said, "I will do that Madam." Helga appeared at the door. Already in her black dress and stiff white apron. "Would you like me to take it to his room?"

"Yes, thank you Helga." I said "A pot of coffee and two cups please and some toast. Otto is with him."

Christina added "And a pot of tea and some toast for us too please Helga we will take it in the morning room."

I followed Christina to the beautiful room near the end of the entrance all. It had large floor to ceiling windows, that flooded the room with morning sunlight. A stone fireplace, a polished oak writing desk, a few winged chairs and a bookcase were the only furniture. It was decorated with Chinese azure blue silk curtains and chair cushions, patterned with white birds and flowers. A rug of the same hue and colour lay in front of the fire. Christina shook her head "I always loved this room. I used to lie on this rug when I was a child and read my books."

The curtains had been torn to shreds and the cushions ripped apart. The bookcase had been toppled and its contents strewn across the floor. Christina picked up one of the few books still intact. "This was one of my favourite books as a child," she said. The book was worn and rubbed at the edges, damaged only by time and love, unlike the rest lying on the floor. The illustration on the cover was of a rabbit with a suitcase. Christina red out the title. *"Abenteuerliche Briefe von Felix. Letters from Felix*. It is the story of a little girl who lost her stuffed rabbit called Felix at an airport. She is devastated till she starts getting letters from him, from all over the world. I loved it so much my mother got fed up reading it to me and used to make my father take turns. She knelt beside the fireplace, put a match to the kindling and the flames burst into life. "Come sit here Erica. You look frozen." I did as she asked, I was cold, being still in my pyjamas and a very thin hoodie. I was glad of the warmth from the fire. "Tell me how James is this morning?" She asked.

"Better, he says but…"

"But what?"

"He has memory loss. He doesn't remember anything, from finding Sean, to waking up in the bedroom here."

"Really! How awful. We must take him to a hospital."

"No, there is no need. Otto hypnotised him, made him forget everything, in order to help his mind, recover from the memory of the torture. Otto also put it down to the strong pain medication he was giving him, and I trust he is telling the truth. He said James' memory will return quickly now his body is healing. I trust Otto."

"Ok, if you are sure." She looked at me sympathetically, knowingly. "Then he does not remember Potsdam?" She asked.

"No."

"Not the tunnel? Or the moment in the church?"

"No, nothing." It was obvious to me then, that she had seen us kiss. I didn't want to talk about it, so I quickly changed the subject. "Take a look at these. I found these pieces of tapestry. I think they are very important. I handed her one."

"Why?" She took one from me.

"Look at them. See if you recognise anything. Where was this tapestry hanging?"

She examined the larger piece, where you could clearly see grass and a tree and a gate. The smaller piece, with the same colour tones had mud stuck to it, but it was still possible to see the gate and a half circle of stones. "It's the garden tapestry, it has always hung here, in the morning room, on that wall above the fire."

"What do you know about it?"

"It's very old. It was a red-haired girl walking through a garden towards a gate. My father used to tell me, that is what I would look like when I grew up."

"Could you see her face?"

"No, she is walking away from the observer. Only her back is visible."

"Were there keys in the painting?" I felt excited.

"Yes, the girl held one in her hand and there were some more keys scattered around."

I stood up. "We really need to find the other pieces of this tapestry."

"Why is this so important?"

"Because I think this tapestry and a painting in James flat, hold the clue to where the gate is. I explained as much as I could to her. "James has a flat in Glasgow. Jonah came down from Aberdeen when Sean went missing. James invited him to stay in his flat. Avoiding a hotel bill, Jonah gratefully accepted, but when he arrived at the flat there was no sign of James. The flat turned out to be a luxury penthouse by the river. It was so not what Jonah expected. He was stunned by the opulence of the flat and asked Katie and I to come and see it. We were as surprised as Jonah. We could not understand how James could afford such luxury. We still haven't got to the bottom of that. Anyway, there was a painting on the wall in the living space. It was a red-haired girl walking in a garden. Walking towards a gate. A gate that looked exactly like the one we found in the cellar at Lanshoud and there were keys, not obvious at first, but when we looked closely, we could see the keys hidden in the foliage." I pointed to the fragment with the girl in it. "Christina it's the same girl and the same garden in these fragments of tapestry. Only on this piece there is that half circle of rocks. I don't remember seeing anything like that on the painting. If it is the only difference, then it is maybe a clue to where the gate is. we must find it and close it, you know that."

"How could the painting be the same as the tapestry? That tapestry is hundreds of years old. Was the painting an old one?"

"No, it was fresh, new, an oil on canvas."

"Who could have painted it? The tapestry has never been anywhere but here in Heiligtum and Heiligtum has never been open to the public."

"Right now, that doesn't matter. That tapestry and the painting carried a message. I believe it will tell us where the Heiligtum gate is."

She swallowed hard. She shook her head. I saw her knuckles were white as she gripped the piece of tapestry and suddenly,

I realised how afraid she was. She was trembling. Selfishly, I had forgotten how she had suffered and almost died at the hands of the things that had come through the Lanshoud gate, and now she knew the same creatures had rampaged through her home. They could come back.

"No." She shook her head violently." There are no gates in any of the gardens here, that look like the one in the tapestry. As you said it, looks like the one you found at Lanshoud."

"Christina, the one at Lanshoud was not a real solid iron gate, it was an illusion. It looked just like that one on the tapestry and painting. It was a copy of the entrance to a Nazi death camp during the Second World War. It was a symbol, carrying a message, that here was the entrance to Hell on earth." I shivered and wrapped my hoodie around, just saying it out loud brought back the terrifying memories of standing before that gate. "According to our mutual biological father Luke Treadstone, Hell is not a physical place on earth, but another world in another dimension. The entrance through it is not a physical passage, but a portal that allows entry to Hell, but not exit. That is why they hunt our planet. Because Luke entered from his own world and exited here. He is the reason the Hunt ride.

They have been hunting him for centuries. He left these gates open. As I see it, there is no circle of rocks on the painting in Glasgow, it's the only difference. I have a feeling those rocks are important." I pointed to the fragments. "They may be a clue, something to do with the portal here at Heligtum."

I was interrupted when the door knocked, and Helga came in with a tray of tea and toast. The relaxed ,familiar way I had seen her address Christina in Potsdam had gone and she had returned to her formal ways. She said, "Madam, I am sure you will be pleased to know that Mr Anderson has already eaten his breakfast and has asked for more." She smiled, something she seldom did. She liked James. "Also, Mr Reinhardt said to tell you that Sean's parents will be arriving at Munich on the 10.30 flight. Kurt and Stephan will collect them and bring them here if that alright with you? Is there anything else you require?" Helga glowered at me. She could see Christina was upset.

Christina pulled herself together "No, thank you Helga, I am very pleased to hear James is eating, do you know if Sean is awake yet?"

"Yes, Sean is awake and sitting on Mr Anderson's bed eating toast. Mr Anderson insisted I leave him there. Mr Frank and Mr Reinhardt are there keeping an eye on him. Sean said thank you for his toast and milk. He then told me his Mummy and Daddy were coming today and my toast was better than theirs, because Mummy and Daddy always burnt his toast. He has requested another large plateful."

Christina said. "He is a little rascal Helga, don't pander to him."

"It is no trouble Madam I am quite fond of the little boy. He promised he will help me to wash up the dishes and I will see that he does."

Helga left closing the door behind her. Christina said, "she will do you know. She believes in gentle daily discipline of children. She was great with him at Potsdam. She will have him up to his elbows in soap suds, even though there is a perfectly good dishwasher in the kitchen."

The moment Helga left we started sifting through the debris, stopping only to drink some tea and take bite of toast. It didn't take long to find most of the tapestry, almost all, except the crucial piece, that was different from the painting in Glasgow. That was the rest of the stone circle.

"It's not here." I said exasperated. "The one bit we need has been stuck to a shoe or something." We need to check the rest of the house." As I opened the door, it dawned on me. "Why do we need to find it? If this was your favourite room and you spent a lot of time here and that tapestry has hung here for centuries, how come you don't know anything about that circle of rocks or stones or whatever they are?"

"I didn't spend my life studying it. It was just there above the fireplace. Anyway, I didn't say I didn't know there was a circle of stones in the tapestry. I said I didn't know what it was, and I certainly have never seen it in the gardens." She thought for a moment. "Though Kurt might. We have a firm of gardeners who look after the grounds and Kurt supervises their work. If anyone knows it will be Kurt."

Helga came in to collect the tray. I asked her where Kurt was, she said he had already left for the airport to collect jack and Gill. I asked her to look at the stones on the fragment. "Do you remember seeing this in the tapestry that hung here. Do you know what these stones are?"

"Yes, I do." It's the well."

"The well!" Christina and I said at the same time.

Christina was surprised. "We have well? I didn't know about. Why has no one ever mentioned there was a well in the gardens?" She turned to me. "Honestly, Erica, I have never seen it or been told of it? Helga why is that?"

Helga shivered. "I imagine it was to protect you. It is a bad place, no one goes there. It is considered bad luck to even speak of it. The local people believe that something very evil lives in that well and many people have disappeared in that part of the forest."

"The forest? We are talking about a well in the gardens." Christina said.

"There is no well in the gardens, near the house Madam. The well lies further down, deep in the forest, but part of the grounds that belong to Heiligtum. The gardeners who are under contract to manage the grounds will not go there."

"I want to go there." I said. "Could you tell me how to get there?"

Helga shook her head violently." I do not know exactly where it is and even if I did, I would not take you there. No", she said emphatically, "no one goes near the well."

"But Kurt must know where it is." Christina said. "It is his job to manage all the grounds belonging to Heiligtum."

Helga very quickly became upset." My son will not take you there, please do not ask him to do this." She looked genuinely afraid of something.

Christina said, "it's alright Helga don't worry. I am sure Frank will know where it is. Have you seen my husband this morning? Is he up yet?"

"Yes, he is with Mr Anderson and Mr Reinhardt. If you need me Madam, I will be in the kitchen supervising the washing of breakfast dishes in the sink."

The moment she left. I said, "that's it, that well is the entrance to the gate. It also explains why the legend of the Wilde Jagg is so strong in this area. We have to find that well."

"Yes, and Frank must know where it is. What I don't understand is why he never told me?"

"To stop you looking for it on your own I suppose. Are you sure Frank knows about it? You didn't."

"Erica, you are here to look for the gate. Even if we hadn't realised the significance of the tapestry. The superstition surrounding the well makes it an obvious place to start looking. Yet has never even mentioned it. That's odd. We need to speak to him."

Jack, Gill, and Katie arrived later that day and we spent the whole day, all of us, clearing the mess and finding the missing pieces of cloth from the tapestry, in the hope there might be something to indicate the location of the well. James sat at the table and worked with Sean. They matched the pieces of tapestry together as we found them, like a jigsaw puzzle. We did find most of it, but in the end, other than what looked like a well, it was exactly like the painting in the penthouse, so we were no further on. When we asked Kurt, he said yes, there was a well, somewhere in the forest, near the old village, but he had never seen it, never been able to find it. He told us, there were tales among local people that the devil lived in it, waiting to catch children. Kurt believed the stories were concocted to keep children from wandering into the forest and getting lost.

Jack said he was probably right. Why would a well be dug in such an isolated place, when the whole purpose of a well is to provide water, in this case either for Heiligtum or for the local village. Frank added that there would be no need for a well even if it weren't isolated because the mountain streams provided all the water they needed. James suggested speaking to the people in the village. Kurt said there were no people in the village anymore nor had there been for at least one hundred years. The village was in ruins now; however, he did know there was one cottage with a roof still standing. He told us the story of when he was at school, when he and his friends who were thirteen years old decided to spend a night camping in that cottage.

Helga helped him tell that story of how the four boys, three thirteen-year olds and one twelve-year-old had lied about where they were camping. Kurt, she was ashamed to say, was the ringleader. The boys told their parents that they were camping in the gardens at Heiligtum, but they had no intention of going there. The whole purpose of their trip was to look for the well.

Kurt interjected at that point, saying it was all about proving how mature and brave they were. Coming back to school with photographs of a place steeped in superstition would have raised their credibility with the other boys, and the girls would have seen them in a new light. Unfortunately, it all went wrong, they just couldn't find it.

It was getting dark and as the evening wore on the boys realised, they were completely lost. By the time they came across the old cottage they had been walking in light rain for at least an hour. They were cold, tired, and grateful for shelter. Shelter they deemed to be better than just the tent. There was no glass in the windows, but the cracked wooden shutters and doors still closed enough to keep the rain out, though the wind whistle eerily through the cracks. Dried moss, stones and animal droppings littered the floor. There was a fireplace and some bits of broken furniture. They gathered wood, heaps of wood Kurt said, and together they cleared all the debris with a fallen a tree branch. There was no way of pitching the tent, so they spread it on the floor, in front of the fire, it was better than putting their sleeping bags on cold stone. With dried moss and sticks they built a fire and cooked sausages on sticks, taking turns at telling ghost stories. It had all been scary fun. Kurt laughed at this part of his memory. Wrapped up warm in their sleeping bags, they were quite happy until, around midnight, when the noises and screams started. They told themselves it was nothing more than owls and foxes, but still clung together like frightened rabbits, afraid to sleep. They lit every torch and candle they had brought with them and stayed like that until they could stay awake no longer. Huddled together on the floor beside the fire, is how the men found them in the morning.

"Think back, "James said, "was there anything out of place, anything unusual?"

Kurt said, "we did find two stones that were highly polished and engraved with symbols."

Jack sat up sharply. "Engraved! What did the symbols look like? And how far apart were they."

"A distance just enough to see one from the other. They were carved in great detail, so much that we wanted to take them home as souvenirs of our trip, but they were too heavy to lift. I can't remember the symbols exactly. I have not looked at them for years, but I can show you," he said. "It was my friend Heinrich's thirteenth birthday; that was the reason we were allowed to go camping, he wanted a tent and a camping adventure as his gift. That and the fact we were supposed to be camping in the safety of the gardens here, was the reason we were allowed to go. Heinrich got a camera for his birthday, from his grandfather. He photographed everything on our camping trip and gave us all copies. I have kept them all in an album. There is a photo of one of the stones among them."

"This could be important Kurt, can you put your hands on it now. We need to see that album," Jack said.

"Yes of course. I will get it." Kurt went immediately.

As he left, a little voice said, "Daddy there is one on the cloth." We all turned to look at Sean. He had been sitting quietly beside James, drawing birds and animals. He held out a little fragment of the tapestry. "Here Daddy, I think this is what you are looking for."

He had been so quiet I had forgotten he was there. Jack took the tiny piece of cloth from Sean's outstretched hand. It was definitely from the Garden Tapestry. It was such a tiny spot on the cloth that Jack asked for a magnifying glass. Frank fetched one from the morning room desk and Jack peered through it at the small dark spot on the cloth. He lifted his head exasperated. "It looks like a stone, but the fabric is so worn it's impossible to see clearly. Hopefully, Kurt's photos will be better."

"What are you thinking it might be? "James asked.

"I don't want to say until I am sure. If it's what I think it is then it's probably what we are looking for."

Otto called "Sean." In a gentle tone.

Sean stood up sharply, with the discipline of a highly trained soldier responding to an officer. "Yes Sir" he said.

Only Christina and I looked surprised. No one else seemed to notice the strange formality of Sean's reaction. I would say a it was a, very strange reaction, for a five-year-old only, I didn't know what age he was supposed to be.

Otto's said. "Sean, your father cannot see the pattern on the stone. Can you see it?"

"Yes Sir."

"Can you draw it for him?" Otto asked.

Sean turned to Jack. "Don't worry Daddy, I will draw the stone and symbol for you." He took his pencil and pad and proceed to draw an extremely detailed copy of the stone.

There have been many occasions in those last few years when I likened myself to Alice in wonderland, only mine was a much darker wonderland and a much deeper rabbit hole, however, that day in Heiligtum was the most bizarre of all. No one seemed to question the fact Sean had not only been listening to the adult conversation but had correctly interpreted the problem. It was as strange as the events of the morning. Let me paint a picture for you.

I would like you to imagine the scene where distraught parents, those being Jack and Gill, are being reunited with their baby, the baby being Sean. Yes, Sean, the baby who was kidnapped only weeks ago. A baby for whom the media and the entire Scottish police force have been searching. The parents are ecstatic. Sean runs towards them. Before he was kidnapped his vocabulary was limited to baby gurgles, but now he was calling out "Mummy, Daddy I missed you so much. He throws himself at Gill with hurricane force and almost sends her flying. "Oh sweetheart!" Gill says hugging him. Look how you have grown. What on earth has Aunt Christina been feeding you."

"Lots and lots of nice things, "he said beaming. He spots Katie. "Auntie Katie! You came too, how nice." Sean hugged her. "I hope you all had a pleasant journey."

Now that was creepy. Not the turn of phrase you would expect from a five-year-old; yet with faces full of love, they showed no sign of surprise that Sean was running towards them. They didn't blink an eyelid but just scooped up this sturdy boy, hugging him, telling him how much they missed him and asking if he had a good holiday.

It was absolutely unbelievable. Katie had come with Jack and Gill, no surprise there then, after all, Katie was not one to miss out on a get together, but strangely she had the same reaction, to Sean. I looked over at Otto and Christina. They were watching me with the raised eyebrows of an I told you so. They had told me, that much was true. I had seen the photos on my mobile and seeing is believing, but this happy family reunion was a stretch of anyone's imagination and believe me, mine has been stretched to the point of snapping. The whole scene was totally bizarre.

Dreamlike as this scene in the hall was. I knew it was real to everyone around me. I knew without a doubt, when I went home, to my flat in Glasgow, there would no longer be reporters hanging around outside and no Valdez sniffing around looking for a crime she could pin on me. The kidnapping of the baby wasn't just old news, it hadn't happened. It had been wiped from everyone's memory

While all the hugging and laughing went on, James and Frank appeared at the top of the stairs. James looked good. He would have looked back to normal only he was a bit stiff and his face had patches of yellow where the bruising had faded. I wondered what slant or twist would be put on the story of his injuries sustained while rescuing Sean, because now, as far as they were all concerned, he had never been rescued in the first place. I didn't have to wait long. Gill immediately launched into sympathy telling him how horrified they were when they heard what had happened.

Heard what? I was still wondering, till Jack said. "At least you got out alive James, it's good to see you on your feet. That bus driver should be prosecuted."

Ah! I thought, that was the cover story, a road accident. They went on to discuss it in amazing detail, which when you consider that it hadn't actually happened, was quite incredible. I wondered how the piles of newspapers, on the coffee table with the front-page headlines of a child abduction had been dealt with. Even if they binned those papers, hundreds of others had been sold and there were the recorded TV interviews.

Sean started drawing, with Jack watching intently beside him, when he had finished Otto held up Sean's drawing of a smooth round stone with a symbol carved on it.

"Do you know what it is?" Gill asked Jack, looking over his shoulder at her son's artwork. "That is amazing Sean, you are a very good artist?"

"Amazing really." James said picking up the fragment of cloth, "considering we can't see it with a magnifying glass."

Jack said, "it looks a bit like a Masonic Symbol." He turned it round and round looking at it from different angles. "Otto do you know what this means?" There was no answer and as we all looked around Otto had gone, and no one had seen or even heard him move."

A serious little voice said. "Daddy, Otto said to tell you he has gone for help"

Otto hadn't spoken. Though I did see Otto make eye contact with Sean. It reminded me of the young men Katie had pointed out, whom we could see from our hotel window in Potsdam. They had been standing in silence just looking at each other. At this point I realised that Sean and Otto were telepathic.

We were passing the drawing around when Kurt returned with photographs. Heinrich had indeed been a prolific photographer, there were at least thirty snaps of the boys in their tent, in the cottage, cooking and eating sausages. The rest were mostly just the boys sitting on grass or climbing a tree. There were three that caught our interest. Two were close ups of flat round stones and one showed their distance apart. The symbol in each stone was different.

"I am going to send this to Eli," Jack said, "he will be our best bet at translating this." He then copied and emailed the photographs and sent a text to Eli's mobile asking him to check his emails. Eli's response to Jack was totally unexpected. For a start it was an instant reply. Eli was notorious for not picking up emails and texts. and he gave no explanation. Jack showed us, it read.

I am willing to come directly. I cannot stress enough. Do not look for the stones till I get there. I have seen these symbols before. I believe these are steppingstones, leading the way to, if I am right, what you think is a well. It is not a well but an inverted tower and very dangerous. This a momentous find Jack." Then he added "*Could you give me directions to get there, please.*"

Jack called Eli and asked him if he could ready for the following morning. Frank arranged everything and insisted on footing the bill. Stephan would pick Eli up at the airport and Jack would go with him.

Chapter 17

The Well

Jack and Eli sat up most of that night pouring over the photographs of the stones and Sean's drawings. Eli, who had not even noticed Sean's sudden and dramatic growth spurt, had been seriously impressed by the intricate reproduction of the symbols and attention to detail evident in such a young child.

When morning came and I came down for breakfast. I found Eli and Jack drinking coffee and locked in a serious discussion with Frank and James. Ironically, James looked well, whereas Eli was pale and drawn and Jack looked haggard. "What is it? What has happened?" I asked.

James answered, "The Hunt were outside last night?"

"Eli and I both saw them." Jack said.

Eli held up his arm. "Look my hand it is still shaking." He made a poor attempt at laughing it off, though he was obviously traumatised by what he had seen."

"I didn't hear a thing." I said, sliding into a chair beside them, with my pot of tea.

"That was the odd thing." Jack said looking to Eli for confirmation. "They didn't make a sound. If Eli hadn't insisted on putting our cups in the sink, we wouldn't even have known they were there. By the way Frank, you might want to have a word with Helga. She was none too pleased, about the broken crockery, even though Eli apologised profusely for dropping the tray. Apparently, there were plenty of mugs in the cupboard we could have used, but unfortunately the cups we used were part of a vintage tea set, which had escaped the carnage of the burglary."

Eli sighed. "Yes, I am so sorry, I will of course, pay for the damage. I am embarrassed to say I was frozen with fear when I saw them. It is one thing to talk about the Hunt but another to see it. Those hooded figures, on gigantic steeds with hot coals for eyes, staring straight at me. It was the most terrifying sight." He clasped his hands together to stop them shaking.

Frank said "Please don't worry about the cups Eli. It could have happened to anyone of us. I might have dropped more than a tray if I had seen them." He said, making light of it. "Helga gets carried away with her importance as housekeeper of Heiligtum. She sometimes forgets that our friends are more important to us than our possessions."

I said, "he's right Eli. The first time, when Katie and I heard them tapping on windows and doors. We were terrified. We didn't even see them. We could only hear them. We were alone in Lanshoud and petrified with fear. I swear, for a moment my heart stopped beating. I couldn't breathe."

Eli nodded, he was so pale and tired, he looked as though he had aged overnight. It was a few moments before his hands stopped shaking, and then only because a Jack put a mug of coffee before him and he put his hands round it He said, "I have always been slightly jealous of the fact you had seen such a well-known mythological entity as the Wild Hunt. I had a great interest in them at one time and I have read many witness reports. Of course, one never truly believes in the existence of such creatures. I now see, now see mythology in a new light. I fear the sight of those hellish creatures will haunt my dreams forever."

At this point, as always, guaranteed to lift the mood, a sleepy Katie came into the kitchen. Still in her pyjamas and hoodie, she was rubbing her eyes and trying to persuade her mane of black curls to stay behind her ears. She said, "good morning everyone" and complained of being jet-lagged. Jack pointed out it was only a three-hour flight and on the same time frame, so how can she be jet lagged. She turned from the coffee she was pouring and retorted that she was jet-lagged because she was on a jet, that lagged and missed it's time slot for landing. There was really no answer to that, so Jack didn't bother to try. He just chuckled.

I asked Eli about the translation he had been working on. He didn't answer at first but sighed and looked pointedly at Jack. There was a moment of silence, broken only when James asked, "Have you been able to translate even part of it?"

It was obvious Eli seemed reluctant to answer, then Jack said, "Eli do you want me to tell them?"

I could see Eli was trying to pull himself together physically and mentally. He pushed the edge of Sean's drawing towards me saying. "It is the language of the dead."

That made my blood run cold. "Do you mean a dead language? I asked. "Like Latin."

He rubbed his forehead. "No, I mean the language spoken by the dead. These symbols speak of despair, spoken by evil to those with no hope." He pointed to Sean's drawing. "I have seen these symbols before. They are a corruption of those, found in the journals of John Dee and Edward Kelly. Do you know of John Dee?" He asked me directly.

"Yes," I replied, he was..." that was a far as I got, when Katie asked, "You mean the people who make tractors?"

"Tractors!" Eli eyes widened, he as was confused as was Frank and that set James and Jack off laughing.

Katie was offended. What's so amusing?"

"I'm sorry Katie." James said still chuckling away. "Yes of course, John Dee are a firm who make tractors.'

"So?" She asked, still rattled, "what's your point."

"I was referring to a historical figure, Katie." Eli said

Now she cut him off. "I am well aware of who John Dee was Eli. He was that dodgy guy who tried to turn metal in to gold in Elizabethan times. I just thought you were going to say the stones had been dug up by a tractor. A lot of strange things have been found in farmers' fields you know." She was so serious it was too much for Jack and James who were off again, in a fit of childish giggles.

Eli tried to placate Katie who was getting annoyed." You are quite right my dear, only much more. John Dee was a mathematician, astrologer, and occult philosopher. He was an advisor to Queen Elizabeth the first. He and his spirit medium Sir Edward

Kelly were heavily involved in occult practice and spent much of their time in alchemy and divination. When John Dee died in 1608 his journals contained a language, he believed to be the language of angels. Which he supposedly wrote down after it was given to Sir Edward Kelly during a séance. It was named the Enochian language after Enoch who according to biblical tradition lived till he was 365 years old, then went to heaven without dying first. There were many theories around Enochian. There is a school of thought that it was manufactured by Edward Kelly to fool John Dee who had been heaping pressure on him to achieve results. No one truly knows. All I can tell you is, that it is the Enochian language that is carved on these stones. The message on these stones speak of pointing the way. It reads

For you who must pass through the Gates, these steppingstones lead the way. Climb down to the top of the inverted tower. Illusion to reality, light to dark, life to eternal damnation."

"I don't understand, a well is a well. Why suddenly call it an inverted tower?" I asked.

Eli explained. "A well is built to provide a water supply. An inverted tower is built for an entirely different reason. There are only two inverted towers in the world, both lie in Sintra in Portugal." He opened his notebook and took out a card and put it on the table and then there is this" This is a tarot card from the Major Arcana. The most important cards in a Tarot Deck. Look carefully at it. It is a tower struck with a lightning bolt through the top, look and see the flames. The figures are falling, escaping the flames through the windows cut in stone wall of the tower. It is said to represent, upheaval, chaos, and revelation. Now…" he put a finger on the card and turned it. "…if the card comes out reversed, from the deck, it then called the inverted tower and is said to represent, fear of change, and averting disaster. Make of that what you will, but look at the card, inverted now the figures are escaping fire and flying upwards to the top of the well or tower." He pointed to the bottom of the inverted card where flames burned.

He placed a photograph on the table. "In the town of Sintra in Portugal lies the incredible Quinta da Regaleira. A gothic palace built on a gothic landscape full of weird and wonderful things. The whole area is a world heritage site. It has two inverted towers in the grounds both linked by underground tunnels. The largest is called the Initiation Well. And it is believed that Masonic initiation rites may have been performed there. I have been there; many years ago. it is an incredible sight. Shaped like a large deep well it has a staircase between outer and inner walls spiralling downwards. There are nine platform on the way down, with fifteen steps between each one. These numbers nine and fifteen are significant and linked to Masonic, Rosicrucian and Tarot mysticism. Also, there is speculation that they may represent the nine levels of Hell in Dante's Inferno. The staircase spiralling downwards is supported by large carved columns. Arched windows cut in the outer wall follow the staircase down, allowing a dim light for those following the staircase to the bottom. At the bottom, Templar, Masonic and Rosicrucian symbols are everywhere including a compass on a Templar cross painted floor."

"It's amazing" Frank said, "I have never heard of this place."

I said, "If there is something like this here. It is exactly what we are looking for. Luke left us clues to help us find the gate at Lanshoud. I think he has done the same here, with the tapestry".

Eli continued to tell us about the Portuguese businessman who was a well-known Freemason and had built the Quinta da Regalia, but he was interrupted when the door burst open and Sean ran in, followed by Gill. Sean ran straight to Jack and climbed on his knee, breathless with excitement he said, "Daddy did you see the big scary horses last night. He laughed. "Mummy was so scared it was funny." He put his fingers around his eyes, shaping them into specs and in the deepest tones he could muster he croaked, "they had big red eyes that glowed in the dark."

Gill her face pale and drawn, was obviously not happy. She didn't even glance our way, she looked straight at Jack. In clipped tones she asked him. "Have you been sitting here all night?"

218

Jack was taken aback at the anger in her voice, he got up and walked over to her presenting a show of repentance that did not convince her. "I'm sorry, time just ran away with us."

One look at Gill's face and Eli hastily added his apologies, saying it really was his fault, since he had asked Jack to help with the translations. Gill was not interested in this excuse; she didn't even look at Eli. Focussed on Jack she said, "Time ran away with you did it? The Hunt was out their Jack, you must have heard them."

Eli in his attempt to help Jack just made it worse. He said. "Oh yes, they were right outside the window. Even though Jack reminded me they could not get in." He said placatingly, ringing his hands. "I was terrified."

Gill slowly turned her head to Jack. She nodded, and in what was almost a whisper and full of disbelief, she said slowly. "You knew, you knew they were out there, and yet you left us, your wife and child, all alone." She shook her head.

Jack probably would have been better saying nothing, rather than making the mistake of reminding her how important it was to translate the stones.

"Oh yes Jack, that's you all over. Get your priorities right. "You... stupid.... big...idiot." She was punching his shoulder. "They could have taken your son." She screamed at him. "He was standing at the window Jack," she punched his shoulders again and again. "He was trying to open it." Her eyes were filling with tears. "That's what woke me. He said he was trying to open the window to see the horses. You knew they were out there, and you left us alone," she shouted at him and then burst into tears. Jack stunned by her outburst caught her hand and pulled her close. She sobbed on his shoulder.

It would have gone on like that only a little voice said, "Mummy I told you they cannot come in unless you invite them."

Gill turned to look at Sean, he looked so upset she knelt beside him. "It's ok darling Mummy is just being silly".

"Please don't cry Mummy, you mustn't be angry with Daddy." Sean's little face had a pleading look. Daddy's work is important"

"Who told you that... Daddy?" She glared at Jack.

"That's enough Gill." Jack was getting angry. "You're upsetting him."

"I'm upsetting him? She said furiously." You've been drinking" she said in disgust. "I can smell it on you."

"I said enough." Jack shouted at her his face contorted in anger". He held up a warning hand. "I said enough." Such was the level of threat in his voice it brought James and Frank to their feet.

"You've been drinking she said in disgust. You are reeking of alcohol."

His finger almost in her face, shouting at her, he retorted "Don't you" … that was as far as he got when scraping his chair back. James shouted "Jack." It was loud enough to make Jack falter.

Gill looked over at the table as if, until then, she had been unaware we were watching the little tableau.

Eli was about to defend Jack when James stopped him. "But he only had one glass of whisky", Eli whispered. That left me wondering if the glass was a pint glass.

Jack tired and defeated, knelt beside Sean, and gently grasped both his arms. He hugged him. "I am sorry Sean that I wasn't with you and Mummy to see the horses, I won't ever leave you again at night,"

Gill her cheeks flushed red, turned, and almost ran out of the kitchen. I stood up to go after her, but Katie pushed her chair out and said, "you stay, I'll go". She poured out two coffees and went after Gill.

Sean with eyes, like saucers was staring straight into Jack's eyes. His little face looked ready to crumble. Jack softened immediately when with a trembling lip, Sean said, "I want to go with Mummy." The accusation was apparent in the child's voice and it hit the spot.

Jack still kneeling hung his head. "We will both go, in a moment Sean, "he said softly. "Sean, tell me first, when did Otto speak to you about the horses? What did he say?"

"When I was drawing the picture of the stone for you, "he told me I might see riders, on big horses. He told me the riders cannot come inside any house unless someone invites them. I wanted to see their faces, I would have asked them to come in, but Mummy wouldn't let me, and Otto told me you must never let them in." He said all of this very seriously with wide-eyed innocence."

Jack took a deep breath and hung his head. "I didn't hear Otto say anything. What else did he say to you? Did he say why he left?"

"Yes." Sean thought for a moment. "Yes, he asked me to help you with the stones and he told me not to worry about anything, because he was going for help."

"What kind of help?"

"I don't know. Why does he need help Daddy? Can we not help him?"

"I don't know son." Jack hugged him, stood up and said "ok, let's go see Mummy."

The moment they left the kitchen, Frank, who had only met Jack for the first time the day before, shook his head, he said "He is a bit of a hot head that man."

"Yes," we all agreed.

I said "Jack is getting worse. He was out of order. I feel so sorry for Gill. She had domineering bully for a father who made her mother's life a misery and now she has ended up with him. How did he come to be like that? He seemed such a nice guy, fool of fun. He made her laugh; she was so happy with Jack."

James agreed. "He was such a nice easy-going guy when we first met him. You're right he was out of order, Gill had good reason to be upset."

Eli took off his specs and rubbed his eyes. "I have known Jack Docherty for many years. As you know we taught together at Glasgow University. Jack has always been an insecure man. A clever man, but lacking faith in his own ability. He was going through a bad patch when he met Gill. He told me he could not believe this beautiful woman could love him. You can see he loves Gill very much but always the fear of losing her hangs over him. He told me in confidence he was devastated because he could not give her a child. Yet now, look, they have a beautiful little boy. He should be happy, but for some reason, he is not. His paranoia and insecurity cause him to seek refuge in alcohol and so he swings between a Jekyll and Hyde persona and in fear that she might leave him, he thinks by dominating her he will prevent it."

I sighed "It could not be worse. If he doesn't want to lose her, he is going the wrong way about it."

"Ah yes, you are thinking Gill will not want a repetition of her childhood." Eli said. "It is I am afraid, a difficult situation." He yawned, "I am so sorry, but my lack of sleep is catching up with me. I must go get some rest."

Frank stood up. You will have to excuse me too. I have some estate business to take care of with Christina, but we will be back by lunchtime. We can talk then. Yes?"

The sun had come out from the clouds and was shining warmly through the window." It's a lovely morning Janes said. Do you fancy a walk in the gardens?

"Yes, if you feel fit enough."

"I wouldn't have asked if didn't, but we will have to wrap up well, it looks nice but there is no heat in that sun. Up here in the mountain it's still very cold."

"Oh well, it will be just like home then." I'm a Glasgow girl remember." He laughed at that.

The gardens were beautiful, full of unusual shrubs and rock formations. We walked for ages finding paths winding in different directions, leading to alcoves with stone seats, statues of Nymphs, even a fountain. Another path led to stone animals, a gigantic Grizzly bear, a tiger, an elephant. "Oh, Sean will love this. "I said.

"Yes, a lot of work has been put into this place."

I could see he was faltering, limping a bit. "Is your leg sore? I asked.

"Yes, a little, let's sit down for a bit. We sat on a stone curved bench in one of the alcoves.

There was a little warmth in the sun and the alcove sheltered us from the bitterly cold wind. He sat rubbing his leg." Come closer "he said, "we can keep each other warm""

222

I shuffled up beside him. Though I was wearing a fleece lined hoodie. I was still feeling the cold. It was lovely sitting there, keeping each other warm, and we sat like that for a while listening to the birds singing and the leaves rustling in the trees. It was a magical place.

"How is your memory now? I asked. Is it coming back?"

"Some of it. The last thing I remember is getting on a plane at Glasgow airport. Frank and Stephan told me I was coming here to give advice to a client who was bringing charges against a UK Newspaper for defamation of character. Apparently, she has got herself another lawyer now, which is just as well because I don't remember anything, not even before the accident."

"Maybe it will come back to you in time," I said knowing full well that Otto had erased the whole episode from James' memory. "You seem to be healing faster than anyone expected."

"I know, and that's down to Otto. I think he must have some medical training or been an army medic maybe. He is a German security officer did you know? Stephan told me a lot of guys leave the army and join the BND."

"Yes." Remember he took Katie and I to Garmisch-Partenkirchen"

"Oh, that's right. There is something I remember after all. I think you will have to keep filling in gaps for me."

We sat quietly again, listening to nature around us. I was trying to find the right moment to ask about the flat, when he saved me the bother by asking, "Do you know if Jonah stayed at my place?"

"Yes, he did. Bye the way, I saw your penthouse,"

"Jonah gave you a tour, did he? I take it you would like an explanation".

"Yes, but please don't bother spinning me a tale."

"Erica there are things I can't tell you."

"There are things you don't have to. I know already you are MI5 or MI6. According to Jonah you are the living and breathing James Bond. Jonah made that very clear."

What can I say? Handsome, suave, brilliant. You can see how Jonah made the connection."

I had to laugh at that. "Just you keep thinking that if it makes you feel good."

He leaned forward hands on his knees. He was scanning the view in front of us. "The penthouse belonged to Chloe Harkins. She had been living there while she passed herself off as a budding solicitor. When she vanished, she was listed as an illegal immigrant and I was given the penthouse to use as a base."

"We suspected she had been there. The shoes and the clothes."

"What shoes?"

"A pair of very expensive red shoes that Katie had seen her wear and the designer collection in the wardrobes. It wasn't you somehow."

"You went through the wardrobes?" He was surprised.

I suddenly felt guilty as if I had been trespassing and refiling through his belongings. I became defensive, "What did you expect? You vanished, no one knew where you were. We were looking for you. Your office was looking for you. Of course, we searched the flat. Are you annoyed that we cared enough to look for you?"

"Who cared?" He was looking straight into my eyes. I wondered if he would ever remember that moment in the church at Potsdam. I wondered, did wiping someone's memory wipe out their emotions too?

"We all did. Are you really asking me that? Katie, Jack, Gill, Jonah, we were all worried about you, even Jonah's girlfriend."

"Jonah has a girlfriend!" he said surprised and laughing at the same time." Well he's a dark horse."

"Yes, Valerie. I really like her. She was a colleague of Jonah's from way past. They met again on the Edinburgh train. I think it's quite serious."

"Really! Well I'm glad. I have a lot of time for Jonah. He's one of life's good guys. It's nice to know he won't be living alone."

I plucked up the courage to ask." Did you live alone? or did you share the flat with Chloe?"

He raised his eyebrows. "Why? Are you jealous? Are you asking me if I slept with her?"

I got a bit flustered, "No, I just wondered." He was grinning like a Cheshire Cat and I was blushing like a stupid teenager." I suddenly felt ridiculous.

In a serious tone he said. "No, I didn't, although it was difficult, because she found me irresistible, still I managed to keep her
at bay."

"Oh, don't tell me? You had to fight her off?"

"Yeah. I did. She was far too glamorous for me, too devious
and too self-obsessed. She wasn't my type."

I groaned. "Really, then what is your type?"

He thought for a moment. "Sensitive, strong, kind, intelligent
women who don't know how beautiful they are."

"Well good luck, you will have a hard time finding one of
them."

He said. "Oh, I don't know. Sometimes they are right under
your nose."

The wind was picking up. I shivered "I think we should go
back," he said." It's getting cold again, I had to agree, though I
would have sat there with him forever, if he had asked me too. As
we strolled back to the house, he asked me, "How did you know I
was here? At Heiligtum."

"Jonah worked it out. He found your stash of weapons and
documents behind the picture. thought you might be travelling
under an alias."

"He is a regular Sherlock Holmes that guy. How did you
know about the accident?"

"Christina told me," I said thinking to myself, it was a good
cover story, but it would not stand up to too much questioning. I
wanted to tell him the truth. That he had been nearly killed
rescuing Sean but that meant explaining the kidnap and as far as
James was concerned it had never happened.

Christina had arranged for Helga to serve dinner at seven
that evening. The atmosphere was strained and conversation
difficult, as Jack and Gill had not yet reconciled their differences.
It transpired that Frank and Christina had gone with Kurt to
visit his old friend Heinrich, the boy whose birthday had led to
the finding of the steppingstones. Heinrich's father was a forest
ranger and knew the forest like the back of his hand. He knew

exactly the location of the well, but Heinrich said he was sure no amount of money would persuade his father, now in his seventies, to go anywhere near it. The reason he gave was that the Wild Hunt was riding again. He said his father might risk his life for money but not his soul. Heinrich told them a local farmer had sworn on his son's life that he had seen the creatures, furthermore, two people from the new Village were found dead: an elderly man and his wife. The door of their cottage was lying open and they were found lying together on the floor. The bodies went for Post-mortem. and the cause of death was Myocardial Infarction, in other words a heart attack. They both had a heart attack at the same time, on the same day. The local doctor said it looked as though the life had been drained out of them. Now everybody was locking their doors and saying it was not the life that was drained from them but their souls.

Chapter 18

The Steppingstones

Sean asked if he could eat in the kitchen with his knew best friend Kurt. Gill said no, because he would be in Helga's way, but Helga said it was not a problem as Kurt was very good with Sean and they both found his comments very entertaining.

Doria exhausted by the journey had stayed in her room since we arrived, now refreshed she joined us for dinner at seven. She had been reading and watching television most of the time and was anxious to tell us of a late-night news and current affairs pro-gramme she had watched, where they were discussing a recent series of mysterious deaths. They mentioned an elderly man and his wife, found lying outside the front door of their home. There was no sign of physical injury. The coroner said it appeared that both their hearts had simply stopped beating. They also inter-viewed a farmer who had found one of his farmhands dead in a field. The young man had been working late into the evening and had failed to return. The farmer and his son went out looking for him and found him lying in a field that had been churned to mud, by what looked like hoof prints. The farmer said it was a crop field and there were no horses, nor any other livestock kept in that field, nor in any of the neighbouring fields.

The interviewer then spoke to a woman whose fifteen-year-old son had been cycling home from football practice. She told him the boy had fallen through the door shaking and in tears, saying he had been chased by dark hooded figures on horseback. His mother locked the door behind him and looked out the window. She said she saw a huge dark horse with a hooded figure standing right in front of their house. She screamed, and her husband came running, but when he looked out the window the figure was gone. The cameras followed the woman outside, where she showed them the actual hoof prints in the grass verge beside her house. Then the interviewer spoke to a senior police officer, who said they were investigating numerous sightings of hooded men on horseback. He said they were taking the reports seriously and until they could apprehend the riders, he advised people to lock their doors and report anything suspicious. He also dismissed as superstitious nonsense the numerous phone calls from the public saying they had seen the Wild Hunt. He then appealed to the general public to be vigilant and to be aware of the harm caused by scaring people in these isolated communities and by spreading ridiculous stories about the Wild Hunt riding again to collect souls for the devil.

"Did you record the interview Doria." James asked.

"No, I'm sorry. Of course, I should have but I was engrossed in the discussion and when I thought about it, it was too late and anyway I didn't know which was the recording button."

Frank and Christina talked about their meeting with Heinrich's father. Helmut Schmitt whom Christina described as an elderly man with startling white hair, a ruddy pink complexion, and an enormous smile. Frank added that it was a smile that faded rapidly when Helmut realised why they were there. They had tried hiring him as a guide, offering to double any asking fee he thought appropriate, but to no avail. He was adamant he would not take them to the well. He asked them if they had seen the recent news bulletins, of hooded riders seen on the roads. When they said yes, he told them there were many more sightings that had not been reported to the authorities. These sightings had been in the woods near the old well.

Given what Heinrich had told them about his father, Christina said she asked Herr Schmitt if he believed it was the Wild Hunt these people had seen. She said he gave an unconvincing laugh and dismissed it as no more than superstitious nonsense. She said he told them, that though he personally had not seen any riders, one of his friends had. An honourable man, who would not lie about such things, had seen men in hooded cloaks riding in the forest. Real men, dressed in costume, not ghostly figments of imagination. He then pointed out that it is near Halloween, and most likely irresponsible teenagers out for a laugh. He had no doubt the local police would quickly track them down and put an end to their dressing-up games. It was a contradiction in terms, one minute he was hinting it was dangerous to go near the well when riders had been seen and the next, dismissing it as childish pranks.

Christina didn't give up, but said she pressed him further to tell them why he would not take them there, saying the well was on the grounds of her home and she was going to find it, whether he helped her or not. She told him they had respected archaeologists and historians, guests from Scotland, one of whom was an elderly man whose life's ambition was to see the strange well. Eli laughed when she said that.

Frank said trying to pin Herr Schmitt down as to why he would not take them was impossible. He was evasive, coming up with excuses like, the path was on a slope with loose rocks and led to a dense and almost impassable part of the forest. Then saying the elderly man would have difficulty walking there and it had always been a dangerous place. Then he told them that few years ago a man, a tourist, went missing in the forest. Herr Schmitt said that he was one of the volunteers helping the police to search for him. At the end of that day, some of the searchers reported hearing what sounded like a pack of wolves howling and since no trace of man had ever been found, there was speculation that he may have been killed by wolves.

Christina asked how big the well was and Herr Schmitt admitted that he had only seen it once. He and a friend had come across it when they were part of the search party for a missing tourist. He said the well was much bigger than you would expect a well to be, and in a strange place. He said that it was always dark in that part of the forest because the trees were so dense that they cut out the light. He described it as a jungle they had to hack their way through. When they finally came close; they found a well in the centre of a clearing surrounded by a circle of giant fir trees.

They didn't realise what it was at first. It looked no more than a huge circle of stones. When they went to investigate, they were knocked back by a stench like rotten eggs. Herr Schmitt described it as though a gas were emanating from the well, a stench so foul it made them retch. He said the other man described it as the smell of rotting flesh, thinking perhaps curious animals had fallen and died there. They decided there and then, to suggest to the authorities that they get the estate owner, that would have been Frank and Christina, to fill it in, or cap it.

Frank said no one had ever approached them on the subject and asked Herr Schmitt to describe the well in more detail, he replied that he couldn't. They would have looked closer but there was a flash of lightening and a rumble of thunder. That made then turn back and so they left quickly not wanting to be caught amongst trees in a lightning storm.

Frank said when he asked Herr Schmitt why no one had ever approached them on the subject. Her Schmitt looked down at his cup and took a moment to answer. Then he told them it was never reported. He said it was the worst day of his life and it had taken them all of that night to find their way back. Then told them sheepishly We never reported it because we were afraid to go back, afraid to even talk about it. It is a bad place.

Christina said she asked him outright if there was any inducement that they could offer that would tempt him to take them there, because they were going to find it whether he took them or not, In the end, he would do no more than draw them a rough map.

Frank placed the drawing on the table in front of us. It was a simple drawing, it showed Schloss Heiligtum and a path leading South towards the old village, then it turned West and went in a straight line for around one kilometre to where the first steppingstone could be found.

Now we had a map, it should have been simple, but a stupid argument broke out over who should go look for the well. In Frank's opinion, we would be best to set out first thing in the morning after breakfast. He said the sensible thing to do was locate the well, have a look at what we were dealing with, see what equipment, if any, we might need to go down it.

Eli agreed saying he believed it would be better if we knew beforehand what messages there were on the other steppingstones.

Jack who had been quietly consuming most of a bottle of red wine, pushed back his empty plate, sat back in his chair and said, "look this is what we are gonna do. You will all stay here. Frank and I go first. We will check out the route, make sure we are on the right track. Take some photos. Make sure it's safe for you to tag along. We will decide when, if at all, the rest of you go or not. You can stay here till we see…"

It wasn't what he said, for some of it might in other circumstances, have been considered thoughtful, but he delivered his opinion in such a demeaning fashion that I was livid and cut him off. "Hold on a minute! Tag along? Stop right there Jack. If anyone is going in the morning it will be me. Grateful as I am for the company, this is my task Jack, mine, and mine alone. I know those creatures are coming from that place and terrorising the local people. I am the one going down that well. I am the one with the key, I am the one who must close that gate and as soon as possible."

Jack laughed at me. He sat forward, placatingly he said." Hey! Look I'm just trying to help you."

"Really," I said with a smile." Is that what you're doing?"

He said, "of course it is, what do you think I'm trying to do, steal your thunder or something?" He looked as though he was threatening me. He stabbed the map with his finger and raised his voice, practically spitting the words very slowly into my face. "It is a difficult place to reach, deep in an ancient forest. Silent as the grave." He swung his arms in the air. "An overhead canopy of branches that blots out light. Dead and decaying vegetation on the forest floor. The smell of the decomposing flesh of dead animals. No clear path. You could wander in circles through the gloom and be lost forever." He leaned forward. "Do you get it?" he growled. "Do you get it? Do you?"

James raised his hand and shouted "Hey! back off, that's enough Jack, she gets it. What the hell is wrong with you? What exactly are you trying to prove? That you know more than the rest of us about that place? You make is sound like you've been there before."

Jack did a double take. They glared at each other and for a moment. It looked as though there would be a standoff, but then Jack sat back, and his voice changed to a softer, soothing tone. He looked at his empty wine glass and refilled it saying. "Piss off Perry Mason. You don't know what you are dealing with."

"Jack" Gill cried out." Stop it, what are you doing?"

He grinned stupidly in her face." I'm telling it how it is my love"

"No, no you are out of order my friend. "Eli said shocked.

James was furious "Don't push me Jack you're going a step too far"

I quickly caught his arm, "Please James ignore him, he's drunk." James calmed down quickly.

Jack continued with his rant. "No, it's the useless people at this table you need to ignore. Listen to me Erica. It will be an amazing find. Exclude the locals and the rest of the world doesn't even know of the well's existence. Eli and I were discussing the fact that magazines, like the National Geographic, would pay a fortune for photos of an unknown inverted tower. Give them a hint that a gateway to Hell is at the bottom, well you would be talking thousands. Book deals, movie contracts, documentaries, the sky's the limit." He was animated, like someone who had just won the lottery. He was grinning like a Cheshire Cat. "When I take this to the press. I am gonna be a rich man."

Eli gasped, he looked at me and then Christina, his cheeks flushed red as if he had been caught doing something, he was ashamed of. He shook his head. "No, no Jack, that is not how it was. Of course, I discussed it with you, but I did say, the very idea of going to the press was inappropriate and I would have none of it."

Doria who was astounded by Jack's unmitigated effrontery, his assumption that this story would ever be his to make public, glared at him. "You do not have the right to do such a thing," she said.

"Doria is right. That well is on the Schloss Heiligtum estate." James said, "legally you couldn't sell the photographs, or the story, without Frank or Christina's permission."

Gill obviously embarrassed by Jack's behaviour, strangely didn't comment. I wondered if she was afraid that challenging him with her opinion might start another embarrassing argument.

Jack turned to James. "Oh, pardon me. I forgot we had a legal expert on German law here. No, wait, sorry, I got that wrong, didn't I? You know nothing about German law. What's it to you anyway you're not an archaeologist or a historian, your just here to chase that expensive piece of skirt sitting doe-eyed beside you. You're not fit to take part in any of this. So maybe you should just keep your opinions to yourself."

That was too much for James, "You drunken fool. Keep your mouth shut I'll shut it for you. He pushed back his chair to rise

I think it's time for you to leave the room Jack?" Christina caught James' arm and I caught the other."

Jack laughed." Oh, hold him back ladies. I am shaking here."

Frank in a loud voice said, "Jack that is enough. This my home and my table. I would ask you to curtail your behaviour or leave us."

Gill on the verge of tears pleaded, "stop it Jack. Please."

"Stop what?" Jack asked surprised, then he laughed, reached for the bottle of wine and shouted, "ok Frank. I know I'm overstepping the mark." He reached over to touch my hand, but I pulled it away. "I can be a bit of a plonker sometimes. I'm sorry Erica but what you don't realise is that this is a big deal for me. I know what I'm like. I get carried away sometimes, but I've been waiting all my life for a find like this. An inverted tower, it's like finding the Holy Grail or maybe an unholy grail," he laughed again. I mean even the stones engraved with Enochian language, unknown to the world's historians and archaeologists. It's a momentous find and important enough to make me lose sight of my need to defer to you, whose task is to find the gate," he said dripping sarcasm. "You who has ownership of this find or at least share it with Frank and Christina. He sighed deeply. Me, I am just a hanger-on, a loser, only here because I married into this wealthy little circle of friends. Yeah. Sure, I want a piece of the fame that will come with this find. I mean what have I got to show for all the work I've put in, nothing."

No one answered him. He looked around at the faces, no one gave him the sympathetic response he was looking for, so he lifted the glass of wine and emptied it in one swallow. "I know I've been out of order." He was talking to himself now. Staring into his glass having a private pity party, his voice was almost croaking. Funnily enough, Katie remarked the other day that his voice was always coarse these days, He seemed to have lost that beautiful Irish lilt that had charmed Gill.

"I very sorry Ewica." There was no contrition in his voice." He said it with a stupid pout and a baby voice. "Will you forgive little Jackie for being a bad boy." It was bizarre behaviour. Then just as quickly his voice changed, and his face softened. "I have worked so hard on this. I know I have overstepped the mark, but I get carried away when I am on a project like this." His Irish accent had suddenly returned. He looked around the table. Then he turned to Gill. He gripped her arm and, in the process, sliding her sleeve where I could just see the edge of a dark bruise. "My darling wife here has been putting up with a lot from me. I am very, very sorry for my behaviour. "he said to Christina and Frank.

Frank said coldly, "your touching display, of self-knowing and contrition is misplaced Jack, I think it is your wife who deserves the apology."

The tension broke when the door opened, and Helga came in to say a fire had been lit in the sitting room. She asked if Christina would like tea and coffee served there.

We wandered through, James and I helping Doria, who was always stiff after sitting for any length of time. Katie said she was going to help Gill bathe and settle Sean.

Jack said "No, I'll do that." He stood up and pulled Gill's chair away from the table. He actually jerked it back startling her in the process. They left the dining room and didn't come back down that night.

As we walked along the hall Doria said "There is something not right, something unwholesome about that man."

It was all we talked about that night, the change in Jack's personality. Frank who had only met Jack and Gill for the first time when they arrived to pick up Sean, said he was nothing like the description Christina had given him.

Christina said, "but it was true, he was charming when I first met him."

"Jack has changed," James said. "Sean's kidnap hit him hard. He started drinking heavily, even so the change in him is quite dramatic."

"His behaviour is very much out of character." Eli said. "I have been quite worried about my old friend."

Katie added "Eli is right. Jack used to be a lot of fun. He was an Irishman with the gift of the gab. He used to say he had kissed the Blarney stone. I don't know what's happened to him, but I am worried about Gill. I helped her bathe Sean, the other night, when she rolled up her sleeves, I could see she was bruised on both her arms. She said she was tired with travelling and had carelessly bumped her arms. When I said that was nonsense and it looked more like finger marks to me, as though someone had grabbed both her arms, she pulled down her sleeves. Then she said it was nothing and added she didn't want to talk about it. She looked me straight in the eye, on the verge of tears, swallowing hard as though she wanted to say something but couldn't get the words out. She is frightened of him Erica, I'm sure of it, but all she did was ask me to go downstairs and leave her to put Sean to bed."

Frank was leaving in the morning with the direct purpose of locating the well and photographing the stones. He would take Kurt and Stephan who were both familiar with the terrain. James who wanted to go with Frank had the sense to know he would slow him down.

Frank insisted he was leaving without Jack. "I don't trust that man, but he was right James about you staying behind. You have injuries still healing, it would unwise to come with me. Give your body a little more time to heal."

That worked for James, he agreed, whereas, I can't remember the exact words, but Jack had riled James by saying to him something like, "don't be ridiculous, you're in no fit state to go anywhere. You stay here." It might have sounded like Jack was expressing concern, but it was delivered more like an order, and in such a derogatory tone that its angered James, who then warned Jack not to try telling him what to do.

In the end we could see the sense in checking out the area first. Frank said they would go as early as possible, at daybreak, because going earlier would be foolish as the terrain was rough and downhill. To begin with, the ground is littered with loose stones where one false step could cause a slip and fall.

"How do you plan to get away without Jack. He thinks he is leading the…" James stopped mid-sentence when the door opened. Sean stood there in his bare feet and green pyjamas with the Pinocchio on front.

Katie got up. "Sean! What on earth are you doing out of bed? Do Mummy and Daddy know you've come downstairs? You look frozen." She took his hand and led him over to the fire where we were all sitting.

The little boy shook his head. "Mummy is sleeping I am looking for Daddy. I can't find him" He said. "Do you know where daddy is?"

Katie asked, "Is Daddy not with Mummy in their bedroom?"

"No." Sean said, "The man is there."

"What man?" Katie and I asked at the same time"

"The man who looks like Daddy, but Auntie Katie …" he rushed out the words as if he were afraid, she wouldn't let him finish ". … he's not my Daddy. I told Mummy but she won't listen. She doesn't believe me." The silent tears were now running down his cheeks. "I don't like him, he hurts Mummy." Sean's lip was trembling, Tears glistening in his eyes he looked around the adults asked. "Can you help me find my Daddy?"

Chapter 19

The Dybbuk

That evening was a turning point. Till then, though disgusted by Jack's behaviour, no one had considered the possibility that Jack wasn't Jack: Surprising I know, when you consider that James, Katie, and I had experience of the demonic possession of Caleb. Molly's son-in-Law. That is Molly, the housekeeper at Lanshoud.

Listening to Sean, by unspoken mutual agreement, no one attempted to disagree with him. No one suggested he was talking nonsense. James muttered. "Given Jack's personality transformation, you can hardly blame the boy." Then he asked Sean. "Daddy looks and sounds like himself, why do you think he's not Daddy?"

"No!" Sean almost shouted at James. "He doesn't always look like himself."

Christina asked him. "What do you mean Sean. Who does he look like then, if not himself?" The reply he gave made me shiver.

"Sometimes..." he hesitated to look around at our faces, reluctant to say something he thought we might dismiss as imagination..."sometimes he looks like a different person, like when he gets angry, his face changes, it goes in and out of Daddy and a different man." Then he rushed out, "I told Mummy, but she wouldn't listen. He looked up a Katie and said sadly, "I told her, but she said I was being silly."

"What did the different man look like Sean?" Frank asked. "In what way does he look different from Jack can you describe him for us

Sean swallowed hard. "I saw him once, in the mirror, Daddy was standing at my back holding my shoulders telling me to brush my teeth. I looked in the mirror and Daddy had gone; it was a man with black hair and a crooked nose and a kind of beard. I was so scared. I cried out and Daddy's voice told me to shut up, or he would drown me in the sink. I couldn't move. It wasn't Daddy it was a different face; he was a different man. Then Mummy called me, and the man's face went all wavy in the glass and it was Daddy again. Daddy pushed me against the sink, and I couldn't move. He hurt me. I got a bruise on my chest. See?" He pulled up his shirt to show the faded bruise now turning yellow. "Mummy called again, and Daddy let me go. I ran away to Mummy I tried to tell her, but she got angry with me and said I had to stop telling silly stories, because it would make Daddy very angry." He was rushing out the words, trembling and half crying, choking back tears, sounding just like the little boy he was. "I showed Mummy the bruise, but she said I must have got that when I fell off my scooter, she didn't believe me."

"Oh Sean." Katie sighed. "It's alright sweetie, everything is going to be ok." She pulled him close, hugging him, tears in her own eyes as she wiped his away. Then Sean quite suddenly pulled himself together and said firmly. "She knows, Mummy knows, just like I do, that the man is a stranger, but she is too afraid to say so. I know she is, and..."he hesitated... "and he hurts her, he hurts her bad. She always says it was an accident, but I have seen him do it. He twists her arm and stands on her feet till she cries out. He says he will kill me if she tells anyone. I am telling the truth." He was almost shouting." There is another man inside my Daddy, and I can't find my Daddy." He huddled into Katie and, shaking, sobbed his heart out.

Christina held her hands up. "How have we all missed this?" No one answered.

It was hard to watch Sean so distraught, Katie stroking his hair, holding him close, allowing him to cry it out. When he calmed down. "Sean." James asked gently. "When was the last time you saw your Daddy, without the other man inside him?"

Sean thought for a minute. "It was at our house. You were there, you came to stay. It was the night the dark people came.

Daddy lifted me from my cot and gave me to them and they took me away." I gasped in disbelief. "Daddy gave you to them!" The child nodded, so upset he couldn't speak. He was describing his kidnap, a memory from a time when he was still only a baby. Sean's shocking statement should have invited a reaction from everyone, except Christina and I, but no one else seemed to notice.

"Yes." Sean said from the security he found hanging onto Katie. "He carried me downstairs and out into the street. He gave me to the dark people on the horses."

Again, as Otto said would happen, no one except Christina and I looked surprised at Sean recounting his experience as a baby torn away from his mother, recounting a memory in detail, it was incredible.

James continued to question him. "The dark people, were they men, Sean?"

"I think so, I don't know. They wore hoods and smelled bad. They brought me here and gave me to the men who spoke German. Then I was taken to Potsdam."

Right then I thought the realisation that something wasn't right had caught Eli, because there was one awkward moment when Eli seemed to realise the absurdity of a four year old remembering something that happened when he was a baby, and being able to describe it in detail. He said. "My God who is this child, who can speak so eloquently. It is not possible; he was only an infant." He shook his head, then rubbed his forehead roughly, as though it would clear his mind. He took off his spectacles, cleaned them and put them back on his face and looked at us blankly, as though he hadn't said a word, or had forgotten what he had just said.

Frank, James, and Katie didn't seem to notice anything odd either. Christina gave me a knowing look. I suspected she had that same sudden thought that I had, that someone else, sitting there, must surely remember that Sean could only be around two now, and only about five months in real-time when he was taken by the Hunt. Yet here he was, just weeks later, looking around four years old. It was just as Otto said it would be. By some miracle they were unable to see the rapid growth and maturity of Sean. As for Eli the sudden realisation that something strange had happened seemed just as suddenly disappeared from his mind. Instead he continued to rub his head as though he had lost his train of thought and couldn't get it back. Neither James, Frank nor Katie looked confused, nor did they question Sean.

Katie said. "We will find your Daddy. Don't you worry. We'll find him."

Refusing to go to his room. Sean sat with us until he fell asleep, then Frank carried him upstairs and Katie settled him down for the night. Katie said she listened at Jack and Gill's door but heard nothing, and so assumed they were already asleep. We sat talking till around one o'clock in the morning, going over events, everyone putting forward their own opinion of Jack's behaviour, which was so out of character. The shock revelation by Sean that it was Jack who had taken him from his room and handed him over to the Hunt. That Jack had physically hurt him in the last few weeks, was so horrific, that the conversation inevitably led to the possibility that something else had taken over Jack.

We had all seen changes, not just in his personality, there were physical changes too. He had lost weight. The skin on his face seemed loose. His eyes sagged a bit. Jack was always well groomed, but not anymore. He didn't shave as often, he seemed to wear the same clothes day after day. He was argumentative. Minor quarrels had broken out with Gill, because he came to the table unshaven, with unkempt hair and clothes that looked as though he had slept in them. That and his aggressive manner had made the possibility of possession cross my mind, but the very idea that Jack was possessed, and right now upstairs sleeping in the same bed as Gill, was too terrifying to contemplate.

James reminded us of how easily we had been deceived by Emilio the clairvoyant. That terrible night when Caleb, that big gentle giant of a man, had been possessed by a demon. He turned into a dangerous, foul-mouthed imitation of the real Caleb. I shuddered at that memory because James was right. Jack's personality transformation was along those same lines.

240

"Oh God, surely not. I think it's just the drinking, I think he is turning into an alcoholic. Poor Gill, she has been going through hell with that man. What can we do?" Katie asked.

Doria who had been very quiet, just listening to the conversation, slowly struggled to her feet. She tapped her stick on the floor. "Nothing" she said, "we can do nothing, it is for Otto to deal with. Remember, Sean told us Otto had gone for help. Well, we are not alone. He told me he would return by daybreak. Otto is a powerful being of light and he will return as he said he would. I suggest you all go to bed and get some rest." We did and she was right.

After a restless night with little sleep I came down for breakfast early the next morning. I came downstairs with Katie to find James, Frank, Christina, and Otto sitting in the kitchen. There were two other men in the room. Katie whispered, "look it's them, the two guys we saw from the window outside the hotel in Potsdam."

It certainly looked like them, the two tall slim young men, who had stood in silence with Otto. Only they no longer wore dress suits, now they were dressed in jeans and hoodies

Otto introduced them as Jehoel and Daniel. Jehoel, who later, Otto referred to as Joe, sat on a chair with his legs stretched out in front of him and his hands behind his head, he didn't so much as nod at our introduction. Daniel who was sitting on the window ledge, looking out at rain that was lashing down onto Heiligtum' s courtyard, simply nodded his head. They didn't try to communicate; in fact, they made no attempt to interact with us the whole time they were with us. Their faces devoid of emotion reminded me of the first time we met angels.

"They are like you?" I asked Otto

"Yes," he said. "Don't be afraid."

"Afraid! Why would we be afraid?" exclaimed Katie "We have met angels before you know. Though these two are a bit better dressed."

Otto found this amusing. "Yes Katie. I know you were rescued by angels of a much higher rank than us. You met archangels; you are therefore very privileged human beings. You saw something few humans have ever seen."

Katie studied the two silent young men, then as blunt as always she asked Otto if these were the two guys he was talking to, outside our hotel in Potsdam. "Only you weren't talking exactly," she said "just acting a bit weird, standing in silence, looking at each other. Telepathy was it?"

"You are very observant Katie," Otto said. "I think perhaps you have missed your calling as a detective."

"Why are they here Otto?" I asked.

"They are warriors Erica, but of a lesser rank than the archangels. However, it's not you they have come to help. It's Jack. They are here only for Jack,"

"Jack!" Katie and I exclaimed at the same time."

"They are here for Jack!" James asked. "Why Jack?"

"Because Jack will accompany us to the well..."

James interrupted him. "That's not a good idea. Jack's a loose cannon. He's not himself just now, so much so even his son doesn't recognise him. He seems to be having some kind of mental break-down. Otto, he is aggressive and argumentative, you should think twice about taking him with you. Though if you don't, he will put up a fight because he is determined to go, but I think taking him along is just asking for trouble."

The door opened and Eli came in, just in time to hear what James had said. He wore black waterproof trousers, turned up at the ankles, and a cream fisherman knit sweater. He was obviously dressed to go somewhere. He smiled, and his face flushed at the surprised comments of not recognising him. Especially Katie's comment of, "you look good Eli; you should dress like that more often; it takes years off you."

Shyly and self-consciously smiling. Eli said. "These are the clothes I keep for fieldwork and I also have walking boots with me." He noticed the two young men.

"This is Joe and Daniel," Frank said. "Otto's reinforcements"

Eli politely smiled and said good morning to them. In return he received a perfunctory nod of the head. He sat down at the table and Christina poured him some coffee.

I asked him, "are you planning to come to the well with us today?"

"Yes, of course. I am looking forward to it. I would not miss it for the world." Eli said.

Suddenly without any warning, at the same time Joe and Daniel stood up. With no more than a glance at Otto they quickly left the kitchen. "Jack is awake and quarrelling with Gill." Otto said. "This is the day of the well. Jack will be more agitated and more dangerous than usual, but they will deal with him."

I stood up I think I better go and check on Gill."

"It's alright Erica. Gill does not need you just now" I pushed back my chair. He said "I promise you Gill and Sean are safe. Daniel and Joe will see that Gill sleeps while they take Jack away from her. I promise you they will take care of her, but I need you here, so that I can explain about today. They will not harm Jack, but they must control the thing inside him."

James said, "So you're saying Jack is possessed?"

Otto didn't reply at first.

"It's alright. I said, "We have been discussing it."

Otto said. "Yes, he is, sit down Erica please. I have a lot to explain."

For the next twenty minutes we sat riveted to the story that Otto told us. He started with the night that James and I were involved in a car accident. The night we met the Wild Hunt on the road and were rescued by the messenger Abdiel. He said "Abdiel told you and James that a gift would be given to your friends. That night Sean was conceived. On that same night, the Wild Hunt who have been riding for centuries, were dispatched from the dark world to collect souls. They collected the evil soul of a man called Harry McGuire, the leader of a drug and human trafficking gang, who was shot dead that same night by a rival gang.

Distracted by the presence of Abdiel, McGuire's soul, in spirit form, escaped from the riders. It followed you Erica, and James, back to Gill and Jack's house, and there it found Jack to be the perfect host."

"It's unthinkable. A demon. "Katie said.

"No Katie, not a demon but a dybbuk."

"A dybbuk. What's a dybbuk?" I asked

Eli exclaimed, "A dybbuk Ah! Yes! I understand. I know of dybbuk." He looked around." Should I explain?"

"Carry on." Otto said.

Eli clasped his hands on the table. "There are many instances of a dybbuk in Hebrew literature. It is a dispossessed soul, a malicious spirit seeking to escape its punishment. It is opportunistic and seeks possession where there is weakness."

"Jack's not a weak person." I said.

Otto disagreed. "He is weak and vulnerable when he drinks. The dybbuk would use that to control him and force him to hand over Sean. Jack would have no memory of it."

"But Otto, all the men had a drink that night." Katie said.

"Yes, Otto agreed, "but Jack had drunk more alcohol than most. McGuire took over Jack's body and Jack gave the baby to the Hunt, to protect himself.

James said. "It took me a while to realise Jack's personality had changed completely. It was only last night the possibility of a possession crossed my mind and again only because Sean led us in that direction."

Otto nodded. "A dybbuk is more difficult to recognise than demonic possession. They slowly and quietly take control. A demonic possession can be seen instantly but a dybbuk is more subtle, it can go unnoticed. Jack has been changing for some time has he not? And you have seen or have evidence of the Hunt around you. The riders of the Hunt cannot return to their master empty handed. They are compelled to find the soul they lost, or an alternative and they would kill Jack to get it, taking both souls back to their master."

Otto continued. "While this was happening in Scotland, in Germany Dietrich Oppenheim a man steeped in occult practice like his predecessors, the original Nazi's, in search of money and power, had succeeded in conjuring a powerful demon called Balaam, the demon of avarice and greed. Balaam made a deal with Oppenheim that he would give him everything he wanted, in exchange for the four keys. Balaam offered Sean to Oppenheim, the child the Hunt took from Jack. The Hunt could not use Sean to appease, their master for the loss of McGuire's soul. The child's soul was too bright, to pure, but it was a child the Hunt could use. Balaam ordered the hunt to take Sean to Oppenheim who with his henchmen had set up residence in Heiligtum. Oppenheim could use the child and claim the keys in ransom. It all went wrong for Oppenheim when James and Stephan tracked Sean to Heiligtum.

Frank working undercover in one of the Neo Nazi cells found out Sean was at Heiligtum and helped Stephan and the now badly injured James to get Sean and escape. It was Frank who took them to the safe house in Potsdam.

Oppenheim desperate for power, again conjured Balaam, but he no longer had Sean. With no child and no keys, he had nothing to bargain with. Balaam killed Oppenheim and that was the body that Katie and Erica found in the cellar. The body was removed by the police, but the soul was left behind. The Hunt still searching for a soul, evil enough to replace McGuire's soul, collected Oppenheim's instead and wrecked Heiligtum in the process."

Otto sat back in the chair. "So, you see your suspicions were correct. Jack is possessed and it was McGuire's face that Sean saw in the mirror."

No one spoke. We sat in silence, the horror of it all sinking in.

Otto said. "All is not lost, Jack's insistence that he go to the well, is coming from Jack's soul. It is attempting to fight back, but the soul of McGuire is in terror of that outcome. It will not go there willingly, for it knows it will be dragged from Jack's body through the open gate. That is why we must escort Jack to the well."

"Why did the Hunt not just kill Sean and take his soul to their master in place of McGuire's" Eli asked.

"That was their intention, but because Sean's soul was too pure, too bright, it blinded them. It could not be taken to Hell. They could not use it. So, they did what Balaam asked and took it to Oppenheim for him to use as a bargaining tool to obtain the keys."

We sat in silence, understanding at last, not knowing what to say and horrified at what Otto had told us.

Otto broke the silence by saying" We cannot wait any longer. We have to take Jack to the well today. You must know that Joe,

Dan, and I will take you, but we cannot go down it, the proximity to Hell would damage us and put you in even greater danger. You must go with Jack." Otto pushed back his chair and stood up.

Stunned. James said "What? She can't go alone, just with Jack, that's insane. A young woman and a possessed man who has lost his mind." He was adamant. "That's madness she is not going with only Jack."

Otto held up his hand. "Let me finish" he turned to me. "Erica you have a number to call."

"I know I was thinking about it. Do you mean Humphrey." I asked?"

"Who is Humphrey?" Eli asked

Otto laughed, "Humphrey is not a who but a what. It is highly sophisticated communication device, designed by Luke the father of Christina and Erica. Break the name down into letters using F instead of the PH and I instead of Y, it then becomes. HUMFRI. It stands for High. Undulating Modulated Frequency Replicating Intelligence. It is a form of communication that stretches across endless galaxies. To someone, like the alien being, you call Luke it was no more than providing his children with access to an emergency service. It enables Christina, Erica to call for help."

"The help being Sentinels." I said

"Yes, exactly"

I sighed with relief in the knowledge that those beautiful ephemeral beings, who wrapped calm and security around me when we went to the gate at Lanshoud, would be with me again. If they were with me at the well, I wouldn't be afraid. At least that's what I decided to tell myself. The truth was, I woke up that morning feeling almost sick with dread. I had a panic attack thinking I couldn't do it again. That feeling was still hanging over me, but now, knowing I could summon the Sentinels, I felt calmer.

"Did you know about the Sentinels Frank?" I asked him.

"Yes, Christina told me."

Christina said "I told him that when I was attacked and recovering in the nursing home. A man came to see me, a stranger. He said he was the messenger, the man who helped Erica and James on the night of the car crash, his name was Abdiel. He told me that me that a guardian had been sent. One who would look after Gill and her baby in the hospital. He said Raphael was coming to heal me. He said he was there to teach me about the Sentinels and how to summon them. He told me I had to help Erica. It was madness. I was weak, terrified and in a lot of pain. I thought he was asking me to perform some sort of ritual to summon these creatures. Then he gave me the number on a piece of paper, told me to call it. If I did not, then all would be lost. The whole episode was so bizarre I thought I was hallucinating. Angels using mobile numbers. I thought I had lost my mind. You know the rest; you know how that played out."

"I have seen them they are bewitching; What are they Otto? Are they aliens or angels? "Katie asked

Otto answered. "They are beings from another world therefor alien to you. They are an advanced race of beings, who like my kind, also serve the Supreme Being. Long ago Luke created H.U.M.F.R.I, as a means of contacting the Sentinels. The device enables you to summon them, because though they do not speak, they do understand your language so you can speak to them.

Erica when you call the number, HUMFRI will connect with the Sentinels. The Sentinels will go down the well with you and Jack to the actual gate where the soul of McGuire will then be sucked in. Then it's down to you to close the gate. We may have a problem with Jack. Daniel and Joe may have to drag him there."

"They won't have to 'drag' him there. He won't resist" Katie said" He has been planning to go all week."

"No, he never intended to go to the well." Otto said

"Never intended!" I said, "he has been planning it for the last few days. Otto, he will insist on coming with us."

"Jack may well insist. but McGuire has no intentions of going to the well, he never has." Otto said. "McGuire will not go near it. Even if Jack fights back, the entity inside him that is McGuire, is stronger."

247

Chapter 20

Thanatos

By the time Gill came down there was only James and I at the breakfast table, we were discussing Jack's behaviour. She overheard us. "Don't stop on my account," she said. "I have been thinking worse than anything you can say." Her voice was hoarse, and she looked awful. She wore loose grey leggings and an oversized pale blue sweater that emphasised how painfully thin she had become. Dark shadows framed eyes that were swollen and red and the hoarse voice suggested she had been crying for some time. She looked worn out. Her long black hair was scraped back into a tight ponytail, emphasising the prominence of cheekbones in her gaunt face. I pulled out a chair beside me, "Here Gill, sit here and I'll get you some breakfast."

She slid into the chair saying. "Don't bother, just coffee thank you. Where is everyone?"

I poured her coffee. "Katie has gone to get dressed. Eli is buried in his books in the study, he planned to come with us. Otto explained why that was impractical, on more than one front. Doria is being spoiled by Helga and is having breakfast in bed again.

Gill's voice was flat and emotionless. "I know that. I saw Sean sitting on Doria's bed eating his breakfast with her. I was looking for Jack?"

"He said he was going to get ready." Did he not tell you they were leaving soon?" James asked.

She shook her head and licked her dry lips. "No, he doesn't tell me anything. He doesn't speak to me unless he has to. I don't know why I asked, I don't really care if he's gone or not." She sipped the hot coffee, not making eye contact with either of us, looking only at her cup.

Nothing was as I thought it would be that day. I made my call to H.U.M.F.R.I. I stupidly expected to open a door and find the sentinels waiting, appearing suddenly, just like they had at Lanshoud, but it didn't happen like that. As the morning wore on, I became worried that they might not come at all.

Otto came and asked me to go get the keys. I did as he asked, and he was waiting for me at the foot of the stairs. I told him I was worried and asked him if he thought I should call H.U.M.F.R.I. again as there was still no sign of the sentinels. He said, "have a little faith Erica they will be there when you need them." He asked me to show him the keys. I offered them to him, but he declined. Well, more than declined, he drew back as though I was handing him hot coals. He said "keep them, they are for you to hold. Get ready now, we are leaving soon".

Anxiety was taking a grip as I went to the boot room to dress in my walking boots and raincoat. It was a small room with a tiny window and a door into the garden. Multiple jackets hung on the hooks. Boots and wellingtons were lined up in orderly fashion, under two bench seats on opposite walls. Sitting on the bench, pulling on my boots. I looked around and saw Gill's purple and Katie's vibrant green rain jackets. They hung together beside Sean's little yellow fisherman coat. There was something yellow lying on the floor beneath it. It was Sean's yellow rain hat. I picked it up and something fell from it. It was a small figure of Marshall, his favourite character from Paw Patrol. Sean carried it everywhere, so upset was he at losing it, that everyone had been searching for it. Gill was demented. It was not as if, in this remote area of Bavaria, there was a toy shop selling them. I don't know if she tried, but somehow I couldn't see Amazon delivering it to Schloss Heiligtum, a castle halfway up a mountain. Sean, extremely intelligent in more ways than one, was way ahead of his years, but not when it came to Paw Patrol, in that he was the same as every other child on the planet. I put the small toy in my pocket. For a brief moment the thought of seeing his face when I produced Marshall made me smile.

I suddenly realised that the jacket at my back belonged to James. I touched the sleeves then put them around my shoulders and closed my eyes, comforted by the fact that it was part of him. I imagined he was standing at my back, holding me close. Feeling cold I lifted it put it on and wrapped myself in it. It was miles too big for me, my hands only came halfway down the sleeves, but I felt cold and the jacket was heavy, warm, and comforting. There was a smell that was James, shower gel or deodorant or just my imagination, it didn't matter it was just comforting.

I wasn't just cold I was afraid; I could feel my heart thudding in my chest. My palms were sweating, and my mouth dry. I took a drink from my water bottle and my hands were shaking so much I couldn't control them. I felt alone and more anxious than I had ever felt in my life. I wanted to stay there in that jacket wrapped up warm inside it forever.

The last time I had to face a gate James the others had been with me. Now for company, I had Otto, whom I hardly knew, Daniel and Joe two total strangers, and a demented lunatic in the form of Jack. I thought, I can't do this again. No, I won't do it. My biological father had left me rich, but he had left me with the burden of these keys. No amount of money or property in the world, was worth the stress and fear of the task I had in front of me. When I closed the gate at Lanshoud it had been dreamlike. Part of me had never believed it was real and I was surrounded and supported by my friends, and those alien creatures called Sentinels. That was adventure, this was reality and I was not ready for it. Hiding under that jacket seemed a better alternative.

The sentinels hadn't come. Maybe I could use that as an excuse not to go. Otto said he could go no further than the well. Surely he wouldn't expect me to go down it alone   I couldn't go alone. I would tell him now, firmly, I was not going to do it. He was better equipped than me for that task. Fear was paralysing me.

The door opened. Otto stood looking at me. I must have looked pathetic wrapped up, shivering, and snivelling in the oversized jacket. I felt stupid and embarrassed.

He smiled. "I think you have the wrong coat. That one doesn't look your style."

"I am not going," I said, "not today, nor any other day." I slapped the key on the bench and said," here you take it." I slunk down inside the coat like a child.

He sat down on the bench beside me.

"Don't try and persuade me," I said, "I am not going, there's the key; you take it, you close the gate."

He took a deep breath." If I could do this for you, I would. Look at me." He touched my chin and turned my head to look into his deep blue eyes. They were mesmerising. He said, "come Erica, don't be afraid, you will not be harmed." It had the effect he was looking for. I wiped my eyes and just managed to pull myself together. I was ashamed that he saw me in that state, huddled in James' jacket. I took it off, tried to hang it up but it was so heavy I missed, and it fell to the floor. I was shaking so much. He lifted it and hung it up. Still shaking uncontrollably, I struggled to put on my own jacket. He helped me, with the gentleness of a mother helping a child. He even zipped up my jacket. "There," he said. "You are ready."

Shaking my head, I said "Otto, I am not ready." I wanted to say more. I wanted to tell him how terrified I was, but I knew if I voiced that fear, I would lose my control.

He stood in front of me and said "hold my hands."

I hesitated.

He said again, "hold my hands. I am feeling nervous. It will help to calm me. "He held out both hands.

I laughed. "You are nervous!"

"Yes," Given where we are going why are you so surprised.

"I am more than surprised, "I am flabbergasted"

'Flabbergasted, what does that mean? I am not familiar with that word."

"It means I am incredulous, shocked really."

"Is that an English word?"

"Yes, please don't tell me you're nervous. I am relying on you, you are an angel for God's sake, how can you be nervous?"

Otto Sighed "Ah yes! Angel, that word again. Erica, to you it means something immortal, but indestructible we are not. We are beings of light, the proximity to the miasma of the dark world, you call Hell, could destroy us."

"You don't like being called an angel, do you?"

"Not particularly, though I do not find it offensive"

"What's wrong then?

"Truthfully?"

"Yes truthfully"

"Angels, well, the word has a childlike association. Do I look to you as though I have fluffy white wings?"

"No, but angels do have wings. I know, I saw them at Lanshoud."

"That was an illusion. We do not have biological wings. Our technology is thousands of years ahead of yours so, yes the answer to your question is that in times of danger, I can fly. It would appear to you that I have wings, because you have never seen anything like this technology before. Your brain tries to make of sense of what you see, and it appears to you as wings."

"What about the halo."

"The halo, yes, well depending on circumstance, I have a device that sits over my head and controls the atmosphere I need to survive. These things are not always visible to the human eye. The halo, as it is called, is a device that controls the atmosphere around us, maintaining the levels of oxygen we need and the temperature we need to survive, anywhere in any universe."

"I imagined angels were indestructible. But you said you are not going down that well."

"That is correct the sentinels will take you to the gate. You think I am an angel and therefor fear nothing? There is a song I have heard, which says fools rush in where angels fear to tread. Do you know it?"

"Yes."

"Well, there you are, we fear just as you do. Now, take my hands and close your eyes."

I did and I felt a warmth travelling up my arms and a sense of calm flowing through me. It was the kind of feeling you get from drinking a glass of wine too quickly. It lasted only a minute, but it wiped away the feeling of panic that had been ready to overwhelm me.

"Ok? Better?"

"Yes, thank you. Is jack down yet?"

"Jack is outside with Daniel and Joe."

I followed him out into the hall. There was a heavy silence in the air. Turning into the kitchen to say we were leaving, I was surprised to find it empty. I didn't understand. The breakfast dishes were on the table. The fire Helga had lit was crackling away in the fireplace, but there was no one there. I thought they must be waiting in the morning room or the sitting room. I tried the dining room, the study, but they were all empty. Surely, they had not gone upstairs, they knew we were leaving I thought they would have stayed to wish me luck.

Otto was no longer standing at the door. Maybe they were outside with Otto, but they couldn't be. I had seen all their jackets, there in the boot room and there was torrential rain outside. They had all gone, where was everyone? A chill washed over me. I felt panic setting in again. Upstairs, maybe they had gone upstairs. I put one foot on the bottom stair when a firm no nonsense voice said, come Erica." Otto held out his hand. It is time to go.

"I will just tell them we are leaving"

"There is no need. You will just upset yourself."

"I want to."

"It is not necessary."

"I think it is. They will think it odd if we just up and leave. They will want to wish us luck. I don't want to go without…"

"Without what?" He said, "an emotional scene? Tears, hugs, good wishes?"

He was right of course. Could I honestly hug James and then walk out the door, maybe never see him again? I stood there, silent, feeling deflated and insecure.

Otto's turned me away from the stairs, his deep soothing voice washing over me said, "There and is no need to say we are leaving. They are all asleep, they will not wake until our return."

I stopped "What! You drugged them?"

I fully expected to see Daniel and Joe outside, struggling to control Jack. Instead Jack was chatting with them. Well I should say Jack was chatting and they, stony-faced, appeared to be listening. Jack turned, all smiles looking and sounding just like the old a Jack he said "Erica, at last, what's kept you, You are all the same, you girls, can't take a step out the door without a makeover.". It was odd, he was obviously excited. He almost shouted. "Come on, let's get going, I can't wait to see this place." He turned onto the path and strode off with Daniel and Joe following him, keeping pace with him, like dogs on a leash. At one point he started singing the Irish Rover at the pitch of his voice. It was bizarre.

Otto said. "The power from behind the gate, is calling the soul of McGuire, inside Jack. It's drawing him to the well. As we get closer to the well McGuire will recognise the pull for what it is".

We followed them down a path winding downhill, which was difficult in parts where the heavy rain had turned the path into a mud slide. I had to hang onto Otto, who had a walking stick with him, to keep myself from falling. Once we reached the trees the ground levelled out, but the terrain was still hazardous, with fallen tree trunks that we had to climb over. Within thirty minutes we had reached the first steppingstone and already I was feeling tired the rough terrain was as tiring as walking through heavy snow.

At first, excited, Jack knelt, wiping the rain from the stone with a cloth he produced from his backpack. "Amazing isn't it?" He said beaming. It must be thousands of years old." He handed me his mobile. "Take a photo please. "I took the mobile and Jack posed beside the stone, grinning like a seasoned explorer for the National Geographic. He asked me to take several of him standing, kneeling, pointing at the stone. After the last snap, he rubbed his head looking confused he said. "You know I've forgotten what it says. Otto, remind me."

Otto was watching him closely. He crouched down and wiped the fallen leaves of the flat surface of the first steppingstone and read aloud.

"For you who must pass through the Gates, these steppingstones lead the way. Climb down to the top of the inverted tower. Illusion to reality, light to dark, life to eternal damnation."

254

For only a moment Jack stared as though he had never heard these words before. He shuddered and there was a subtle change on his face, he looked scared, confused. He ran his fingers through his hair and rubbed his face hard. "I think we have done enough for today. The weather is getting worse, we should maybe turn back, wait for a better day Otto." He was furtive, rubbing his hands together, looking slyly at Otto. His voice had changed his. The Irish lilt had gone."

Otto picked up his bag "Come on Jack, you were desperate to see the stones. We do it today, you see the rest of the steppingstones, you take some photos back and you make Eli happy. Look over there, there is the second one."

Reluctant to go forward Jack turned away, only to find Daniel and Joe blocking his path. He stepped to the side. Joe caught his arm. Jack tried to pull away swearing at Joe. Joe turned him, pushed him forward then released him. Jack was swearing like a trooper. He tried side-stepping Joe again but then Daniel blocked his path. Jack called to Otto asking what the hell his mates were playing at? There was now more than just a hint of fear in his voice.

Otto replied." Just keep walking Jack. Look, you can see the next stone from here. They are steppingstones, Kurt said the rest are mostly no than three meters apart."

With no option, reluctantly, Jack picked up his things. He said, pathetically almost pleading. "Erica come and walk with me, please." Before I could answer. Otto said, "No." Daniel gently pushed Jack forward, ignoring his foul-mouthed complaints.

The dirt path eventually led to a dense area of the forest. There was no option but to go through a wall of thick bramble bushes. "In there," Otto said." follow the path."

With no other choice, we stumbled through, while leafless branches tore at our clothes and skin. We fought our way through the undergrowth, ignoring the stings of resisting bushes and soon we were free and stepping into a small clearing. "I can see it Joe called out," he pointed, "look on the other side, over there."

The second stone that lay in front of ,what appeared to be, a tunnel. A strange, dark tunnel formed by trees and decaying vegetation. Daniel stepped inside, flashing the beam of his powerful torch around, but it barely penetrated the gloom.

Joe went down on one knee beside the stone and scraped the mud and leaves that had built up over the writing. Jack didn't move. He just stared at it keeping his distance. He was nervous and agitated again. He seemed unable to stand still. His hands shaking, he pulled a notebook and pencil from his pocket and said jovially. "C'mon Otto what does this one say?" Otto watched Jack carefully as he read aloud.

Step forward
He who takes the life of the innocent.
The Murderer

A wave of fear washed over Jack's face, only it wasn't Jack. It was I supposed, McGuire's face; it was the weirdest thing. I remember thinking this must have been what Sean had seen. The little boy must have been terrified. Jack's face kept changing like a 3D hologram, moving, fading in and out as though there were two people in one. Then he shook himself violently and he was Jack again. He began writing in his notebook as if nothing had happened.

"Keep moving." Otto said placing a guiding hand on Jack's shoulder, easing him towards the tunnel, a tunnel that was a strange work of nature. The walls were formed by stout mature trees, and the roof a canopy of intertwined branches and leaves. They were so tightly woven together that it almost completely blocked out the light. The strange atmosphere was enhanced by the rustling of the leaves and the remnants of rain dripping through and onto the narrow single dirt track. A track made uneven by gnarled tree roots that made walking difficult.

Daniel and Joe switched on torches and led the way keeping Jack between them. I walked behind and Otto with another torch walked at my back. The tunnel twisted and turned, the air was cold, damp and very quiet. It was around ten minutes before the tunnel widened out and we could see daylight again. There we stepped out into a large clearing and in front of us lay the straight line of steppingstones.

We followed the stones. Otto clearing moss and mud, translating each one as we went. Jack now firmly in grip of Daniel and Joe was melting and reforming into a complete stranger, a stranger who trembled with fear.

One by one Otto translated the engraving on each steppingstone.

Step Forward
The one who has destroyed the innocence of children.
The Paedophile.

Step Forward
The one who bears false witness.
The Liar

Step Forward
The one who takes what is not theirs to take.
The Thief

Step forward
The one who unelected, controls and persecutes his people.
The Dictator

Step forward
The one who defiles the integrity of another's body.
The Rapist.

Step forward
The one who consorts with darkness.
Welcome home to your home.
The Satanist

"We should be able to see the well now." Otto said. From the last stone we could see the well only a short distance away. As we neared it Daniel stopped abruptly. He covered his eyes with his hand, as though he was afraid of what he had seen. Something

257

had moved. Peering from behind him I could see a strange dark figure. At the sight of it Jack started moaning and squirming away, but Daniel and Joe kept vice like grips on him. Neither they, nor Otto, looked surprised. Joe his gaze fixed on the figure whispered, "Otto."

"I know, I see him. We go slowly," Otto said, "meet him halfway."

"Do you know who that is?" I whispered, feeling very afraid.

Otto nodded, not taking his eyes off the figure. "That is Thanatos, called Ankou by some. His hood hides his face Erica, do not look at his face. Only the dead see his face. If you do, he will claim you. Now we walk until he stands, then we only take steps when he does. Walk beside me, but remember, once he stands, we stop and take steps only when he does. Do you understand? Answer me." He said loudly, shaking me out of my trance.

"Yes." I said hearing the tremble in my own voice,

The grass was damp and had been turned almost swamp-like by the relentless rain. We ploughed through it, Jack slipping and sliding as he repeatedly tried to escape. Almost as soon as we started towards him Thanatos rose, he turned towards us and seemed to glide over the grass. He was very tall, well over six feet, dressed in a black cloak reaching to his feet with pointed curved black shoes peeping out below. The hood of the cloak was large and pointed, making him seem even taller. I had no need to worry about seeing his face, it was completely hidden concealed within the depth of the hood. However, two ghostly red eyes like burning embers glowed in that depth. He carried a staff that towered above him, that was topped by a large curved blade, it looked like a scythe for cutting grass. The skeletal fingers wrapped around the staff had incredibly long curved fingernails.

It suddenly dawned on me and I felt my blood run cold. I whispered "Otto who is Thanatos? Is that? Is that? ..." I couldn't get the words out.

"You may have heard him called the Grim Reaper. He is here to collect the soul lurking inside Jack, it is time Erica, for Harry McGuire to pay for his crimes."

It moved, the thing, gliding over towards Jack, in a weird majestic, graceful, and chilling way. Jack stood transfixed and had to be forced to move. Each step the creature took, Jack had to be dragged forward. He fell into the mud a couple of times. It was horrendous to watch. Finally, the creature stood in front of him. It towered over him, stretched out a long thin skeletal hand and grabbed his shoulder. Jack started screaming. He screamed and screamed as though he were in agony. I couldn't listen. I covered my ears. Then his face dissolved completely into McGuire's, only it looked like black jelly. The creature laughed it was a sickening sound, it drew back its hand and the black jelly came out of Jack's face. Jack fell to the ground in silence. The creature immediately vanished.

Otto knelt beside the now unconscious Jack. He held Jacks face in his hands and spoke in a language I had never heard before. Jack stirred and opened his eyes. Otto helped him to sit. "Rest a moment," he said.

Jack look around. He looked at his own torn and muddied clothes. "Mother of God, where am I? What happened? Why am I here? "The Irish lilt was back in his voice. "Erica, where's Gill?"

"She is at Heiligtum with Sean, Jack. They are both fine."

"And we need to get you back to them Jack." Otto said. "Daniel and Joe will take you."

"Daniel and Joe?" Jack said looking at them. "And who would you be?" he asked them.

"They are friends of mine Otto said. "Jack they will take you back to Heiligtum. We went for a walk You had a fall and it is affecting your memory. Everything is fine now."

Jack stood up stiffly rubbing his head looking around. "Oh my God look at the state of me he said brushing of the caked mud. Gill will kill me. I wasn't drinking, was I?" he asked me quietly

"You were a sober as a judge Jack." I said lying glibly

"Good then we best get moving." He was off.

When I didn't move, he turned. "Are you coming?"

"No Jack, I have to stay with Otto."

Jack raised his eyebrows. "What about James, will I let him know when you will be back."

259

He made me laugh. I said, "it's ok James knows where I am."
He persisted," and he knows who you are with, does he?'
"Yes Jack, he knows."
"Well, we best be off then. I'll be seeing you later." He nodded to Otto and went off reluctantly with Daniel and Joe. We watched them until they were out of sight. "What now?" I asked Otto.
"Look over there he said."
I did and I saw them, the two bright glowing figures. The sentinels. "Thank you God," I said to the sky.
"Come," Otto said, "I will take you to them."

Chapter 21

The Gate

The Sentinels stood like two bookends at either side of the steps. Seeming to float just above the ground, their bodies undulating with soft hues of lavender, white and blue. They were beautiful creatures. It was hard to believe they were the warriors Otto portrayed them to be. They stared at us, their huge black slanted eyes unblinking in their long faces. Otto stood directly in front of them. He was deeply focussed. I hadn't ever seen him like that before. "They are greeting us." he said." When we reach them, bow to them, they will understand that."

"How do you know they are greeting us?"

He was surprised. "Why do you ask that? You have met them before."

"They didn't communicate then."

"They probably did, but you could not understand them. They are telepathic."

"Like you?" I asked.

"Yes, in a way. It is like the difference between German and English, so sometimes it is hard for us to understand each other's meaning. Come, we should walk slowly forward now, and you and I bow to them together."

"I never did any of that before."

"Well, just do it now. They would have thought nothing of it before, but I am with you now. Most alien races accept the fact that human beings are quite ignorant."

I was about to respond, when I realised, he was joking and just trying to lighten my mood.

He said. "When we bow Erica, I will turn and leave. You must not worry; you cannot be in safer hands. Just follow them."

"Wish me luck," I said

"You don't need luck; it is a fate accompli. You need courage and those two beings will give it to you. Now, let us go forward."

This was it. There was no turning back now. I tried move but I couldn't, my legs had that leaden feel that rooted me to the spot. I started praying...

"Dear God, it's me Erica, again. I know you have sent your angels to protect me. Otto is wonderful, and I am very grateful but..." my prayer was frantic... "I am not capable of this. I realise you must be fed up listening to me. I am hoping that I have not used up more than my share of your mercy and good-ness, but please, please make me strong enough to go down the well. When I have no one but these strange aliens for company. Please God, give me courage, keep me safe and let me back out of that place alive."

As if he had heard my silent prayer or received a divine message by telepathy. Otto said, "take my hand." I did so willingly, knowing the strength that it gave me once before. His hand was warm and strong, and I felt the warmth travel through me. Then like a five-year-old child, he led me forward. We bowed to the Sentinels and he immediately turned to face me. "Do you have the key." I took it from my pocket and showed him. "Follow them." he said and walked away, without once looking back.

One of the Sentinels took the first step down the well and the other indicated with his staff that I should follow him. I have been afraid so many times in my life, that I should have been able to handle it, but this was a different kind of fear, the kind that leaves you helpless. I stood at the top of the stairs and looked down and the sight of the stairs spiralling down into darkness was terrifying. I was filled with such dread, I would have bolted after Otto, but my legs wouldn't move. I was frozen again and trembling from head to foot.

The second sentinel came so close to my back that the ephemeral light that emanated from him. He, if he was a he and not a her, shone over and through me. There are no words I know that can describe it, but it felt a bit like a shower of warm water. It had the desired effect of taking my muscles out of the paralysis that had set in, and I took the first step down onto the spiral staircase.

There had never been water in this so called well, but still moss covered the walls and the air smelled of dampness and decay. The steps were slick with mud and dangerous. The arches on the inside wall followed the spiral down. They reached floor to ceiling, allowing air to come in, but very little light. I switched on the torch Otto gave me, for though the glow from the sentinels lit the steps, the penetrating beam of the torch was much more effective.

There were fifteen steps down to the first platform, I stopped and shone my torch around the wall and there again, just like at Lanshoud, graffiti covered the walls. Some were carved into the stone, some painted, all I presumed gave dire warnings of where these steps would lead. At least I took that to be what it was, as they, like at lanshoud, were written in every language under the sun. I played the torch over the walls till I found English. Carved with the precision of a stonemason it read

'Lest you wish to join the damned, Fool, turn back now, only horror awaits you below.'

I wanted to scan the walls for more English, but the Sentinel kept moving. The second level had more pictures carved into the stone. One looked like the grim reaper punting down a river. There were bodies impaled on sticks, stretched out on racks, burned at the stake and other atrocities. They were so horrendous, that I was afraid if I didn't look away, they would haunt my dreams forever and eventually drive me mad.

The second sentinel waved back and forth over me, to move me on. The sentinels were not solid creatures, but rather they were ghost-like, even so I did feel something. It was like something was pushing me forward from inside my own body. I followed the first sentinel down the next set of stairs. There were nine platforms with fifteen stairs between each one. As we descended, the graffitied walls came closer and the spiral tighter. By the last level there was no longer any light coming though the archways, and the tightness of the spiralling stairs was like a corkscrew, and claustrophobic.

I took the final step onto bottom of the well, behind the first sentinel and found myself in a high vaulted chamber. The smell was stronger too, but very different. Not of sulphur like the stairs to the gate at Lanshoud, but of damp and decay. So pungent was it, it seemed as though the very walls had died. The light from the sentinels was too dim to penetrate the gloom and though I worried about the battery life of my torch, I kept it on. Scanning the walls there was no gate. Only an entrance to a tunnel on the opposite side from the stairs.

A sudden movement startled me. There was something there, near the entrance to the tunnel. It was a figure, difficult to see because it was dressed like the Grim Reaper. Not in black, but in a mouldy grey colour from top to toe, that made it blend into the walls. It sat in an alcove carved out from the rock, its head bowed, its face buried deep inside the hood. Not knowing what to do, I turned to the sentinels, but they just looked at me with their huge expressionless, unblinking eyes. The figure moved again, and I froze, too afraid to take another step, or I would have run back up those stairs and come back another day. As if he had read my thoughts when I turned towards the stairs. I found one of the sentinels blocking my path.

In my head, to calm my fear and lighten my mood, I had been thinking of the sentinels as Hughie and Louie. Hughie was a deeper shade of violet than Louie, and always went first. It was Hughie blocking the stairs. He blocked my escape route so completely, there was no way past. I stood there trembling afraid to turn back and on the verge of panic.

The only way I can describe what happened next, is that Hughie walked over me, enveloping me completely. Trapped and unable to move he brought me to stand before the grey figure, then released me.

There was a deep silence, so deep, it could be felt in the air, I took a step away from the thing and… it lifted its head. I almost lost control of my bladder. The figure began to rise. "Speak" it said. It was very like a voice I had heard before, it sounded like the chilling voice of Christopher Lee, an actor, who could send shivers down my spine, just watching a movie. "Why are you here?" It asked. "It is not your time. What do you seek?"

My tongue had stuck to my mouth. I managed to croak out. "Gate. I am looking for the gate."

It laughed a loud, deep guttural laugh that made me shiver. Holding out its bony skeletal hand. it cried, "pay the coin" again and again.

"Pay for what? I don't understand?"

"Pay" it's voice boomed. " Pay the coin". The voice echoed around the chamber bouncing repeatedly off the stone wall, then it screamed out a blood curdling sound. "Pay the price or be damned to Hell." It rose above me; it must have been at least eight feet tall. The hooded robes were ragged and torn, but I could see the face was that of a skeleton. To my shame forever, my bladder gave way and I passed out.

Someone was calling my name. I opened my eyes, nauseated, and disorientated. The voice whispered. "Erica, Erica, wake up." It took me a minute to focus. It was James, on his knees, holding me close. "Can you sit up?" he said supporting me and holding a water bottle to my lips. "Sip it slowly. You're bleeding. Did someone hit you?'

I felt the side of my head it was sore and there was the stickiness of blood. "No, I think I fainted." Remembering why I fainted, I whipped round, looking for the figure, at the same time scabbling closer to James.

Blending into the wall the figure was still there, silent, its head bowed. I tried to get up, but I was dizzy and couldn't. James caught me. "It's ok. It's ok. he said, "you're alright. Just sit, just take a moment you've taken a crack on the head."

"How are you here?" I asked, confused. "Otto said he put you to sleep. How did you find the well?"

"Jack's here." he said. "You can thank him for that. I don't know how he persuaded him, but Otto woke us up and Jack brought me here."

Jack came over and knelt beside us. His voice, his face was the old Jack, and he was smiling at me. I said, "You came back Jack? that must have been a hard thing to do."

"Truth" he said "I don't remember anything. James had to fill me in, and he didn't hold back. It's hard for me to believe I behaved like that. I don't remember anything, other than bringing you here with Otto. Which is maybe not a bad thing."

I looked around; the sentinels were still there, standing together against the wall. "Look over there, do you see that thing?" I whispered. James hugged me closer as I shivered, and Jack shone his torch on the figure, which was sitting, again with its head bowed.

"Well what have we here?" Jack asked. Given his recent encounter with Thanatos I was surprised that he seemed more interested than afraid, but then he did say that he didn't remember anything.

I watched him move hesitantly towards the figure. When he reached it, he touched it gingerly? There was no movement. "I see him alright." He shouted back.

I called out," he spoke to me and he screamed at me, when I didn't understand what he was saying."

"What did he say?" Jack asked.

"He asked me why I was there and when I told him I was looking for the gate, he told me I had to pay with a coin."

"A coin." Jack repeated playing the beam of his torch over the figure. "Now that's interesting." In his Irish drawl, he said. "Now, are you sure it's alive, your mind can play funny tricks on you when you have had a bang on the head. "He laughed "Look" He lifted its hand and dropped it. You have been spooked by a skeleton. It is no more than just a bag-o-bones." Though he said it. he did seem reluctant to investigate further.

"It was before I banged my head. I am telling you Jack, it spoke to me."

Jack turned the torch beam back on the figure. "This dusty old skeleton's been here for a while. I am afraid Erica, you have allowed your imagination to run away with you." He reached out to pull back the hood, and the dusty old skeleton lifted its head.

Looking back now, I can laugh, because cocky Jack, I suspect also had a bladder incident at that time. He staggered back, lost his balance, dropped the torch and we were plunged into darkness, but for the glow from the sentinels. James felt about for his torch, found it in less than a minute and switched it on to see Jack standing frozen, with the figure towering over him, its hand outstretched, saying "Pay the coin." in that deep Christopher Lee voice."

Jack backed away from the figure. It repeated its script "Pay the coin." The voice boomed, echoing through the cavern. Stepping forward, its ragged gown trailing on the floor, it held its hand out, palm flat. Jack without taking his eyes off it, in a suddenly weak pleading voice, with a definite hint of a tremor cried. "Anybody got a coin? Quickly"

As the thing grew closer. James tossed a pound coin to Jack, it landed at his feet, he lifted and placed it in the skeletal hand. "Pay the coin" it screamed again.

"I think it wants more." Jack said in tremulous tone. "I think he wants one for each of us." James threw him two more coins and immediately the figure turned and walked, disappearing into the tunnel mouth.

Jack stood shining his torch on it, till he could see it no longer. James said, "What is that thing?"

Jack was hesitant to answer. "I know this will sound crazy, but with his dress and the coin thing. I think it's Charon or at least some kind of trick making it look like him. To scare people away."

"He does that alright. It's got a name. How do you know his name?" I asked

He whispered "I think we have just seen the ferryman. Do you know what that is?" He mused, still looking down the tunnel after the figure. "If it were real, what a find that would be. Charon, the ferryman, who in Greek mythology ferried the dead across the river Styx. Who demanded a coin from each passenger? Don't you see? Do you know that still to this day some cultures place coins in the mouth, or on the eyelids, of the recently dead, to pay the ferryman?" He sat down on the floor beside us, his gaze fixed on the tunnel entrance.

"Greek mythology! Seriously Jack We're in Germany." James said. Why would something like that appear here."

"Because it's the right set up for it. Think about it." Jack said. Erica has been directed here to the second gate. The gate to Hell. We are underground, there is a tunnel. Can't you smell the damp and decay. Yet this well isn't a well at all, there has never been water here. What if that tunnel leads to an underground river? A river you may have to cross to reach the Gate." The legend states the ferryman must be paid by the recently deceased. If they could not pay the ferryman, they could not go on to the afterlife and their spirits were left to wander the banks of the river Styx forever.

In the last fifty years archaeologists have found plenty of evidence to support the theory, that there was an elaborate set up. Grieving relatives were walked down tunnels and ferried across underground rivers to the land of the dead. There someone would be waiting to help them communicate with the deceased, they were desperate to communicate with"

James said. "There are no tunnels leading to rivers here Jack. That will just be a passageway that leads to another well like the one in Portugal, or hopefully the Gate. We're in Germany not Greece.

Jack stood up. "I am afraid you are wrong. I think there might be a river, it's cold and damp enough. Listen, I did some research when we first met Christina and she told us about Heiligtum. This part of Germany is known to be riddled with underground tunnels. There could well be an underground river down there. Maybe not with the same set up as the Acheron in Greece but with something similar. The Acheron was thought by many to be the mythological river Styx.

A new book on the ancient highways claimed Stone Age man created a massive network of underground tunnels criss-crossing Europe from Scotland to Turkey. A German archaeologist Dr Heinrich Kusch said evidence of the tunnels has been found under hundreds of Neolithic settlements all over the European continent. In his book - Secrets of The Underground Door to an Ancient

World - he claims the fact that, since so many have survived after 12,000 years it shows that the original tunnel network must have been enormous."

I shook my head. "Knowing the tunnels are real, doesn't confirm the existence of the ferryman. And why would the ferryman be here? There are no traditions like that in Germany. He can't be real."

Jack looked up at the Sentinels "You mean like those things aren't real? Why is any of this real or even believable?" When I didn't answer, he said," Exactly. That is because they are only ever real when you see them with your own eyes. Can't you smell the water? I willing to bet that tunnel leads to an underground river. It is a well-documented fact that in this area of Bavaria, there are over a hundred tunnels more than a thousand years old. That is a fact, and no one knows who built them, or what they were built for. Before I came to Heiligtum I did a lot of research on this area. These tunnels stretch across Europe from Scotland to Turkey. Theories on why they were built run from, a place to hide from predators, or warring tribes, even that they were roads, to be used in dangerous weather. Whatever the reason for these incredible tunnels, the scientific community has not come up with an answer yet. I would say it's a safe bet, there is an underground river and we have just paid the ferryman, to take us across it to the underworld, and that is where you will find the Gate. Oh! and another thing, in Greek mythology the river Styx was a black river that encircled the whole Earth underground. So, it could be down there."

"It's unbelievable. We could be walking into a nightmare." James said. I think we should stop right now, just turn back. Enough is enough. Erica, I say turn back!"

I pushed myself away from him and got to my feet, feeling a bit dizzy from the bump in the head. "Turn back are you crazy? You know I must do this. You know that. Everything about this is unbelievable James. Are you on a different planet or something? What about those sentinels standing there, what about the keys? I can pretty much guarantee that if I ever tell my story, no one will ever believe it. I will be locked up in a mental institution because it's 'unbelievable', but here's the thing. I know it's real. I know no matter how insane it makes me look. I must close that gate." I picked up my backpack. "The sentinels will protect me; you can go back."

James said, "hold on, you were out cold a minute ago. You were terrified when you woke up. Now you are going ahead with this."

"Yes, I am following that creature. My life will never be normal till I carry out these insane tasks I have been allotted by Luke." I was gutted by James's 'attitude. "I am closing those gates and then I can put it all of this behind me. Of course, you think I am weak and scared and stupid, but I will do this James, with or without you, just so I can live a normal life again." I was so disappointed in him. "Just go back James. You too Jack. I appreciate you coming but I understand perfectly if you want to go back."

"Enough" James said picking up his backpack "Stop playing the martyr, it doesn't suit you. Anyway, Jack wouldn't miss this for the world."

This time the sentinels didn't lead the way but followed us down the tunnel, that was so narrow the mens shoulders rubbed against the walls, forcing them to walk sideways in some parts. The walls carved from solid rock in places and built of impacted earth in others, were so close together that my arms often bumped on the sides. The ceilings had been carved into an arch which was fortunately just high enough to allow the sentinels through, and like jelly in motion, they slimmed in when it was necessary.

Jack led the way, shining his torch on the horrendously large spiders and cockroaches that scuttled past, making my skin crawl. Never mind the ferryman, those insects were enough to make me turn and run, only, even if I changed my mind, there was nowhere to run. The tunnel was so narrow there was no room to get past James or the sentinels at his back.

The tunnel twisted and turned in different directions, all the time continuing the descent. The further we went, the bigger the spider's webs and their inhabitants were. Their eyes and their huge hairy legs made me shudder. We walked in silence, our boots making little sound on dirt track underfoot.

The further we went, the deeper the gradient of the tunnel, turning and twisting, spiralling down towards the bowels of the Earth, relentlessly carrying us forward to an inescapable destiny.

At last it levelled out. Now a straight path lay in front and at the end there was light. The air changed too. It was hotter and foul smelling, of not just rot and decay, but of putrefaction.

We stepped out of the tunnel and into an alternate reality, for as Jack had predicted, we stood on the bank of a river. We were in a huge cavern, lit by an eerie greenish blue light. Stalactites hung from the roof like daggers, ready to drop on unsuspecting visitors. The slow-moving river that lay before us was wider than any I could have imagined. It flowed from a tunnel on our left-hand side and disappeared through another on the right. On its surface floated unsavoury looking white scum that Jack said was probably mineral deposits.

A boat that looked like a very old and worn Venetian gondola was lying alongside the riverbank. Charon stood at the rear holding a long pole, like those used by gondoliers.

No longer nauseated or lightheaded, I still didn't feel right. I was scared and nervous, my heart again pounding in my chest. I had a strange feeling that we were seeing something, no living person should see. A place that had existed since the beginning of time. I was in awe of a scene so strange, so macabre, yet it was believed by academics to be no more than fiction. A place our ancestors in the distant past knew and feared, a place of mystery and terror.

The boat had moved and was now crossing towards us. It pulled up beside the riverbank. Reluctant to step into to it, I turned to the sentinels. They stood back watching, unmoving, unblinking, and unemotional. With unstated agreement we stepped into the boat and were ferried to the other bank. Reluctantly we left the sentinels behind, as they made no attempt to follow us.

We sat together the three of us on the bench with the ferryman towering over us at our back steering the boat over putrid water with his huge paddle.   Halfway across something bumped the boat and it shuddered. It happened again. Jack looked over the side but couldn't see anything. Then suddenly leaning over the other side he cried out. "oh my God it's bodies, corpses, floating in the water, hundreds of them. James looked over his side and gasped and I looked away. I didn't try to see. Instead I closed my eyes but not soon enough to prevent me seeing the bloodied arm, the hand with only two fingers, reach out of the water, not of its own volition, but by the force of bodies pushing against it. Jack and James were silent, transfixed and so over-whelmed by the scene in front of us, they were incapable of speech. Jack just couldn't look away, he was completely unable to free himself from the grip of his own morbid curiosity.

The boat slowed, the path to the bank hampered by the increasing mass of dead. Charon used his pole to push them away but was making little progress. The stink made me wretch and I had to pull my scarf into a mask, around my mouth and nose. When the boat stopped, we stepped onto the shore. I didn't look back. In front of me there was nothing to see but another tunnel. Jack said his voice dry and almost croaking. "In Greek mythology those bodies are the dead, who did not pay the ferryman."

There was nowhere else to go except into the tunnel. It was smaller and narrower than the last one and with water to wade through. Finally, we were brought to an iron gate. A gate small and as unassuming as any garden gate, with nothing but a wall of solid rock behind it.

"This isn't it. It can't be. There is nothing here." I said. "We must be in the wrong place. Surely this is not the gate we are looking for. Look" I said pushing it. "It's open." As I moved to step through, Jack grabbed my arm. "Wait!" he cried. "Look it's not real." he picked up a rock and threw it. The wall wavered and dissolved and in front of us stood a man in a dinner suit, immaculate white shirt, a bow tie, and highly polished shoes.

Shocked and confused by the incongruity of this man, in this place, we all stepped back.

"Don't be afraid the man said, "all of that," he waived his hand in the air and at the river. "All of that is illusion, come," he waived us forward. "Come and dine with us. Step this way we have been expecting you."

Baffled by the absurdity of this man and this place, no one moved. The man held out his hand. "Come please, your reward is here"

James asked him," who are you?"

At that question, the man's face seemed to change, it melted and just as quickly reformed. It happened so fast. I thought I had imagined it. He turned around, waived his hand at the wall that had appeared again at his back, and the wall dissolved again. "I am the host, "he said. This time we could see a large room full of men in dinner suits and women in evening gowns. They were all drunk, pouring wine down their throats and over their clothes. Some were half naked, their gowns ripped and stained, they were laughing and crying. Some were vomiting onto the floor, then gorging again on food, the remnants of which was smeared across their faces.

"The key" James cried, "where is the key Erica." I held it up as soon as I took it out my pocket. The man in the dinner suit lurched forward to grab it. Startled, I accidentally pressed it and immediately the man and the whole room started screaming. The gate slammed shut and they all disappeared. We were left staring at a closed gate and a stone wall. "I don't understand," I said. How could that little gate to that room and the orgy, be the second gate? How could that be the second portal, letting demons into our world."

"They were demons, and this is just another part of Hell" Jack said. "C'mon the boat quick   before it disappears.

We ran back to the boat were Charon stood patiently. We clambered in and he pushed off from the bank. Very quickly I realised he was not crossing the river but heading down it. Jack cried out and tried to grab the pole but couldn't reach it. James tried to help, but the boat rocked and almost capsized, filling us with dread. I am sure my heart stopped for a moment. James staggered and almost fell overboard in among the teeming corpses.

I honestly felt we were going to die or worse, instead we were bathed in the violet light of the sentinels. The light fell on the ferryman. He screamed as though he had been burned with acid. and jumped off the boat onto the water. He ran across it as though it were a solid surface. The boat slowly turned. I was gripping the side watching the violet light play over my skin, calming me. It was pulling us. The sentinels were using their light like a traction beam and with that they brought us safely to shore. Then they both pointed to the tunnel. We didn't wait to see what happened behind us. We hurried as fast as we could, back through the tunnel, struggling and out of breath, because the way back was a twisted climb uphill. Even when we reached the well, we didn't stop to look back, but climbed, running, and falling, back to the surface.

Stepping out into the fresh sunlight was like stepping into heaven. I turned to thank the sentinels. They both lifted a hand to say goodbye and then just seemed evaporate into the air like a fizzy drink. Without looking back, we returned to Heiligtum.

Everyone was waiting, watching for us, praying for us? As soon as we reached the door, crying with happiness, Gill threw herself into Jack's arms. Sean screamed," Daddy" to Jack and ran to him. The whole ordeal was worth it just to see them united again. We showered and changed, drank tea, and shared our story. Mostly told by James and Jack.

Otto came to sit on the sofa beside me, he said "you are very quiet. What is wrong? You did it, you closed the second gate. You should be happy it is over."

I played with the spoon in my tea." It was small gate Otto, like a garden gate. I am afraid that it was the wrong one."

"The key closed it." he said firmly. "it was the right one. You were exposed to deception at highest level. It's all illusion. The gate is closed Erica, I think you can relax now."

"You think, do you? Well, there are two more gates"

"Yes, "Otto agreed, "but that is for another day, another place, and another time. Rest now, this is a momentous day. Good has overcome evil."

Yes, it was a momentous day, not only because the second gate was closed but, because. later that evening James and I went for a walk in the garden and he asked me to marry him.

I think because it had been such a traumatic day, it was the last thing I expected. It was the wrong time and the wrong place. I was physically and emotionally exhausted when I left the well and the things we had seen were still haunting my mind. We sat on a bench and talked about the unbelievable horror. Trying to make sense of it all.

The night was drawing in and the birds were singing their evening repertoire. Beside the bench, a beautiful flowering shrub grew, it had a vibrant deep pink flower that neither of us could identify. "I must get a cutting from that before I go home," I said. "I am going to start a secret garden. "I suddenly shivered, a cold wind had whipped up. I said, "this garden is so beautiful, when I go back to Lanshoud. I am going to take a piece of my land and turn it into a secret garden, and I will have masses of flowers and bird boxes to encourage songbirds. You know, I think getting back to nature is healing., Somehow the perfume of the flowers and the birdsong penetrate the darkness in my mind and soothe it. I feel better here." I smiled I don't know if it's the garden or maybe it's just because I'm with you." I rubbed my arms. "It's getting cold, we should go back now."

"No, wait." he said taking off his jacket and putting it round my shoulders. He put his arm round me and pulled me close. It was warm and comforting.

"Is that better? "He asked

"Yes, I feel better, I have been secretly wrapped up in this jacket before you know."

Surprised he asked. "When was that?"

"Just before we left. Otto found me huddled in it. I must have looked ridiculous. I could smell you in it."

"Smell me! Well thanks for that." I laughed. "I was scared witless and trying to be brave. The jacket was warm and comforting."

"Comforting eh. Well I'm glad I could be useful for something."

"We sat in silence for a while till I said, "I could stay here all night, but you will get pneumonia." I held the jacket open. "It's big, do you want to share? I put my head on his shoulder, he turned my head round and kissed me. It was so gentle and so loving. I almost forgot where I was and returned his kiss.

Erica, he said "Did anyone ever tell you, you give out mixed messages?"

"What do you mean?"

"I mean you blow hot and cold."

I knew what he meant but deliberately misunderstanding, I stood up, held the jacket open, laughing. "There's room for two in here, we can share. I tried to put it round him and staggered almost landing on top of him. I was happy and a little dizzy, not because of mild concussion or anything like that, but because I had two very large glasses of wine at dinner."

"I think I'm a little tipsy." I broke into a fit of giggles.

"Yes, you are."

"Oh! You look very serious. Am I being censured?"

"Maybe. Be serious Erica, it is not my jacket I want to share with you, it's my life. Look at me," he said. I looked up and he kissed me again, but this time there was a hunger in his kiss. Erica I love you. I have loved you from the first moment I set eyes on you. I have been besotted, since the day I drove you home from the office. I want you to be my wife. He produced a ring box from his pocket and opened it up to show a sparkling diamond. He went to kneel. I stopped him. He said, "Erica will you marry me?"

I was speechless for a moment, stunned, lost for words, and immediately sobered.

He said, "well if you have to think about it. I guess the answer is no. Are you afraid I will run away with your millions?"

"James, the ring is beautiful, but I can't marry you, not yet." I said sitting back down. He put the ring back in his pocket. I could see he was hurt, and I hated myself. I reached for his hand. I said, "I know you won't believe me now, but I have loved you too, from that first day we met, but it's the wrong time."

"What! Why is it the wrong time? Is there someone else? Is it Otto?"

"Otto!" I laughed. "Otto isn't even human. No, there is no one else. I love you James, just you, I really do, there is no one else. I just need time. I know; I owe you an explanation."

It was hard for me to explain, even though I was baring my soul, to the only person on earth I needed to be part of my life. "I have no secrets from you," I said emphatically. There is truly no one else...not now...but there once was someone else."

"I loved my husband Paul Cameron from the day I met him too, but when he died, I discovered, that like my adoptive parents, he had lied to me my whole life. He was put in place by Luke Treadstone to look after me. You have no idea what that feels like. It's the biggest betrayal of all, when the people you love the most, make a fool of you." I was suicidal when I found out, I was so depressed I couldn't open my eyes in the morning. If it wasn't for Gill and Katie and you. I wouldn't be here now. You three pulled me though and then... it happened all over again. How? Because you behaved the same way James. You, like Paul, never once told me the truth. You lied about your job, you pretended to be a solicitor, when in truth, you are a government agent. I am sure you had good reasons, but also I refuse to believe you didn't know I was in love with you.

I had to find out the hard way that you had been living with Chloe. I can't, I won't go through that again. I am sorry, I want this more than anything, but I need time to sort my life out and I have two more gates to close. I need to heal James. Can you even give me this time?" I could feel tears running down my face. "It's getting dark now I am going back."

He stood up saying nothing.

"No, please wait." I said, I want to go back alone."

I left him standing there. He called after me. "Erica, I will wait till you feel the time is right. I will wait forever if that's what it takes."

I had a crushing pain in my chest. I cried myself to sleep that night.

Lightning Source UK Ltd.
Milton Keynes UK
UKHW010635280422
402201UK00001B/26

9 781839 751424